MOTHER'S JUSTICE

A COWBOY CAT MYSTERY

CHRISSY WISSLER

BLUE CEDAR PUBLISHING

 Created with Vellum

ALSO BY CHRISSY WISSLER

Cowboy Cat Mystery Series

Women's Justice

Mother's Justice

For more information about Chrissy Wissler's other works, go to
ChrissyWissler.com

MOTHER'S JUSTICE

A COWBOY CAT MYSTERY

To Kate and Eric—
Who taught me about the fierce love and hope of being a parent.

PROLOGUE

Evie Blonberg sank into the uneven wooden chair in her tiny kitchen. The skirt of her dress, heavy and thick, suddenly weighing her down. Trapping her. Binding her.

The chair, as off-balance as it was, and for the past year-and-a-half of her constantly telling Lou it needed fixin', and no surprise, still remained as it was. Broken. Uneven. The whole thing feeling as if it were about to tip her right down onto the dusty, ash-strewn floor.

As she deserved, apparently.

Or, at least, as Lou believed, apparently.

No sunlight glinted in through the tiny, cracked window, though she'd pushed those curtains back as far as they'd go. She did this every morning, hopin', prayin' that today might be different. That the sun just might come piercing right through those thick and heavy clouds, shine past all that ash and sulfur which clogged the air, stung the eyes, made her wish for a future that she knew was never meant to be.

Couldn't be.

Certainly not now.

And except for a brief glimpse of the sun 'bout a week ago, that had been all. As if the sun and had forsaken her, just as the Lord—and Lou—had.

A sob trapped there in her throat and she held it there. Kept it in.

Just like the tears.

Had to.

Because there, playin' on the floor with the little doll Evie had made from bits of buttons and cloths that couldn't be used for mending no more, was her dearest little girl, Rose. Rose, with her still-chubby face, somehow holding onto all the beautiful bits of childhood and joy despite the darkness of Butte.

Butte, Montana, with its never-ending chorus of miners trudging up and down the hill, all day, all night, and those piercing whistles that preceded the miners' arrival. The ash and smoke that just about made up their life, certainly now in the dead heart of winter. All those smelters, burning their heaps without a care 'bout the rest of 'em, especially how that smoke liked to stay hunkered down, right on top of the hill, and no amount of praying would move it.

It just... stayed there, and they, to a one, had to live with it.

There was never any beautiful white snow for Butte, nothing at all like what she'd grown up with. Just the sharp, cold bite of wind and the blackness that came, regardless if it were day or night.

Evie doubted she'd ever get used to it, and yet, there was Rose who simply never seemed to notice. Always there with a smile on her face, always a joy and a bounce in her step while her long hair, braided in two as she always wanted, flopping and hopping against her back. Didn't matter that they spent their recent days making their way through that black daylight, dropping Peter off at school, then picking him up again. That they could barely find their way and relied on the others in their neighborhood, mothers and families who were aiming to do the same as Evie, and how they all bunched together so they didn't lose their way. And yet, through it all, Rose was smiling. Simply filled with such joy that she went skipping along on those mud and gravel frozen streets without a care or concern in the world.

The exact opposite of who Peter had become. Harder. Closed off to her.

Peter.

Oh, dear God, what was she gonna tell Peter? What was he going to think—

Evie could barely glance at their small kitchen table. The wood there, which had been gouged in a few places from an angry knife thrust downward, along with the black, burned smudges near the center from Lou's mishap one evening while in the bottle. It'd only been the one time, and it'd been easy enough to drape some cloth over it, dressing the table up some, for when they had guests over. Friends.

But then she needed the cloth for mending, using it to patch up some of Rose's clothes, and it hadn't mattered much since they didn't have guests over no more, anyway. But that one time, Lou's single angry outburst had slowly turned into many.

Too many.

Evie's stomach churned. She felt the sour taste rising up her throat and she did her best to keep on breathing, in and then out again, calming her insides as best as she could.

Couldn't let it out... couldn't let it show...

Instead, she focused on the sourdough bread she'd baked fresh just that morning, which now sat there in that curved bowl, nearly gone because her dearest children were growing and always, always so hungry. And yet, there was still bread because Lou hadn't taken his customary four slices before heading out in the morning.

Not for work, because he didn't have a job no more and couldn't keep one, though God only knew why. Or at least, the real truth of it. And if Lou wasn't workin' and he wasn't here, either it was because... because...

Evie squeezed her eyes shut.

Peter and Rose would finish the bread, and then it'd be a luxury she couldn't replace. Not now.

Maybe, not ever again.

And yet, despite her best intentions, Evie's gaze strayed to the opened newspaper laying right there beside the bread, beside the slab of butter she'd left out for Peter when he got home and was hungry again.

The newspaper that had sealed her fate, and in a way she'd never expected, never imagined or dreamed would ever happen to her...

Her fate.

She pressed a hand to her stomach, but it didn't still the uneasiness swirling inside her, the nausea that had been waiting just for this opportunity. A quiet moment. A still moment when it was just her and her thoughts and she wasn't needed to kiss a bruised knee or get some food out for endlessly hungry tummies.

A boy had come by with the paper this morning, knocking hard on her door, and when she'd answered, was greeted to the sight of this scrappy kid. News cap squashed low on his head, looking no older than Peter, and with them piercing green eyes that seemed to cut right through her. The look, the intensity in those eyes, it'd been so unexpected she'd taken a step back, placing a hand on her chest as if needing to catch another breath or two of that foul, smoky air.

This boy wasn't Peter's age, at least not exactly. Something about him had him seeming... older.

Even now, sitting in her chair that was still broken, just the memory of this boy and the way he'd looked at her made her shudder. It was the kind of look she'd never want to see on her children and yet... and yet...

She knew in her heart, in her gut, it might just very well be their future.

Especially now.

Especially when the boy had handed her the paper, right then and there, as if he'd known it, too.

Not that she read the paper much to begin with—that had been more of Lou's interest—but she found herself reaching for it, accepting it, even. Almost as if some part of her had already known. Maybe it was the way the boy was looking at her, or maybe just this feeling she had swirling in her gut, like her mother's intuition, telling her, warning her what was coming.

Evie glanced at the headline, saw it was from the *Butte Bystander*, one of Lou's favorites, and that it was the morning's edition.

So fresh, in fact, it immediately left black smudge stains on her fingers.

"I, I don't understand," Evie had said.

But the boy didn't ask for no payment, didn't ask for anything, really. Instead, he just glanced past her and into their small, one-room home, to Rose who looked up at that moment, and her eyes met his and the smile she always wore, the one she went bouncing along with her braids even in during these black daylight hours, faded. Just... gone... like it'd never been.

Their eyes had met, Rose's and the boy's, and yet not a word being passed between them.

Well, Evie *had* asked a few words, though none went answered. Least not that she could tell, anyway.

The boy merely gave her a slight tip of his news cap and an apology.

"I really am sorry 'bout this. I just thought... just thought you'd want to know. And that, well, you're not alone in this. Just remember that, Mrs. Blonberg."

And *that* had caused Evie to start because she knew for a fact that she didn't know this boy. Knew that he wasn't no friend of Peter's, cause Peter didn't know the kinds of kids who walked around with these haunted, aging looks in their eyes. A look that didn't come from growing up in a poor, though loving, home as her own children had.

Evie had closed the door then, her whole body shaking and shivering, while the door decided to stick before shutting it properly, as it always did 'cause the latch wasn't workin' right and had never worked right and Lou had never cared enough to see it done proper. Evie had stood right there with her back against her front door that didn't close, holding that crinkled paper in hands, debating what to do, debating if she should open it or toss it right into the fire.

Running never solved a problem. Pretending like it didn't exist didn't make it go away, neither. And the boy, clearly kind, had brought it to her to see. Specifically. Which meant there would be no running from this. No hiding.

So, with her intuition coiling around her stomach like a flustered rattlesnake, Evie opened the paper and immediately saw the classified, listed right there.

A classified that Lou had written.

About Evie.

Naming Evie.

This time, sitting there in her broken chair, trying to understand her future, Evie's will, her control, could not catch the two tears that slid down her face. And though she quickly brushed them aside, little Rose looked up, as if sensing her mother's distress.

Those deep brown eyes of hers, starin' just so, just like Lou often would, at least, when he'd been sober enough to remember she was even there.

"Mama?"

"It's, it's nothing, dear heart."

The lie sounded untrue, even to her ears. But Rose said nothing more. Just got up on her little feet, the stockings already wearing through at the knees and toes, and oh dearest Lord, how was she gonna pay for another? How was she gonna pay for anything at all? Their rent, their, their *food*—

More tears.

She couldn't stop them. Even if she wanted to.

And then Rose was climbing onto Evie's lap, using the heavy layers of dress like grooves on some rock or tree. She climbed right up and wrapped her arms about Evie's neck and held her, just so.

Just... held her.

How could Lou do this? Do this to Rose? To Peter?

If anyone should have held sway over Lou's heart, it should have been Peter. But Peter... his only living son, well, he'd always resembled Evie more. Thick black hair, his lighter gray eyes that sometimes looked a bit yellow. And his spirit, a stubborn and righteous all in one. No, it wasn't a surprise that concerns for Peter and his future hadn't held enough sway over Lou's heart. Not Lou, at least the Lou he'd become. Angry and bitter. Always saying how his loss at the Spectacular Mine was somehow Evie's doing, blaming her cause he couldn't go and blame the real person at fault: himself. She didn't why it'd all happened, but she suspected, just like she suspected the reason for her son's hardness. Lou and his drinking, which had only gotten worse while he worked at the Big S. And after?

Evie's hands shook at the mere thought.

She might not know the whole story of what happened to Lou, losin' his job, and why he couldn't keep another—God forbid the man actually tell her and be truthful—but she was pretty darn sure his drinkin' and his temper had something to do with it. And when it came to drinking and being drunk down in the mines, when life and death held in such a tight balance... no, it wasn't the kind of infraction to be allowed, regardless of how close you were to a person.

Lou knew it, and yet he'd blamed her.

Blamed her enough that, even after all their arguments, her begging and pleading him to go out there and try again, sign up for another mine and maybe this one would be better, have a better crew or shift boss or foreman—whatever the heck it was that Lou thought he was needin'—and sure, he might try. Might slam his fist down onto that table before stomping outside, grabbing his lunch bucket on the way out... but he'd always come back.

Empty pail and another pink slip in his hand.

She'd done everything, absolutely everything she could to get their family a little extra money, food, anything at all really, especially with Rose always tagging along with her... she'd done everything in *her* power... and he'd gone and left.

Just... just left.

Left her and the kids all alone just so he could start another life somewhere else, somewhere better without the baggage of three extra mouths to feed, at least, so she assumed. It wasn't like he'd gone and told her any of this. No, of course not. Instead, she'd woken up yesterday morning, saw that he was gone and had taken their one suitcase.

No letter. No goodbye. Not even a hug or kiss for Rose or Peter.

Just, just gone.

But the worst part of all was he'd gone and told the whole town of Butte. He'd placed his classified and made it clear as day to everyone that Mrs. Evie Blonberg was not to be trusted.

Evie's hands shook as she brought Rose closer to her, kissed the top of her daughter's head, while the tears, they kept on coming.

No one would hire her now.

No one.

Cat stood there, wearing her cleaned, pressed blue jeans, and her boots planted firm on the smooth, wooden floor of Mrs. Allen's boarding home. Standing almost within spitting distance of the front door and being unable to reach it.

Her boots, which were still scratched and worn in a few spots but had been cleaned and nicely shined, brushing away all that filth and grime she'd picked up from the underground tunnels. As if by ordering her boots cleaned, it'd wipe away any memory of the event, of those who'd lived down there down in that darkness, of those naked light bulbs hanging overhead. Half of 'em broken. The other half just given up on living.

And her boots, now nice and cleaned and shining in their worn leather, as if... none of it had happened.

Cat knew better.

Hell, she had the bruises and bone fractures in her shoulder to prove it. And underneath the bruising, there lay a different kind of ache. Uncertainty. It held onto her so tight, like it was doing its best to reach her soul and straight-up live there, snuggling all good and close. A feeling that made her hands shake, sweeping over her at the oddest times and always when she least expected it. In the middle of the night, or now when she was doing her best to sneak out of the house and get the hard, cold ground underneath her feet.

Being mad was a hell of a lot easier than lookin' to closely at what she was tryin' real hard to *not* look at.

Cat breathed in, then out again. Focused on keeping herself centered.

See, it no longer mattered how comfortable that sitting room was, with all them couches and chairs, all them lace and curtains, which were just about the spitting image of her parents' home when she was a child. All those years ago, ghostly memories that were more fuzzy and gray about the edges than real. And yet... and yet... all she had to do was close her eyes and she could hear her ma banging away in that kitchen, humming and singing to the tune of those pots and pans. The smell of some roasting meat dripping away in the oven.

It wasn't a comforting memory either, but a reminder.

A reminder of everything she'd had, and lost.

Her and her sister, Alice.

It was the kinda memory that, even now, even with her trying to keep calm and breathing, to not let the frustration come shootin' out her ears, caused her heart to twist. Those bits of her, ones she'd thought gone and buried, were tugging awake. Like the longer she stayed here, rested here in this sitting room, spent her days staring out that big, recently fixed window, the more those memories stirred.

The more she felt.

The more she remembered.

Which had made this little healing venture that much more painful to suffer through, and Cat wasn't exactly the sit-down-and-do-nothing type to begin with. Or the type who let others take care of her.

Instead, she liked to move.

She liked to live—to simply *be*.

And those couches, sure they were so worn-out and comfortable that they simply wrapped around a body and coaxed tired, tender muscles to relax. Which, she knew quite well, and had been quite grateful for them, especially those first few days of healing. God, it'd felt like she'd never move the left side of her body again, or ever do something as simple as lift her arm and *not* feel intense agonies of pain.

But there was only so much relaxing and resting a person could do and Cat was comin' hard up on her limit.

Real hard.

And Mrs. Allen wasn't listenin'. In fact, she was doing the opposite. She was doing her utmost damnedest to make the whole room so enticing you *wanted* to simply sit down, open up one of them many newspapers, and reach for a plate of that delicious, mouth-watering apple pie.

The pie, which again was freshly baked with scents of cinnamon swirling off that steaming, perfectly browned top.

The whole thing practically begging you to take a good-size forkful of said pie right into your mouth and simply spend a lazy day staring out that big window, the glass still shiny and new. To sit back and merely watch the world outside go by—least as much as one could see with all them dark and smoky clouds hanging 'bout the hill like they owned it—but still, there were glimpses.

Enough to make Cat yearn to be back out there... stretching her legs, her boots smacking hard into the mud and gravel frozen streets, feeling that cold, chill air bite right on through her overcoat like she wasn't wearing a thing.

There was the sun, too, which even if it weren't exactly shining, she'd know it was still there, could sense it... hiding somewhere up high, on the other side of that blackness, glowing its bright gold for the rest of the world but not for Butte.

God, did she miss it.

All of it.

Missed feeling the wind tugging at her hair, pulling it loose from her braid as it always did. The bits of rocks and gravel flinging at her as those hacks drove on by, riding their horses hard enough that the whole carriage nearly tipped on over, a sure sign that Fat Jack was the one doing the driving, yet his hack never did tip or fall. Then there were those miners workin' their way on up the big hill of Butte, shoulders and backs already bent and broken though they hadn't yet started their lengthy shift down there in the dark. But they always had a ready grin for Cat, a friendly air about them as they shared tales of their families and whatnot.

Which was the whole point.

The *seeing* and not the living.

And Cat knew, without a doubt, that the only way she'd really get back on her feet was being out there. Only way to quell this uncertainty riding herd in her stomach, causing her hands to shake, causing her to doubt just everything she'd done and everything she'd set out to do since coming to Butte.

As if someone like her was good enough to help others seek justice.

And that, right there, was what Cat had been doing for a week now. Stewing and watching and more stewing. Stuck right there, right there on that damn couch, watching the whole world move on, and she was plum sick and tired of it.

And why was she forced to sit?

Cause Doc Griffin had warned otherwise.

"Push too hard," he'd said, "and you might damage those muscles more."

The doc, who'd examined Cat up in her room just that morning with the door tight and closed, while the others were off and doing who knew what. Mrs. Allen probably baking yet another pie or a tray full of cookies for all the visitors that had come by, lookin' to get a gander at Cat and hear the tales of what'd taken place down in the cribs of Grace's Gardens. Chin probably off cleaning something, and Dusty... well, he'd been keeping to himself lately, avoiding her, not meeting her eyes, as if he had something heavy on his mind that he wasn't ready to share with the rest of 'em. Certainly not with Cat.

Which she understood.

It wasn't like she knew Dusty well, or any of them. It wasn't like they were family.

Not really, anyway.

Doc Griffin pushed his thick spectacles further up the bridge of his nose, right there in between those white, bushy eyebrows. He gave a careful look over her shoulder and all the damage that'd been done to it. To her, it looked like it was still just one big black-and-blue bruise that was just barely starting to take on the tint of yellow, hinting that, just maybe, she was finally on the mend.

Though it often felt like it wasn't ever gonna get better.

"Truthfully," he'd said, "I'm amazed you've got so much movement in your shoulder as it is, especially after that wallop you took. A lesser person, hell, even a lesser man, would have been out for a month with an injury like that. Certainly taking his fair share of substances to dull the pain."

He'd pushed and probed at the bruises there, making Cat wince and her eyes tear up, which she was careful to hide. He'd seen, of course, and she was sure nothing slipped by that man, and yet he'd said nothing.

"Still causing you quite a bit of pain?"

"Just a bit."

"You know, I can give you something for that—"

"No drugs," she said.

"All right. Fair enough."

Doc Griffin was an ancient man with more wrinkles than a crushed-up map, but his hands were always steady, soft, and comforting. There also wasn't a thing dull or ancient about his mind. Nor his kindness. He'd taken to seeing the working girls in all the big houses, and when he had time, the smaller ones as well. It was how they'd come to meet, though not in the way he met other girls.

See, Doc Griffin didn't really need the extra money no more, but he did it cause his soul demanded he do so.

Not that he'd said as much to Cat.

But then, he hadn't needed to.

When she looked into his eyes, it was like staring into a mirror. The past haunted him. Haunted so real and vivid he couldn't help but reach out to these working girls, girls who the rest of the society deemed fallen and now worthless, completely brushing its hands of the circumstances that might put those girls in those houses in the first place.

It was why Doc Griffin had originally stopped his hack and had stumbled into this strange mess of a family: a boarding house owner with her own colored past, a boy who lived and breathed the shadow world, and then, well, Cat. While she hadn't met Doc Griffin until recently, until this business with her shoulder, she'd been looking for him. See, he'd been the one who'd come upon a fallen, dying prostitute and tried to save her. He'd failed, cause there wasn't a whole lot one could do when poison took its hold, but he'd stopped and he'd tried to save her.

Just as he was now coming here, doing what he could for Cat. Maybe, even, trying to save her, too.

While Cat didn't work the line no more and never planned to again, the line would never leave her, and truthfully, like him, she couldn't turn her back on it, either.

This was Doc Griffin's way of atoning and she'd understood.

Perfectly.

Doc Griffin had finished examining and Cat had tugged her shirt back on, getting one arm in the sleeve and the other, moving real, real slow-like. No point showin' him just in the hell how much it hurt, not when she herself had a point to make: she needed out of this house and needed out *now*.

When Cat struggled with the buttons of her blouse, pushing those little bits through one-handed being no easy task, Doc Griffin had kindly helped her. He'd given her a sympathetic look, as if he'd known just how much she was simmering over needing this help, over sittin' on her hands when the whole world out there was practically begging for her feet to start walking over it again.

And like his last visit and examine, he made no comment about the blue jeans she wore or the holster at her hip. He'd accepted her for who she was as soon as he saw her, even if that acceptance did not extend to her leaving the confines of Mrs. Allen's home.

At which point, Cat reminded him that her bones and all those bits of fractures there, *were* healin' quite nicely and to her mind was perfectly sound reasoning that she be allowed outside for a bit, to move and stretch her legs.

But of course, the doc being a doc, shook his head.

"Too much and you might not regain your strength there, Miss Cat, and that'd be a real shame. A real shame. I hear you did some good in town that night."

"I want to stretch my legs, Doc, not get in a gunfight."

"I heard there *was* a gunfight on your last adventure."

"One shot went off."

"A person died," he pointed out.

"The right person. And I wasn't even the one doin' the shooting."

Though that hadn't been from lack of wanting to.

When she'd been down in those cribs right on the heels of a killer, she'd gotten smacked, good and hard, by a real heavy chunk of wood by Mr. Rippi. Rippi who, it turned out, was an angry, disillu-sioned miner who'd fallen in love with, and been fooled, by a woman's smile.

A damn intelligent, if trapped, smile. And the very reason why Cat had found herself drawn into that mess and this family.

Well, Mr. Rippi, he'd worked real hard down in those mines, and his swing and the way he'd connection with Cat's shoulder certainly proved that point. At least Cat had taken the blow to her shoulder and not where it'd originally been intended.

Her head.

And understandably, the small derringer Cat had pulled free of its holster, hidden under all those layers of silk and lace, had flown right out of her hand. Finding it again, little thing that it was, would have meant crawling around in that torturous corset, huntin' in the dark, while Mr. Rippi stood behind her, poised and ready to take another swing. Finding the gun hadn't been the best option to keep herself alive and breathing.

So, she hadn't.

Another girl had, and she'd been the one to do the shooting.

Not Cat.

A fact that everyone was so keen to forget.

And Doc Griffin, as if the man was reading her mind, shook his head, causing that snow-white mustache of his to bob up and down.

"And what if something *did* happen to you?" he asked. "You're in no position to defend yourself, and there are quite a few powerful people who aren't happy with you. Can't say they wouldn't mind seeing you disappear, either. And those girls you helped, they need a bit of goodness, a bit of hope. I know Norma sure did."

Cat felt a chill at the woman's name, spoken aloud.

Norma.

The hairs on the back of Cat's neck rose but... no ghost appeared. No cold touch of the dead resting on her shoulder, making her feel that tremendous chill from her fingertips to her toes.

Norma was well and truly gone.

Norma, yes, but not Alice, her sister. Never Alice. In fact, Cat very much doubted the shade of her sister would ever leave her, could ever leave her.

Peace was not something meant for the likes of Cat. Atonement, maybe, but not peace.

Still, Norma's name was enough... enough of a reminder.

Norma had been the woman, the prostitute, Doc Griffin had tried to save. And right from that moment Cat had stepped off the train and spotted Dusty selling his papers and his haunted, shadow eyes, she'd felt the pull of this lost woman. They way it'd tugged on those very strings from her own past, of Alice.

There was no ignoring it. No denying it. Certainly when Dusty had handed her that paper and she read about Norma's story. Not that there'd been a lot there, written in that article. But it'd been enough to not sit right with her, to get all her senses and awareness tingling, and put her on this very path.

It'd been enough. Enough for Cat to commit body, heart, soul, into finding the truth.

Justice.

Because this world here had just wanted to sweep Norma and all her troubles under some rug to be forgotten, to let the dirt settle where it lay, though preferably out of sight.

Truth was, Cat had come to Butte looking to do some good, to help out those who had nothing left for them. No hope. No light. No chance at all of justice.

Someone exactly like Norma.

Doc Griffin finished the buttons on Cat's blouse, breaking through her thoughts of the past.

"There you go. Won't be long at all before you'll be back to dressing yourself. I imagine you're eager for the day."

"Very."

"You know," he said, "if it wasn't for you, Norma would never have gotten what peace she had in the end. And those girls, they can't have that anymore either if you go and tear something in that shoulder of yours."

He gave Cat a pointed look.

Then Doc Griffin put on that tall dark hat of his on his head and tipped it to her, understanding, shining and bright, reflected in his eyes. "They need hope, Miss Cowboy Cat. Hope. I'm sure you understand my meaning."

She had. Even if she was doubting herself, she'd understood it.

Which was an unfair blow, and he damn well knew it.

Which, of course, was why he'd said it.

Hell, it wasn't like she gonna push herself; she wasn't that stupid. Jesus, that *was* the point about the body doing the hurting. It told you, right darn true, when you were being stupid and pushing too far and too hard.

Cat could listen to her body just fine.

What she wasn't good at was listening to *other* people. Certainly when they were telling her what, and what not, to do.

Like now.

Like with Mrs. Allen who'd taken it up as her personal responsibility to see Cat whole and healed, which apparently meant seeing the doctor's orders carried out to the letter. Including his final insistence that Cat have more "rest" before she "venture outside and find herself in another heap of trouble."

Which was why she and Mrs. Allen were in their current standoff.

And the winner... well, let's just say the outcome wasn't exactly clear yet, and any man with a half a sense in his head was far, far away from Mrs. Allen's boarding house.

At the moment, though, there wasn't a person in sight. Not a single shifting of feet on floorboards. No one.

Not even Mrs. Allen's faithful Chin.

Cat crossed her arms, slow and careful-like to keep the bruises from pullin', giving her body time to adjust as pain flared right on through her shoulder at the movement. Hurt like hell, it did, but she wasn't about to let an inch of it show.

She had a point to make, after all. A mighty good one, too.

Course, Mrs. Allen's gray eyes narrowed at the sight, which just went to prove nothing much got by that woman.

But Cat was done caring about the doctor's orders.

There was only so much damn pie a person could eat before she went crazy and started shootin', before she lost what little hold she had over the woman she was tryin' so hard to remember, and to be.

Enough was enough.

CHAPTER TWO

To be fair, she could see, clear as day, that Mrs. Allen was getting mighty darn tempted to shoot Cat herself.

All the signs were there, practically humming off the other woman. She stood there in her heavily-layered dress, and it flowed off her like she was some dark, avenging angel or something. Yet, she wore it in such a regal manner that each movement became one of grace... and a bare hint of hardships survived. That underneath those wrinkles and her silky dark hair, except for that silver streak right down the middle, was a kind of strength most men didn't come in contact with their whole lives. That they wouldn't even recognize if it bit 'em on the ass. That they, almost to a man, had no idea the truth depth and strength living and sparking behind those gray eyes.

Truth was, everything about Mrs. Allen, from her dress to her presence, was one which men nodded in welcome admiration. They saw her and they felt... well, mostly safe. After all, she was a strong woman with a keen intelligence, and while they might not be exactly comfortable, Mrs. Allen managed to toe that line between acceptance and discomfort.

And somehow, never once steppin' over it.

Mrs. Allen was accepted and respected by polite society and she fit... nice enough, anyway... into their little world views. To them, it didn't matter that, like now, she was dusted head to foot in flour, and that there were a few mended bits of her dress, though only a careful eye could spot this. And regarding Mrs. Allen's past, well, it *was* in the past and she did nothing to remind them of this.

Other than the fact that she was allowing Cat to board in her home.

Cat, who was another story entirely.

Oh, Cat drew the eye, same as Mrs. Allen, but it certainly was not in admiration.

She wore her true self, her essence, right there, right out in the open for the world of men to see. And the men, well, they usually got so pale so fast, their faces turning right quick into an ashy white, like they were gonna faint themselves dead at the sight.

Her blue jeans hugging her hips just so, her boots smacking hard onto those boardwalks, leaving clumps of mud and whatnot behind her. Her revolver fitting snug and comforting at her hip, the holster swaying in tune with her gait. A place where both belonged, and there being no question, none whatsoever, of her knowing how to use it.

Course, then there those who got so enraged at the sight of her that she often was mighty glad for the revolver at her side, and the ease she moved with it.

She could tell, in a mere glance, their thoughts and their intentions. They didn't have to speak one word; she just knew. Could see it in their movements, like the way their muscles tightened at the corner of their mouths or just above their eyebrows. Could hear it in the sharp inhale of breath. Could feel it in their eyes, their gaze, as they looked at her.

This was a skill her daddy had taught her during those few years when she'd been blessed with his presence. And she'd continued to hone this skill, this gift, of seeing all the truths, all of them right there in the open, all those little details that seemed so small and insignificant, but which were, in fact, so much more. They told the whole story of a person.

And Cat was doing it, right now, with Mrs. Allen.

Her wrinkles pinched together right at the corner of her eyes. The slight tightening of her hands, poised as they were on her hips, leaving a deeper stain from the white flour that even Chin would have a hard time dealing with.

She was certainly angry, though that was pretty much a given.

Fear and concern, however, were the underlying truths. The very ones which Mrs. Allen wasn't about to admit, and one, too, Cat wasn't about to admit, either.

Initially, when Cat had first started healing, Dusty had pushed them both to talk, to get the worst of those feelings out and then move on again. But he'd let the matter go after a day or two, falling into his own quiet, his own shadow, one that seemed to lengthen with the days.

But the truth was, the hurt Cat felt wasn't about to just let go. She'd trusted Mrs. Allen, and like it or not, as new as that trust had been, it still hurt like the devil. And it'd only grown worse as shut up in the house as they'd been.

Not that Mrs. Allen was trapped.

She could leave any darn time she wanted. She'd simply *chosen* not to because she knew damn well the second her back was turned Cat would be snagging her hat, slapping it on her head, and heading out that door so fast it wouldn't hit her heels on the way out.

In truth, there were a whole lot 'a words being left unsaid and unspoken, festering right there between them, becoming just as dense and suffocating as the relentless smoke outside. They both knew it, both had their issues, and both were too darn stubborn to admit it, either.

Hence, the standoff.

Mrs. Allen stood there, her shoes rooted to her nicely polished floors, floors which showed not even the slightest hint of what had transpired here a week ago, including the near burning of the house.

But Cat remembered, just as she remembered the state of her boots when she'd come trudging out of those tunnels.

All of it... the memories, her mistakes, and near failures, and those who'd nearly paid for those failures. It was so very raw and just standing here was reminding her of it all.

Cat found her hand reaching up to her injured shoulder completely of its own accord. She touched the spot gently there, just enough to cause her breath to catch from that sharp sting of pain, which shivered right down her arm to her fingers and stayed there.

All the choices she'd made... the good, the bad... and all those disappointments. Could almost see her ma's gaze looking up at her through the past, and a disappointed frown that just about mirrored Mrs. Allen's.

Mrs. Allen, whose gray eyes narrowed at Cat's hand, which was still resting there, just so, on her injured shoulder.

Cat dropped her hand.

Then she shoved aside the lingering memory of that night, of all those questions that had followed, like what *would* have happened if she'd waited for Blake instead of running headfirst into the cribs. Christopher Blake, a police officer and Mrs. Allen's nephew, a man who'd hated everything Cat was on principle and yet, somehow, in such a short time, stirred up a whole lot of confused, mixed feelings—

No.

Cat shook her head. She had enough to deal with without bringing Blake, and his continued absence, into the picture.

Mrs. Allen's frown got all twisty then, which meant Cat hadn't been doing a good job hiding her feelings in the first place.

A misstep she'd been making ever since she'd stepped off that train and into Butte.

"You'll have to get used to it, you know." Mrs. Allen stayed where she was, hands slapped there on her hips, but they weren't digging into her dress and staining the fabric as bad. "You're part of the family now, for better or worse, and there's just no hiding truth. Or pain. Or hurting. Which you clearly *are* still hurting."

Cat flinched at the word.

Family.

And did her best to ignore it.

"Course I'm hurting," she said. "Injuries take time to heal, and I'm more than willing to give it the time it needs. What I'm *not* willin' to do is sit here like a plucked hen any longer. I need air. Fresh air. I need wind on my face."

"'Three things you're not gonna find in Butte, as you well know."

Which Cat did, and really didn't care.

"I'll settle for the earth under my feet," Cat said, "frozen and cold as it is. I'll settle for simply walking and moving my body."

They both kept staring at the other, and Cat had a feeling that, like her, Mrs. Allen was feeling the anger leach out of their insides, replaced instead by a kind of tiredness that went right to the bones.

Neither woman willing to nudge, neither woman willingly to back down, either.

Christ.

Dusty was probably right; they *needed* to talk.

Cat tugged and pulled at the long strands of her dark blonde hair. She'd already redone that braid a thousand times today, purely out of frustration. Hell. It'd be a whole lot easier if she could just pull her gun and start shootin', let out her own pain by lettin' loose a whole volley of bullets at some unsuspecting target.

Except she knew, from experience, that such actions didn't do a damn to dull the pain.

Neither did breaking open a bottle of whiskey.

Still... even if whiskey wasn't exactly the right choice, it certainly would do for now. Certainly if she was thinkin' about having an honest conversation, especially when she still felt the ghosts of her parents nearby. Her ma in that kitchen back there, banging away with the pots and pans, her pa sitting right there at the couch, smokin' on his pipe, legs crossed at the ankles. They were so close, Cat could almost feel their icy touch.

And with them, of course, came Alice.

Alice...

And right along with Alice were all of Cat's mistakes and missteps, and the consequences that'd followed. Choices she'd made and maybe ones she could have done better. Just like that night at Grace's Gardens, when she'd gone headfirst into the cribs and gotten surprised, and nearly killed, by Mr. Rippi.

She hadn't waited for Blake. There'd been no time. Not with an innocent, another girl—Abigail's—life at stake.

No time.

And yet...

Cat's shoulder, all those bruises there, the injured, fractured bone, they all tingled in both pain and something deeper. Something that felt an awful lot like realization.

There was no turning back that clock. Couldn't change what had happened in the past. She knew it, hell, she lived it, every day, when she remembered her sister.

But the real truth was harder to bear.

She wasn't some western legend right out of those dime novels. She was just a woman, and one who had some grand notion of helping those in the shadow world no one else cared about. It didn't take some soothsayer to tell her what her ma would think about that. And just how foolish her little quest was, regardless of what Doc Griffin had thought.

She could, and did, bleed. And she hurt, too. Both her body and heart. And right now, they were hurting.

She wasn't invincible. She wasn't Cowboy Cat and she certainly wasn't Miss Justice, either.

Maybe she never would be.

CHAPTER THREE

Mrs. Allen took her hands right off her hips and shook a hard, pointed finger at Cat. "That's it, girl. You need a drink."

Cat blinked.

It was about the very last thing she'd expected Mrs. Allen to say.

"I see that look you've got," Mrs. Allen said. "All that pity shining in your eyes, and yes, I can see those tears you're trying so hard to keep from spilling. Trust me, it won't work. The heart will do as it will and it will cry as it will."

Mrs. Allen grabbed two glasses from the small table there, poured out that amber-like liquid, drops of it dribbling down the side as Mrs. Allen quickly pressed one glass into Cat's hand.

Her good hand.

"I'm willing to talk," Mrs. Allen said, "and I daresay that you are, too. This situation isn't working anymore for the either of us, and I'd like to do what we can and fix what we can."

Cat breathed in, let it out, and felt part of her old self stir.

The girl her daddy had taught to stare down a rifle's sights at a deer, how the whole world fell away and became that one, narrowed focus. The girl who'd became a woman and found herself in Butte, determined as all get out to find the truth of a deceased fallen lady few others cared about.

Healing from a physical injury wasn't just about healing muscles and bones. It was healing the insides, too, the parts that got shaken real good. The parts that one didn't know if you'd ever heal properly again until you got up and tried.

She needed to try.

Had to.

"Now," Mrs. Allen said, "are you gonna tell me what's really going on or are you just gonna keep pretending that you're mad being stuck in this house. If you're willing, anyway."

The real reasons. All of them.

"I'm willing," Cat said.

Mrs. Allen smiled. It was a small one, and sad, one that just about summed up all of what Cat was feeling, all her uncertainly, how unsteady she felt right to her soul... as if Mrs. Allen knew the feeling herself.

She probably did.

"Good." Mrs. Allen took a sip of the whiskey and shuddered. "It's been awhile. I seemed to have lost my tolerance on the stuff. No matter. The occasion certainly calls for something stronger than tea."

Cat took a few sips of her own and felt it burn all the way down. Not burning through those emotions and feelings, certainly not the lingering sense of her parents nearby, but then, one couldn't hide from the past. Or from yourself.

Much as a person could try, anyway.

Cat sighed and felt the burn from the whiskey, but also another kind of burn, tears and the like that she still held onto and wouldn't dare let fall. Not when it wasn't safe to do so. Not when she could still feel the shame from her past, her parents, her sister, so very close by.

Mrs. Allen sat at her chair and gestured for Cat to take her usual spot on the couch. After only a moment's hesitation, she did.

"I know I've been pushing you," Mrs. Allen said. "And I knew darn well when you walked into my house and told me right what you were thinking of doing, of finding the truth about Norma's death, the dangers you might be walking into. 'Course, I hadn't quite expected you to go tangling with a copper king of all things—"

"I never even met Daly."

"Doesn't matter. Those were close personal friends of Marcus Daly, and you were sure close enough to feel the heat of *that* fire, as you well know. But my point is, I knew who you were and what you were aiming to do. What you *still* are."

A shiver slid down Cat's back. Again, the uncertainty and her hands started to shake some.

She put the glass down on the table.

Mrs. Allen noticed, of course, but said nothing. Maybe she knew that part, too. Maybe.

"I suppose," Mrs. Allen said, "I just wasn't expectin' to take such a liking to you, and the thought of you not getting back on your feet, of being your whole self again—I feel responsible. I wasn't there to help and I should have been."

Cat closed her eyes, already feeling the part that'd been left unsaid.

Like family.

They were a long, long way from being family, even though they'd all started to feel it—Cat, Mrs. Allen, Dusty... even...

Blake.

But it hadn't lasted long, though, that quiet moment in time, almost like a pause, almost like the way Cat's gift worked and the whole world slowed down while she took each and every tiny detail. Instead, it was like life itself had finally caught up with them. After the adrenaline of that night faded away, as the truth of Norma's life, and death, finally settled around town and the parts they'd played in reaching that truth settled and nothing but ash and soot and dust was left.

Just like she'd received no offered invitations from Blake to dinner, to dance.

Cat glanced down and saw her hands will still shaking.

Mrs. Allen reached out and took Cat's hands in hers. "I am sorry."

"You lied to me," Cat said. "You broke my trust."

"I did."

Mrs. Allen didn't bother denying it, which Cat was grateful for.

The truth, any kind of truth, really, was rarely a nice and neat answer, certainly never clear cut and obvious. Instead, it was messy. Lines blurred and crisscrossed, where nothing was black or white, just gray and shadows.

And while Cat understood the reasoning, understood that Mrs. Allen had taken Dusty's word and trust over Cat's—Dusty, who was just a boy but very much like family—how could she fault the older woman? Hell, the only reason Mrs. Allen had gotten involved with Norma, sought and pushed the police about her death, had been because of Dusty.

Norma's brother.

See?

A right plum mess it was.

Mrs. Allen's hands tightened on Cat's as if she knew exactly what she was thinking.

"I apologize for my actions," Mrs. Allen said. "I know I hurt you and broke your trust, and I know there's nothing more valuable to you, to *us*."

To women who'd both walked the line and survived it.

"It's all we have left," Cat said.

"It is. But you also know why I made the choices I did. Believe me, it just about drove me mad knowing you were here, standing in the middle of that rattlesnake's nest. And me? I spent that whole time hiding out with Blake like a little old lady, and not being able to do a thing to help you."

Cat leaned back, slipping her hands free, and closed her eyes.

Her hands weren't shaking but her insides were. All thanks to those memories, which were stirring up like crazy again. Harder this time, too, like they didn't want to be denied.

Refused to be denied.

Cat knew all about denying feelings, knew that regardless, they found a way to surface again and it wasn't ever in a way, or a place, you wanted them to.

Still...

She couldn't do it. Not now. Not here.

It just hurt too damn much.

Somehow this place, this woman, this home—hell, everything about Butte—still kept finding a way to get under her skin, crawl to those dark corners, those shadows in her soul she didn't want to look closely at.

Cat opened her eyes, and this time she didn't stop the tears from welling up. She didn't look away from Mrs. Allen, either.

"It was too dangerous," she said. "For you. And you were all Dusty had left."

"*He* helped you. A boy. *He* got to get right in on the action while I sat on my hands and did nothing."

"I didn't want him to."

A boy, not even twelve years, who'd already seen too much.

A shadow soul somehow finding a way to survive, somehow seeing Cat for who she truly was and roping her into doing the one thing he needed more than anything else:

Finding the truth about Norma.

Oh, Cat had, and in doing so, pretty much everything Dusty had loved and cared for, what little he had left, was at risk—thanks to all the players who'd been involved in Norma's death and the following cover-up.

See?

A right mess of a situation and no clear-cut answers for her, or for Mrs. Allen. Or for Dusty, who'd turned back into that shadow self and was only seen in the quiet of the night when he thought no one else was up and looking, and saw that same flash of hurt Cat now wore. The ways his hands seemed to shake as hers now did.

They both had more than a few things they needed lettin' go of.

Somehow.

Some way.

And for Cat... that meant taking a risk again. If she was willing to put herself out there, to look into those dark, shadowy corners of her soul, and let them out again.

She didn't want to. Though she didn't know if she had much of a choice, either.

"I'm putting my faith in you again," Cat said. "But you need to do me the same."

Now it was Mrs. Allen's turn to take a long, long sip of that whiskey, and boy, the woman that she was, she didn't shudder one bit as it went down, either.

"You want outside."

"I do," Cat said.

"Even if it's not safe."

"I never asked it to be."

"Before you're completely whole and healed."

"I was never whole, and a great part of me was in need of some healing." A part that Norma and her story, her truth, *had* helped heal.

"God help me," Mrs. Allen whispered, "I know it. I know, too, that you won't stop. Won't wait for help, either, even if I did hire a man to keep step with you."

"No, I wouldn't."

Mrs. Allen put her glass down with a light chink.

It was empty.

"Well, to be fair," Mrs. Allen said, "I think Doctor Griffin was wrong on one account. Healing the body is important, but so is healing the soul. You need to be outside. You need to see who you really are under all that, and you can't do that by sitting around here eating my pie all day. And whether I like it or not, you're a grown woman, though I'd feel a lot better if you had some escort with you."

"Like who? Chin? Blake?"

Mrs. Allen's gray eyes widened, but in sympathy. "Regarding my nephew, I know he hasn't—"

"It doesn't matter."

Cat waved her hand, her right one, the one that didn't hurt with so much as a finger movement.

"Blake's got a right mess to clean up, finding all those bits and trails of corruption, and, well, he's also entitled to his own opinions."

Regardless of how much it hurt in the end.

Mrs. Allen shook her head, though Cat guessed it had more to do with Blake than her, which made her feel... marginally better about the situation.

"I know," Mrs. Allen said. "Don't I know it. He's not available, and the Lord knows where Dusty's run off to. He's not been right himself these past few days, and I'm worried, but with his sister and all that ugliness, I suppose it's to be expected. All right, Miss Cat. I'll trust in you and you'll learn to trust in yourself again. I think that's probably the best thing for everyone right now."

And Cat agreed.

She *was* having a hard time seeing who she was these days, seeing beyond the bruises and the woman she'd strived so hard to be. How on earth could a woman like her, a fallen woman no less, do something so grand and important as find justice?

Doc Griffin had thought so.

And all those girls in the cribs, the ones who'd come to her aid when she'd asked for it, when it'd just been her and Rippi and MacDonald, and poor Abigail trapped there between them, all those girls had thought so, too. Enough to rise up and help.

Cat didn't get a chance to think more on the matter because that's when she heard the unmistakable slight creak on the floorboard.

The sound of someone quietly approaching.

Someone who didn't want to be heard.

Or discovered.

CHAPTER FOUR

Cat shifted on the couch, slowly lowering her hand until it rested against the cool metal of her revolver. Its presence, familiar, comforting.

Again came the sound.

The slight creak of a floorboard, of air that had gotten trapped underneath and no longer rested flush against its foundation. The sound was so slight that most people would miss it, including Mrs. Allen. She tattered on, moving onto the subject of some gentleman who'd wanted to meet Cat but she'd sent away, not liking the way his eyes had squinted, like a hungry little mouse, apparently.

Mrs. Allen hadn't heard the continued quiet, the small shift of feet moving lightly from the entryway and then towards the stairs. There was also no telltale sound of the door and its unusual temperament, the one which required a good shoulder slam to actually shut the darn thing, which in turn caused the whole house to shake.

Instead, there'd been no slam, no shaking house. As if the person knew exactly the door's temperament and just how to close it to make the house unaware their presence.

There were only two people who could do that.

And while Blake was one, he was also a large, muscular man. He could move quietly enough, blending in with the shadows and the people around him so smoothly, so effectively as if to make him invisible, which Cat knew from experience, but she also knew he couldn't move *that* quietly.

There was another slight creak, just a bare whisper of wood pressing down, as if the person were purposefully walking with their heels up in the air, and the clear, hopeful intent, to skip the sitting room entirely and return upstairs without anyone being the wiser.

Cat dropped her hand away from her gun and rose. "You'll have to excuse me, Mrs. Allen. I've been cooped up long enough and need some air, fresh as it can come by in these parts, anyway."

Mrs. Allen's mouth tightened, clearly unhappy, but also not going back on her promise, either.

"Of course. Do be careful."

"I'll do my best."

"Yes, I know. And that's what I'm afraid of."

This last, though, she said to Cat's back because Cat was already up and out of the sitting room, her longer strides taking her out quick as possible in case Mrs. Allen had a change of heart—and in case Dusty wanted to scramble for those stairs.

She certainly wasn't in a mood to scramble up after him, though she would if needed. She had this feeling, this feeling, this tingle in her gut. It told her she needed to be here, needed to see him. As if even though he'd been avoiding her, he actually needed her.

Thankfully, there was no reason to scramble and twist her body and shoulder in ways they wasn't interested in doing at the moment.

Dusty stood there in the entryway, one foot raised in the air, the other planted firm and quiet. He looked up, quick-like, as if a startled rabbit caught snacking on some farmer's prized carrots.

Which was, in itself, fine.

Everyone was allowed their privacy, allowed to keep to themselves when they so wished. Cat certainly needed that more than most folk.

What wasn't fine, however, was the look of Dusty himself.

His dark hair, which was usually stickin' out from under his cap, springing each and every way it could go, now just... sagged there. There were dark smudges round his face, like he'd gone and scrubbed it with a dirty cloth before trying to sneak on in. And underneath his eyes, too, looked so deep and black, like the very bruises lining Cat's shoulder, as if he hadn't slept a wink this past day or two. But that wasn't the worst of it, wasn't what made her stop dead in her tracks, made the breath in her chest catch and hold right there, and a sorrow she felt right to her soul.

Those green eyes of his, the ones she'd first seen getting off the train from Miles City, they'd literally pierced right through that smoke and ash. Practically begging her, daring her, to come over and ask for a newspaper, ask what kind of local news he might know.

They'd been the kind of eyes that stirred her own passion, made her believe in such a silly dream of justice for those who lived in the shadow world.

Now, though, his eyes were dull and tired.

And... sad.

A kind of sadness that ate away at a soul, right through the middle, and left nothing behind.

A look she knew well. And still did.

"It looks like you spent a day in the mines," Cat said, keeping her voice low.

And he did.

"Yeah?" He asked. "What of it?"

"That's not where you were, was it?"

All that ash and grime and soot. Sure, he'd tried to clean it off, but it was still there. It clung to his dark clothes, the trailing ends of thread along the cuff of his pants, clearly a mending that couldn't hold up any longer. There was also the ink stains on his hands, smeared and stained now, probably came right from freshly printed papers.

"Does it matter where I was?" he asked. "No one sure cared before this mess with my sister."

Cat took a few steps towards him and reached out, again with her good arm, and tugged on the sleeve of his coat. This green-blackish grime came right off onto her fingertips and she held them up.

"I care," she said.

Truth was, it sure looked like he went down and toiled in the darkness, in that sweltering heat for twelve straight hours before gettin' hauled back up to the surface. But for Dusty, his toil had lasted longer. A whole life, in fact, and all his recent losses—his sister—looked like it'd finally come crashing down around him and he didn't have a whole lot left in his body to keep himself upright.

As if, as if he were about to lose even more.

Most likely himself.

Christ, and she'd missed it. Missed all those signs. She'd been right there, watching it happen, and hadn't seen it. She'd been so wrapped up in herself, in her own aches and frustrations, her own memories and her ghosts, she'd missing someone who needed her... someone right in front of her. Someone she cared about.

Almost like family.

Dusty deliberately wouldn't meet her eyes. Another piece of the puzzle, of what she'd missed, fell into place.

Cat let out a breath.

Of course.

He'd avoided her 'cause he knew damn well she'd start putting it together. That she *would* start seeing the signs and reading 'em. All those little details, those emotions that leaked 'round even a person's strongest defenses for the whole world to see.

Well, not the whole world. Just Cat.

Right then Cat felt the small pieces of herself, the parts that had lived and survived by her gut, her instincts, who'd dared come to Butte and help shadow souls—like Dusty—find some small measure of peace and justice, *that* part of her... stirred a bit. Woke up, almost.

Just a little. Enough... to feel like her old self before everything that had happened down in those cribs.

Her hands, they still shook, as if reminding her she wasn't invincible, she could, and did, fail.

But whatever was going on with Dusty, she couldn't fail him now.

"You went to the tunnels again," she said.

Dusty shrugged. "I've been a few places. Someone has to."

"Dusty," she said.

And still, he wouldn't meet her eyes.

Which was fine.

Because Cat knelt and went to his.

Now, it wasn't like Dusty was a young lad, neither tall or short, but he felt small in that moment. Felt just like the child she'd been so many times long ago, the same child who haunted her own memories. The single, deliberate look as if her ma came out of that kitchen right at that moment, hands pressed on her hips, disappointment lit in 'bout her every feature because of the wild daughter she'd had instead of gettin' the boy who fit such a personality.

"What's going on?" Cat asked, pulling herself hard and away from those ghosts.

"Nothing."

She touched his chin, though she didn't raise it. "I want to help."

"You're gonna leave."

His words startled her so much that Cat dropped her hand.

"Why?" she asked. "Why would you think that?"

He shrugged. "I've seen the way you've looked. Starin' out the window. Lost. Alone."

He finally looked up and met her eyes.

Now it was Cat's turn to want to look away.

She didn't, though.

"You look just like me," he said, "and you can't. You can't. There are people, they need you, Cat. You can't be like the rest of us."

"I wish it were that easy."

And she did. Truly and sincerely.

"Well, if not you, then someone will have to."

He went to pull away from her, but Cat saw the movement.

Apparently some parts of her, while shaking and uncertain, were still part of her, still in control and awake. Everything her daddy had taught her. She saw it in those tiny details. The way Dusty's muscles moved, first from the tight frown around his mouth, carrying down to his neck, then to the rest of him, his shoulders, torso. All those small, barely perceptible movements and tensing, in preparation for him actually pulling away—

No. Running away.

So Cat moved first, without thought, just on instinct alone. She trusted it, just as she used to before Norma, before coming to Butte.

Cat gripped his shoulder, holding him, just enough to keep him from pulling away... and running.

The very same instinct she'd felt in herself not long ago, standing there in that sitting room, with all the ghosts and memories piling on out of her.

And from said sitting room, Cat heard the unmistakable swoosh of a heavy dress risin' and moving. Then the clink of glasses, the rims, most likely, coming together as if a single hand picked them both up.

Dusty followed Cat's gaze, and his whole body tensed right quick.

He didn't want Mrs. Allen to see. He didn't want her to know...

Well, what exactly, he hadn't yet revealed, though she hoped he would. Not here, though, that was for certain.

"Come on," Cat said. "I need some air, and Mrs. Allen wasn't keen on me going alone."

"I can't."

"Why on earth not?"

She thought maybe it's 'cause he was tired from being up all night or for how many days straight as his own ghosts did the haunting, but then she saw a glimpse of something else.

Sorrow.

One that didn't have to do with him or Cat.

And that got her insides tingling again. That feeling in her gut, the same one when she'd spied in from all the way across that train station.

The knowing of something important was coming.

"Come on, before Mrs. Allen changes her mind 'bout letting me outside. And then, when you're ready, you can tell me what this is all about. What say you, Green Eyes?"

She called him by the nickname she'd given him on that train station and she saw, if just a small amount, of relaxing from him, from herself. As if they both needed to know that under her own shadows, her own ghosts, Cowboy Cat was still there.

Maybe.

CHAPTER FIVE

Truth was, Dusty didn't say yes right away.

In fact, it took the growing sounds of Mrs. Allen cleaning up, the clink of glasses, the swoosh of her dress as it caught on the couch for a moment before swishing free again. Cat could almost see Mrs. Allen as she slid that untouched pie onto another plate, saving it for later and for a more appreciative audience—and no kidding; even from here, Cat could smell those baked apples, that slight dusting of cinnamon.

Maybe Dusty had smelled it, too, and maybe he knew that his stomach's growling was about to give them both away because he immediately turned and headed out the front door again.

He said nothing to Cat, just turned and walked out, pulling his gloves back on as he did.

Cat grabbed her coat, slapped her wide-brimmed cowboy hat onto her head, and followed after him. Not that she moved with her usual crisp, determined pace. In fact, she had to pause there and shrug the coat on, slow and careful like, feeling her face heat and that kind of frustration she'd felt earlier come roarin' back.

She hated being weak. Hated needing help, and by damn she

wasn't about to ask Dusty to string through her coat buttons as Doc Griffin had done earlier.

Instead, she left the front open.

Still, Cat could practically *hear* her ma's opinion on the matter, and just what in hell she thought she was doin', going outside as she was, as if she were some officer or detective out solving the great crimes of the world, when they all knew she wasn't. When they all knew, point blank, who the real Cat was.

Dusty, though, said nothing.

Not about Cat following after him or how long it was takin' her to actually get out the door. Instead, he merely waited. And when it was clear Cat was dressed, he gave her a questioning look, specifically glancing at her undone buttons, then headed straight into those thick folds of smoke and cloud and darkness.

She'd been waiting for this moment, practically bouncing on her heels to get outside, to feel the hard, cold earth under her boots again, but it took a whole five steps for her body to start aching from the effort. Her shoulder, already startin' to twist and throb like the muscles there had forgotten what it felt like to *sway* as the body moved, one of the many aspects needed to keep a person upright, balanced, and comfortable.

Though, when it came to Butte, comfort certainly wasn't a word commonly used. Especially when they were trudging through suffocating clouds of sulfur. It burned Cat's eyes, causing her to tear up at the same time as that thick smoke slid on down her throat, causin' it to scratch and scrape raw just from trying to breathe.

And breathing?

Well, that was a laughable attempt at best, though she kept trying.

Just as she kept trying to see the boardwalk in front of her as she followed Dusty, and that her boots actually landed on some hard, solid surface and not accidently a missing plank or, well, the *end* of the boardwalk.

Such was Butte in winter, when those mines were burning off all their ore and whatnot, and not a wisp of true wind came down from those mountains ringing it so—not that Cat had ever seen the mountains, mind you, but she'd read up about them.

She followed Dusty's small form, he slowing his pace so she wouldn't lose him in the dark and ash, which in itself was a reminder of just how far she had to go before she was well and truly healed. And she did her darnedest to not get overly frustrated on this matter.

Doc had told straight; she had a ways to go before she was healed.

If she ever would be again.

Didn't make it any less frustrating, though.

Still, Cat followed as best she could, moving her legs and feet a bit faster than they seemed comfortable with, knowing she'd be sore as all get out tomorrow, but she couldn't seem to help herself. For his part, Dusty clearly had some destination in mind. His steps were sure and even—purposeful, even. He turned this way and that with the kind of surety she'd seen in him back at the train station what felt like a lifetime ago.

And Dusty, well, he knew Butte.

Really well, in fact.

He wasn't needing to read no street signs or nothing, but seemed to have his own internal map and markers. Cat had a similar one, herself, though the thick smoke was makin' it a bit more challenging to see where was up and where was down. Still, it was one of her gifts, her skills, that her daddy had taught her when it came to surviving in a wilderness. And truth was, Butte felt a whole lot closer to a wilderness than a city at the moment. Especially when it felt like she and Dusty were completely alone amidst all those empty, silent brick buildings, as if not even their ghosts were willing to open up a window and peak outside.

Even the streets were a bit quieter.

Sure, she heard the bells and whistles in the distance, hacks and their whips crackin' the air, but it felt like those sounds came from a great distance off. There wasn't even the faint traces of golden light from lamp posts or lanterns.

Just the darkness and the smoke.

And not a one of it seemed to bother Dusty. He just dodged down one street, then onto another. He turned up some ally only to head back out at another point, one that Cat had no idea was even there, and even if it had been bright and sunny and daylight, she still would have missed it.

Dusty squeezed on through this space between buildings, it seemed, as if a builder had forgotten to finish this one little section here. After a moment, Cat followed him.

At this point, it was past noon and about every inch of her was aching. The muscles in her shoulders tense and hurtin', and her stomach even growling a bit, which was a good sign. It was good to have an appetite again. Maybe they were even near enough to that noodle house, the one where she and Dusty had eaten once, the one that had also been a favorite of his sister's.

Finally, when Cat was about sure her shaking legs were gonna collapse right underneath her, Dusty popped out onto yet another street... and Cat saw they weren't alone anymore.

In fact, it wasn't just one or two folks braving their errands in the smoke and darkness, but a whole group of 'em.

She squinted her eyes trying to see, which only made them tear up and burn all the more. The first thing she noticed was there were two types of individuals—adults, and all women for that matter, and the rest were children.

Young children.

The whole group was movin' together, as if one giant mass, through them dense, thick clouds. Each of 'em bundled up good in their heavy skirts and coats. Hats and bonnets pulled so low and tight around faces while scarves wrapped even tighter 'round necks and throats, as if each speck and stitch of clothing was doing everything possible to keep those young ones warm and cozy.

Instinctively, Cat reached up to gently touch the faded pink scarf she always wore—but it wasn't there.

Panic gripped her for a moment. A heavy weight slammed into

her chest so hard and fierce and fast she almost couldn't breathe... and then... she remembered.

Not lost, just forgotten.

Alice's scarf, the one her sister had made for Cat a lifetime ago, was upstairs. Left there, dangling across Cat's bed with that neatly folded floral quilt. Because why *would* she be wearing it, cooped up in the house as she'd been for a full week? She'd no need to wear it, not inside as she'd been. And then, well, she'd been in such a rush to leave, had been so concerned about Dusty and what he'd said, she hadn't thought twice about it.

For the first time in years, she'd forgotten Alice's scarf. It wasn't with her.

Cat's gut twisted fierce at the thought that she'd actually left it behind, something she'd have never done before coming to Butte.

But... it was only a scarf, right? And hadn't she earned some sympathy from Alice's ghost after what Cat had done for Norma? Some small bit of atonement for all those mistakes she'd made?

Maybe.

Maybe not.

Still, it'd be waiting for her back in her room when she got back. It could wait.

At least, that's what her rational mind said while her insides told a whole other story.

"You okay?" Dusty asked.

Cat dropped her hand. "Yeah... just forgot something."

Dusty eyed her neck, those sharp eyes of his probably immediately noticing the difference. He was a lot like her in that regard, noticing all them details, putting all the pieces together. Yet he said nothing about the scarf, just like he said nothing about why they were here—and why they'd stopped right as this group of mothers, and those children, passed by.

Cat's attention immediately went to the children.

Really, she couldn't help herself.

Couldn't help but be drawn in by the light shining out of their eyes, the kind of joy and excitement that even the most suffocating, dense clouds of ash and soot couldn't dampen. And watching them, watching their light, it helped Cat breathe a little easier, made her aches and burning eyes hurt a little less.

Not much, but enough.

Enough to tease out a smile of her own.

Many of the children were toddling as best they could over the frozen mud banks of the street and the half-rotted boardwalk, while others, babies, were wrapped up tight against their mothers in some sling or wrap. Others held onto each other's hands and a fair few had grabbed fistfuls of their mother's skirts, clutching that fabric so tight like their lives depended on it. Those ones, they were clustered together and holding on, as if afraid they'd be left behind and get lost in the cold, heavy smoke around them.

But... not all children kept themselves tight and safe with their mothers, and *those* were the ones that really brought out a smile in Cat. Those kids, and there were a fair few, ventured to the very outskirts, as if pushing against some invisible ribbon tying them to mothers, who wanted to go farther, explore and walk where none others dared walk. And yet, even those listened, as if they understood this common, accepted knowledge that one simply *had* to remain close.

Except for one.

One child, in particular, stood completely apart from the group.

A little girl, who to Cat, seemed fearless.

This girl was up front and center, and was literally dancing to her own tune.

She had her arms lifted above her head as she twirled this way and that, like it were really some bright spring day and not the cold, dark one it was. The hem of her dress was drooping, unraveling along the bottom, but it never once touched that frozen ground or dragged on the cold dirt there, all thanks to that dancing.

It was like this girl didn't care one whit about what was accepted and expected, or what was going on behind her.

The very sight of her got Cat's heart twisting and twisting hard, and for more than one reason. But despite it, despite feelings and memories she felt stirring up inside her, she simply couldn't take her eyes off the girl.

Nor did she want to.

Neither, it seemed, did Dusty.

He too, was watching the girl, but he'd shifted his body so it was harder for Cat to get a good, clear look at him. As if he didn't want Cat to see all those details, see beyond the surface to what he was feeling underneath, all his own uncertainties and fear.

But she felt him, though. Felt the waves of hurt rollin' off him like it were her own. Noticed, too, the small shaking of his shoulders, as if he were wrestling with some deeper kind of pain, one that was refusing to let go.

"You gonna tell me what we're doing here?" she asked. "Why you were sneaking into the house? Why it looks like you've got the whole of Butte weighing on your shoulders?"

"There's someone... who needs help. Someone who needs your help."

Cat's breath caught in her throat. She hadn't expected it, hadn't expected *this*...

And she should have.

Hell, Dusty had told her as much back at Mrs. Allen's, especially since he thought she was gonna up and leave.

Yet another sign that Cat wasn't herself and maybe would never be again. She didn't know if that person was in her anymore, if she could even be that person again... not after everything that had happened with Norma, with Abigail and all those other girls, how they were put in such danger because of her, digging for the truth as she'd been. And she hadn't a clue just how deep or how dangerous that rattlesnake's nest had been.

Dusty turned and looked at Cat.

His green eyes were blazing, daring her like they'd done that day at the train station, staring at her through all that black smoke and ash, as if a shadow of himself were peakin' out and around all his own hurt, the loss of his sister and truth of who she'd really been.

Stand up, his look seemed to say. *Go and be someone different.*

"I don't know if I can," Cat said, keeping her voice quiet, and low. "But I don't know if I can't, either."

He didn't look away. "Won't know unless you try."

"Yeah, kid. Yeah."

She gripped his shoulder, using her good arm, and squeezed slightly. Somehow she found her voice, somehow she found it even through all that fear and uncertainty that was doing its best to take over her senses.

Somehow she didn't let it.

Couldn't let it.

"All right," she said. "You brought me out here, so you gonna tell me what my being here has to do with her?"

Cat nodded, tipping her hat towards the dancing girl. A smile tugged at Dusty's lips, as if he knew, better than her, that Cat really was in there. That the real her, the her who was aiming to do some good for those who needed it most, wasn't gonna go away anytime soon.

"You tell me, Miss Justice. What do *you* see?"

CHAPTER SIX

That name smacked hard into Cat.

Justice.

It hit harder than even Mr. Rippi when he'd swung that giant piece of wood as he'd done, connecting hard with her shoulders and sending a shockwave of hurt that Cat had felt all the way to the tips of her toes.

That, however, was nothing to what she felt now standing there as she was.

Her boots on the cold, hard planks of the boardwalk. The winter chill and blackness which ate right on through her coat and laughing all the while. Fingers and heart, numb. Frozen, almost, at the mere thought. The mere name.

Justice.

Cat couldn't claim the name anymore; she didn't have a right to claim it.

All her uncertainty, her fears, her mistakes—not to mention that downward, disapproving frown of her ma, one that Cat could see without even closing her eyes—it all came roaring back at that moment and nearly took her out at the knees.

Nearly, but not quite.

Dusty certainly wasn't helping matters as he crossed his arms, narrowed his eyes, almost daring her to say otherwise.

"I don't know if that name suits me anymore," she said finally.

"Does it matter?"

"Yes, it matters a great deal."

Because to someone, in fact, probably the very reason Dusty had brought her here in the first place, that name—and the implication behind the name—mattered a great deal.

Someone needed justice. Someone who the law and justice itself no longer cared about—if it ever did.

Cat let out a breath, one she hadn't realized she'd been holding.

Sure, she was shaking a bit at the knees and her thighs protested simply standing there, as still as they were in all that cold, though both were to be expected after her injury and her rest that'd followed. But the real point of the matter was that she *hadn't* collapsed into a heap, hadn't turned and walked the other way at the mere thought of needing to be that person again, of stepping into that role, of being Cowboy Cat or... Miss Justice.

She was still standing.

And for the first time since her injury, she felt like herself.

Settled, almost.

Not her full self, but enough. Enough for Cat to see the truth before her and all those small, tiny details coming together as it were, into one bigger puzzle.

The first truth came from the group itself, which was almost entirely made up of women and children. These children, however, appeared to be entirely made up of the younger variety. She couldn't be sure, of course, faces and size being a bit hard to see with everyone as bundled up as they were, but Cat was almost certain she didn't see any who were older than four or five. And if there's one thing she'd learned from living in a small town and having grown up in one herself, was that families always came in all shapes and size—and ages.

"They're heading to the schoolhouse," Cat said. "The time fits. Early afternoon. Older kids being let out for the day and these ones headin' out together to pick them up." She nodded towards them. "I didn't know they did that here."

"Mostly during the black winters," Dusty said. "And yeah, everyone does it."

She gave him a look, raising her eyebrows. "Everyone, huh?"

He shrugged. "Most everyone."

Because for all intents and purposes, *he* should be in school just like all those brothers and sisters were.

He could be now, if he wanted to. Cat knew Mrs. Allen had attempted the subject with him once or twice since the incident with Norma. And sure he had a home now, a clean place to live, food to eat, all the essentials, really. He didn't need to scrape by with his wits to survive, picking up all those odd jobs, running errands in the tunnels for different parlor houses, selling papers to folks who got off the train and miners gettin' off shift for the day.

But the truth was, Dusty wouldn't ever be like those kids there, heading out to school and then back home again. He couldn't turn back that clock. Like Cat, his life had been changed livin' in the shadow world... and there was just no going back from that.

Didn't matter how much you wished it, it changed a person, through and through. Dusty knew it, and hell, Cat would bet any of those kids there would take one look at him and know it, too.

"They go mostly by neighborhoods," Dusty continued, "all the families there, coming together, heading out in a group. It keeps kids from getting lost."

"Makes sense."

Which probably also meant that more than a few had gotten lost at some point. And with it being this cold out, the kind of cold that numbed the tip right off your nose, it was no surprise why these mothers were going together, making sure all their school-age children got themselves home, nice and safe, and weren't wandering about lost in that blackness.

"'This one here's headin' to Grant School," he said,. "A right mix of kids from the East side."

Which also made sense.

Cat heard quite a few languages passing amongst the group, though their voices were too hushed for her to catch specific origins and languages. Though, and it was pretty darn clear, there was still quite the dividing line between who was who, and who walked nearest to who.

Dusty didn't add anything more, simply stood there by her side, rubbing his arms and that grime-dusted coat from time to time. Clearly waiting on Cat to go on, to tell him what else she saw.

He didn't have to wait long.

Because the real truth, the one he'd wanted her to see, while a bit harder to glimpse, bit harder to tease out, was right there, naked and bare and brutally honest. Now, if you weren't the type to notice the details, if you weren't paying attention, you would have right missed it entirely.

Cat didn't.

And what she saw made her insides twist even harder.

The dancing girl with her two braided pigtails which bounced up and down off her back. Her smiling, chubby face that stood in that small space between babyhood and childhood. A face that cared nothing at all for what was happening behind her—

Like how the whole group, minus one, were keeping their distance.

Clearly, the one following close behind was the girl's mother. There was just no mistaking the way she hurried after the girl. How she grabbed her skirts in an almost painfully tight grip, the rim of her bonnet flapping up and down again as she moved as quickly as propriety allowed, as if that alone would allow her to catch up those tiny, dancing feet.

To which she didn't.

Cat glimpsed a face through that smoke and ashy black, a face that was desperate to grab her young daughter and pull her back into the safe folds of her dress.

A face that knew darn well she'd never reach her daughter.

The woman's eyes slid to Cat's and, in that moment, they saw each other. A flash of deep brown, darker than even Cat's eyes, and a haunted, terrified look that Cat knew all too well.

Desperation.

Acceptance.

And what was worse, a complete loss of hope.

A feeling that cemented further inside Cat when her gaze slid to Dusty, who'd tucked himself closer to Cat. But the mother saw him anyway, and the way her eyes went wide, that stab of fear and panic and something else, something going sharper and deeper as if reaching right to the soul—

Then the moment passed.

The mother's attention snapped back to her daughter as if Cat and Dusty and all those mothers in the group no longer mattered.

Only the girl mattered... and whoever else this mother was picking up from Grant School.

Cat saw all this in an instant.

Felt it even quicker.

This feeling of seeing the other woman, the hopelessness as it shined out her eyes, but also something more. The determination to keep on going, to keep on living because there were those who depended on her.

That there, that was real strength. True strength, the likes of which Cat had seen all too often living in the shadow world, especially in those who had no choice but to seek this fallen life.

For Cat, this was the kind of feeling that caused her knees to shake and her chest to pull so tight like she had some giant lump that was making breathing near impossible. The small hairs on hers arm standing straight up again.

And there was something else, too, something besides that clog of fear in her chest, that came straight up out 'a herself, something

Dusty swore was still inside her, and now, now Cat glimpsed it for herself—

A certainty. A knowing. And a tingling, one that circled round and round her gut and refused to settle because...

Because someone needed help.

Her help.

And it was about damn time she stopped feeling sorry for herself and accepted it. Accept who she was, and who she was always gonna be.

Mistakes and all.

CHAPTER SEVEN

Cat reached out and gently touched Dusty's shoulder. The movement pulled on her aches and bruises, but even that felt right. Necessary, even. If she was aiming to heal, she'd need to heal her whole self and not just the physical hurts.

Dusty looked up at her, those narrowed eyes of his softening a little, as if he, too, sensed the change.

Cat dropped her hand and nodded towards the mother and the dancing girl. "What can you tell me about them? What do you know?"

"I'd rather hear your guesses. I'm sure you've got some."

"A few," Cat admitted. "Startin' first with you."

"Is that right?"

"I noticed the ink stains earlier on your hands. You were out sellin' papers this morning."

"It's my job."

"One of them. So, were you selling before or after you went down into the tunnels?"

He shrugged. "It don't matter."

"Sure it does. Timing always matters."

"How so?"

Again, Cat tipped her head in the direction of the mother. "You knew exactly who she was, and that little girl. Your attention went right to them and you noticed immediately how those others were pulling away, keeping their distance. That tells me you'd already met them, this mother and daughter, even if only from a distance."

"I know a lot of people in Butte."

Which he did, and she gave him that.

"This time, it was something more," Cat said. "Specific. Like you read something, or someone else did, probably right from the papers they took from you. And that's where you heard about this woman. In fact, you went out of your way and found her, met her even. She recognized you."

Dusty said nothing to this. His silence being more than enough acknowledgement for Cat.

"Also," she said, "you went down into the tunnels at some point, though truth be told, I haven't the faintest idea why unless it was to find out more."

She raised her eyebrows at this last, but Dusty shook his head.

"I had other unrelated business there."

Then he said nothing more on the matter.

Fair enough.

Cat wasn't about to him push if that's what he wanted. Each of them were certainly allowed their secrets, not to mention the tangled mess that was their own past, hers included.

"All right," Cat said. "So are you plannin' on telling me their story? What those papers said about that mother, or are you just gonna have me guess that, too?"

Dusty grinned at her.

It was a real grin, a joyful kind. Full and toothy and completely reminding her, right clear, of the old Dusty. The kid who well and truly lived in that shadow world, and who enjoyed the heck out of it. Enjoyed living each moment on that knife's edge, balanced there, ready fall or ready to jump up even higher, even as those piercing green eyes of his missed nothing.

God how she'd missed him. Missed his spirit during this long week while they'd each suffered in silence in their own hearts and souls.

Dusty tipped his cap at her. "I always liked hearin' your guesses. Hearin' how you put everything together like. But no, this time there's no need."

"Oh?"

But then his grin faded and with it, that small bit of joy Cat had felt faded, too.

"Give it a moment," he said, "and you'll hear plenty."

He was right.

She did.

But hearing and learning the story, that wasn't the real problem. The real problem, for Cat, anyway, was staying quiet. Staying right there, silent and still in the shadows and darkness, like she was just as unimportant and inanimate as those brick buildings looming around them.

Everything inside Cat raged for to act, to move, to do... *something*. Instead, she stood there and listened. Listened at the exchange of hushed and not-so-hushed words passing between those ladies. All the while her heart breaking, just a bit, with every word spoken.

One mother, older than Cat by at least a decade, or it seemed so with all them lines pullin' at her face, around her eyes, her mouth. She had a young one hiked up high on her hip and the poor thing had his face buried full against his mother's chest, as if seeking the warmth of her coat there.

"You *read* the paper this morning, didn't you?" this mother asked another.

"You mean the *Bystander*, Flossie?"

This second mother's hands were free of children, but her skirts, however, were not. Two kids clung to her, holding onto that heavy fabric like their little lives depended on it, as if their feet couldn't take them a step further in that black daylight air.

"You know there's just too many papers to keep up with," the mother continued. "Specially now with all that competing going on between Daly and Clark. Lord, I just wish they'd settle that senate race and get back to matters we care here about in Butte."

This last comment had several others nodding and mumbling agreements to this fact, though for the most part, most seemed more concerned with keeping track of their charges and hurrying through the cold—the quicker they reached their destination, the quicker they'd get themselves home.

Flossie huffed out a breath. "Yes, the *Bystander*, Marybell. This morning's edition. Did you *read* it?"

"No, in fact. I never got the chance. You see, Harold, bless him, well, he just took right off with it this morning. One of the few times I've been seeing him, you know? Busy as they've got him up there at the Big S. Workin' late. Leavin' early. Always so tired and worried with what they've got goin' there, well, anyway, he went and rolled that paper up good and tight, lookin' none too happy, too. He was out the door and long the shift was to start and well, I didn't even have a chance to ask what was in it cause he was just gone. Out the front door in a puff of smoke!"

"*Well*," Flossie said, drawing out the word long as she could, "I can certainly imagine why."

That seemed to perk Marybell's interest. "Oh?"

"He came to my house, in fact. Headed right over, with Reverend Jacobs right beside him as usual, banging on the door until Joe got up and answered it. Indeed, I'm surprised—no, *shocked*—that Harold didn't speak with you before leaving as he did. That was not a kind thing to do, not at all. To think all of us were caught unawares by this... this tragedy." Flossie shook her head again, as if emphasizing her point. "Not right at all."

"Tragedy? Dear Flossie, what on earth do you mean? What should Harold have told me?"

At this, Marybell's voice rose higher, as if not concerned in the slightest about her voice carrying and reaching the others.

Which, in fact, it did.

Suddenly the group seemed to care a whole lot less about the cold and their charges because they were suddenly clustering together, those heavy skirts and coats and bonnets, getting in so good and close Cat had a hard time telling where one woman ended and the next one began.

All except the lone mother with her dancing daughter, which separated even further from the group.

Which, Cat knew, was deliberate. Especially when Flossie there went and sent such a cold, narrowed, and angry look directed right at that poor mother's unprotected back.

This mother, however, did not turn around at their words, even though there was nothing hushed about them no more. Instead, she held her skirts up higher, trying in vain to reach her daughter. Her pace quickened as she hurried even faster, her tightly-buttoned boots striking hard against the frozen mud and the gravel of the street.

Cat's gut tingled.

Hell, her whole body was tingling. She knew, even before Flossie spoke, what was coming next.

They all did.

"It was about Evie," Flossie declared.

"Evie? Evie Blonberg?"

"Of course. That's what I said, isn't it?"

No one replied. No one, most likely, wanted to as if they each knew, in their hearts, that nothing good would come from this moment. But at the same time, nothing could unring that bell or could unwind that clock.

"Why on earth would she be in the paper?" Marybell asked. "It's not as if her family's well off any more, much as I hate to say it, us being friends and all. At least, that we'd been before, well, before the incident when Lou and Joe and my Harold all worked together. I'd always thought they were such good fellows but then... anyway."

Marybell shook her head. "The poor things have been barely holding on, least from what I've seen."

Marybell went and straightened her coat, which Cat noticed had threads hanging loose off the cuff.

"A sad situation," Marybell went on, "and with Lou not being able to keep a job ever since. Like the bad luck's been following him ever since."

Flossie's eyes seemed to go dark. "It's not bad luck that's following him and you know it. You hear it, almost every godforsaken day. And night. Can't go nowhere near their house when he's home with the way he's—"

"You know," Marybell easily cut in, "some say he's got more pink slips than even Matty Kiely! Well, Harold, *he* said—"

"Will you *hush*, Marybell, and allow me to finish? It was a classified. Lou put up a *classified*."

No one spoke in the stunned silence that followed Flossie's near joyful declaration. The only sounds came from the slow shuffling of steps as boots moved over hard ground and the occasional muffled cough from some child whose poor lungs couldn't take the thick smoke and sulfur snaking down their throats.

This particular silence touched everyone, from the mothers to their young kids. There was no longer any squirming or mumbling about it being cold or dark, not even the young one who'd been coughing moments before.

Just... silence.

Enough so that Cat heard a few whistles sounding off in the dark. A train rolling in or out of some station, maybe filled with passengers, maybe filled with the copper ore that just about equaled gold in these parts.

No one spoke.

For her part, Cat didn't dare breathe.

Not when she knew, as well as those mothers, as well as Dusty, exactly what a classified meant.

Especially one put about by a husband about his wife.

This time, Evie, Evie Blonberg, stopped right there in her tracks. Even from here, through all that choking, stinging ash, Cat saw Evie's back going straight and tall. While too far away to see Evie's face, to see the hurt and shame on her features, Cat knew they'd be there. Especially when Evie's fists, though hidden by black gloves, were now clenching her skirt so tight her nails would've drawn blood if they'd been able.

And then, as if by some unspoken command the group started walking again. But... slower this time, and no doubt about it, keeping their distance.

From Evie.

"Flossie," Marybell said, "you... you can't just say something like that. Are you absolutely certain? Are you sure it was Evie's name and not someone else, someone of similar calling?"

"Of course, I'm certain. I read the paper myself, and Lou, bless the poor man and all he must have gone through, because he went and listed Evie by name, and named himself, in fact. There *is* no mistake, Marybell."

Cat found it quite interesting the sudden change in this Flossie. Hatred for the man suddenly turning into sympathy and pure disdain for Evie. Interesting, that's for sure, and probably what they went and concerned their lives with, all the gossip and hatred and whatnot. The kinda life Cat wouldn't touch even if she were hanging by the end of a rope.

No, thank you, sir. She'd much rather live in the shadow world than *that* one.

Flossie leaned closer to Marybell, and Cat found herself leaning a bit closer just to hear.

But then it wasn't really needed cause Flossie, well, she didn't lower her voice one bit. Not one whisper.

"Lou told the whole of Butte that he was leavin' town, that Evie had left his bed and board, and he wouldn't be responsible for any debts she acquired."

No one said anything to do about this.

But Flossie, of course, wasn't yet done.

"And the fact that it was there," she said, "right there for us all to see, well, makes it true."

And... it did.

In this world, the civilized one that Cat and Dusty were no longer a part of, everything Flossie had said was true. Lou's classified, whatever the reasoning behind it, whether or not it was actually true, didn't matter. He'd gone and sealed Evie's fate, just like that, as well as his children's.

Cat's whole body shook, and not from the aches and pains from being outside and moving for the first time in a week. This was a different kind of ache, one that she felt searin' right to her soul.

Right along with a good dose of anger.

Dusty edged closer to her, his shoulder lightly touching against hers, as if he, too, needed the same connection Cat needed in that moment. And to remind her that standing here she was just as insignificant, just as unimportant, as those hulking brick buildings whose outsides had already been stained by the black clouds hanging about them.

And damn it, it hurt.

Hurt something fierce to be standing there, doing nothing but watching and listening. And there was that little girl, dancing away, filled with such joy that Cat couldn't help but feel it, too. Feel the own bits of her past, when she was just as old as that girl, bouncing along in her own set of braided pigtails, not knowing how quickly and swiftly joy could be taken and snuffed right out.

Joy which she'd never felt again.

At least, not like that.

The hurt Cat felt got worse when one of Marybell's kids, probably four judging by the quickness of his steps and the surety with which he walked, tried to run up and join the dancing girl. And how Marybell, faster than a striking viper, reached and grabbed hold of his arm, yanking him right back to her.

"But, but ma!"

"You will not play with Rose."

"But—"

"Absolutely not."

The boy shrank within himself, as if those words alone stole a fistful of his own joy.

In a town like Butte, rumors might as well be clad in solid gold. Iron bound. Undeniable. Cat had even used that to her advantage when she'd been hunting for the truth about Norma's death, strong-arming a few wealthy, powerful businessman and forcing them into a position that suited her needs. But now in this situation with Evie Blonberg and her young children, it didn't matter if a rumor were going this way or that, if it were sproutin' legs and flyin' off into the sunset (if there were even a sun, which there wasn't).

Rumors had been, and always would be, more than enough evidence—to convict and condemn. Truth, honesty, justice—none of that actually mattered. Certainly not when it came to reputation, which was even more true when it was a man's word against a woman's.

Which was precisely what this was all about.

And there wasn't a damn thing a woman like Evie Blonberg could do. Not a damn thing, not now with her name blasted about all over the papers. Which, in turn, begged the real question. The very reason Dusty had brought Cat here to begin with:

What was she gonna do about it?

CHAPTER EIGHT

C at didn't have an answer.

Much as she wanted to march right on over there, right to that gaggle of mothers and haul them up by the scruffs of their necks, shake them hard, give them a good talking to until some of that decency their parents had supposedly taught them *actually* sunk in... she couldn't. Nor could she walk over and defend Mrs. Evie Blonberg. Even if she'd been dressed more appropriately, as a respectable sort of a woman, the kind Mrs. Allen portrayed perfectly, instead of sauntering up in blue jeans and a revolver hanging at her hip.

A sight which, no doubt, would have a few of those ladies fainting dead, their faces smacking hard into some frozen lump of horse shit.

Nor could she haul in the so-called husband Lou and demand an apology, either. Generally, in Cat's experience, the kinda men who put up classifieds weren't usually remorseful kinda fellows to begin with.

And in all honesty, none of it would make a damn bit of difference either.

Those mothers there, and everyone else in Butte, had their minds made up.

Evie Blonberg was soiled goods. A woman not to be trusted. A woman one didn't dare be seen near in public, or private, which also meant there wasn't a respectable, legitimate business that'd take her on, either.

Well, that wasn't entirely true.

Cat had a feeling Mrs. Allen would, and would do so in a heartbeat, but the ties to Mrs. Allen's past would too easily bite both ladies in the ass. And as much as Cat hated to admit it, there were a dozen or more mothers like Evie Blonberg. Every day. In Butte, in other western towns, and more than likely straight up and down their country.

Mrs. Allen couldn't save everyone, and neither could Cat.

"*Shit*," she whispered.

"Yeah," Dusty agreed. "A right shit of a mess."

"Did you meet her?" Cat asked, nodding towards Evie.

"I did. I went to her house and gave her the paper myself. I thought it was the right thing to do."

"It was."

Most women wouldn't have been granted even that small kindness, such a small warning before stepping out into this rattlesnakes nest of bonnets and handbags.

Dusty looked at Cat. "She didn't know. I could see it. She suspected about her husband leaving, I think, but the paper? The classified? She didn't know, Cat."

Shit was right.

Cat let out a breath. "And the children?"

"Word on the street was he left them, too."

"I didn't realize the street cared about some poor mother from the East Side."

And the woman was certainly poor, even before this mess. Marybell's comments had pointed Cat in the right direction, even though Marybell herself wasn't exactly lookin' up in the world, judging from the tears around her dress's trim, the near worn-through shoes she had on. Sure enough, though, the signs were there for this Evie. She also had the same frayed hem along her dress and her little girl's, the latter of which even sagged a bit in the front as if it'd been stepped on a few times too many.

"It doesn't, usually," Dusty said. "But I did. I cared enough to ask around."

Which was all the explanation needed.

And despite Dusty's instance earlier, Evie and her children probably were the reason he'd gone down into those tunnels, a place that Cat was sure he'd be done with. But Dusty had wanted answers and the folks who knew answers... well, they didn't always live in the nice big houses on the street corners. Dusty was well known, both in the shadow world and the civilized one, and more than a few, by Cat's guesses, owed him some favors.

Or wanted favors owed to them.

Truth was, if Dusty was asking, then someone, somewhere, would be willing to trade for answers. She didn't ask him how much the trade had cost him, though. If he wanted to share, he would.

What he did share, however, was that Lou and Evie Blonberg had two kids. The girl, Rose, and an older boy.

Peter.

Cat nodded towards to Evie and her now solitary, straight back. "You get a sense of what she's gonna do next?"

"Nope." Dusty shook his head, his cap slipping down lower on his forehead. "I don't think she knows, either."

More than likely she'd never quite faced that kinda choice before.

Cat crossed her arms. Her shoulder muscles pulled in just that way that made her whole side hurt, but the cold helped numb that bit of pain. A little, anyway. Enough that Cat could focus in on Rose, watch her, watch Evie, and certainly watch that group of vengeful, spiteful mothers.

Flossie, in particular.

All the while, Cat was thinking and wondering...

"All right," Cat said. "Let's say I help. You *know* I don't got a lot of options here. What are you wanting me to do about this?"

Dusty's shoulders drooped. They shook once, then twice, as if wrangling with something heavy inside him that he didn't want to see.

Finally, without looking up at her, he shook his head.

"I don't know, Cat. Hell, I don't know."

Dusty understood all too well just how badly Evie's hands—and theirs—were tied.

"I just..." Dusty went on, "I just know she's gonna need help. If nothing else, a friend."

"Yeah. You're not wrong about that."

Which was clear, even from here. Even with all those different nationalities and cultures, all those languages slamming up into each other, there was somehow more than enough understanding to pass between them, a solidarity, almost, against the one person who threatened them all just by her presence.

Christ, what a mess.

And it wasn't a mess that Cat could simply snap her fingers (or shoot a gun) to solve. There was no mystery to solve. No murder and murderers to uncover, and just how high that deceit went up to the top.

This was merely a husband's word against his wife, and the husband always won.

And yet Cat couldn't turn away, either.

She couldn't just shrug her shoulders, pull her hat lower, and head back on home to Mrs. Allen's where she'd be warm and have another bellyful of delicious, fresh apple pie and a whole pot of tea or coffee. And from the looks of Dusty, he had no interested in forgetting this, either. In fact, he probably couldn't.

Cat could either try or she could stand back and let Dusty throw himself against that solid brick wall of ruined lives and reputations. A wall that no amount of torches or rocks was gonna bring down.

"Come on, Green Eyes. Let's follow and learn what we can."

"That almost sounds like the old you talking."

"Maybe... maybe."

Because one thing Dusty was dead right about: What friends Evie had started the day with were gone. Long gone. And Cat had a feeling the same would be true for Rose, and certainly for Peter when the news finally broke to him.

And it would. Soon.

No doubt about it.

CHAPTER NINE

Dear Lord above, Peter's eyes *burned*.

Heavy smoke and ash hung about that small classroom, shoved to the walls with bodies and desks, every inch of free space taken up and used until there was barely enough room to stand, barely enough room to bend and swivel your knees, especially when your backside startin' hurting from that hard-backed chair.

And *everyone* was fidgeting.

Didn't matter if you were girl or boy, brown-noser or not. Those chairs hurt by the end of the day, and each of 'em were goin' cross-eyed just waiting for the bell to set them free.

Peter heard a chair scrape and light footfalls tapping on that hard, ash-smudged floor. He turned as some fussy school attendant opened the metal grate of that little stove in back and tossed something inside. Coal or wood or leftovers from the scrape heaps. Whatever it was didn't matter much, just that it was thrown in there with the sole purpose of warming the room and keeping little fingers from freezing right off.

Now it was too warm.

Too hot, too stuffy, and Peter's eyes, way too red.

And there was that Polack kid in front of Peter, with his greasy hair and the garlic and whatnot tied about his neck by a thick string. It was creating such a fume that Peter could barely breathe.

As if *that* was gonna cure the Polack kid of his cough.

Everyone with a sound mind knew the coughing wasn't gonna stop until the sun came out and the smoke burned away. Which wasn't gonna happen anytime soon.

Throw in a handful of kids like Polack there, with their mama's remedies from their home countries, used for colds and ailments and whatever else mamas deemed appropriate, and they tied it there, good and tight, tight as a noose 'round their necks. Between them and the stove with the bent pipe, which seemed to get more smoke back into the room than the outside, it really was amazing Peter could even see at all.

And the way his eyes hurt, red as he knew they were, it was amazing. Still, he wasn't bawling like a little girl.

Which he'd never do.

Ever.

Miss Big Eyes Bertha was in the front of the class, those bug-eye glasses of hers perched so high up on her nose it looked like she'd been born with them attached to her, just so. Her yardstick, the one she likened to use, and always with her left hand, was nearby. Laying across her table like the threat it was.

She just kept drawling on and on about something she thought important and the rest of 'em just thought plain boring. Half the class were sleeping. The other half were whispering.

Heads bobbing up and down, looking this way and that, a note getting passed around by grubby, dirt-crusted nails. It looked like it'd been folded up and folded back so many times the thing was just gonna fall apart right then and there.

It didn't, though, and neither did the whispering stop.

If anything, it seemed it got louder. Just a bit, here and there, faces turning and looking...

Right in Peter's direction.

He leaned closer into his desk, into that length of wood someone had thought'd be a great idea to slap onto the front of some chair. He felt the wood etchings he'd made just that morning, little bits of scrawling, really, not even pictures, certainly not drawings. But hell, it was better than paying attention, way better than noticing just how much his eyes hurt, and there Susan Hoy sat across from him, crying her eyes out, probably cause they were so red and swollen any white left was just about gone.

"His *mother—*" a voice whispered.

"*Shhh!*"

The whispering got louder. Gathering speed. The volume increasing, bit by bit.

Didn't matter that Peter was pretending to not notice, it still kept on, like a little wave through his class. Even Bugsy over there—Bugsy, his friend and next door neighbor—he suddenly got so red in the face that he looked at Peter, looked *right at him*, and then looked away.

As if Peter didn't exist.

All the while, shame and humiliation burning so bright in Bugsy's eyes that Peter didn't have a choice no more.

He noticed.

Right along with a sinking, sinking feeling, one that circled 'round in his stomach. And, for a moment, he forgot all about his burning eyes. Because, much as he was pretending otherwise, much as he was doing his best to ignore the whispers, he finally heard one or two.

Which was more than enough.

"...his father. Gone."

"Abandoned them. Picked up, he did, then up and left town."

It was more than enough to smack hard into Peter. The air just about whooshing from his lungs as if Giant-Nose Gibsy gave him a hard shove, just like he'd done last summer at the side hill. Gibsy had knocked so hard into Peter he'd wheezed for about a month, as if he'd gone and rattled something loose inside.

Peter got this terrible, terrible dark feeling that his entire world wasn't ever gonna be the same.

Couldn't be.

He clenched his fists, digging his dull nails as hard as he could, even as Big Eyes Bertha kept drawling on and on, either not noticing the whispers were pickin' up, or not caring. Which, of course, was when Big Eyes Bertha's gaze landed right on Peter and he knew, without a doubt, it's cause she didn't care.

She looked right at him and didn't look away, either. Unlike the rest of his class. His friends.

Bertha looked... and the sneer she gave him was so ferocious it about took Peter out at the knees. If he'd been standing, anyway, which he hadn't been.

Peter's mind was a roll of thunder. Lightning that flashed down and burned whatever it touched. He couldn't... couldn't quite make sense of it... of what the were all saying.

He knew things hadn't been right with his mother, his pa, not since he'd lost his job at the Big S and then just couldn't keep himself straight in another job. Just kept gettin' handed those pink slips and no one, nowhere, had bothered to tell Peter why. Not his mother, certainly not his pa. Maybe Bugsy mighta known, their pas had worked together at the Big S, and they'd been friends until... well, until then. But if Bugsy knew, then Peter knew, without a doubt, he'd have heard something from him. He hadn't. Still, Peter knew money was tight. His mother was doin' what she could, helping out with cleaning and picking up jobs from those who needed a cook or what-not, but she still had Rose to take care of and only so much his mother had been able to do with her there. Money was tight and Peter was no fool. And... and his pa hadn't been around all day yesterday. But that, but that didn't mean...

The words he didn't want to hear came back anyway.

Haunting him. Taunting him. Went and swirled round and round until there was nothing at all he could do but to hear and listen.

And... why should Miss Bertha care? Why would anyone when his mother... his mother...

She'd—

Peter couldn't even think the words. They wouldn't even come to him.

Hell, he was surprised that he somehow got to his feet as the bell went ringing. A sound he barely noticed, like it was some faded thing and he was deep under water.

He just... just stood up.

Got to his feet, grabbed his coat, tugging it on, always careful though not to tug too hard—wouldn't want the stitching along the armpit, the one his mother had sewn up just last week, to come undone again. They didn't have money to replace it. And wouldn't have money if...

...if what they said...

Was true.

All the while, eyes were watching him and they weren't making no pretend now, not bothering in the least, to be quiet. And then there was that water, surrounding him, kept on pressin' all around him. Pulling him down and down, and farther still.

Peter's lungs burned more than his eyes ever had, and he knew, damn well, that he couldn't take a breath.

Couldn't.

How... how could his mother do this? How... how could she drive his pa away?

"Peter."

Someone called his name. At least, he thought they did. Maybe.

And then, when he didn't respond, they did it again.

Peter blinked. Somehow got his head moving and his eyes working again, and saw that it was Miss Bertha standing in front of him. That black dress of hers hanging off like a twig, one hand perched right there on her hips, fingers digging in. The other... the other holding tight to the yardstick.

Real tight.

Tight enough where her knuckles were goin' and turning white.

She even had a toe tapping on that stained floor, a clear sign on impatience... and disgust.

"Yea, Miss Bertha?"

She frowned at him. Her mouth twisting so hard he doubted she'd ever smile again.

"Is there something amiss?" she asked. "In your household?"

"Not that I know, ma'am."

Which he didn't.

Even if... even if that feeling he had, the one circling 'round in his gut, told him otherwise.

Peter swallowed. Felt revulsion just about filling him, right from his toes all the way to the tips of his hair.

"You sure?" she pressed.

He nodded.

"I see," she said. "I am... glad to hear this."

Except there wasn't a smidgeon of kindness in her voice, in her manner, in the way she looked at him. Her mind was made up, and they both knew it.

Just as they both knew she didn't want him stepping one foot back into her classroom.

The thought just about knocked him over.

And it seemed, in addition to those big eyes that missed nothing, Miss Bertha always knew how to read thoughts cause she said:

"I suppose you will be attending school tomorrow." She paused, her smile somehow twistin' even tighter. "Yes?"

He nodded.

What else could he do? What else could he say?

"Good." She slowly lowered that yardstick, but it sure didn't make Peter feel much better.

Not at all.

And not that saying or speaking was much on Peter's mind, though that was at complete odds to the thousands of questions swelling up in him. Demanding to be answered. Answers that no one, no one *but* his mother, could answer.

If she even would.

His next thought, realization more like, was that he was back outside again. Like his body had been moving this whole time, going through those motions without a real clear thought or sense. Just... moving. And now, instead of being near Bugsy and laughing about something Big Eyes said or how Susan Hoy was at it again, crying her eyes until she was red in the face, Peter was alone. Trailing behind the rest of his schoolmates, which, he realized in a distracted kinda way, they'd done on purpose.

Bugsy and all the rest, how they picked up their pace, running and shouting after someone else. Anything, anything at all, to keep from being near Peter.

And the ones who wanted to get close... well, Peter was just as glad they kept their distance. Those narrowed looks. Like because of who Peter now was, because of who everyone thought his mother now was, made him less of a person. Made him a target for all that anger and hatred. And the hatred, it was there, there for the whole world to see, no question 'bout it. The way those boys, most of 'em bigger than him, too, glared at Peter. Eyes that burned with such hatred and something else...

Something Peter couldn't look at too closely. Didn't dare to, in fact.

Why? 'Cause... he knew it was right there. Right inside himself. And... how many times had he done the same thing? Had he heard about a family fallen on low times, and it was *him* who'd done the turning away. Him who'd done the teasing and... and the bullying.

It was a sense and a knowing that didn't leave him. In fact, the very moment he saw Rose, with her little braids and she standing right there, on her tiptoes and waving at Peter for the whole world to see, that bright and shining smile on her face, it hit Peter so hard he nearly collapsed right there on the ground.

Or stumbled, anyway.

Because right there, standing beside Rose, as always, was his mother.

And she stared at Peter, stared with a face so bleak, so lost. So filled with sorrow—

All his questions, all his demands died in an instant.

They no longer mattered.

In that moment, he knew everything he needed to—and all of it was her fault.

Hers.

CHAPTER TEN

Cat recognized Peter instantly.

He had the same look about him as his mother. Tall and serious, with a stark kind of intelligence just sparking out of their eyes. This, unfortunately, was not the only way she recognized him.

The sadder truth was that Peter already had received the same treatment as his mother.

Exiting the school alone. At the very back of the group while the others rushed to hurry by. Not a single kid, boy or girl, daring to meet his eyes. Hell, not even brave enough to look at him, to acknowledge his existence.

And Peter knew.

There was no doubt about it.

He knew about his mother and father, about the classified. It was there for the whole world to see if one just looked close enough. The way his feet shuffled on that frozen dirt ground, shoulders bowing and a coat that was both too worn and too big, as if it was a hand-me-down from his missing father.

In that moment, he looked so much like Dusty when he'd fallen to his lowest after losing his sister, of being alone with nothing and no one else to fight alongside him.

Cat's heart hurt.

It did.

And she didn't need to look at Dusty to know he felt it, too.

Or Peter's mother.

Cat did, though, because she needed to. She needed to see Evie Blonberg, to acknowledge what happened here, what no one else was brave enough or daring enough to simply witness.

The breaking of a family.

And it was, make no mistake.

Not when Peter came within a few feet of his mother. His mother, whose arms were outstretched and almost... almost begging him to come to her. As if she needed to hold him, hold him tight and never let go because that was the only thing she could control, the only thing she could do, could make right—

But even that wasn't true. Not any longer. 'Cause no matter how tight Evie Blonberg held her kids, kept them close, she couldn't keep them safe from danger or from the shadows of this world.

And soon enough, those arms, that love, wouldn't even be able to fed those children.

Peter... he just stood there. Stood there with such anger and such hurt Cat was surprised a hole didn't just open up and swallow the whole family right in. So much hurt that Cat couldn't help but feel it.

And part of her lived it.

She knew Dusty felt it, too, the way he was shaking beside her, fists clenching and unclenching at his side. He stomped his feet once, then twice, on those poor frozen tufts of mud and horse dung, as if seeing Evie, or maybe... maybe seeing Rose and Peter, were bringing back some bits of his own past.

Cat didn't know Dusty's whole story and probably never would.

She didn't know how he and Norma had found themselves in Butte, or what had happened to their parents. There'd been no mention of a mother or father. Just he and his sister alone, and Cat had a hunch it'd been that way for awhile.

A long, long time, in fact.

But there was something about this, something about... Rose, in particular... and the way Dusty kept looking at her, maybe even reminding him of himself, that told Cat there was more going on, more just below the surface.

And Cat knew from experience, that the past and all those emotions that got stirred up had a way of resurfacing. The past didn't like to stay good and buried. It always found a way to the surface.

Something she herself was even now struggling with.

Cat reached out and touched Dusty's shoulder. It wasn't much for comfort, really nothing at all, but it was all Cat had. All she could do. Especially when her own insides were shaking, demanding that she go and do something—even though there was nothing at all for her to do.

She watched, helpless almost, as the other mothers picked up their young charges and took them in hand. When they looked at Peter and his mother, Evie, they showed not one ounce of kindness or sympathy.

Nothing at all but cold disdain.

It infuriated Cat. Got her blood boiling so high she really did think about pulling her gun and letting loose some frustration.

She didn't, though, as tempting as it was. Her pa had taught her that, taught her how to use a gun and to respect it. And if one wanted to do the shooting, that was the worst time ever to pull that trigger.

She didn't.

Instead, Cat kept on breathing, and kept noticing. Everything. Every little detail. The look of each mother and those kids, remembering them, memorizing their faces and names if Cat was lucky enough to hear them... and also, those children who really *did* pause in their steps. Who looked back at Peter and shared with him a moment... of sadness.

And loss.

Especially as Evie finally lowered her arms, recognizing that Peter would not go to her, and the look on her face at that moment... such rejection and hurt, the kind which a soul might never recover from. A look that seemed to understand...

Her son hated her.

Rejected.

A boy who hadn't even heard the full story, hadn't heard from his mother the truth of what had really happened between father and mother. Peter, who probably knew better than all of them here, including Cat, the full truth, yet even he couldn't give his mother the benefit of the doubt.

Even he couldn't accept her.

Cat moved closer, her boots barely making a crunch as she stepped on that mix of frozen gravel, mud, and horseshit. Dusty followed beside her, making not a sound at all.

"*Peter*," Evie whispered.

"I've got nothin' to say."

"Please, if, if you'd let me explain—"

"Pa's gone. *Gone*. Because of you. That's what everyone's been saying. Your fault."

Peter's voice dropped so low that if Cat wasn't paying close attention, wasn't holding her breath to not miss a sound, she'd have missed it.

"Your fault why he left. Why he hated me. Enough to leave me behind. And Rose."

Peter turned, right then and there, and ran. Ran right off into the smoke and shadowy darkness of the early afternoon. Ran right past the group his mother had dutifully followed and silently put up with just so she could see him home, safe and sound.

Peter ran right past Rose, his shoulder barely brushing against hers. Not pausin', not saying anything, in fact.

And Rose, her smile, it finally fell.

The whole exchange, all of it, from mother to son to sister, a right tragedy.

Thankfully, *Cat's* presence was finally being noticed, especially by the nearby kids, who glanced away from Peter and noticed the woman dressed as a man right in their midst. Kids who also quickly pointed out the revolver at her hip, which they dutifully shared with their friends and they, then, to their friends.

Soon enough, the whispered words were circling around their small group, her name passing off their lips and spreading like wildfire.

"Cowboy Cat."

Well, looked like gettin' tangled up in some Copper King business really had done wonders for Cat's name and reputation, certainly the one she was lookin' to build. And if there was one good thing that came from this whole horrid affair, it's when news of Cat's presence finally reached those righteous, upturned noses of the ladies in charge of this reputation lynching.

Like Flossie.

Dear Lord, Cat would never forget the look that Flossie gave her, especially with Cat literally standing right there, close enough that she could reach out and touch a few bonnets. Oh man, the disdain Flossie had shown for Evie earlier was absolutely nothin' compared to the disgust she showed Cat.

As well as her face gettin' so pale and bloodless, like she was gonna faint dead over, right then and there. Topple head first into that frozen mud and horseshit.

Though, Cat hoped, if such was the case, Flossie would hand off her baby first and *then* faint dead away.

Sadly, Flossie stayed upright. Though the surprise and horror at seeing Cat had certainly been worth it.

But what really mattered was when Evie Blonberg saw Cat again. Right as Flossie was recovering some of her color and a might smidgeon bit of anger that Evie saw Cat and Dusty again.

Her eyes going wide. As if... as if she knew that Cat, along with everyone else, had overheard her exchange with Peter.

Cat tilted her head a bit and studied the other woman. At the...

recognition shining out of Evie's eyes. Recognizing who Cat was, her former life on the line, of earning her livin' and her keep in a way that these other mothers saw as nothing but shameful. To fall so low, to become a soiled dove and forever be tainted, and through it, becoming a lesser being.

A fate that nothing in the world could change.

But there was something more. Something else that passed between her and Evie in that moment. Cat couldn't quite put a name on it, not right now. It was just a feeling, really, almost like a stirring in her gut. Her noticing a... change in the other woman, if you will. Oh, there was still hurt and loss there 'a plenty, but also the strength Cat had seen in Evie earlier.

A strength and a will. A determination.

This here, this was not a woman who'd give up. Who'd lie down on that floor and just wait for death to finally claim her.

No.

Evie Blonberg was a fighter, make no mistake. And there was no way she'd be lettin' her kids fade away from her or starve, even if Peter hated her with his whole being now. Evie wasn't about to give in, wasn't about to let go, much as Peter may want to in this moment.

Cat tipped her hat to Evie, acknowledging the woman in such a way that connected them, as well as offering out her hand, in a way. She would be there if Evie Blonberg needed her. Her door would always be open.

It was up to her, to Evie, to come around and knock.

CHAPTER ELEVEN

Evie felt more alone than she ever had in her life.

It didn't matter that she sat in the entryway of the police station, one that was bustling with movement, with officers and other individuals who, like her, sought some aid or guidance. Heads bowed low, hats pulled lower still, and everyone always moving, always talking too, though not always hearing. Or listening. The loud voices of the men just about echoing off these close walls made Evie flinch when their harsh tones went searing through her.

Men in their suits with their tall black hats, their dark shoes shined to a perfection, which was in complete contrast to their counterparts—miners and the like, who stood side by side, shoulder to shoulder, and not a man from either side seeming to notice. Or care.

Such was Butte, and one of the few things she'd loved instantly about it.

The miners there with their overalls, which had clearly seen a hard life's work. Many were worn out along the knees and the ankles. Where the hems were already failing and trailing along the floor, a dark blackened color that no amount of cleaning could undo. There were the carefully stitched patches and mends, which barely kept the fabrics in place, as if those threads were holding it together by sheer will alone.

Then there were their faces, and the look Evie knew all too well.

The dark smudges along their cheeks and jaw, the dirt staining their nails, and the way their shoulders seemed to bow under the some heavy, unseen weight. As if, even here above the surface and in what little clean air there was to be had, they still carried that weight with them.

The push and press of rock. The heat and sweat. The endless hours down there in the darkness.

It was a look Evie had seen on Lou every day, even on Sundays when he was home with her and the children. It was one the whole neighborhood knew and what it meant, yet did nothing. Said nothing. Not even the Reverend Jacobs whom she'd taken solace from, advice on how best to keep praying, to keep believing in that good man buried someplace far down inside Lou.

It was a look that had stayed with him, that, in fact, became harder and colder—especially after he'd been fired from the Spectacular. And then every time after? After every pink slip he acquired?

It'd only gotten worse.

And it was a look she was seeing mirrored out of Peter's eyes, and *that's* the real reason she'd spoken with Reverend Jacobs. She simply could not allow Peter to become his father, to let all that anger and rage claim him and rule him.

Couldn't because it was already in his soul, just like it was in Lou's.

This was the reason they were here now, Lou having skipped out and destroyed everything, everything she'd worked for, and her being in this police station, doing her utmost to hold onto what ounce and shred of dignity she had left in her, and he... and he...

Simply gone. Left town, left her and Rose and Peter—

As if *that* would ever change a damn bit of what he felt on the inside. As if running was going to do anything about all that rage in him.

Evie's chest tightened. Tears filled her eyes.

She did not let them fall.

Not now when she needed all the strength she had, when she had Rose with her. Rose, who sat on the cold, rickety chair besides Evie's. Rose, who'd laid her head in Evie's lap as if sleeping, as if a part of her still believed her mother could, and would, keep her safe.

Each of the men here, from these wealthy bankers and other folk with their nicely shined shoes and pressed jackets, to those miners with the weight of the mine holding about them, each of them gave her a kind nod and a tip of their hat, which she gracefully accepted with a nod.

Tomorrow such gestures would be less. And even more so the day after.

There was no doubt about it.

Word of Evie would spread, of who she was and what had happened. They would know her, recognize her, upon sight. Soon there would no more kind, polite gestures.

She would well and truly be alone.

And yet today, in this moment, she wasn't that person yet. She hadn't been fully known and seen throughout town as the wife of Lou Blonberg, who'd warned them of her unfaithfulness. And yet, it already felt like she was.

She ran her hands down Rose's back. They were still gloved because of how cool the police station was, as if they didn't dare use enough of heat to take more than a bit of frost off a person's nose. She'd never been here before, and already this building, its presence, was enough to set her nerves on edge. Made her breathing, which was already shallow and painful, having grown tired from the long walk to Peter's school, even more difficult.

Rose hadn't asked why Peter had run off, why he was so angry, why he'd said such things to Evie. In fact, Rose hadn't asked about their father at all, either. Rose, Evie believed, knew more, understood more, than any of them had given her credit for.

And as much as Evie didn't want Rose to be here, the truth was

Evie had no choice. Sure, she could leave Rose at home by herself, but that was not an option that sat well with her. And... they had no family or relatives to call upon for help. Certainly no... no neighbors who'd watch Rose for the short while that she spoke with the detectives here.

So they were here. Together.

The station itself was small, barely bigger than her home, though it had the added bonus of an upstairs, where she imagined officers and the sheriff called such offices home.

And, of course, there was the cold, cruel jail, which waited patiently underneath her feet.

She could almost hear the desperate shuffling of those down there, locked up with all their sorrow and sins that had found themselves in such a place. Not that Evie had ever been in such a situation herself or had even seen the jail firsthand, or to visit with the ghost of a hanged man, who rumors said now claimed it as his home.

Nevertheless, Evie felt it.

Felt the hollowness and the depressive weight, as if it had seeped into these very walls and now, just as the ghost, claimed it as their own. As if... as if all those dark feelings were so strong its entire desire was to swallow up this building here whole, and one day, it would indeed. Such was the depth of its pain and its cold attitude towards all things and manner of life.

To Evie, it felt as if she were the one standing there, alone amongst the iron and bars. And perhaps, it should be her, for what she'd caused to happen to her family.

To... her children.

Rose shivered and coughed quietly into Evie's lap. Evie stroked her dearest daughter's back, wishing she could do one small thing and make the simple act of breathing easier. Better.

She couldn't.

The thin doors of the station did nothing to keep out the suffocating smoke or the chemicals floating there on the air outside, which stung her eyes and gave her another excuse, another reason, to claim why they were so red. Why it looked like she wanted nothing more than to cry...

And yet didn't dare to.

Just as she didn't dare think to closely on Peter and where he was. The thought of him... of the look he'd given her... all that hatred and anger... her chest tightened so hard. She pressed a hand against her, willing herself to be strong. To keep breathing.

It was so very hard.

As if the thought of Peter, the look he'd given her, was destroying her from the inside out. It ate right through her heart, stabbing straight down with such a fear it felt like she could barely breathe—

She somehow kept this all at bay. Somehow, she kept her back straight and those tears and fears from falling.

Peter knew his way around Butte.

Peter, also, close enough to be a man, would be safe. She had to believe that, just as she had to believe he would come home to her again. That he would forgive her... even if so much of this was on Lou... Lou's choices, Lou's stubbornness. His fault and not hers.

But then, the truth didn't really matter, not when it was Lou's word against hers.

Which was why Evie had no choice but to come here. To speak with an officer, to see exactly what her options were. She knew they were few; she wasn't a fool. But she had to try. Had to ask.

For Rose's sake.

For Peter's, though he now hated her.

Evie would suffer this humiliation, as word would spread like a lit fuse of dynamite in this room, these men who'd been cordial and kind suddenly pulling away as if she carried some terrible, catching disease.

Still, she stayed.

Even as an officer approached her, taking off his hat and revealing hair as blond and golden as the sunshine the whole town so dearly missed. He gave her a kind though sad smile.

As if... as if he already knew her story.

"Mrs. Evie Blonberg?"

Somehow, she found her voice. Somehow, she found it in her to not only stand and nod... but to accept the officer's hand in greeting, something she knew wouldn't happen again, at least not after today.

"I'm Officer Christopher Blake," he said. "I was told you might be in some trouble."

CHAPTER TWELVE

Evie froze. Her entire being going still. Cold.

Around them, all the movement and the noise, even the sorrow living within these walls, seemed to still. Go quiet. As if it were only her and this officer. Even Rose, who watched this exchange, seemed to fade into the distance.

Officer Blake, who still held her hand, gave it a gentle, kind squeeze.

"How..." Evie's voice was dry, unused, uneven. "How do you know? About my troubles, I mean."

Could it be possible? Could news of her have spread so quickly? She didn't dare think on it. She still had hope, after all, hope to find someone willing enough to take her on, to pay her a decent wage where she might care of their children on her own. Maybe cleaning. Maybe laundry. Maybe in some boarding house, if they were willing, with her new reputation and all. Maybe. Maybe. Maybe—

"A concerned boy," Officer Blake said. "Someone I know well, who sent me word. He thought you might be in some trouble and asked me to keep an eye out for you."

"And I'm here."

"You are."

Officer Blake dropped her hand and Evie instantly felt the loss of his warmth, though not the loss of his kindness.

He was a handsome man, taller than Lou by at least a foot, and filled out in such a way that it appeared *he'd* been the one working down in those mines as opposed to the girth that Lou had acquired over these past few years as the heaviness of the mines claimed him, inch by inch, and Lou caring less and less after his own health and happiness.

"Mama?" Rose looked up at Evie, her eyes wide and... sad. "Why are we here?"

Again came that twisting, heavy feeling in Evie's chest, in her heart.

"Oh... dearest..."

She didn't know what to say or how to say it. But there was no more hiding the truth from her dear heart Rose, nothing that could protect her from what would happen next, nothing to save her from the childhood that Lou had so selfishly stolen away.

Officer Blake knelt in front of Rose. "Your mama's looking for some help, little one."

"Is she in trau-ble?"

Rose spoke with her beautiful little inflections, still learning the words and the way in which they all got put together, and Evie's heart nearly broke right there. How could Lou do this to Rose? To Peter—?

Evie breathed in quickly, then let it back out.

Officer Blake noticed, of course. She'd a feeling this wasn't a man who missed anything. And he probably guessed the real reason her eyes were so red, why the those tears hung right there, so desperate to fall and give in.

Yet he said nothing.

Instead, he turned back to Rose, tipping her chin up a little, giving her same kind smile he'd given Evie.

"Nah," he said to Rose. "She's not in trouble with me."

Officer Blake met Evie's eyes. Acknowledgment of what had been left unspoken, and her accepting this gift, small as it was, and giving thanks as well. All without speaking. All without saying a word.

Just a shared look. A shared understanding.

And yet... it was clear Rose wasn't fully convinced.

She pressed her lips together, thinking long and hard. Her young mind not picking up the distinction and the particular words Officer Blake had used, yet somehow knew there was something being left unsaid.

Clearly, her child's intuition *had* noticed the difference.

Rose might not understand it, but she noticed it. And even with such knowledge and how it clearly wasn't sitting right with her, still Rose nodded her head, in both agreement and understanding, to Officer Blake. It was all very sage-like, as well, and very serious, even when those two braided pigtails bobbed up once and then down again. Almost as if Rose were the one giving permission for Officer Blake to help her mother.

Evie gripped Rose's shoulders, holding her close, wishing to God this wasn't happening. That it hadn't happened to her, to their little family, and then accepting that it had and it was up to her to survive it.

"Thank you, Officer Blake. I hadn't expect this... this kindness."

"I learned recently that a bit of kindness, even if a smile, goes a long way in this town."

"Oh? And who taught you such rare wisdom?"

Blake's smile faded. "She's gone, I'm afraid."

"I'm sorry. I didn't know. I hope she was not close with you, a family perhaps."

"No," Blake said, his tone a bit brisk. "Not to me. And nothing at all to be sorry for, the line of work she did..."

His voice trailed off.

Those blue eyes of his held hers, and Evie found herself swallowing around a lump in her throat. Of fear.

No, he did not need to answer that question.

He did, anyway. At least, in a way.

"It wasn't an easy life she walked, but she left an impression. And quite a few cared for her. Enough to give her some small justice in the end."

His words perked some memory in Evie, like a little tug on her mind, but then it was gone as he kept talking, changing the subject to one that she truly, in her heart, didn't want to have.

"We can talk somewhere else if you like?" he said. "Alone, if you prefer. I understand this is a quiet matter."

An offer. Another small kindness.

Evie didn't know why she deserved it or even why this boy—and she had no doubt which boy—had been looking out for her, had sent word to this kind officer, a kindness she'd never expected, not after Stan's classified was printed.

"No," she said, "it's all right."

"Are you sure about that?"

He glanced around the room, deliberate like, but Evie only nodded.

"Yes," she said. "It won't be long anyway. Before the day is out, or at least by the morrow, everyone in Butte will know."

They'd know from her story, to her kids, to what Evie herself looked like. Those strangers passing by her on the street or shopping in some store, they might not have ever seen before in their life, but they'd know who she was. The looks, the stares, the whispers, all of that would follow her the very moment she stepped outside her small home. It would follow her, dodging her heels every breath she took from here on out.

Evie held Rose tighter, just for a moment.

"Everyone will know," she said.

Evie lifted her head and looked at Officer Blake, right in the eyes. She did not raise her voice, though she didn't lower it, either. She would not run from this. She would be strong for both her children. Peter may hate her but she hoped, someday, he would see her for who she really was, and what she would do to keep her dearest hearts safe.

"I'm here about my husband," Evie said. "And... and the classified he put up about me. In the paper, the one that ran just this morning."

The room, which had faded from her view before, her awareness, now came into sharp, clear clarity.

All movement had stopped.

Everyone was looking at her.

She felt them. Felt, too, the judgments already seeping into their minds and hearts. Of what she could have done to warrant a classified, though she knew the very first thought they'd have. And it was not a kind one.

She watched from the corner of her eye as one man even reached for a newspaper.

Evie closed her eyes briefly. Felt the same stabbing shock, the pain, the hurt all of it. Then she looked squarely at Officer Blake and would *not* let herself look away.

Or the tears fall.

"I need to know what my options are," she said. "I need to know what I can do about this, about these lies he's told, and the slander to my good name."

Blake let out a heavy breath. "There... is not much. Yes, you can go in front of a judge, state your case, but... but unless there's significant signs of abuse towards you or your children, there's very little, if anything, to be done."

"And abandonment?"

She knew his answer even before he spoke. It was in the way he breathed, the heaviness suddenly pulling on his shoulders, pulling him down as if that ghost in that jail below wanted to yank him right through that floor.

And it was in the sorrow as he looked at her and slowly shook his head. Once. Then twice.

"I'm sorry, Mrs. Blonberg."

"There's... there's nothing legal? That I have no legal recourse? No legal defense? That he can say whatever he wills, but I can do nothing? That he's gone and stolen away my only options, my only ability to feed and shelter our children, the ones *he* left, and *I* can do nothing? Nothing which the law will help me?"

Help her.

Protect her.

"No," he whispered.

It was a whisper that everyone in the entire room heard and felt.

In all honesty, she was prepared for this answer. She'd known it before she walked in those thin doors that didn't keep out the cold or the smoke. But at the same, she'd had hope. There was no harm in asking for help and guidance. And yet... she'd been wrong, and the blow itself, hearing *that* word...

No, she couldn't have ever prepared for this moment. No way she could have anticipated what such a simple, small word did to her. How this small bit of hope she had, a spark, really, burning there in her chest that perhaps, just... just maybe... they'd be okay. That she would find some way to survive, to clear her name enough to make an honest wage for an honest day's work.

That hope was gone.

"Mama?" Rose asked. "Where Papa go? Why make you sad?"

"I... I don't know."

Rose tugged on Evie's coat sleeve, but Evie found she couldn't quite move or respond, or even think.

Ever since the boy with the green eyes had handed her the newspaper, Evie discovered all she'd had left was her own children and... hope. Now, now Peter was gone, hating her with his whole being, believing that she was the reason his father had left, had abandoned them.

And Rose? Would she soon look at her the way Peter did? As their life fell around them, as hunger burned in their stomachs and the cold ate away what little they had left?

Whatever hope Evie had felt earlier, that small spark, winked out. Just, just gone.

"You're sure?" Evie asked again, somehow finding her voice. "There's nothing, nothing at all I can do?"

"I'm sorry."

"Yes, yes, of course."

She found herself suddenly speaking and moving then, though not truly aware of it. Couldn't be. Too much pain, too much... disappointment. Loss.

"Umm, yes, right," she said. "Thank you for your time, and I apologize I wasted it so. And also, for your kindness. I mean, thank you."

Evie held out her hand in farewell, not catching herself in time that now, now people would not want to touch her, to be cordial or polite. They would not wish to greet her or say farewell.

Not anymore.

"Right, sorry." She lowered her hand—

Then Officer Blake took it, gently. Just as gently and kindly as when he'd first greeted her.

"It's I who should be apologizing to you. That you have no recourse, that the law can't protect you and so many like you, it shames me."

"The law," she said, somehow keeping her voice from shaking. "It wasn't written for the likes of me, for women."

He just looked at her for a few moments, as if considering her and thinking hard behind those blues eyes of his, eyes that went again to Rose and stayed there. She watched as he struggled with his own inner demons and hurts, as if, for whatever reason, she and Rose brought all of it up to the surface.

And then, there was that sorrow in him again. The one she felt just as clear as she felt the ghost downstairs in the jewel.

"No," he finally said. "The law isn't fair to you, certainly not for mothers with young children who need them. I'm sorry."

"I... expected as much. But thank you, anyway. I will find my way, I will see to my children's needs as best I can."

With the only option left remaining to her.

And with that thought, that acceptance, Evie nodded to Officer Blake, mustering up as much regal and grace as she could.

Officer Blake released her hand.

She raised her head and gave one final look to all those men here, standing and watching and judging as they were, each of them witnessing her fall from the life only a good woman could walk. They witnessed and saw, saw her doing what she could to restore her name, and not a one of them said anything, not a one showed an ounce of empathy.

Except for Officer Blake.

She nodded to all those men there. Her hope might be gone, but she had some strength left in her, and pride.

Officer Blake, apparently the true gentleman she'd first pegged him for, opened the door for her and Rose, and when she expected him to go back inside, shutting the door and forgetting all about her and ruined reputation, he did the opposite.

He came outside with her. He slapped a hat, black with a wide-brim, onto his head. She'd no idea where he'd gotten it or the coat he was now shrugging on.

"Come on." He nodded down the street.

Evie didn't move.

Officer Blake stopped and turned, raising his eyes at her and his brows just about disappeared into that sunshine-gold hair of his.

"You coming?"

Evie shook her head, her bonnet falling low. She pushed it back. "I, I don't understand—"

"I told you the law wouldn't help, and it can't. Judges and their like, even officers like me, rules are pretty darn clear. But what I can do is introduce you to someone. Not that she can change what your husband did or what the town thinks, but... maybe, maybe she can do something more for you."

Evie's mind raced. Twirled. Spiraled.

"Sh-she?"

Evie swallowed, tried speaking again.

"What ever could a woman do for someone like me, someone no better than myself?"

"Don't know, for sure. But she a has a thing, a way, really."
"And what's that?"
"In a manner of speaking, justice."

CHAPTER THIRTEEN

This time when Mrs. Allen plopped a giant slice of apple pie down in front of Cat, that fine china clinking together as she placed it on the sitting room table, with the fork nearly unbalancing itself and toppling right off, Cat didn't protest. Or complain.

Instead, she grabbed the fork and dug right in. And savored every bit and bite of that cinnamon-apple goodness.

For a week now she'd been itching to get outside, to feel the earth under her feet, but now she was just so damn glad to be back home. Back in the warmth and the light that seemed to live in this house, as if it were coming right out 'a the walls—even if the house reminded her so much of her own childhood home.

Cat's stomach gave a delighted gurgle, which made Mrs. Allen beam with such a light.

"It's about damn time." Mrs. Allen propped her hands onto her hips. "And to think, all I needed was to let you outside, get worked up a nice appetite, and then there'd not be a word of complaint."

"Should have listened," Cat said around a mouthful of stickiness, not caring one bit about the usual manners.

"Apparently so." Mrs. Allen smiled. "I'll remember that for next time you almost get shot."

Cat rolled her eyes but said nothing more on the topic—she'd been in no danger of being shot after all, not once—and instead focused on what mattered most: her food.

Damn, she was hungry.

And *damn* was she sore and hurting. It was like every inch of her body had a thought and a complaint of its own. Even the parts of her that *hadn't* been injured and didn't need healing had quite a loud opinion regarding their current state of disuse and what felt like sudden overuse.

Still, despite it all, despite the turmoil rolling inside from her and Dusty's their little outing, what they'd witnessed, Cat felt good. And maybe a little bit at peace. As if she were reopening parts of herself that had found themselves lost after her battle with Mr. Rippi. That maybe some of those parts were startin' to come together again, repatch themselves, if you will.

She wasn't the only one doing some healing. And some hurting.

Dusty sat beside her, probably for the first time in a near week. He'd come home with Cat when she'd asked, and to her surprise, he hadn't gone straight upstairs to hide or sulk as he'd been doing. Instead, he went and sat beside her and was now digging into his own slice of pie with a gusto that made Cat mildly envious.

Especially when, in two bites, the whole thing just about disappeared.

He held up his plate for more.

"You can't just be eating pie, you know." Mrs. Allen waved a finger at him. "You may think I don't know what all goes on in this house, but I do. I do, indeed, and I know exactly what you've been sneaking out of my pantry, and pies, young man, aren't going to cut it. You need meat and potatoes and some good greens in you, especially if you plan on skulking around those tunnels again. Which you will."

Dusty squirmed in his chair.

"And," Mrs. Allen went on, finger still shaking mightily at him, "you *will* catch more than just a cold if you keep it up. Certainly if you don't start eating and sleep right. And yes, I noticed that, too. Barely sleeping a wink. Barely even laying in your bed, and when you do, spend the night tossing and turning like the devil's after you."

Cat raised her eyes. She hadn't realized just how light a sleeper Mrs. Allen was, if she could hear all that. Chin, her Chinaman servant, Cat knew about *him* being a light sleeper, guarding the halls downstairs where so much as a creaking floorboard and the man was up with his little lantern and his narrowed eyes that missed nothing that went on in this house.

"I will, Mrs. Allen, I surely will." Dusty raised his plate up higher. "After just one more?"

And then he smiled at Mrs. Allen, and sure enough, it was a straight-up Dusty smile. The kind that both Cat and Mrs. Allen were not immune to.

Not one bit.

Mrs. Allen frowned at him, but it was playful and filled with joy. "All right. So long as I have your word?"

"Promise."

"Then just one more."

She went and cut him another slice then, before sliding it easy as pie onto Dusty's plate, with an ease and a practice that made Cat shake her head. The whole thing had stayed together in that perfect little triangle, not breaking into about three pieces as what usually happened when Cat did the serving.

Domestic life, clearly, was simply not suited to Cat, and she was just fine with that. Just fine.

It was clear that Mrs. Allen was happy to see Dusty being himself again after his little fall there down into his own darkness, his own demons. Not that it was gone completely, which Cat could still feel coming off him in small waves. Nor was it gone completely in her, either. How could it? How, after everything they'd seen and witnessed earlier, Evie and her kids, could they simply laugh it all away, enjoy their pie, and *not* be affected by it?

Truth was, you couldn't.

And it was all still there. Haunting Dusty. Haunting Cat.

Just as Alice, Cat's long-gone sister, was still there right by her side. Alice with her pale, fading hair, straight and lifeless, and her sad, sad eyes. Eyes that even now looked at Cat with such overwhelming sadness. Something that Cat couldn't ever make happy again. But at least, for now, Alice was silent, though always present.

She would always be with Cat.

And it wasn't just Alice haunting Cat, either. It was Evie Blonberg and her little girl and Peter. No, they weren't ghosts in the way Alice was, and dear Lord Cat hoped it wouldn't be so for a long, long time. Yet nevertheless, she felt them as if they were beside her.

Truth was, while this little homecoming here felt right, she and Dusty and Mrs. Allen, even if not Blake, felt like it was needed, it also didn't mean things were right in their world, with this little gathering of a sorta family. Maybe they never would be. Maybe they couldn't when there were others out there, suffering and finding themselves down in that shadow world through no fault of their own, and with no way out, and not a damn thing she or Dusty could do about it.

Of course, the moment Cat thought that, she heard the clear stomping of feet outside coming up that small, wooden porch. The door knob turning, hard and loud, not purposefully silent as Dusty had done earlier. Almost as if newcomer was makin' a loud and clear announcement that someone was here.

This time even Mrs. Allen noticed. She was just beginning to sit in her usual chair across from Cat when she paused.

"Why, I wonder who that could be? I wasn't expecting any more guests for the day."

"A boarder?" Dusty asked.

"No. They've all moved on. Except for you two." Mrs. Allen rose, wiping her hands on her flour-stained apron. "I guess I better go see—"

The door opened fully.

There was no knock, just an opening of those rusty hinges

announcing the newcomers, followed by footsteps. Hard, determined steps, in fact. Purposeful, even. Boots smacking onto the newly polished wood floors without an ounce of forgiveness or concern.

Footsteps that Cat immediately recognized.

She somehow kept from reaching up to her shoulder. Kept from touching the sore, injured muscles there, the bones that, through time, were refitting together or whatever it was that they did.

Officer Christopher Blake.

The one person she wanted to see, and the one person she didn't dare to.

CHAPTER FOURTEEN

No amount of healing, no amount of time would ever be enough to prepare her for seeing Blake again.

Or for the ridiculous and unreasonable hurt she suddenly felt swelling up inside her, as if she were some frilly, silly little schoolgirl with big, shining, sad eyes ready to startin' crying. It was almost enough to make her mad and forget all the rest of the crap turning and twisting 'round inside her.

Almost.

Cat's hand, which currently held a good forkful of apple pie, froze mere inches from her lips. Her stomach both rolled and tightened, as if the darn thing couldn't decide what it was gonna settle on.

Blake's footsteps entered the house, hard and purposeful, then they paused.

She could almost hear that rush of air underneath the floorboards, the shifting of his sudden weight and the intensity that fell off the man in constant rolling, unyielding waves.

At least when he was around Cat.

Not long after Cat had arrived in Butte, Blake had followed after her, havin' gotten wind that she was interested in the recently deceased Norma. Especially, as it later turned out, with Blake's own investigation, which was pulling up more questions than answers. And at the time, Cat hadn't gotten a good look at who was following her—he really was a master at hiding amongst the crowd, though nowhere near as proficient as Dusty and his shadows—Cat had still recognized Blake's gait.

Had, in fact, memorized it, as she did with most things. The surety of his stride, the way he moved with such purpose and conviction, she'd known instantly he was a police officer.

Cat only knew bits and pieces of Blake's history. She knew this was, indeed, his childhood home and where he'd grown up, helpin' out with the boarders, and also where he grew a large resentment towards his aunt—and her former profession.

Something that even now as a grown adult, Blake could not forgive.

Regardless of that history, Blake was an honest, upstanding cop and Mrs. Allen had trusted him to help when the situation regarding Norma got tense. And help he did. In fact, Blake and Cat, despite his initial, personal feelings towards her and *her* former profession, they'd come to some sort of... not quite agreement, not quite arrangement, not quite trust... but something in between all three.

Something she couldn't define and doubted he could either.

Still, Blake hadn't set one foot in the boarding home since they, together, had uncovered the true means, motive, and calculation behind Norma's death. He'd stayed away, declining Mrs. Allen's continued invitations to coffee and pie, along with Mrs. Allen's hint or two that they all attend some local dance, something that would suit them all, in a celebration sort of manner, even with Cat's injury.

Blake, had again, declined.

In fact, he kept them all in the dark with his life and with his business, from his aunt to Dusty, claiming he'd been busy tying up loose ends from Norma's case—though the police couldn't and wouldn't technically try it in the courts.

But the real reason he'd stayed away, one which everyone knew, was a simpler one.

He'd stayed away because of Cat.

And now, apparently, he was back and Cat didn't know the first thing about what to think about it.

Or feel.

Finally, Cat managed to get her body workin' again and lowered the fork with that apple pie, no longer feeling the slightest bit hungry. She took a few deliberate breaths, centering herself as her pa had taught her, getting control, least as much she could, of all that hustling and bustling going on in her insides right about then.

Blake was not someone she was interested in seeing right now.

She had enough problems on her own. Especially... with her injuries, the healing she was doin' on the inside, all that relentless uncertainly rolling 'round in her, doubting just about everything she did or thought.

Blake would only complicate matters.

Cat thought briefly of heading upstairs and avoiding the whole thing. After all, wasn't that what *he'd* chosen to do? But she doubted she'd be movin' fast enough and she certainly wasn't about to explain why *she* was the one running away.

And... that simply wasn't her.

To run away.

Then there was Dusty to consider, who immediately noticed her reactions right then, and made no bones about staring at her so... openly, in fact, and with the kind of intensity that she really didn't want to think about. Or look closely at.

Cause both he and Mrs. Allen knew exactly who was coming across those nicely polished, wooden floors, all thanks to Cat.

Scary to think how well they knew her after only a short bit of time together.

Still, Cat pushed those thoughts aside, did her best to keep her breath even, slow, and centered, and got to her feet. Somehow. Just like she somehow managed to keep standing when Christopher Blake walked into the sitting room, as if the place were home.

What they all didn't know, including herself, were the dual, quiet, tentative steps of the individuals following behind Blake.

Now, Cat should have known. Logically speaking, of course. After all, she'd purposefully gone and started making a name for herself around town, and the papers had quite a field day when it came to the story of how Marcus Daly's close, personal friends had gotten tangled up with a prostitute and murder.

Maybe she would have noticed, would have figured out what those light footfalls meant—if her insides weren't tingling and twisting like crazy.

Which they were, especially right then as Blake stepped into view. He wore his all-black officer uniform and his wide-brim hat, which was nothing at all like his fellow officers.

He swept the hat off his head and nodded—to Mrs. Allen.

Blond hair a bit darker, as if the same ash and soot that dusted on his face and gotten in there, too. He wasn't nearly as clean and cut as she last remembered.

Though, to be fair, he'd been wearing a borrowed black suit at the time. Perfectly pressed and polished, along with a matching bow tie and hat. And she... well, she'd looked better as well, sportin' that pink, frilly dress of lace, layers of it, too, that flowed off her like it was a river.

The kind of dress little girls dreamed about in fairy tales and happy endings.

Together she and Blake had gone inside that rattlesnake's den called Grace's Gardens, arm in arm and undercover, to confront two of the most powerful men in Butte. If they'd gone in wearing nothin' but jeans and the guns at their hips they'd have never seen the door, let alone the knob.

Course, when they did get inside, thanks to the fancy getups they were wearing, the whole room had stopped and stared. Which she was pretty darn sure the staring was being done at Blake, and not at her, though she'd looked mighty fine for the part.

But the intensity in Blake's blue eyes that night? As he took in the whole room with all those lights and crystals glistening from the chandelier above?

It was still there, even now, and not an ounce of friendliness that Cat could see, as if such a visit here warranted gettin' a pulled tooth as well.

Blake's gaze flicked from Mrs. Allen to Dusty, and finally settled on Cat.

The look he gave her now was nothing like the last memory she had of him, rushing down those stairs into the cribs below the Gardens. Cat, who'd been just about ready to fall flat on her face from the pain in shoulder, thanks to Mr. Rippi. But at that moment, Blake had looked at her with such worry and fear that she almost believed she'd imagined it.

She probably had because it was nothing, like now.

Just the same hard eyes as when they'd first met, him being a police officer, her being a former prostitute.

Not a smile to be found.

So Cat didn't smile back, either, though she was really glad she was still sitting down. Her body really was aching, and she was just about to do so when she finally heard those soft, faint steps coming up behind him. Footsteps that barely touched down on that floor, barely made an impression on the creaking, polished wood. Steps as if from a child.

A little girl, in fact.

One who both Cat and Dusty immediately recognized, as the little girl peeked around Blake.

Rose.

And, of course, who followed behind Rose was none other than her mother, Mrs. Evie Blonberg. There was no question, either, that the hour or so it'd been since Cat had seen Evie Blonberg hadn't been an easy one.

Oh, no.

If looks mattered, and they did, Evie Blonberg had had a hard hour, indeed. One that wasn't gonna end until she left Butte, changed her name, and prayed no one recognized her ever again.

CHAPTER FIFTEEN

E vie did not want to be here.

Did not want to be sitting down at this lovely table with all the trims and trappings, with the pot of hot coffee along with an unchipped mug at her hand. The white lace and white table cloth, neither of which had a single stain that she could see, though both appeared well-worn and well-loved. Just like the rest of the house. Of course, the greatest slight of all was the perfectly sliced apple pie just sitting there, just so, right in front of her. As if this pie alone was all the reminder she needed at how badly she'd failed.

As a wife.

As a mother.

So Evie just sat there, not touching a bite, not drinking any, either, simply because she couldn't trust her hand to stay steady or her eyes to keep from tearing up again at the thousands of reminders presented in this little room alone.

Evie hadn't known what to expect when she'd followed Officer Blake, but it wasn't this.

Or *them.*

The very people she'd seen outside Peter's schoolhouse. Who'd been there, on purpose, to witness what had happened there.

When Evie and Rose had entered the boarding home, following behind Officer Blake, it was Mrs. Allen, the owner, who'd made the introductions. She got right to work as hostess, as if the mantle never fallen far from her shoulders, despite her flour-stained apron and the dusting of the same on her face and in her dark hair. In fact, she showed Evie the same kindness and politeness that Officer Blake had shown at the station. And there was certainly a resemblance between the two. Not so much in looks, but in... manners and their way of speaking, though neither Officer Blake or Mrs. Allen offered any explanation.

Mrs. Allen didn't miss one beat in the role she played, nor did she pepper Officer Blake with questions regarding Evie and Rose. Instead, Mrs. Allen had simply accepted the situation as it was.

Though the look she gave Evie as their hands clasped in greeting, the slight tightening of the older woman's fingers around hers, left little doubt.

Mrs. Allen knew her troubles, and yet spoke nothing of it.

And the same was true of the other woman standing there. A woman who Evie could barely bring herself to look at, at least at first. In truth, Evie found it difficult to follow Mrs. Allen's conversation. To say she was shocked was... quite the understatement.

You see, she'd gone with Officer Blake because she'd had nothing left to lose. No choice but to set out searching for a job, one she knew no one would hire her for, leaving one last option remaining. She hadn't expected him to bring her here, to the very boy with those piercing green eyes, the same boy who'd handed her the newspaper that morning and forever changed her life. The boy, Dusty, who looked nothing at all—and yet everything—like her Peter.

Nor had Evie expected the woman that stood next to Dusty.

Cowboy Cat.

Oh, she'd heard some stories of this Cowboy Cat. Everyone in Butte had, especially with all the rumors runnin' round about Marcus

Daly and his ties to two gentleman being looked at for murder. And perhaps if Evie hadn't been so lost in her thoughts and her fears at the time, she would have recognized Cat for who she was, out there on those streets and in the smoke, waiting for Peter.

After all, how many women, even in a place like Butte, went around wearing jeans and a cowboy hat?

Just one.

Yet at the time, while the sight of this woman had shocked Evie, it hadn't been enough to put the pieces together. To draw the right connections. Too distracted. Too emotional.

Even now... she didn't know what to feel or what to think.

But then, Officer Blake's words kept circling around and around in her head, haunting her, almost. Justice.

But... that was impossible.

Blake had said so himself. There was no justice for Evie and her situation, nothing the law or the courts could do to help her or secure a job that paid well enough to keep Rose and Peter sheltered and fed. Nothing else mattered.

And yet... yet Evie felt something, almost... very close...

Like hope.

And hope was the very last thing she could trust right now. The very last thing she could afford.

Evie bunched the fabric of her dress in her hands and squeezed where no one else could see.

It was now just her, Officer Blake, and... Cowboy Cat.

Mrs. Allen had taken the young ones to the kitchen and set them up with something more filling and appetizing than just pie. Even this comment, as innocent as it seemed, was not entirely so. As if Mrs. Allen had taken one look at Rose, saw the slenderness in her face, arms and legs, and knew what it meant. And even then, kept the comments to herself.

Just as Cowboy Cat now did.

Just as Cowboy Cat now waited. Patiently so for Evie to tell her story.

She sat across from Evie, sipping her mug of coffee with a hand that did not shake and brown eyes that saw everything. Seeing deeper into Evie than she dared want anyone to see, yet knowing she couldn't hide who she was, how she was hurting, and... how she was longing right at that moment.

Longing to be sitting there as this Cowboy Cat did.

Confident and sure, as if both radiated out from her whole being in a way and a manner which was completely foreign to Evie.

Not that this Cowboy Cat was some legend from the famous dime novels. Far from it. Evie could see the hurting in Cat's eyes, especially when her gaze, though rarely, glanced at Officer Blake. In truth, Evie recognized the look in herself, one she continually saw these past few years as Lou fell further and further away from her and their little family.

But even with all that hurting, Evie saw strength in Cat. As if the blue jeans and boots Cat wore and the gun holstered at her hip were part of her. The same way Evie's dress and done-up hair and bonnet were part of her as well.

Defining them both. Defining their roles.

True strength.

Something a housewife and a mother couldn't dare to achieve. But then, Evie was now being called onto being something more, something... other. And she didn't know if she had that kind of strength in her.

Cat lowered her mug, setting it on the table. All the while, her gaze never once left Evie's.

"You do," she said quietly.

As if she were reading Evie's thoughts.

"You do," Cat said again. "Have strength. A great deal of it."

Somehow Evie managed to swallow the lump that got stuck right there in her throat. And the tears that again wanted to slip free.

She couldn't let them.

Wouldn't.

"How did you...?" Evie began.

"It was easy enough to see where your thoughts were goin' and how they were makin' you doubt yourself." Cat gave her a sad smile. "Believe me, I know the look."

They sat silent for a moment, neither speaking, while Officer Blake shifted at his spot on the chair. The furthest one from Cat, Evie noticed.

There was certainly history there between them, though Evie couldn't begin to guess what or why. It was in the way the two *didn't* look at each other. And sure, they acknowledged the other's presence, but nothing more. Nothing shared.

"I've got to be honest," Cat said, finally looking at Blake. "I'm not sure what you're expectin' me to do. We both know the law. We both know she's got no recourse against her husband."

Blake's lips tightened. "You have your ways."

Cat crossed her arms. "Short of tracking down Lou and stringing him up by a horse to get an apology out, it's not gonna do a load of good."

Blake said nothing, just narrowed those blue eyes at Cat just so, and Evie had a feeling the two were having a whole conversation without ever once speaking.

But not speaking or not, it *was* about her.

And... she had to try, to reach for and ask for help...

For Peter, for Rose, if nothing more.

Evie sat up a bit straighter. "I'm, I'm not sure what you can do for me, either. Officer Blake was quite clear on my predicament. And my options. I knew them beforehand, but thought it best to... check, anyway. And the truth is, I haven't any. And the law, it won't support me, either."

Cat turned her attention to Evie. "No, it won't."

"Then I've wasted your time. Both of you." Evie stood. "Truly, I'm sorry. I am aware of my...predicament, and also what I need to do."

Both Cat and Officer Blake rose as well, but while the officer stood there, silent and stoic as ever, it was this... this Cowboy Cat who suddenly reached across the table, took Evie's hand in hers, and held tight. So tight, it was as if Cat thought she were about to fall over.

Maybe... maybe she was.

Because there was, indeed, a heaviness in her heart. And a resolution, too.

"See?" Cat whispered. "Strength. You've got it in you, to do what needs to come next. My question, how can I help? How can I ease some of that?"

"You said it yourself, there's nothing—"

"There's always something. I spoke true. I can't change the law, and I can't change what your husband said and how the selfish man went and splashed it across the papers as he did, but I can help. All you need do is ask."

There were a hundred, no, a thousand questions and needs that Evie had in that moment. How to feed her family, how to support them and keep them in their home that was too small and a neighborhood that would, no doubt, not want them. But it was theirs and it *was* home, even if it barely held against the cold winter winds and the black smoke that found every inch and crack to slip on through. And Lou... Lou and all his black moods, his foul temper that got even fouler when he drank... Lou was gone.

Sure, he left her a mess to deal with, a reputation in shatters and no hope ever of it getting better. And the neighbors? Everyone? They'd hate her. Despise her. See her as everything sinful and wrong in this world and it'd all be laid at her feet; her fault.

But in that moment, the only thought and desire Evie had was for Peter.

Peter, who hated her. Peter, who despised her. Peter, who without intervention, without help, would never again see her in the way that mattered most.

As his mother.

This time it was Evie who gripped Cat's hand. Evie, who looked Cat in the eyes with a kind of strength she didn't know she had, but was there, nonetheless.

"My son," Evie said. "Officer Blake says you know justice. Then I'm asking you for this. I need justice. As a mother. I need you to find my son, speak with him. Help him—"

Tears finally slipped out from her eyes. She did not fight them.

"Help him understand. Even if he won't ever return to me, I need him to know the truth. Can you do that? Can you?"

Cat met Evie's gaze, and for the first time, Evie didn't feel alone.

"I can," Cat promised. "I will."

CHAPTER SIXTEEN

Evie's words slipped in and out of Cat's conscious thoughts. Up and down, drifting in and out. First as simple thoughts, then ideas. They stayed with her, haunting her as surely as Alice did. And never once leaving.

But perhaps, just maybe, she'd find a way forward.

For Evie.

It was just Cat and Evie now, sitting on the couch together. Evie, with her head pressed against Cat's shoulders as heavy sobs wracked her poor body and stained Cat's blouse with all the sorrow she finally dare let go. Meanwhile, Cat had one arm around her and let the woman simply be a woman at that moment.

Not a mother or wife, but just a woman who had her heart broken.

Whose whole life had gotten flipped over, turned upside down and inside out. Who, from this day forward, could only show strength and resilience to the world.

Cat let her cry.

The coffee had long gone cold and the apple pie remained untouched. Which was fine. Evie more than likely didn't have much an appetite now, though Cat would be sure to wrap it up good, perhaps for Evie's children to enjoy later.

If, of course, Peter returned home.

Peter.

Cat remembered clearly the look in his eyes as he'd stood before his mother, fists clenched as they'd been, all the rage and frustration flowing off him like a dam suddenly breaking, timbers splintering, brick and concrete, crumbling.

What had he heard in that school? What rumors and twisted truth? Lies? What had pushed him so far that he couldn't stand the sight of his mother, even long enough to hear her truth?

One thing Cat was sure of, there'd been nothing but pain in Peter, pain which he'd directed at the one person he felt safe with, the one person he clearly loved.

And who so dearly loved him in return.

Cat let out a breath. They would find him.

She'd gone into the kitchen, quietly telling Dusty about Peter, and Dusty had gone without saying a word. Just a nod. He knew what he needed to do. He'd put out the word, see anyone had caught sight of Peter. The shadows would find him. They would look out for him because Dusty had asked.

The shadow world, to a degree, took care of each other.

When they weren't busy trying to tear the other down.

It was a hell of a balance, a knife's edge, really, but it was the life they each lived, Cat included. And now soon, Evie.

Which made her all the gladder that Blake had gone.

Truth was, she had no stomach to hear what would happen next. His resentment towards the profession, the one he knew intimately both from his work as an officer and because of his aunt. Yet at the same time, he understood the choices women like Evie had, and that there were just about none. Especially when said woman had two young, growing children. And Blake knew, just as well as every man and officer in that station had known, what *would* happen next with Evie and her choices.

Cat hadn't asked Blake to leave, but he'd done so on his own.

Still, as he quietly stood up from the table, slipping his hat onto his head, there was an understanding in him. She'd felt it. He'd said not a word, but the truth was there, holding in the air right there between him, between Cat, and the kind of justice Evie was seeking.

Along with his own, unspoken promise:

He would help in whatever way he could.

Cat was both glad for such a promise... and glad that he was gone. For many reasons.

Part of it was the look they'd shared. A mere glance, really. Maybe even the barest of a nod.

If one could call it so.

Truthfully, Cat wasn't entirely sure her mind hadn't made it up how tired she was feeling right then, all the emotions swirling about this sitting room, as if living in the very walls, witnessing was taking place here. She missed the wind blowing through trees, tugging at her hair and all those times she'd let it loose from her braid. And the wind and they way it'd go right on tugging and tangling, and finally taking with it all those negative thoughts and feelings she didn't want no more.

Except here in Butte, there was no wind.

And no trees, either.

Just a woman, also a mother, allowing herself to feel and grieve in the safety of someone who understood.

Evie, a mother who was barely holding on, and somehow even knowing what was to come, finding the kind of strength Cat could only envy and strive to find within herself. Out of all the things Evie could have asked help for, from putting a good word in with the more trustworthy and kind madams, to even a place she, herself, could rent. Neither had been what Evie asked for.

Instead, she'd asked only for Peter.

A mother's justice, Evie had called it.

In Cat's mind, the only justice would be finding her deadbeat of a husband and tying him to a steer before lettin' the beast drag his sorry ass all over Montana. Since that wasn't an option, Cat just allowed them both this moment to feel the sorrow and grieve for the life neither of them could ever have again.

And while Cat didn't let herself cry on the outside, she did on the inside.

Cried for that girl she'd been when Alice's husband, Stan, had died, or to be fair and honest, when Cat had killed him. It'd been her only choice at the time, the only way to save herself and Alice. But then, that truth there, the act to save them both, had been the very thing that broke that sisterly bond. The act and not the truth itself of *why* Cat had taken that gun, lifted it there just so as he'd broke through that wooden, pathetic lock. How he'd charged in with both fists raised and bloody. His angry, red face and the mouth that smelled of sour whiskey and rotten food, all the while dirt from the ceiling fallin' loose, hanging in the air about them.

Cat had fired to save their lives.

And she did save them, that was. But to Alice all that mattered was what Cat had done. And the good, Christianly woman that Alice had been couldn't look Cat in the eye and see her sister no more. Instead, she'd demanded that Cat leave their childhood home, their town, and never return.

Which was exactly what Cat had done.

She'd made a choice. It was the very same one Evie was making now. Cat, though, had a heart that carried a wildness all her own, one that both her parents had known, with her father accepting and her mother rejecting. But in the end, what mattered was the outcome and the consequence. There were simply no actual, decent, paying jobs for a woman in Montana.

Except one.

Except becoming a night lady and living a life in the shadows, forever shunned from the civilized world of Sunday churches and family gatherings. And while Cat had made that hard choice and lived with that choice as best she could, including the very reason why she was even here in Butte, holding this crying mother because she wanted—no, needed—to atone for her part in all this. As if maybe one day the ghost of Alice would forgive her. That, that there was the real reason behind why Cat was sittin' here, trying to help those who couldn't help themselves.

And simply too, she just couldn't live with herself sitting back and doing nothing.

But the other truth, the harder one, was that Cat *hadn't* had two children of her own when she'd been faced with this life... like Evie did. Evie, who would be forever tainted. Forever seen as a lesser being because of her husband's rash, unkind words toward her.

Finally, Evie's sobs quieted a bit and she lifted her head. Her eyes were red and puffy, and her nose was running something fierce.

Cat went and got her a handkerchief from where she knew Mrs. Allen kept them on hand.

Evie thanked her. But Cat wasn't looking for thanks. All the while Evie had been hurting and grieving, while Cat fought her own ghosts from the past, she'd been thinking and planning. All those ideas and thoughts that had slowly taken shape of their own.

But first, she needed some details, and when she asked Evie for them, Evie told her...

About Peter.

Not Lou.

In fact, Evie said nothing at all about Lou, about what had happened in their marriage, why the man, the one she'd married and pledged her life with, went and turned her out as he did, destroying every chance she had of any good manner of life. And yet, true to Evie's word, she said nothing at all about him, and when she did it was in the context of what mattered most.

Peter.

Peter was who she cared about. So that's what she told Cat.

Who Peter's friends were. Where he liked to play and go for fun. Who he had troubles with at school and around the neighborhood, the east side of Butte, and all them kids and gangs they were in, sorted by ethnicity, of course.

"But then," Evie said, "I guess that won't be a problem no more. It's not like I can afford our place and the neighbors, they certainly won't have us—"

Cat took her hand. "We'll come to that when we get there."

"Yes, yes of course."

Even though they both knew every word Evie had spoken was true. Cat was even bettin' Peter's teacher had said something to him, inquiring if he'd be continuing to school. While the school was there for everyone to attend, so Cat assumed (she wasn't exactly versed whether Butte law required mandatory schooling), she did know many children were forced to leave their schooling behind because the family needed them to. To instead pick up work around the house or boarding homes, become nannies for the wealthy folks, doing anything and everything they could to bring some extra money home.

Or there were kids like Dusty. Kids who simply chose another kind of life.

Regardless, it wasn't a happy prospect for Peter, nor a chance for a happy reunion.

Cat sat back on the couch, the cushions worn yet still comfortable and they wrapped around her just so. Her shoulder hurt a bit, but not as much as earlier. Instead, it just reminded her of exactly what she could do—and what she couldn't.

Evie wiped at her eyes. "Do you think you can find him? Do you think he'll talk with you?"

"I can find him. Dusty's already sent out word with the folks he knows, and trust me, he knows a fair few."

"Dusty." Evie lowered the handkerchief. "Why did he help me? Why... why did he come with the paper? He didn't need to."

"No, he didn't."

And whatever his exact reasons were, Cat didn't know. Nor would she ask. It wasn't her business.

"You'll have to ask him yourself," Cat said, "though I suspect it's because of your children, and seeing them probably reminded him of something from his own past."

"And you? Why are you helping me?"

"Because I can. And because, because someone needs to." Even if she wasn't the woman who'd first stepped off that train in Butte. Maybe never would be again.

Evie nodded. A strand of her hair had fallen free of its knots and ties, and it just lay there, curled against her cheek. She tucked it behind an ear, her mind clearly far, far away from this sitting room.

"Do you... do you think Peter will listen?"

Cat let out a breath. That certainly was the question of the hour.

"I don't know," Cat said. "I don't know him yet, how his mind thinks or how he feels, but I will."

And it was in the learning, in her getting to know who Peter was, on the inside and the out, that she'd find her answer. Hopefully it was the one Evie so desperately needed. Without it...

No, Cat wouldn't think on that. Not yet.

Instead, she gave Evie another squeeze of her shoulders. "We'll figure this out. In the meantime, let me call in Mrs. Allen and the both of you can talk."

"I don't need—"

"You do." Cat stood, wiping her hands on her jeans and at the apple crumbs that weren't there. "Mrs. Allen knows enough folk around here to point you in the right direction, if nothing more, and believe me, *that* will be doing both of your children more a favor than settling Peter's feelings."

"All I care about it—"

"Peter. Yes, yes I heard you. And as I said, I *will* find him, but you've got more than just Peter to worry about."

As if Cat's words brought her, there was Rose, peaking her head around the corner. The joy Cat had seen earlier was gone from her face, and a sadness settled there instead. Gone was the little girl dancing down the frozen mud road in a pitch black early afternoon to pick up her brother. Careful. Joyful. All of that gone.

"Mama?"

"Ro—Rose!"

Evie got to her feet, so unsteady she nearly knocked over that cold slice of apple pie.

Cat steadied the plate, then she steadied Evie.

"If I were you," Cat whispered, "I would sit your daughter down now and tell her the truth."

Evie paled. Got so pale she looked like the white of the moon's surface—if they could ever see the darn thing.

"I-I couldn't! She's just a child. Barely more than a babe—"

"And one who surely will hear it from someone else. Someone very soon, probably even the moment she steps out of this house." Cat gently touched Evie's shoulder. "Do her a kindness. Tell her the truth. Let her hear it from her mother."

"I, I can't."

"If you don't, it'll be Peter all over again."

Evie closed her eyes. Fresh tears slipped down her face. One, then two. And then none at all.

"Yes," Evie said. "Yes, of course. You're right."

Cat let her hand drift away just as Rose was coming around to them.

"Mama?"

Cat let mother and daughter be, not quite sure who was holding who, but even from here, she felt both those hearts breaking as they curled up on that couch together, Evie pulling her little girl onto her lap and Rose burying her head in Evie's chest.

And, truth be told, Cat's heart was breaking, too.

Mrs. Allen waited just beyond the doorway, watching the whole thing as well. Her face looked more aged than it had earlier, more wrinkles, too, and also a sadness. The deep end, the one that a person felt right to their soul.

Something they felt.

"That was a kind thing you did," Mrs. Allen said. "For Rose, for asking her mother to tell her the truth."

"Maybe."

She certainly hoped so.

Cat stretched her shoulder a bit, the muscles there having gotten bunched up and cold from the position she'd been sitting in with Evie. So many thoughts swirled around in her mind, wondering just which way she had to turn next.

She'd promised to find Peter, but she still knew so very little about him. That would be a problem. Maybe she needed to find one of those close friends of his in the neighborhood... Bugsy, Evie had called one of them. Maybe he'd point Cat in the right direction. And if not her, then Dusty or one of his fellows.

"Have you heard from Dusty yet?" Cat asked.

Mrs. Allen shook her head. "Not yet, though I wouldn't be expectin' an answer before tomorrow. From everything I heard, Peter was just a normal, ordinary boy."

"You sure? Dusty's already put word out on the streets." And he'd gone into those tunnels, lookin' for whatever information, Cat didn't know.

Mrs. Allen shrugged. "Maybe, but from everything I heard, Peter's not the kind of kid who'd stick out to those boys living in the shadows."

No, no he wasn't. He was just a normal kid with normal parents who, until this morning, lived a normal life.

"Damn," Cat whispered.

Mrs. Allen touched her shoulder, the uninjured one. "You know he will. You know Dusty's good for his word."

She did.

"Just like you," Mrs. Allen said.

"I just hope it doesn't come back to bite me in the ass." Because one day, one day she wouldn't be able to keep a promise and it would sure hurt, hurt something fierce when that day came.

First, though, there was someone she needed to talk to.

Cat first went upstairs, grabbing her scarf her sister Alice had made, paused a beat before, decidedly, she wrapped it around her neck. No matter what rattlesnake's nest she was walkin' into, having it would make her that much stronger. At least on the inside, and remind her just what she was doing all this fighting for. Then Cat came back down, boots clomping on the wooden staircase where Mrs. Allen waited on the bottom, hands planted right there on her hips.

Cat ignored her.

Instead, she made her way to the closet where Chin kept all their coats and slowly, carefully, shrugged hers on.

Mrs. Allen followed, the heels of her black, buttoned shoes clicking on that polished floor with the kind of intensity she'd had when they'd first started this day—and their fight.

Which felt like a lifetime ago.

"You're not seriously considering going back out there?" Mrs. Allen said from behind Cat, keeping right at Cat's own boot heels. "I agreed to give you time outside, to move and regain your strength, but not to injure yourself more. Which is exactly what you'll do if you push yourself—"

"And what would you have me do?" Cat turned and looked right at Mrs. Allen. "Would you have me stay here? Do nothing?"

Mrs. Allen huffed, squishing her lips together, crossing her arms. She even got to tapping her toes, which told Cat she was both really frustrated and really mad.

"No. No, of course not," Mrs. Allen said. "All I'm saying, it's not wise, throwing yourself back into things like this. You're not healed and Doctor Griffin *was* perfectly clear about that."

"And so was Mr. Lou Blonberg when he posted that damn classified." Cat grabbed her hat from the stand and shoved it onto her head. "That family doesn't have time to wait for my wounds to heal, for my shoulder to stop hurting."

"That wasn't what I was talking about and you know it." Mrs. Allen uncrossed her arms. Let them fall to her side. "You're not yourself, Cat, and you're not doing a damn thing to hide it, either. Everyone can see."

"Except for Blake."

Because he hadn't been around. He'd chosen to not be around.

Cat shook her head. "I know what you're saying. And I'm not, I'm not saying you're wrong. What I *am* saying is that I don't have much of a choice here."

Cat glanced back towards the sitting room. There were no voices coming from there, just quiet sobs, the kind that went right through a person's body and straight down into their soul—and stayed there.

"No," Mrs. Allen finally agreed. "You don't. That doesn't mean I have to like it."

"Good."

Cat adjusted her hat, feeling how foolish the whole thing was and hopin' like hell she had the energy to get herself outside and then back home again before her whole body simply gave out. She *was* tired. She *was* exhausted. And doing what she needed to do next—it sure as hell wasn't the state of being she needed to be in.

But what choice did she have?

What choice did any of them have?

"You'll watch after them?" Cat tipped her head towards the sitting room. "Make sure they get home safe enough?"

"You know I will. And what about you? Where, exactly, are *you* going?"

"Dusty's trying to find out what he can about Peter, but that's only one problem, and Evie's got a whole helping of them on her plate right now."

"You mean, where she's going to find work?"

"Yep, that's what I mean."

Mrs. Allen sighed, and to Cat it looked like there were suddenly more wrinkles there. The vibrant light of the older woman slowly fading, and right in front of Cat's eyes, too. It was a sad thing indeed to see.

"I can help with that, you know," Mrs. Allen said. "The girls keep me appraised of the madams, who the honest ones are, who stay clear of."

Mrs. Allen, though no longer living the life on the line, hadn't cut all ties with it. Like Cat, she was haunted by her own ghosts, her own failures and slights. One of the ways Mrs. Allen appeased her ghosts was havin' the mail from the working girls delivered here. This gave the girls a reputable address, helping to keep their secret, and their profession, a bit longer from friends and family.

And while she'd advised Evie to listen to Mrs. Allen's advice, Cat had this feeling tugging in her gut, a tingling, really, that told her this time... this time it wasn't gonna be enough.

"Can you?" Cat asked. "Can you really help? The red light is just as pissed at you as they are with me right now."

And while the red light district was made up of a whole bunch of independent owners and businessmen, the truth was there were only a few major players to take into account. And the biggest one... well, let's just say Cat's recent learning of the truth about Norma had inadvertently led her straight back to one of the biggest fingers in that pie. And while that particular finger had no way of getting in trouble with the law, truth was, the law was now *looking* at him regardless.

Meaning, he wasn't none too happy with Cat... or anyone else she'd tucked her lot with.

Including Mrs. Allen.

Cat buttoned up her coat as best she could with her one good arm and shoulder, and feeling all the more tired from her earlier outing. It really was pulling something fierce on all the parts that were healing.

Mrs. Allen sighed and helped with the buttons. "Mr. Nadeau knows me. We have a relationship, of sorts, and there he sees a great deal of respect for me, despite what Madam Grace has managed to do to my name. Besides, of the two of us, I know how to be civil."

"You do."

Certainly no argument there.

Mrs. Allen finished with the buttons but stayed close. "I should be the one to go."

"Any other day. Any other time. And that's the problem. He's plum pissed with us and it ain't been long enough for the steam to stop coming out his ears."

"I'm well aware he's unhappy."

"And between the two of us," Cat said, repeating Mrs. Allen's phrase, "I'm the one with a gun."

"He won't help."

"Not me."

Cat nodded towards the sitting room. The sobs had quieted, though she almost felt their sadness as if it were a living, breathing thing in there. True strength, she reminded herself. Which was exactly why this was a stop she needed to make, even if it turned out to be fruitless at best, and at worst downright dangerous.

Probably the latter.

"But maybe," Cat said, "maybe Mr. Nadeau will be willing to help them. And I won't know unless I try."

And she intended to try. For Evie's safe. For Rose.

For Peter.

Cat opened the front door, got a blast of cold air and smoke that immediately started stinging and watering her eyes. Or just maybe the tears had been there to begin with and she just hadn't noticed until now.

"Besides," she said, "I made a promise. I aim to keep it."

CHAPTER SEVENTEEN

P eter *ran.*

Ran as fast as he could. Ran as fast as his legs would move.

Up and down over that cold, hard ground. No rain, no water falling down from the sky so there was snow, but it was still cold. Real cold. And slippery, too, and ice had glazed over the ground in some spots, hiding there, patient and biding its time for some wayward foot to touch down and send 'em sprawling.

Somehow Peter stayed upright. Somehow he kept running.

Didn't stop. Couldn't.

He stayed near the boardwalk, but not on it. Couldn't see well enough in front of him through that thick, rolling black smoke, the sulfur that clogged the air and choked him good. He couldn't see if someone might be coming out of some store or home. The same went for the street with all them horses and hacks and their like.

Not that he saw anyone.

Neither horses or people, but he sure heard them. Heard the smacking of whips and that hard clomp of hooves. Heard voices like they were whispering right there in the smoke, right into his ears, taunting and unkind. Like them voices were living right inside that smoke, each and every one of them, and they sounded exactly like the other kids.

Mean. Angry. Like suddenly all their hurts had been caused by his mother.

One foot landed down. Then another.

Peter kept running.

His thoughts, though, those voices, they stayed with him. It was like they kept pace with him, whispering right there in his ears, loud and hurtfully clear.

"I heard 'bout yer mom, Peter! They say she's nothing more than a fallen lady now!"

The laughter that then followed, that hugged close to Peter's heels and he was tying, so very hard, to outrun—

And couldn't.

Including, including Bugsy.

"You best stay away, Peter. My ma isn't gonna want you 'round no more. No. Not even at the side hill. You can't come now. You ain't one of us."

Peter's foot slipped a bit.

A patch of dark ice sleeping quietly over an even darker patch of crushed-up gravel and bits. He nearly went down. Nearly cracked his knees right there on that street, but damn it, Peter wasn't about to give up now.

Even if he was running.

Or trying to.

But worst of all had been the mothers, the ones picking up their kids and walkin' home through that black smoke. It had been their words that had chilled Peter, that even now kept him running, as if doing so, just maybe he could run fast enough. Hard enough. To change their future.

"She can't be trusted."

That's what Bugsy's ma had said, and the look she'd given Peter, the way her mouth pinched into that tight line, like she was smellin' something foul just by looking in his direction.

Peter's lungs and chest were hurtin'. The smoke and all them chemicals and whatnot he was breathing in, dear Lord did it *hurt*. He'd take in one breath just to want to cough it back out again.

Still, though, he kept going. Had to. Didn't matter that his whole body couldn't keep up, couldn't fight back all that anger he was feelin'.

And all that hurtin', too.

His sides were hurtin' now and he was even startin' to limp cause he'd stepped on something a little too sharp, something he felt right on through his thin, worn shoes. And at least, for this moment, as he ran, arms pumping up and down, he didn't feel the cold.

The hurt, though... try as he might, run as hard and fast as he could, the hurtin' stayed right with him.

Tears stung his eyes and he wiped them, wiped them away good and hard.

He was *not* a sissy girl like Susan Hoy.

So what if his pa had left? So what he he'd gone and said all those things about his mother? So what—

If his life and Rose's weren't ever gonna be the same again.

All that, though, just made the tears keep coming, and keep coming harder.

Finally Peter couldn't take it no more, the pain in the side or that stupid need to breathe. He slowed down, taking big, painful gulps of air—and did his damn best to not cough them back up again.

Running during a black winter—silly, stupid idea.

He'd keep going, if he could.

Peter bent forward, bracing his hands on his knees, and just kept breathing and trying his best not to cry. Which didn't do a damn thing, and those stupid tears, they just kept coming, and made him all the more madder.

Then he started walking.

Just walking, not really knowing where he was going and not seeing anyone else, either. Wiping at his eyes that just couldn't seem to stop tearing up and crying like the sissy he was.

How could his mother have done this to them? To Rose? How could things have gotten so bad with his pa that, that he'd do this? Leave them. Leave them and ruin them?

Some part of Peter, the rational part—at least he thought so, anyway—kept trying to break through all those swirling voices, kept trying to pull Peter up and out of that spiral.

His pa had a temper.

His pa hadn't worked in months.

His pa was angry all the time, and Peter *knew* his mother tried. She brought in extra money, much as she could, except it just made his pa all the angrier. And sure, Peter had been spending more and more time out of the house, draggin' Rose with him, too, even though Bugsy didn't like when his little sister tagged along. But Peter couldn't let her stay in that house, stay near the fire he'd see sparkin' in his pa's eyes. Couldn't live with himself if anything had happened to her.

But still—

The town had said it was his mother's fault. That she was the unfaithful one. The town *believed* it, so what in the hell mattered if it wasn't actually truth?

Because now, now it was truth.

Truth.

Peter kept walking until he nearly twisted his ankle on a rock, one 'bout the size of his fist that seemed to just appear out of the smoke. He got so mad right then that he kicked it as hard and far as he could and sent it flyin'.

Heard a small ping echoing in that smoke, like the hard rock striking thin, warped metal.

Peter looked up. He squinted his burnin' and tearin' eyes, and realized where his feet had taken him.

The side hill.

The place that he and Bugsy and the other kids played. After school, before school, even when no school was happenin'. It was their place. He could just make out them sagging wood beams from the bridge, the place where some kids would stand under while yellin' up top to the others.

Now, however, there wasn't no talkin' to be had.

Probably wouldn't be any, either. Not when it was so black out and all them mothers who'd be worrying about them getting lost and other such nonsense.

For a moment, though, Peter turned and looked behind him. Waiting and almost expecting Bugsy to come out of that smoke and smile with that crooked smile of his and call Peter some name 'bout him being a sissy doing all that crying he'd done.

But Bugsy didn't show.

No one did.

Though for a brief moment, Peter thought he saw someone. Someone like him... same height and build, skinny and wearing a too-big coat like his. And possibly a glimpse of green.

But then Peter blinked, and the person just up and vanished, meaning he'd been alone this whole time to begin with.

It was just Peter and the whispering voices, the hate and hurt swirling inside him, refusing to leave him alone, refusing to even let him breathe. And all the while, the realization slowly, slowly sinking into him.

He had no where to go and no one to turn to.

For the first time in his life, he was well and truly alone.

CHAPTER EIGHTEEN

Cat was just about itching to be any place but here. Any place but the grand mansion of businessman and owner of at least half the red-light district (if not more), a one Mr. Joseph Nadeau.

Mr. Nadeau who had quite the healthy... frustration... where Cat was concerned.

Deservedly so, in truth.

Just as there was another simple truth: Cat couldn't move from her spot, right here on the gleaming, wooden floor, without feeling like she was gonna knock something over with her too-long arms and pointy elbows, or drop a pile of dirt right from her boots. Sure, she could have gone and put on her cleanest, most pressed pair of blue jeans and blouse (which she hadn't done), and it wouldn't have made a damn bit of difference. Neither she nor her clothes would ever be considered acceptable to a place such as this. As everyone from the butler who ungraciously and grudgingly allowed her entrance, to the maid who took her coat and hat, made quite, quite clear.

Cowboy Cat was not welcome or wanted.

Yet, they'd allowed her entrance, anyway. Which she was gonna take as a good sign, though a small one.

Everything, *everything* about this house had been polished and cleaned to within an inch of its life, from those gleaming, hard-backed wooden chairs, the kind that gave your ass a bruise in about five seconds flat, to the dainty little serving table there that—no surprise— remained completely empty of refreshments.

Which was just fine.

Cat was pretty darn sure if she so much as looked at any of their fancy china teacups they'd shatter on principle.

Best to keep her hands, her feet—hell, her whole body—to herself.

Where Mrs. Allen's home had felt almost comfortable to Cat, even with it bringing up all those memories as it did, Mr. Nadeau's place set her skin itching. A crawling almost, right there between her shoulder blades. Like this wasn't a home to be lived in, and instead a place to be admired and gawked at like the silly, bumpkin little cowgirl that she was.

And who could blame her?

Hell, who could blame *anyone*?

Sure, it might be grand, might be beautiful, but it wasn't a home. That was for damn sure.

She'd also never seen such a waste as this place, either. Intricate, carved wooden sculptures lining the walls before the fanciest kind of wallpaper she'd even seen, about the same color as the wood, too, took over and reached all the way to the ceiling. It was like the two blended together, these carvings of birds and swirls and blooming flowers, then faded away, perfectly so, the same way a fawn hid in the tall grass from the hungry wolves, stomachs growling from the long, lean winter and just waiting for that perfect midday snack.

The feeling was not lost on Cat, either.

Or the imagery her instincts were pullin' up.

She might still be healing, might still be learning who the new her was, but all these bits and parts that had kept her living and breathing for all these years... well, it was good to know they were still there. Still lookin' out for her.

She was gonna need it.

And while she could appreciate the display of craftsmanship here, a true artisan really, it was also completely empty. Its only purpose to be admired.

And envied.

Which was the point. A point that the very lady of the house, Mrs. Nadeau herself, seemed quite clear and intent on making.

Cat had come calling on Mr. Nadeau to speak with him about the situation surrounding Evie Blonberg in hopes he might have some soft spot in his heart for a single mother with children of her own, and him being a father himself, would hopefully understand. Cat hadn't been holding out much hope. In fact, like Mrs. Allen said, it probably *was* downright foolish for Cat to come here.

Alone.

He was, after all, a bit unhappy with Cat regarding that business with Norma and ties that had, unknowingly, led back to him. And while Cat had partly expected him to deny her visit, what she hadn't expected was his wife.

Mrs. Nadeau.

Mrs. Nadeau, who entered the receiving room with a swish and swirl of the severest, darkest dress imaginable. Her collar so tight and high that it was a wonder the woman could even breathe. Which, thanks to Cat's near-perfect memory, reminded her exactly of Mr. Nadeau. She'd met him one time and one time only, in the great ballroom of Grace's Gardens. He wearing his formal suit and his shoulders and head up so high that the rest were simply rodents and other such desirables underneath him.

At least the two Nadeaus seemed quite perfect for the other.

And Cat was in no way, shape, or form envious of this nasty, bitter woman, whose cold eyes narrowed into slits as she regarded Cat with such disgust.

Nor was Cat jealous of her wealth. Far as Cat was concerned, Mrs. Nadeau could keep it—and all the pain and blood and sorrow that went with it.

Cat raised her hand in greeting, the way such things were done in polite company, at least according to her ma. Mrs. Nadeau, on the other hand, seemed disinclined to follow such polite society rules because she glared at Cat's hand, ungloved too, as if it were a hairy, beastly little rodent. She also made no move or motion in offering Cat a place to sit, either.

Which was just fine.

Sure, Cat could have used it about now. She was tired and sore, and truthfully a bit hungry since it felt like she'd been ridin' hard for these past few hours. Still, she wasn't about to let any of that discomfort show.

Cat stayed right where she was, polite as she could be, the faintest bit of a smile poking through. Because what did bitter, nasty women hate more than anything else?

A smile.

And there was quite the power in a smile, as Cat had learned, all thanks to Norma. The thought, which really *did* get her smiling, and poor Mrs. Nadeau glowering so fierce it looked like her face was scrunching up into a map of unhappy wrinkles.

Mrs. Nadeau, however, said nothing.

And for the second time that day, Cat found herself in a standoff with yet another formidable woman.

Cat was perfectly content to stand there and wait, even if her stomach was startin' to grumble, but thankfully, such stoic silence was unnecessary.

Either Mrs. Nadeau wasn't as patient as Cat, or... she simply couldn't stand the sight of Cat in her home, probably dusting off the smoke and ash from her trek over here on her beautiful, polished floors, which simply would not do. Not do at all.

"Why have you dared come into my home?" Mrs. Nadeau demanded.

Cat raised her eyebrows. "I thought my message was pretty clear. I came to speak with your husband."

Mrs. Nadeau's mouth pinched in a tight line. So tight and thin it looked like her lips were bloodless. Probably her heart, too. Dusty had told her a rumor that Mrs. Nadeau knew exactly what her husband's business was all about, and in fact, her name was on the very papers for several of his businesses.

And Mrs. Nadeau was just as cold a being as her husband, no question about it.

Cat's hairs were standing so straight up on end, her skin feeling like it was crawling with the wrongness of the other woman, as if a piece of her had broken off and crumbled away a long, long time ago.

"My husband is indisposed," Mrs. Nadeau said.

"A shame."

Cat crossed her arms. Carefully and slowly, not betraying an inch of her hurts. Though Mrs. Nadeau's eyes narrowed right on that spot of her shoulder, the one where Mr. Rippi had gone and done a hell of a bit of damage to her.

And that simple glance, that simple movement, told Cat more than Mrs. Nadeau had ever wanted Cat to know.

Cat smiled and kept her tone, her words, nice and pleasant. Perfectly cordial, so perfect, in fact, her ma would be pleased at the uncouth barbarian her youngest daughter usually was.

"You know how long he'll be?" Cat asked. "I've got a urgent matter to discuss with him."

"He will be away for some time. I do not recommend you wait for him."

"Fair enough. I imagine you're wanting me gone from your home."

"That would be a correct assumption."

"Though, though I suppose... I could make this all a bit easier on all of us, I certainly don't want to kick my heels up here to wait for him, either, but I suppose I *could* discuss the matter. With you."

"Why on earth would you do such a thing?"

"For starters, you know quite a bit about his business. All of them."

The legal ones, the illegal ones, and the ones that straddled that world of both.

The shadow world, itself.

Mrs. Nadeau straightened, though how she managed in *that* dress... the thought alone made Cat shudder.

She'd had enough of corsets to last her a lifetime. Two lifetimes, in fact.

"My husband keeps his own counsel, Miss Cat, and I do not appreciate your insinuating otherwise."

"Don't blame you, really. A good move, in fact. Probably works on most people."

Cat turned then, making a big show of searching the room. Then took two long steps to one of those uncomfortable wooden chairs, the kind with a cushion so hard just looking at it made your ass hurt—

And sat down.

"I mean," Cat continued, "you being a respectable lady and all, you certainly wouldn't want to talk about those deplorable conditions the ladies in your husband's employ live in. You know the ones I mean, down there in the tunnels underneath..."

Cat wiggled her fingers, and Mrs. Nadeau stood even taller in that dress, sucking in a big long breath, too. Well, as a big a one a corset like *that* would allow.

"Stay with me here," Cat said. "You've got the tunnels underneath the Dumas there. A fancy place, I hear, though haven't a chance to visit myself, yet anyway, and oh! Of course, your newly built Copper Block. I did get a good look at it, first coming to Butte and all, mighty impressive. Mighty fine plans your husband has for it."

"What is your point, Miss Cat?"

"I'm just wondering..." Cat leaned forward, staring hard at Mrs. Nadeau. "You have a chance to tour them yet? The tunnels, I mean. Or do you limit your visits just to the Dumas? Cause, you know, city records are pretty darn clear on who owns *that* property."

And, like Cat had suspected earlier, Mrs. Nadeau was not her husband. Oh sure, there were similarities, a coldness that simply lived in each of them like all that wealth had slowly taken over, corroded really, whatever kinda heart they'd started life with. But Mrs. Nadeau was something more.

Sharper.

More dangerous, even.

The look she leveled on Cat, it would freeze a lesser being. It would make their knees shake, and probably loose their bowels, too, maybe even out both ends. See, it was the kinda look that no longer had a speck of humanity, the kinda look that priests and rabbis and whoever else believed in some God or religion or whatever warned against. Not evil, no, but simply... lifeless.

Soulless.

But then...

That made sense, too.

Mrs. Nadeau would have needed to become this person, to shed her humanity, especially if she wanted to acquire all this wealth here, especially when such wealth, such living, was all thanks to the sorrow and tears and degradation of others, and Mrs. Nadeau here, she was pretty much neck deep in it.

And Cat, how dare her, was calling her out on it.

Yet, Mrs. Nadeau showed not an inch of anger at this. It was like the anger itself caused her to withdrawn even further. Even the disgust at Cat's presence, this deplorable creature seated in the heart of her empire, faded away.

There was no doubt, none at all, that Mrs. Nadeau was every inch the businesswoman as her husband, perhaps even more so. And Cat had this thought, this small, nagging worry of just *whose* idea it'd been to go into the flesh trade.

Mrs. Nadeau gave Cat a cold, curling smile, not hiding one inch of who she really was.

Cat slowly sat back, all her senses tingling like crazy.

This whole time, she'd been led to believe that Joseph Nadeau was the dangerous one. Now, upon meeting the missus, Cat saw a completely different picture, a completely different understanding.

Cat had been wrong. Everyone had been wrong.

CHAPTER NINETEEN

There were a hundred things Evie should be doing. Preparing, going out and finding new... employment for herself.

Yet Evie couldn't move from her spot by the window. Holding back the curtain and staring out, far as she could in the darkness, and the tears that seemed insistent on filling her eyes.

And her soul.

Rose had fallen asleep by their small bit of fire. It hadn't taken long, either. Two steps inside, both of them almost stumbling under the weight they felt from the cold and from what tomorrow would most certainly bring, and for once Rose didn't fight Evie on getting ready for bed. If anything, Evie couldn't get her ready fast enough, as those heavy lids of her daughter's slid closed.

They'd stayed some hours at Mrs. Allen's, both of them recovering in both body and soul, though Evie had known it was only meant to be a small pause, that quiet intake of breath before the real storm hit.

But she was grateful for those moments, if nothing else, for Rose.

Rose, who slept huddled up there on the floor with quilts and blankets wrapped around her. There was her small doll, too, the one she'd grudgingly left behind when they'd gone to the school to walk Peter home. A lifetime ago. And now... now there was a sadness within Rose's features. As if her forehead couldn't relax, couldn't release the hard, dark thoughts now plaguing her. Her hair, no longer in braids, spilled about her face just so.

But she slept and with a fully tummy as well, thanks to Mrs. Allen and—

The other.

The woman who wore both confidence and gun like they were part of her.

Mrs. Allen and... and Cat, they'd been the only two people, other than Officer Blake, who'd looked at her, looked her right in the eyes, and held kindness for her.

Kindness and sorrow.

No one else. Just them. The very ones that her world had rivaled against and demonized her entire life.

How? How had Evie allowed her life to fall to this?

To be sitting here staring at the window, knowing in her heart that neither husband or son was gonna walk through that door? How had she done so much wrong? To have her family unravel in such a way that, that she was needing the help of strangers, of former night ladies for that matter! And all because no one else, *no one*, not even Marybell who used to invite them all over for Sunday dinner after church back when Lou was workin' for the Big S, and they'd all been welcome. Not even the reverend himself had offered forgiveness or understanding, the reverend who'd been driving by in a hack just as she and Rose had climbed out of theirs. The hack that Mrs. Allen had kindly called and paid for (even if the driver was a bit on the frightening side with how he quick he took those turns). But Reverend Jacobs and his usual patient smile and kind demeanor, one which she'd relied heavily on since Lou had lost his first job at the Spectacular, listening to her worries and offering her council, especially with Lou and his continued anger, continued interest and desires in drinking, even that patient smile was gone.

There wasn't one inch of kindness. No hint of a smile.

Certainly no understanding.

Instead, Reverend Jacobs had sat up so tall and straight and looked as if she'd gone and slapped him in the face, as if her... her betrayal was somehow a personal, hurtful one.

For him.

For a moment, she'd thought he'd stopped. To call out to his driver and order him to stop. Maybe even to get down and share those kind words her heart so desperately needed to hear. But then that must have been her own imagination because Reverend Jacobs said nothing and then, he was gone.

For now, anyway.

Until he came knocking on her door to remind her the trials of her evils and the path of sin he knew she was on—which he would surely do. Eventually. Hopefully not today and not tomorrow or the next one, either. Maybe at least give her enough time to... to figure out what she needed to do.

A sob caught in Evie's throat, and this time it stayed there.

She let the curtain fall, and then, before she could move away, picked it up again.

Somehow, in some manner that she didn't understand, there was hope. It beat there, strong and insistent and true in her breast. But it was fear that kept her there. Kept her right there by the window, as if when she caught even the faintest glimpse of Peter, she could rush on out of the house and plead with him. Tell him how sorry she was, how wrong she'd been and how many mistakes she'd made.

She should have taken Lou seriously.

She should have listened to her heart years ago. Should have done the hard thing and left him before, before—

Before their life had been ripped away from them.

Tears fell down her cheeks, staining them, probably making a right mess 'cause of all that ash and soot she'd collected from being outside for so long. Yet couldn't find the energy or will to wipe herself free of it, or any of the dust and dirt she'd gathered. Couldn't drum the effort to even care. Because why *did* it matter? Truth was, it didn't. How she looked, how she presented herself to the world, no longer mattered now.

It also didn't help, either, that their home, the one she and Lou and the kids had slowly added to, put together bit-by-bit, didn't feel like theirs anymore.

Nor did the neighborhood.

No one had left their homes. No one had said anything to her.

But then, no one needed to. Their opinions of her and her new situation had been made quite clear, in fact.

It seemed like their entire block had done what Evie was now doing, staring out those curtains, waiting patient as could be for Evie to come home. Then, each of one to a person, went and pulled back those curtains as far as they could, made sure that she saw them standing there, glaring at her for all their worth. The disapproval written clear across their faces, their... their disgust and resentment that a woman like *her* was now in their midst, now sullying their neighborhood.

Didn't matter that she knew most of them were poor, real poor, though they tried like hell to hide it. Evie's gaze strayed to Marybell's home, a place that'd once been welcome to them and even with their own change of fortune, having less to go around, though none of that was ever said, Evie always welcomed her home to Bugsy. Never asked a question and was never offered an answer, either. Then there were those other families, ones who'd faced a similar choice as hers, choosing whether a family was to live, starve or... or do what was necessary, take the kind of jobs no good Christian family would ever take, yet not having the choice not to.

Course, none of those had been made so public as Evie.

Frustrated, angry, and not being able to do anything about it, Evie wiped at her cheeks.

Hard.

Hated, too, that she was even still crying.

Crying solved nothing. Crying would not find her a job or put food in her children's bellies. What's worse, though, was she'd hoped she'd gotten all her cries out at Mrs. Allen's, that she'd left those fears and worries in the safety of that warm, welcoming home, but apparently not. Apparently the act of being awake and breathing was enough to keep all those feelings all right there.

Or maybe it's just because she was so desperate to see Peter.

Even if only a glimpse.

Even if she knew that a glimpse wouldn't ever be enough, that nothing she could say or do would be enough to fix what Lou had done, what he'd so carelessly thrown against the wall and broken.

Their family.

Rose stirred from her spot beside the fire, pulling up the quilt closer to her chin, as if she was sensing the slowly dimming cold as the last of their wood became red, glowing embers, and how the darkness crept into their home.

Bit by bit, of course, the slow, lengthening of shadows, her breath puffing out white before disappearing. Not that there really was much difference between day and night, certainly not if one gauged by the appearances outside that window, and yet Evie still felt it. Felt that slow drop in temperature. The depth of cold that stole right through the thin walls of their home and that broken door. And she felt it, too, in her heart and knowing that Peter wasn't gonna come home tonight.

Maybe... maybe not ever again.

It wasn't yet late, but Evie found she didn't have the strength to keep her eyes open any longer. Or maybe it was just her soul.

She pulled herself from the window, picked up Rose, who stirred again though didn't waken, as if the events and what she'd learned today had tired her mind and body in ways she wasn't meant to feel. Not for some years anyway.

Evie carried her little girl to bed where after a long, long day of their world falling apart, crumbling right there as she watched, Evie finally fell into a fitful sleep herself...

And never once stopped thinking about her son and this small, tiny hope she had left for him. A hope given to her by the most unlikely person. A woman wearing a man's clothes and a gun strapped to her hip. How... how had her life come to this? And why, why couldn't she do anything about it?

For the third or fourth or tenth time that day, Evie cried, though this time she wasn't aware of it. This time she slept, and in her dreams, dreamed of Peter...

And justice.

CHAPTER TWENTY

Mrs. Nadeau swept across her elegant, polished monstrosity of a receiving room, moving in them layers of silk and fabric like it was nothing, like breathing was not an effort at all. She also wore these little black gloves, so snug and perfect, but not the kind that actually did the job of keeping fingers warm.

Which wasn't a problem.

Not in this house with the heat goin' so high Cat was startin' to sweat in her coat. Not that she was about to take it off. The coat, like the rest of her—jeans, hat, gun, all of it—were a type of armor all its own. Hers.

Mrs. Nadeau graciously sank into the chair.

Right beside Cat's.

Every inch of Mrs. Nadeau now resembled a lady. Every inch of her, a predator. One who suddenly didn't seem to mind that this rough-coated cat was lounging around her sitting room...

Which made Cat very, very wary.

She was quite glad, quite glad indeed, that she'd left Mrs. Allen at home. Least this way one of them would be safe.

"What can I do for you, Miss Cowboy Cat? Or would you prefer I call you by your other name? Miss Justice?"

"Cat will do."

"Will it? You're... quite sure? Because last time, as I recall, your form of *justice* resulted in an increased scrutiny of my family, of our lawful business, by the town, by the law itself, even. As if we could ever find ourselves involved in something unseemly as... murder."

Cat slowly stretched out with her legs, crossing them at the ankle, acting as if she hadn't much care in the world. Or much worry, either.

Mrs. Nadeau noticed.

"From the start," Cat said, "I was upfront about my business and interest in the deceased woman, Norma. How you and your husband, and your upstanding family business, got involved in such a matter, that's on you."

Mrs. Nadeau's eyes narrowed, just this minor, slight crack along her perfect mirror.

"As you said," Cat went on, "a *family* business. But that's not why I'm here."

"Then I see absolutely no reason for your being here at all."

Mrs. Nadeau stood just then and reached for a little sliver bell. The thing, so tiny and small and hidden by an equally shiny, silver lamp. Even Cat, with her keen eyes, had missed its presence.

Mrs. Nadeau rang the bell and the little chime echoed and danced in the air. Almost pleasant sounding... which was the absolute furthest thing to the look Mrs. Nadeau was giving Cat.

"I allowed you entrance," Mrs. Nadeau said, "in hopes of an apology, but I see such an act is anathema to you, which my dear husband warned me would be so. Telling me that my good heart would be hurt if we were ever to meet. I am sad to say, he was right."

Uh-huh. Right.

Though Cat bet Mrs. Nadeau *did* get sad whenever she was wrong.

"Fair enough," Cat said. "I won't be taking up your time any longer, then."

She untangled her long legs and got to her feet, and then slightly... adjusted the revolver at her hip. Nothing threatening, mind you, but obvious nonetheless.

Mrs. Nadeau knew who she was, knew her power, and Cat had no issue, none at all, reminding her of Cat's power.

And just how damn far she'd go when it was justice that needed done.

Which, in itself, was a small reminder of why Cat had come here. Because as much as she'd love a verbal sparring, of pullin' out the claws, that was *not* the reason she'd come.

So Cat managed to get another calm breath into her.

Then another.

"While I didn't come here with an apology, I did come with something else."

Cat reached into her coat pocket, pulling out the folded newspaper. Just a bit, though, enough to show the curling ends of the paper, the ink that had gotten smudged by fingers before it had fully set. Just enough of a peek to spark... interest.

And opportunity.

Opportunity was the true gold for businessmen. And businesswomen.

"You see, Mrs. Nadeau," Cat said, "I came here for another matter, one that I thought your husband would be interested in hearing me out on. But I see how much my presence bothers you so. Thank you kindly for your time. I'll be on my way."

Cat tipped her hat to Mrs. Nadeau and started walking towards the door. Which, of course, opened right then with a loud, groaning sound, and revealed the surly eyed, grumpy butler who eyed Cat with such loathing, as if he knew darn well that the second Cat left he'd be ordered to get the whole place scrubbed down, from top to bottom. Behind him was a great clock, probably shipped over specially from Europe just for them, and beyond it, the door that led to the ashy world outside and her freedom.

All she had to do was take those handful of steps and all this would be behind her. All of it.

"Just a moment, Miss Cat," Mrs. Nadeau called out.

Cat paused and waited.

Said nothing.

The butler was still there, standing perfect and still as a statue, waiting for the command from the missus on how best to proceed next.

The seconds ticked on by, leading into a full minute. Cat waited, doin' her best to block out all the sores and aches her body was taking that quiet moment to remind her of.

Finally, Mrs. Nadeau cleared her throat. "What, exactly, is this *other* matter, Miss Cat? I am assuming, for your sake and your... livelihood while in Butte, that this is not another attack on my family."

Cat turned. "No, quite the opposite."

Though even as she said those words, she hated herself for doing so. Hated what she was here to do, or attempting to do—bartering with a woman as cold and unfeeling at Mrs. Nadeau. Oh man, were Cat's insides tingling. Her skin feeling like electricity was running rampant all over her, up and down, then back down right under the skin itself.

Deal with the devil, that was for damn sure.

And sure, Cat wanted to turn and walk away. Wanted anything else but to smile in a friendly sort of way at this woman, who pretty much ran rough over the graves and sorrows of so many others.

But then... there was Rose.

Rose, who appeared in Cat's mind just as she'd seen her earlier. Her pigtails bouncing up and down, the joy as she went and danced over that frozen mud in air so black one couldn't breathe without wanting to cough, or to cry.

And...

And there was Peter.

Lost, angry, frightened Peter. Old enough to understand and old enough to know he couldn't do a damn thing to stop what his father had done.

For their sake, Cat reached into her coat pocket and pulled out the newspaper article. She'd clipped it out earlier, takin' the relevant bits only; no need to go walking 'round with that big ol' thing tucked into her coat.

Cat held the folded article to Mrs. Nadeau.

She did not take it.

Very well. Cat laid it on the table, the one where the little sliver bell sat waiting, patient as could be, for another summoning. A summoning which that poor butler still stood at the door, silent and unmoving, awaiting orders that... just might not be coming. At least not yet, anyway.

At least if that glimmer of intrigue in Mrs. Nadeau's eyes was any indication, though she'd tried to hide it so. She failed, of course, because it was those kinds of details that Cat didn't miss.

Mrs. Nadeau reached for the article, her black gloved fingers dancing just mere inches above it. Still, she did not take it.

Cat waited.

"And what," Mrs. Nadeau asked, "is this?"

"A story."

"Yours?"

Cat huffed. "My name may be gettin' round in some circles, but I assure you, I'm not famous."

"I think you'd be surprised."

"I think that wouldn't be so good for me."

"No." Mrs. Nadeau smiled as she finally reached out and plucked the article from the table. "No, not at all. Which, of course, brings me some hope, you see, that perhaps my family will have some justice of its own for the damage you did to our good name."

Right.

As if they needed justice. As if they deserved it.

Shame on Cat, that Mrs. Nadeau's poor husband got caught helping another who *did* commit murder, and how Mr. Nadeau, himself, helped cover it up. All of which was exactly Mrs. Nadeau's very reasonable thinking.

In her mind, anyway.

But then, it really didn't matter what Cat thought because the laws and the courts, with all them big men sittin' on the hill, those gents cared about individuals like the Nadeaus and *not* the deplorables who grudgingly lived in the town. Taking up residence on Mercury Street and Galena and others. Galena, which also happened to be the very street that was pretty much owned and controlled by the Nadeaus.

Cat, however, said none of this.

For once, she stayed silent. For once, she kept her a tight grip on her anger, on all those memories stirrin' up just by standing in the same room as this woman, and all her ties to the sadness Cat had seen since coming to Butte.

For Peter.

For Rose.

And for the own ghosts that haunted Cat. Like... like Alice.

Mrs. Nadeau finally got to unfolding the darn thing, moving with such slowness Cat was sure she could have taken a nap and not missed anything.

Mrs. Nadeau's eyebrows rose. "I see the implications of this classified, and what it means for Mrs. Blonberg, but I fail to see what it has to do with me. Or my husband."

"What that the classified doesn't say is that they had two children."

Mrs. Nadeau folded it back up and placed it back down on the table. "A shame."

Not a single of hint of sympathy or of a heart.

"I understand you have children yourself," Cat said.

"Grown children."

"Now, yes, but they weren't always so. Can't imagine, really, or maybe I can and I'm simply too afraid to, what that'd be like. Working the life with the young ones depending on you."

"The great Cowboy Cat? Afraid? My, I might have to alert the newspapers myself."

"There are plenty of things I'm afraid. Can't say there's anything more than that." Cat walked across to the receiving room and retrieved the paper, tucking it back into her pocket. "I do thank you for your time, Mrs. Nadeau."

Cat nodded again, took two steps before Mrs. Nadeau asked:

"How old are they? Her children?"

"A boy of about eleven, twelve maybe. And a girl."

"And she is?"

"Four."

Mrs. Nadeau slowly, carefully, turned away from Cat. She made her way to the window that, while the curtains were mostly closed, didn't actually matter. It was so darn dark and smoky outside it looked like night. And even from here, with those windows sealed up good and tight, the smell of sulfur drifted in.

Hung there, right between her and Mrs. Nadeau.

"What," Mrs. Nadeau asked, "are you exactly asking for?"

"A good place to work. A fair one."

"It won't be enough, you know. Unless your Mrs. Blonberg is some great jewel, she'll never make enough to afford a place to ply her trade, and another to house her children."

"I imagine you're right. All I'm looking for is a fair deal."

Mrs. Nadeau turned back to Cat, a curling smile on her lips. Not kind, but not unkind either.

"There is nothing *fair* about that life, Miss Cat, as you well know."

Cat nodded.

"And the husband?" Mrs. Nadeau asked.

"As far as Mrs. Blonberg knows, he's gone. And she's not askin' me to find him, either."

At this, Mrs. Nadeau stood straighter. Not much, just a slight raising there of her shoulders. Shock. Surprise.

She hadn't expected this. But then again, Cat hadn't exactly expected it, either.

So Cat told Mrs. Nadeau about Evie's choice, to find her son, Peter.

And it was that, that piece right there, that finally convinced Mrs. Nadeau. Again Cat saw it. Saw that slight change in her eyes, that slight softening of cold to... well, cool.

"I will inform my husband," Mrs. Nadeau said. "Your Evie Blonberg will have a place to work. And a fair deal."

Cat waited because she knew darn well such a deal wasn't coming without its own strings. Certainly not with the animosity hanging between them. And it didn't take long, neither, to hear what Mrs. Nadeau wanted in return.

Cat's stomach sank and all her senses got to tingling. She let none of it show, though. Even when she knew, every instinct in her tellin' her to turn down the deal, Cat said nothing.

Instead, she felt Alice right at that moment, the ghost of her sister, warming through the scarf that Cat now wore. Hidden, tucked out of sight from the woman in front of her, silently reminding Cat of her promise.

It was enough.

Enough so that when Mrs. Nadeau held out her hand, gloved in that gleaming, smooth, black leather of hers, Cat reached shook it in turn.

Their deal was stuck.

CHAPTER TWENTY-ONE

Dusty was waiting right outside the Nadeau's home, waiting for Cat.

Cat stopped there, right in the the doorway, preventing the unhappy butler from slamming it shut, and gave Dusty a long, long look.

While her talk with Mrs. Nadeau had only lasted a few minutes, that grand ol' clock in the entryway hadn't gonged, not even once, and still it felt like hours. And Dusty, from the way he was glaring at her right then, clearly felt the same.

Cat sighed and wished she'd a few more moments to herself, to breathe in what air she could, though not a bit of it fresh, and let loose the crawling feeling she had all over her skin, her whole body.

Her hand.

She gently reached up and touched Alice's scarf. The knitting was safely tucked inside her jacket except for one bit of it, the part that even now was warming round her neck in a way that didn't feel entirely natural. She hoped, deep down hoped, that it'd been worth it. That fighting to keep this promise, one she knew was impossible yet here she was trying anyway, was worth it.

That maybe one day Alice would forgive her.

Her ma certainly never would, especially if she could see Cat now, standing on the porch of same grand mansion, one that wasn't hers, wearing a pair of dirty, ash-stained jeans and a faded scarf, which was the only splatter of color about her person and even that was faded almost beyond recognition.

Cat slowly lowered her hand.

It *was* freezing and after a moment, she got out her gloves and tugged those on, too. Slowly, of course. Her whole body was aching and she wanted nothing more than to curl up in bed and go to sleep.

But now was not the time for sleep.

There was still that promise she had to keep.

Cat got her gloves on, though truthfully it didn't do a damn when it came to the cold, right there, right where Mrs. Nadeau's fingers had curled around Cat's.

Sure the woman's hand had been gloved, all nice and bound in that tight leather, but still, Cat had felt it. Mrs. Nadeau had the kinda touch that a person remembered and felt long afterwards...

Like for a long, long time.

Just like Mr. Nadeau.

Still, even if Cat wasn't settled and wasn't back to her usual self, and even with her instincts were still tingling like crazy from that woman and her whole damn house, Cat knew something was wrong.

She took one look at Dusty, lookin' past the fury that she'd taken so damn long inside that damn house, and knew something was wrong.

Very wrong, indeed.

His tightly pinched mouth, his shoulders pointed right up towards that black, slowly darkening sky as twilight stretched into evening. Though that, in truth, wasn't exactly possible. It'd already hit dark as night sometime 'round noon that day. Still, it felt like it simply 'cause the temperature had gone and dropped a few degrees while she'd been inside the devil's mansion, shaking hands with the devil herself.

Or the devil's wife.

Take your pick on which was worse.

Or better.

Cat certainly had her suspicions, which Dusty seemed to as well, seein' as the look he gave her was downright incredulous. And furious.

Cat stood there, still in the entryway, preventing that butler from slamming the door right on her ass and stared at Dusty while he stared right back at her.

Neither said anything.

Finally, Cat took one step and the butler went and did what he'd been longing for since Cat had knocked on that big brass knocker. The mansion's big, heavy-ass door literally slammed shut behind her, and the whole block knew of the butler's displeasure.

But it was only then, when the latch clicked shut and the lock snapped into place, that Dusty turned all that fury loose on her, as if suddenly it was now safe enough to speak.

Though it probably wasn't.

Probably that butler immediately turned tail and ran to the nearest window, pulling back a curtain, creaking open some of the glass just so he could hear—

Yes, there was a curtain fluttering not two feet from them—

To report back.

Dusty, though, didn't seem to care 'bout this little detail.

Not. One. Bit.

"You *spoke* with Mrs. Nadeau. Mrs. Nadeau! What were you thinking? What were you doing? Sittin' down and having some tea and biscuits?"

Cat blinked at him.

You see, in their short time knowing each other, this was the first time Dusty had ever spoken to her this way, and she wasn't at all certain what to make of it. Or what could have possibly happened in the hour since she'd left Mrs. Allen's.

"*Is* there something wrong with you?" he asked. "That... that you'd come here, that you'd go and practically invite the whole police station to arrest you!"

He shook his head so hard his news cap looked like it was gonna come flapping off.

"Well..." Cat said slowly, still trying to make sense of all this. "I didn't have much of a choice, really, about speaking with Mrs. Nadeau. The mister wasn't exactly home."

"Of course, he's not home. As if he'd be anywhere near here when he got news that *you* were on your way over."

Which... made sense on why *Dusty* was here.

And sure, now that she thought of it, it made sense, too, that Mr. Nadeau knew. Probably the moment she'd hopped onto that hack and told the driver her destination, someone, clearly a runner, had heard. And that runner, doing what he'd been paid to do, set loose a kind of information wildfire which the shadow world, and Dusty, was known for.

And she'd missed it.

Hell, the man had probably paid some neighborhood kid to keep an eye on that front door and let him know the comings and goings of Cowboy Cat. Someone familiar, too, someone Cat would have seen and noticed during all those hours stuck sitting there at the window, but she'd been so damn focused on her own hurts and she'd missed it—

Again.

No.

Cat stopped herself right there, right in that thought's tracks. She wasn't gonna go down that road. If she started doubting, if she started blaming herself, then she'd be no good to Rose and Peter.

No good to the promise she'd given Evie Blonberg, and *that* was unacceptable.

What's done was done. She was here now and she was gonna do her best. She was trying to get back on her feet and there was no reason, none at all, for Dusty to be acting this way. Hell, he should very well have expected Cat to go and do something as foolish, or foolhardy, as having a nice chat with the Nadeaus.

But...

There was something right there in his eyes that he wasn't wanting her to see.

"I get that Mr. Nadeau's a might unhappy with me," Cat said. "Mrs. Nadeau was quite clear on that matter. But all this seems a bit much. Certainly in regards to me being arrested."

After all, the butler could have simply refused her entry.

Dusty looked like he wanted to spit leather right then.

"You *threatened* him," he said.

"Of course, I did. But that was last week. And it wasn't like I'd gone and threatened him all that much."

Only a little bit.

"And," she said, "everyone seems to forget that he had no issues threatening me."

Along with everyone else in Butte she'd been starting carin' for. Like Dusty.

Course, that had all happened that evening in Grace's Gardens while she and Mr. Nadeau had shared a little dance, back when Cat was whole and had the full capacity of her entire body—well, most of it. Least much as one could when one was bound by the bone ribbing of a corset. And again, it wasn't like she could have done much damage to him either, thanks in part to the corset and the little derringer, with its single shot—that also happened to be tied to her leg, so not readily available.

And Cat told him as much, right there on the big, fancy porch of the Nadeaus, right in earshot of the butler—just in case Mr. Nadeau had left out all those *fine* details.

Dusty moved from lookin' like spitting leather to fire. And Cat got the clear, clear sense of something else.

Something that felt an awful lot like fear.

For her.

"If you get arrested," Dusty said, "and you keep going on like this and you sure will, you ain't ever gonna see daylight again. Nadeau will make sure of it. Daly, too! God, Cat, why on earth would you think to come here? Alone?"

"Because, someone needed to."

Those were the same words he'd said to her back to Mrs. Allen's, back before had Cat learned about Evie and her two kids, one of them who was out there right now, missing in that darkness and cold, some place warm, Cat surely hoped, if not at home with his mother.

Which she knew, darn well, he wouldn't be.

Dusty was still shaking his head, but not like earlier...

And again, that sense from earlier when she'd first stepped outside the Nadeau's home and got a good look at Dusty came back.

Cat felt it, that tingling along her senses.

A prickling on the back of her neck.

"It's not me you're angry at, is it?" Cat asked.

She moved in closer, finally stepping off those big porch steps until she was just a foot from Dusty. Then came even closer.

And Dusty, for his part, ground his wearing-thin shoes right there into that nicely laid-out boardwalk.

No, she wasn't yet herself, wasn't that woman who'd stepped off the train and walked into Butte with an idea and a dream in her little head. But part of her, the survival part, it was still there and working hard and finally startin' to notice all the other details.

The little ones. That ones that her own past, her ma and Alice, had clouded over, hiding from her just like Dusty using his anger as a shield had done.

No more, though.

Dusty's frown, too tight and hard. His breathing, too uneven.

And... he wouldn't look at her, not in the eyes, anyway. He kept those piercing greens away from her direct gaze as if he knew darn well she'd immediately know what he was keeping hidden.

And something else, something deeper. She could feel it, dancing right on along the surface of her thoughts, something that had to do with his past—one he didn't want her to know about.

Cat took another step forward. They were inches from each other now.

"What's really goin' on here, Dusty?" she asked.

"Nothin'."

Again, he wouldn't look at her.

Or stand still.

The kid kept on bouncing on his feet like he had a couple jumping beans stuffed down his stockings. And it wasn't like he was trying to keep warm, either. No, that wasn't that kind of movement. Instead, it was like he was shifting... as if every moment that slid on by was a precious one indeed.

Worry.

No question about it. The kind of worry that ate away at a person's soul until there was nothing left but that big, black ball of ugliness, right there, smack dab in your center.

"Dusty."

Finally, he looked right up at her and glared, as if hating her right then, hating her for making him stop moving as if stop moving meant he finally had to *feel*—

"You're here," Cat said, "waitin' for me, getting colder by the second for a reason. You could have gone and done whatever it was you needed doing, but you waited. Now, I'm here but I can't help if you don't tell me."

He kept on glaring.

Now, now she was startin' to get a bit mad.

"You're ticked 'cause I went to talk with Mrs. Nadeau? You know darn well why I did it. Evie's gonna need some place to work and I wanted to see she'd get a fair shake. Now, no, don't go interrupting me. I already had this talk with Mrs. Allen. You want details, you get it from her. You know the streets well enough to know *why* the woman with a gun came instead of sweet ol' Mrs. Allen. Now—"

Cat crossed her arms and glared right back at him.

She hadn't mentioned the deal she'd made with Mrs. Nadeau. Didn't think now was the right time.

Or ever, really.

The deal, after all, was between her and Mrs. Nadeau. And God, probably, who was most likely laughin' his ass off about now. But regardless, Cat had made the promise. In exchange for helping Evie Blonberg, Mrs. Nadeau got herself a favor, one to be called in later, from Miss Justice, herself.

It was risky. It was a hell of a risk, in fact.

But all Cat had to do was think of Rose and Peter and... and Alice.

Cat shook her head. Focus. Focus on what was needing done right now.

"Are you gonna to tell me what you need or do I need to go stomping off on my own to figure it out?" Cat asked. "Cause I'm sore and I'm tired and I'd very much like to hit the sack sometime soon."

Several breaths passed, and neither said anything.

Several more, and this time Cat was feeling her throat itch and burn with the need to cough out this God-awful, foul air.

Still, Cat kept on waiting.

Finally, finally Dusty uncrossed his arms and let loose this big ol' breath he'd been holding in, as if the ash and soot didn't bother him in the least. Lucky kid.

"It's Peter," Dusty said. "I found him. Right before I heard about you, coming here to the Nadeaus. All on your own."

"You knew I could handle myself."

"Like last time?"

Cat didn't reply to that cause there was still that something more going on. "Why did you really come here? You didn't need me. You said so yourself. You found him. You could have gotten him yourself and brought him home."

Dusty looked right at her, and Cat saw a hell lot more than

shadows swirling in those green eyes of his. Something an awful lot like sorrow.

And regret.

Finally, Dusty shook his head. "That's the thing, Cat. I don't think I can."

CHAPTER TWENTY-TWO

Dusty led the way through the smoke and ash, not once making a wrong turn, and if he did, certainly didn't tell Cat about it.

They made their way, inching, it felt like, up that big ass hill of Butte. They were the only ones walking about, though they occasionally heard the clomp of hooves, the rolling of wheels over gravel, the high-pitched whistles in the distance of train cars and ore cars and whatever else kinda machinery always seemed to be running when it came to the mines.

Cat's calf muscles were burning something fierce and it just about felt like her thighs were on fire.

Not to mention the absolute ache in her shoulder, which now spread all the way down to her left hand, her fingers there a bit numb and tingling. Every bit of movement, it felt like, pulling on all the healing she'd been doing.

And probably undoing a whole bunch of it.

This certainly was not the light exercise that she and Mrs. Allen had agreed to earlier in the day, after their little standoff. And Cat was pretty darn certain if the doc were here, he'd have more than few words to say. She was also fairly certain they'd be the kind of words not appropriate for polite company.

Which, thankfully, she was not.

Still, Cat recognized that her body was hitting its limit, and while she wasn't about to speak aloud this, this limitation, she was gonna growl and complain about the walk they were doin'—straight up the damn hill, no less.

"We could very well hire a hack," Cat said. "Save us some time."

"You do that and Peter will hear us coming. He hears us, he's gone. Just gone."

"You sure about that?"

"Yes," Dusty said. "He hears us and we ain't ever gonna find him again, and you can't keep that promise you made."

The one to Peter's mother.

Cat slowed, though Dusty didn't.

He kept trudging through that black smoke and paused, but only a beat, when he realized she wasn't right on his heels like she had been.

"Is that what happened to you?" she asked. "You heard them coming? Family? Friends? Then took off again?"

Dusty glanced at her. It was only for a moment. Just long enough for her to see a heavy shadow 'cross those green eyes of his. Eyes that instead of looking piercing as they usually did, now looked clouded. Sad.

But then Dusty shuttered his gaze, and it was like the moment had never been, like she'd gone and imagined the whole thing.

Which she hadn't.

Cat remembered the details, the feelings shining out his eyes, staring right back at her, along with all those things he hadn't wanted her to see. Yet, she'd seen anyway.

Then Dusty disappeared.

Yep. He went and walked right into that black smoke just to make his point. He knew what she'd seen, and he was pretty darn ticked about it, too, that she'd pried like—and knowing damn well why she'd done it.

Also, Dusty clearly knew, for certain, that Cat would follow him. Which she did.

Still, what she'd seen, those glimpses, really, of Dusty's past were eating him alive. That even now, even after all these years, or maybe just because this circumstance with Peter and Rose was hittin' a little too close to home, they were bubbling up to the surface in a way that was gonna stay contained, no longer stayed buried under some giant mountain of cold rock.

All those little pieces, though, were sliding into place. Bit by bit. Making a picture that Cat could see and feel and start to understand.

Dusty had been Peter, in some way, shape, or form.

The details were for Dusty to know only, unless he decided to share, which Cat wasn't believing he was gonna do anytime soon. Which was fine.

Make no mistake, though, Dusty had been hurt. Same as Peter had been hurt. And both kids had run. In Dusty's case, he'd done the running from whoever it was that'd cared for him... and he must have kept going he got to the point where there was no more turning back. No turning around, no walking across that boundary, that line that separated the civilized world from the shadow one.

And Cat couldn't help but wonder how Dusty's sister, Norma, had fit into all this.

If he'd run because of her, because their family had learned the truth about her occupation and turned her out—which was what always had. Or possibly, it'd been another reason entirely, and it had been Norma who'd finally found Dusty. Norma who'd helped him and took him in as best she could. As best as Dusty would let her.

Both situations, Cat could believe. Certainly Dusty's stubbornness, which she knew firsthand when he set his mind to something.

A lot like her, really.

Probably another reason why they kept coming back to each

other. He askin' her for help (in his own way, of course) and her following.

And for her part, Cat knew she was on the right path. Her instinct was right there, that slight tingle along her skin, almost a hum of tension that she could feel slipping up and over the hairs there on the back of her neck.

The right path... this one, right here, with Peter. With Dusty.

Even if Dusty didn't want her on it.

But that's what family was for. Even this little makeshift one they'd cobbled together, her and Dusty and Mrs. Allen.

"You gonna keep up?" Dusty called after her from the shadows. "I thought you wanted to get home and rest."

"I do."

But what she really wanted more than anything was to not see those shadows in his eyes again. Or for a long, long time.

Cat hurried after Dusty, slipping in between those tendrils of smoke that made her eyes burn and her throat scratch and desperately want to cough. She hurried after him 'cause they were family and 'cause she knew darn well that hiding from the past never worked out well. Always, it had a way of coming back up again.

And always when you least wanted it to.

Like now... as Cat's own thoughts slipped back to Evie, her fierce love and acceptance for her children, compared to Cat's own mother who, as far as Cat could recall, had never once looked at her the way Evie had with Rose.

Or with Peter.

It didn't take her long to catch up to Dusty. Didn't take long, either, for her to get annoyed when, after she asked Dusty about Peter and what he knew, Dusty did his usual.

He kept silent.

Silent as a damn grave, in fact.

Now Cat may have agreed with this whole not-hiring-a-hack business, but she certainly wasn't gonna keep on going with every inch of her sore and on fire, eyes included, without a good explanation. Also, going into a situation with as much knowledge as possible was *how* she managed to survive all this time.

So she made this perfectly reasonable request to Dusty, and when said request was met with his continued silence, Cat stopped.

Yep.

Stopped right there, right in the middle of that frozen, crushed gravel street.

And sure, while the street was a bit quieter than usual, as if everyone, miners included, had hurried their little hides home to where it was warm and at least partially clear of smoke and ash, there were still some individuals about their business. And hacks, even with those lanterns strung up near the driver, were still notorious for clipping a bystander or two.

Or each other.

And there was Cat, standing right there in the middle of the street they'd been crossing, as she crossed her own arms and glared, refusing to budge an inch.

Dusty grabbed Cat's arm and tugged on her coat. "What the hell's wrong with you? Are you hopin' to get run right over?"

"I'm waiting for you. And your explanation."

Dusty swore, and it was pretty colorful, too.

"We need to move," he growled.

As if right on cue, there came the sound of a whip cracking through the air and the unmistakable crunch of crushed gravel and rock bits.

"Cat!" he hissed.

Cat stayed put.

"Fine, fine." Dusty tugged again. Harder this time. "Just, just move and I'll tell you what I know."

So Cat relented and they moved off that road, and in good timing too, 'cause a hack did fly right on by them, the wheels of the side carriage practically picking up off the air, and Cat thought she glimpsed the tall, skeleton frame of Fat Jack riding his horses hard— and that Jack lifted that tall black hat of his at her in greeting. Then both hack and horses were gone, and as promised, Dusty told her what he knew about Peter.

It was all thanks to the word he'd put out this morning right after meeting with Evie and giving her the paper. Peter had gone down into the tunnels just to "see what folks knew."

Cat gave him a look. "I thought you said your business there didn't have to do with the Blonbergs."

"It didn't. Like I told you before, I had other business. Also, I just happened to be near the people who could find out some information for me. So, I asked."

Despite Dusty's again half-truth, Cat *was* glad he'd taken the initiative. It'd given Dusty the insight he needed to find Peter to begin with because, as Mrs. Allen had guessed rightly, there hadn't been a whole lot known about Peter. Peter and his sister and his mother, they all kept to themselves. Nothing fancy known about them, no big embarrassments and whatnot, until today, that was. There *had* been some stories about the father, Lou, but Dusty hadn't asked about those.

He'd wanted to know about Peter.

That got Cat's attention.

"How did you know?" she asked. "About Peter? That Peter was the one to even ask about in the first place?"

And, far as Cat knew, not Evie had known what she was gonna do about him until she'd spoken with Cat and asked her to bring Peter home.

Dusty shrugged. "I just knew, okay."

The movement and his words alone, answering a half dozen questions and giving her another full dozen questions in return. But Cat didn't press.

Right now, this was about Peter and finding him.

Dusty, through his shadow network, found out where Peter and his local gang liked to spend their days when not in school and when not doing forced chores around the home.

"Gangs?"

He nodded. "Every kid's in one, though not in the way you're thinkin'. Gangs go by neighborhoods mostly, 'specially those coming together from their home countries. You know how it is. Kids from the Gulch not liking the kids from Finntown. Kids from Centerville *really* not liking the kids from Walkerville. That there's when the big trouble starts, and they go and meet together over at the Moonlight dump for rock fights or fist fights."

Cat was fascinated.

There was so much more to Butte than she understood, and the children's world was one of them. Well, for that matter, probably most of the adults didn't know how that world worked, and kids being kids, did their best to keep the adults with their big noses out of their business.

Could be another reason why Dusty was being so damn cagey about this business with Peter.

In some ways, it sounded like a similar world to when she'd grown up as a child, but that, though, had been a small town and with mostly one race of people. Maybe two. Though she imagined she would have loved it, would have jumped right into the middle of that fray despite being a girl, because that was what she'd always done.

Her, of course, and not Alice. A point that her ma was always quick to point out and swear at.

"What about Peter's gang?" Cat asked.

"He's from the East Side, and just about everyone there are outsiders. Sure, there are groups and they stick together, as they always do, but... it's different over there."

Interesting. So, not the Cornish or Irish or whoever against the Blonbergs, but a big ol' mixing pot thrown in together. Damn. There really was a hell of a lot about Butte she didn't know.

Thank goodness she had the one guide that probably knew every nook and cranny of this place—and how to get out.

"You'd think," Cat said, "with everyone being on the outside as they are that they'd have treated Peter a bit kinder when news of his mother got out."

Dusty shook his head. "You know the difference. There are some lines that loyalty doesn't cross. Even if they're your best friend."

The way Dusty said that last, Cat knew without a doubt, he'd just given her another piece of his story.

But... she also had the feeling that this time he didn't mind. As if, as if he'd wanted her to hear. Maybe, too, that he was tired of bearing the burden all by his own anymore.

And she wondered, too, if Norma had known the depths of Dusty's own sufferings, his own walk into this shadow world. If she had, would she have still made the choices she had? The very choices that put her in the crosshairs of the likes of Daly and Nadeau and Mr. Rippi, the man who eventually did pull that trigger?

Cat's instincts told her no.

That Norma, Dusty's sister, hadn't known at all. And he'd purposefully kept it from her.

Cat didn't ask why.

Instead, she just stayed by Dusty's side, following him through darkness until they came to a place which Dusty had called "the side hill."

He whispered now, keeping his voice so low that not even the chill, tickling breeze, could carry it. "This is where Peter and his friends go. There ain't no one here, now. All of them went home."

"Except Peter."

Cat also followed Dusty's lead and kept her voice pitched low.

Dusty nodded.

"And you saw him?" she asked. "Any idea where he is now?"

Dusty pointed. Cat could just make out the large, pillar-like shapes of the bridge, wooden posts that seemed to be sagging under the heavy weight from above... and maybe... the huddled form of a young boy right at its base.

Christ.

Peter was out here. Alone. Probably freezing his ass off and hungry for sure.

And as much as Cat wanted to rush on over, do exactly what she'd promised to Evie and bring her son home, Cat stayed put.

Instead, she turned and looked at Dusty. "Now. No more dodges. No more misleading. Are you gonna tell me why you didn't go and get him, seein' as how you knew exactly where he was?"

"Like I told you, he's not gonna listen—"

"So then, *why?*"

Dusty adjusted his news cap. Then fiddled it some more as if he couldn't stand having his hands free and his mind free of distraction. Or more than likely, all those feelings she saw shining out through him. It was in his actions, how he kept shifting from one foot to the other, how he wouldn't look at her. All of it, clear as night, each of them feelings bubblin' up, right there at the surface, demanding to be let free.

"Dusty."

He dropped his hands. Didn't look at her.

So Cat waited.

One minute, then another.

"You're both the same," she said. "You both have similar stories. Why on earth would Peter listen to me and not you?"

Finally, finally, Dusty raised those eyes of his and looked right at her—

And Cat saw nothing but clouded shadows gazing back at her.

Nothing at all like the Dusty she'd first met on that train station. Nothing like the Dusty who, just that afternoon, stood right in the center of Mrs. Allen's entryway and demanded that Cat try and be the person he knew she was.

That kid wasn't there no more.

Now there was nothin' but a scared, scared boy. A boy who, somewhere along the way, had gotten his heart broken.

By family, no less.

"That's thing the thing, Cat," Dusty said. "I was that kid. I was Peter. And it was another kid, another boy, who came and talked to me."

For a moment, she thought she glimpsed the faintest shimmer of tears in those shining green eyes of his.

He blinked and they were gone, but he didn't look away. Not this time.

"I'm telling you now," Dusty said, "I ain't talking to Peter. Not now. Not ever. *You* go do what someone should'a done for me. You go talk to him and bring him home."

CHAPTER TWENTY-THREE

Peter was so cold, so hungry.

He sat there under the bridge of the side hill, huddled as best he could in his fraying coat with the pocket there that had another hole in it, doin' just about everything he could to keep warm. And keep from turnin' into Susan Hoy, who, if she were here, would be cryin' her eyes out nonstop.

Not like Peter.

Peter, who wasn't a sissy, who wasn't gonna cry even though his stomach grumbled and growled so hard it was foldin' up on over itself. Not gonna cry either about his hands and feet, both which he couldn't feel much of anymore, except this tingling bit of numbness. Which he knew wasn't good, but he couldn't find the will to move, either, and besides where would he go?

Not home.

Never home.

The cold, though, it sure as hell didn't care what Peter decided. Stay or go. Cold was cold. It just kept on seepin' up from that hard, frozen ground, and his pants, they were just too thin, too worn, to fight against it.

Peter pulled his knees in tight against his chest and wrapped his arms around them, too. And when that didn't do nothin' to keep himself warm, he went and he tucked his hands tight underneath his armpits.

Which didn't do a damn thing, either.

The cold won. The cold won always won. As if its whole purpose was to chip away at his resolve, get him to start crying and realizing the only place he could go was home, but that was the one place that Peter wasn't ever gonna go again—

And damn it!

He wiped, hard and angry, at his cheeks as if that could stop the tears from coming. As if anyone was here to see or to care, which no one was and nobody did.

The whole town had made that well known. His teacher. His classmates. Bugsy.

All those images, the way they'd looked at him, all those words they'd said, swirlin' up and around his mind, never leaving him, hanging on, pulling what was left of him away, bit by bit, and as it did, it just went and opened up the floodgates of his eyes as if crying was gonna change anything about him being hungry or it being so cloudy he could see, even in the blackness, his breath puffing out white.

Just like he could see his mother as she'd stood there today outside his school, and Peter wished like hell if there was one thing he could forget, it that moment.

The look in her eyes, the look that wouldn't leave him no matter how hard he screwed his eyes shut tight, no matter how he'd yelled or kicked all these damn rocks. Rocks that would just ping against the bridge, dull and sad like, or against all them metal bits and flattened tin he and Bugsy and the others had carried over during the summer months, building their fort and hiding spots.

Each of one of those rock pings became a sudden a reminder of what he didn't have no more. And couldn't ever again.

Just like his mother and her eyes, the image of her that just wouldn't, *wouldn't* leave.

A constant, constant reminder.

The sorrow and shame and, and *hurt* as she'd looked at him—

Hurt that he'd caused.

He, as he yelled at her.

He, as he ran away.

Peter shivered so hard his teeth clattered, so he buried his head into the crook of his arms, hoping it'd help against the cold, hoping it somehow stop the memory, stop her from looking at him in just that way, as if she'd gone and let him down, rather than he letting *her* down.

No.

Peter slammed that thought down so hard, so fast.

It was her fault.

Hers.

The whole town knew it. His pa had said so. Didn't matter if his pa wasn't exactly good at being a father, didn't matter that he'd not worked in months or least kept a job more than a day or two. All that mattered was the words everyone was sayin' about his mother...

Wasn't it?

For that one, brief moment, Peter wasn't sure. All he wanted was to see that hurt in her eyes fade away and look at him how she'd always done. Love. Adoration. Pride.

But then the moment crumbled as suddenly as it came on.

Peter heard a faint rolling of rocks. Pebbles, more like, as if a handful had come loose from somewhere and then tumbled a few paces down the hill.

Or... as if someone had kicked them while walking...

Walking towards Peter.

Peter sprang to his feet. Or tried to. His muscles, they were sore and stiff, so instead of being light on his feet like he usually was he stumbled. Reached out and grabbed a wooden slab of the bridge before he went down hard again. Felt bits of wood, splinters like, the real pointy kind, poke right through Peter's worn gloves.

He didn't care.

Instead he stood there, gripping that slab, bending his knees, prepared to run. To quickly dart away and just keep on running into that darkness.

Peter squinted and tried to see past all that damn smoke and blackness to see who was coming. His heart hammered in his chest.

Bugsy? One of the other kids? Had they gone and changed their mind about him?

No.

Peter doubted it. He'd seen the way their mothers had looked at him, at the way they'd looked at *his* mother. So no, his friends wouldn't be coming, which meant too they wouldn't have sent any of the fathers or older brothers to fetch him. They straight up just wouldn't have cared no more, not like last week or hell, like yesterday. And they certainly wouldn't have sent that git Reverend Jacobs to come save his soul or something. Even if they'd asked, Jacobs wouldn't have come. Peter knew it, knew it for a fact. Saw it in the man's eyes every time he'd gone and looked Peter's way after services. All those times he'd watched his mother going to him, asking for advice and help, guidance on what to do with... with his pa and his drinkin'... how it was all gettin' worse—

Peter slammed shut on those thoughts.

It was dark now. Real dark. The kind of dark that made Peter grip that wooden slab even harder, despite the splinter slipping past those cloth gloves he wore.

Usually coming up here at night, 'specially during the summer months when he and his buddies would look down at the hill of Butte, the whole city seemed to be lit with this dull, constant glow. Like lanterns or fireflies that moved and danced while the rest of the world, the rolling countryside and scattering of trees beyond, lay dark and still.

Not now, though.

Now, Peter couldn't see one sparkle of light. Not even the few electricity ones strung up 'bout the place, though only half worked some of the time, and the other half just hung there dark and cold.

There was another step as gravel and rock crunched under boots, and it sounded... sounded almost purposeful.

Peter crouched low, ready to run—

And then, slowly, coming up out of the smoke and darkness, was a person.

Peter squinted his eyes so darn tight and close that he felt more burn from the ash than from the tears.

Another few steps and the person came closer. A tall form, too, thin like, so nothing at all like his pa—though why that thought even came to Peter, he didn't know. Why in that very moment, holding tight onto that wood slab, the cold bitin' through his whole body while ash and sulfur burned his eyes, why he thought his pa, of all people, would be hikin' up this hill in the middle of a black winter, searchin' for the son he cared nothin' and no matter for, Peter had no idea.

None.

Yet the thought had been there, and he found himself breathing a tad bit easier.

It wasn't his pa.

Breathing that got even easier when he saw the person was not wearing the big skirts his mother and all those others likened to wear, especially now that it was so cold. Them and their equally big coats and those bonnets pulled tight against their throats, it was a wonder they could breathe—no wonder all them mothers had a shortened temper during the cold months.

But this stranger, though, definitely not his mother.

Relief slipped through Peter.

Sure, he didn't know the stranger, but the stranger already wasn't the two people he absolutely *didn't* want to see. Ever again, too, if he could help it.

It wasn't the reverend, either, so Peter stepped away from his spot by the bridge and let go of that piece of safety and security he'd found. Although, he wasn't prepared for that at first, all cold and bunched up were his muscles, so he winced, taking in a big ol' sharp breath, and then coughing when he got a throatful of ash and burnin' chemicals and the like.

The stranger stopped.

"You all right?"

Peter... blinked. Cause... he was pretty darn sure that, while the rest of him was goin' numb with cold, his hearing was just fine. And being fairly certain that his hearing was just fine, it had sounded a whole lot like a woman right then.

Which was just crazy.

And sure, it was pretty dark out and neither Peter nor the stranger had a light, but he was also quite certain that the stranger there was *not* wearing a dress like his mother. But pants and boots. A cowboy hat, too, and right there, falling across the shoulder...

Looked an awful lot like blond hair. Long and braided.

Peter blinked again.

But the image stayed right exactly the same.

He shook his head just in case the cold was gettin' to him faster than he'd first thought.

But no... the braided hair was still there, just like the way the stranger was standing there with her hip cocked a bit to the side. Completely comfortable, completely at ease. And the kind of stance he'd never in his life seen on a man.

Though to be fair, never in his life had he seen a gun strapped to a woman before, either.

Until now.

Cause now, now there was just no mistake. That there was a woman standing there in jeans and cowboy boots and some kind of revolver hanging from a worn holster at her hips.

Standing there, too, like she knew how to use it.

Well... at least she wasn't his mother.

Even if... even if by her clothes, by her being out here all by herself, told Peter right clear who this woman was. Or what she had been.

A fallen lady.

Like his mother. Even if... even if she hadn't been, hadn't been before his pa had gone and put up that classified.

Peter's throat tightened something fierce, to the point where he wasn't sure he could swallow let alone breathe.

Somehow he managed.

"I help you?" Peter asked.

The woman came forward a bit closer, though she stopped before Peter started feeling uncomfortable, as if she knew he wanted distance. Not only that, seemed to know exactly how far that distance needed to be.

Peter, though, didn't relax.

Even if his teeth did get to chattering again. Which they did. And if even his stomach got to growling again. Which it did.

The woman's gaze lowered, lookin' right at his stomach as if she could good and hear the growling from there.

She said nothing about it, though, and he was grateful.

"My name's Cat," she said. "Cowboy Cat."

"Yeah? And what do you want?"

There was something else about her, though, that nagged at the back of Peter's mind. Just there, just out of reach.

Except he was too cold and too hungry and just couldn't hold onto that little thread, and just wanted her to be gone so he could get to huddling again and staying warm and figure out what the heck he was gonna do next.

"Well," she tucked her hands into her coat pockets. "I heard about your family this morning. A friend came by and showed me the papers. He's good at that, you know, bringing me news about folks who might need some help."

Peter instantly backed a step. "Who said I'm needin' help? 'Cause I'm not."

The woman raised her eyebrows and they nearly straight up disappeared under the brim of her cowboy hat.

"You tellin' me," she said, "that you *want* to go and spend the night out here? Hungry? Cold as all hell?"

"Maybe."

She shrugged. "Far be it from me to offer you a warm bed—"

"I ain't goin' into some house of ill fame!"

"I wasn't offering, and no, that's not where I'm staying either. Or working. Haven't for some time. What I *am* offering is a place to sleep, a place I can guarantee you will at least wake up to see the next day. Some hot food, too, and an even hotter slice of apple pie. Or two, if you want. If you're not interested..." Cat shrugged. "It's no matter to me, and I'll be on my way, then."

There it was again...

It was something in her words or her manner, something that just tugged at Peter in just that right way.

Maybe it was that thought of apple pie, something his mother hadn't made in an age, it felt like, apples and such fruit havin' become a rarity ever since his pa had lost his job. But his mother had always made it every fall, and put in more than the usual sprinkling of cinnamon, to the point where the whole house would smell with that perfect blend of sweet and spice.

And for a moment, Peter felt another wave of tears, a stirring there of hurt... and hope.

He wiped at his eyes, but the woman, this Cowboy Cat, had turned her back and didn't see.

Or maybe, maybe Peter just felt comfortable because she'd turned away from him, spinning on her boots like she really was just gonna wander back into that darkness and disappear. Just like that. Just like the way she'd come. All the while, never once tellin' Peter what to do.

And that, that right there, was why he called out again. Why he asked her to stop.

She did. And then offered Peter a place to stay for the night. No strings attached, she promised. Just a place to stay and fill up his belly, and maybe, if he was willin', to listen to a story or two.

It seemed reasonable, and Peter didn't sense anything threatenin' about her or her offer. He was good like that with people, could tell easily when someone was hiding the truth or just flat lying to him. It was a skill he'd needed to learn to survive those days and nights when his pa saw the world with that black despair livin' out of his heart. But from this woman, this Cowboy Cat, sure he sensed a bit more than just the words she spoke—hell, he wasn't a fool, she had to have some other motive goin' on—but it was an honest one. He could tell. Nothin' at all like the kind that set his senses warnin' him off, telling him to run and not look back.

So Peter, being cold and hungry as he was and not knowing anywhere else to go for the night or what to do, or being much able to think straight beyond the thought of promised pie and the kindness she showed him—

Peter said yes.

CHAPTER TWENTY-FOUR

Dealing with the youth of the world wasn't exactly in Cat's wheelhouse. She didn't have no kids of her own and didn't converse a whole lot with them, but she'd always enjoyed watching them from afar, studying them and how they lived life with their whole being until life stepped in and snatched it all away, forcin' those kids to grow up and live in the harsh realities 'round them. But it was that part there that Cat understood, and part of her wanted to protect them from.

At least, for as long as possible.

Peter and Rose, though, they were well beyond that point. Their pa had thrust them hard into that reality, one which no kid should ever have to live with, and it was that part there that Cat understood. And how, even without Dusty's help, she'd known just what to say, what to do, and when to stop pushin' and walk away.

All she had to think was herself, and if she'd been a hands-span years younger when Stan had come bustin' in that door, with red and murder in his eyes, and if Cat had pulled that trigger being years, years younger—

Her sincerity and her honesty had been enough.

Dear Lord, she hoped it'd be enough, anyway. Didn't know if she could have gone and forgiven herself, ever, if Peter had turned and ran, exactly as Dusty had warned would happen if Cat *didn't* reach through to him.

And still, with Peter walking slow and unsteady by her side, she didn't breath easy. And wouldn't, she knew, until Peter was safely back with his mother and being on the same understanding with the world they now faced.

Cat said not one word about Peter's mother or the promise she'd made to Evie. There'd be time enough for that, and for the rage and indignant disbelief and fury that would follow; Cat had been his age once, she knew darn well what would follow.

What mattered more, though, than her promise to Evie was the promise she was making to Peter. Not aloud, but in her heart. Her promise to him...

And to herself.

She came here hopin' to help those who couldn't get it for themselves, and right now there was no one more deserving than Peter. Peter and probably the dozens of kids like him out here, alone and cold on this black winter night, who Dusty hadn't brought to Cat's attention. Who were alone and would stay that way because this world didn't care for the folks who no longer belonged on their civilized side of the line.

Cat couldn't do anything for those kids, and the thought stirred in her chest like her own black sorrow, and it wouldn't leave, neither. But for Peter, at least, she could give him a warm place to sleep and a great deal of warm, heavy food in his belly.

They'd start with that.

And they did.

Dusty, not to Cat's surprise, was nowhere to be found when she came walking down from the side hill with Peter.

Peter, unsurprisingly, didn't ask who she was or why she was interested in helping him out. He'd accepted her words at face value, or at least enough of it. He'd question her later, no doubt about it, when he got the feeling back in his fingers and toes. And truthfully, she'd have been surprised if he *had* questioned her right now.

The kid looked just about dead on his feet and half frozen over.

Yet even still, there'd been a defiance lightin' in his eyes that told Cat true: if she'd have showed up with Dusty or rode up in a hack, Peter *would* have disappeared into that darkness.

And probably wouldn't have survived the night.

That right there was something Cat wouldn't live with. And Peter was a ghost she didn't want nowhere near her. Or the ghost of any child, for that matter.

They made their way from the side hill, smoke and ash seeming to cling to their bodies, filling their lungs to the point where both of 'em were coughing pretty good. At least the shaking was keeping their bodies somewhat warm. And even though Dusty was gone, he'd sent a hack for them.

Peter, who was practically leaning on Cat by the time they reached the sad excuse for a street, tensed when he heard the horses comin', those wheels there spinnin' hard over that crushed gravel road.

Cat reached out and touched his shoulder.

Gently but firm.

But not too firm where he couldn't pull away if he wanted to, which he did. Cat let her arm fall, though she let her body language speak for her: she was there to comfort and help, nothing more.

Apparently it was enough, for Peter stayed beside her, though tense as a board, as if his whole being was prepared, was ready. For anything. For spottin' the wrong person or hearin' the wrong word and he'd be gone. Gone. Right back into that darkness and damn the consequences.

It was hard for Cat, too, just standing there so, not reaching out, not offering comfort or encouragement. Instead, just lettin' him be... and lettin' him make his own choices.

And hoped like hell that'd be enough.

The hack pulled even with them, spraying bits of gravel and rock and frozen brown smudges that wasn't gonna do anyone any good to look at too closely. The driver swept off his tall black hat, revealing his pointy goatee which had been trimmed nice and neat on his equally pointed, skeleton-like face. And with a heavy amount of sparkle in his eyes, the driver swept her such a bow right then and before the horses had even stopped movin', like she were royalty or some other such nonsense.

Cat couldn't help herself.

She grinned.

"Fat Jack," she said. "Fancy seein' you all the way up here."

"You know me." He set his hat back down right there on his head. "Always go where the best tales are to be had. And I heard word you was up this way."

That was Fat Jack for you, and though Cat had only known the man a short time, she'd liked him instantly—and he, her. Though in his case drivin' around a woman such as herself, sportin' jeans and cowboy boots and gun no less, gave Jack the kinda stories that made him legendary round the barbershop. And, she was guessin', amongst those he gave rides to as well.

The more merry and colorful the tale, the more coin.

Though to be fair, besides that joy of livin' a life that was his and only his, Jack *had* been there for her as well. Just like Mrs. Allen and Dusty and Blake. Fat Jack had pulled Cat out of that tunnel, injured shoulder and all, after her dust-up in the Gardens. Dusty had somehow kept her upright and Jack did the pulling, all the while Cat had apparently been doin' her darnedest to pass out. Still, Jack had gotten Cat home and without asking for a word of thanks or payment except for a promise in the future of more tales and adventures.

Cat, for her part, hadn't forgotten it. Nor would she.

Still, she just hoped Jack wasn't gonna call in that favor now. Not in front of Peter.

Peter who, even as tired and cold and hungry as he was, could very well start putting together the real tale of Cowboy Cat and wonderin' why she'd come all the way up here to collect him.

Definitely too much risk.

Cat looked right at Jack, hopin' he'd see the truth in her eyes. If he did, though, he sure didn't show it. But then, that was also Jack for you. The man saw everything, missed nothing, and gave a whole lot of nothing away.

Unless, of course, you were Cat.

She saw that little sparkle in his eyes, almost turnin' into a twinkle as his gaze swept towards Peter. The wrinkles round the outside tightening just a bit, as if he was remembering ever given a ride to Peter or his family, or maybe even passing 'em by in the street. Then the faintest raisin' of his thin, black eyebrows as recognition clearly dawn on him of just who Peter was—

And Peter, for his part, just stared at Jack with open-mouthed amazement.

Jack, she knew, was a bit of a legend himself, giving rides to the big businessman and copper kings and even William Jennings Bryan, which Jack had claimed was the proudest moment of his life—so far, anyway. Cat sure hoped Peter's amazement would hold off any lingering or new doubts about getting in this hack with her.

"I thought I saw you driving earlier," Cat said to Jack. "Goin' a bit hard round that corner back there. Maybe even lifted a wheel or two?"

"What's the use of drivin' if you ain't takin' a few sharp turns? And... a bit of excitement along the way? As you well know, my great lady of many names and many callings. Must say, I sure missed seein' you around town this past week."

"Jack."

There wasn't anything nice or kind the way Cat said his name. It was a warning, plain and simple.

But Jack, being Jack, just grinned back at her with a full mouth of teeth of yellow and one sparkle of gold. The man knowing full well what he was gettin' a bit close to.

Cat knew, without a doubt, that Dusty would have warned Jack to keep his trap shut. Didn't matter that Jack was already waving her off, like he knew darn well what she was thinkin' and that she shouldn't worry her silly little head off. Fact was until Cat had Peter safely tucked into Mrs. Allen's home, this twinge of worry in her stomach there, circling round and round as it was, wasn't goin' away. Not any time soon.

"Jack," she said again. "You headin' down the hill or do I need to call for another driver?"

"I am, I am. Fact is, soon as I got word that you was needin' a ride, both for you and your charge, I came right on over."

He said the words simple enough, though there was nothing simple about all the bits he *wasn't* saying.

There was never anythin' simple when it came to Fat Jack.

"He's my charge, but just for this evening though."

Cat opened the door, whose hinges creaked like they needed a good bit of oiling, and waved Peter inside.

Peter, though, didn't move.

He hesitated, as if unsure. He held his gaze on that door there as if it was makin' everything all the more real—

And all the more uncertain.

Which wasn't good thing.

The temperature had continued to drop as the evening had worn on, and the chill bit right on through her coat and gloves to the point where it felt like she wasn't wearing much at all. And her shoulder, it was hurting something mighty fierce, and all she wanted was to climb inside, rest her eyes, and take a long, long nap.

'Cept, she couldn't.

And if she was cold, she knew Peter really was just about freezing over, yet still the kid stood there, unsure and hesitating. A smart kid, for sure, even if runnin' away from home wasn't the smartest move to begin with. But hurt and anger, they weren't the kind of emotions easily forgiven, and Cat could easily understand why he'd done what he'd done. And why he was still doin' what he was doin'.

Now, though, Cat had a choice of her own.

She could either stand there and wait, holding that door open, or take control of what she could out'a the situation and get inside. The longer she stood there waiting, the more Peter would start to wonder and question. Truth was, neither Cat nor anyone else but the kid's mother should be standing there so, fetching him out of this blackness and bringing him home like this. Anyone other than Evie *would* feel wrong to him. Off.

As it should.

And well, Cat just couldn't give Peter much a chance to think down those lines or she'd really risk losin' him.

Cat decided to risk it.

She got herself inside, doing her best to move slow and even, to not jostle the healing parts and other areas just plain sore, which felt like pretty much everywhere at this point. And you'd better believe Jack was watching her closely for any sign of that hurting, those pointed, piercin' eyes of his—and she was darn sure he didn't miss her sharp intake of breath when she finally settled on that bottom-hard seat.

All the while, Cat kept her attention away from Peter. She wanted him to believe fully that this was *his* choice. His and his alone. No coercion or deception... though there was a minor bit of omission, one she was hopin' he'd be willing to at least look over on the morrow.

Still, it was his choice to come or stay behind.

Cat didn't dare risk one sign or even one hint of worry that Peter might decide he was better off risking the cold and disappearing into the black smoke. She kept her face, smooth and even, not showing the real truth—

Which was that her skin was tingling and her insides were doin' a hearty dance all their own.

Peter continued to stand there, his whole body shivering, his teeth chattering. But his eyes, though, they were shinin' brighter than when she'd first seen him.

He really was a smart kid.

Cat crossed her legs, speaking to Fat Jack, all the while gesturin' at Peter—and using her good arm, of course. "I promised Peter here a safe place to sleep for the night and a belly full of food. In whichever order he chooses, of course."

"Ahh." Jack sat down heavy on his seat, lettin' his coat billow out like he was a great performer—which, he was.

He, like Cat, wasn't paying Peter much mind at all. His attention was fully on Cat even as he pulled out a cigar from his coat and got to lightin' it. He puffed a few times, lettin' the smoke swirl white around them before it, too, got snatched up good by the darkness and the rest of the black smoke that was Butte.

"Let me see now," Jack puffed. "Apple pie, am I right?"

She nodded. "You readin' my mind?"

"Not much of a need, Miss Cat. Which means you'll be headin' off to Mrs. Allen's, then. Best boarding house in all of Butte, and best darn apple pie that was ever made. Wish I could stop in for a spell myself. Always leave feeling a good two sizes bigger."

"She certainly has a way 'bout her."

"Well, best get on with it. Got more stops to make and more poor folk to see themselves home on a cold dark night such as this. 'Side, I don't want your charge here fallin' over from hunger."

That's when Jack turned to Peter, tilting that tall black of his so high it looked like it'd topple right on off. Still puffing away on his cigar, with those knowing eyes of his takin' in each and every detail about Peter, same as Cat.

"What say you, Peter?" Jack asked. "You headin' back down the hill with Miss Cat, or are you gonna stay up here with all them ghosts?"

Peter hesitated.

Still unsure and uncertain, as if realizing just how little he knew about the people he'd be riding with and fear slowly takin' hold and overcoming the hunger and the cold, provin' he was a lot brighter than any of them had really given him credit for. Made Cat wonder, too, if Peter knew just how bright *he* was, or if he'd spent all his time hiding it from his angry father, doin' his best to disguise just how sharp, though hurt, a mind he had.

Cat didn't hold her breath like most folks would do.

Instead, she kept breathing.

In, then out again.

And as she did, time seemed to slow... to lengthen, until it nearly stopped altogether. And all them details, all those little movements and shifts, those muscles tightening just a bit and those blinking of eyes. Jack's horses, which lifted up their big hooves and slowly crunched back down on that half-frozen road.

Cat watched it all. Watched everything and missed nothing...

And waited for Peter's decision.

CHAPTER TWENTY-FIVE

Time didn't pick back up again for several heartbeats as Cat waited for Peter. Just that slow intake of breath and slow exhale. The horses hooving at the ground in great slow-like movements. Sound that seemed to extend and pull 'bout them, like they were inside a bubble of their own world and nothing, not even those whistles from those big ass ore train cars pierced through it.

At least, until Peter finally, slowly nodded himself—

And time slipped back into place.

"Just until morning," Peter murmured, to which Cat nodded.

Peter climbed into the hack, slamming the door shut behind him. The carriage shifted a bit as his weight moved about before settling in. He sat across from her, wrapping his thin coat as close about him as he could. Which from the shivers and chattering of teeth told her wasn't doin' a whole bunch at all.

And yet... Cat saw the truth for exactly what it was.

Yes, Peter was sittin' there, but he didn't trust her. And the look he was givin' her told her just that. It was the kind of look that said he was no fool and he wasn't trusting her, not in the least. He was gettin' in like this cause he didn't have no better options—and he owed nothing to her, nothing in the least.

All of this said without a single word being spoken.

And Cat, too, gave her own promise back without a word.

She nodded to him.

Jack got the hack goin' again, rolling right along, but not at the breakneck speed she was used to from him. Because nothing Jack did was ever an accident. Even the slow roll of wheels had a purpose, and she'd no doubt part of the reason was so he wouldn't miss a word here that was spoken.

Peter, though, he was looking hard at the door handle, as if seriously reconsidering the soundness of decision and the merits of holding out for this supposed apple pie or striking out on his own again.

Like it or not, she had to give him some answers, had to help ease those worries—much as she could without revealing too much. The kinda of stuff that *would* have him jumping for those doors.

"In the morning," Cat said, "you can decide where else you'd like to go or what you'd like to do. In the morning, if you like, we can talk."

"Why are you doing this?"

It was a question she was asked every time and by all kinds of people, too. As if the act itself, her goin' out of her way to help others, to care 'bout the ones no one else cared about, was so unbelievable that everyone immediately distrusted her on sight.

And as much as it hurt to say so, she understood it.

She really did.

"Cause I need to," Cat said simply.

Peter, to no surprise, didn't look convinced.

They never did.

Cat sighed and adjusted her bottom on that seat, shifting her gun a bit so it wasn't pressing hard into her thigh no more. A movement that Peter's eyes narrowed so straight and focused on, like he was suddenly rethinking about himself being in this hack here with her and her gun.

Yes, she was gettin' mighty tired of it all. And it certainly wasn't helpin' matters that *she* herself was pretty darn tired right then.

And sore.

And hurtin'. Hurting a lot, actually, and from more than just the physical injuries.

Peter's look, his distrust, was hittin' mighty close to home to how Blake had first viewed her. And apparently still did. Now, though, was certainly not the time to be thinkin' of matters regarding Blake—all over. Truth was, he wasn't here now and if he had his way, probably wouldn't be ever again.

His choice, not hers.

Just like this here, this was Peter's choice.

"Look, Peter," she said, "I told you rightly. I heard about your family, your story, and I didn't like it. I don't like any of them, tell you the truth. All the hundreds of families like yours, gettin' the short end of the stick from no fault of their own. I've got my own story, which you can see clear as day just by what I'm wearing."

The jeans. The hat. The gun.

They were different for sure, 'specially in a place like Butte where there wasn't a cowboy in sight. But underneath all that was the profession that she'd clearly walked at some point or other, the very one that his mother was being accused of. So, yeah, she understood his hesitation and uncertainty.

She just hoped he'd be like the few who'd actually open their ears and listen.

"Is that what Jack meant earlier? About you and your different callings?"

Curse Jack for opening his mouth and makin' her job harder. Who the hell knew how challengin' it would be to bring a boy home from that black, deathly cold out here.

When Cat spoke, it was slow and careful like, makin' sure she wasn't sayin' anything that would increase his growing distrust in her. "My story's not a pretty one and I'm carrying a whole lot 'a regrets in me. A lot of 'em, Peter, and they're each with me, every day, every night. Livin' right there beside me, like ghosts who ain't ever gonna find rest. Or maybe they will. I don't know unless I try."

"Helping kids like me, you mean."

Cat shrugged. "Today I had the chance to help a kid. Maybe next week or the next day, someone else entirely. Point is, that's why I'm here. My own ghosts and the promises I made to them. If it makes you feel better, think that I'm doing this for myself and not for you."

She'd a feeling Lou Blonberg would be the type to hate all forms of charity, a belief he certainly would 'a passed down to his kids. Sure enough, Peter sat there bitin' his lower lip for a time. Still unsure, but he was sitting there, nonetheless.

Cat watched him careful like, all the while actin' like she didn't care at all whatever he decided. But to her relief and her sore, tired body, Peter stayed.

She was not jumping out of the hack after him, racing into the darkness. That alone helped her breath a tad bit easier.

Sure, Peter was as tense as a board and sat as far from Cat as he could, but she got the sense that her words had eased some of his worry. Not all of it, which was to be expected. After all, Cat certainly hadn't explained who she was and what those stories and her ghosts, were. Nor had she told him the truth behind them, about Alice and the promise Cat had made, those very parts that probably would have helped him trust her a bit more.

Still, for now, it'd been enough.

And as if sensing himself this new change of events, Jack stepped in with his stories of all the folks he'd driven in his hack from the Byran fellow (who Cat herself knew nothing about, though Peter seemed fair impressed) to the actors and actresses and queens he'd driven around. Jack had no end of stories, including how best to cure rheumatism which apparently amounted to putting sulfur down your socks.

On and on Jack went, his voice becoming a smooth backdrop to that slow crunch of wheels and hooves over rocks and gravel and frozen mud. And finally, while Cat watched out of the corner of her eye, exhaustion and cold and hunger won over Peter. It was like they altogether were too much for even a determined, stubborn boy like himself, and before long he was fast asleep.

It didn't take long, neither, just a few blocks it felt like—if Cat could even see the blocks—which she couldn't. And it wasn't a deep sleep by any means, but it was enough. Enough so Cat could breath a bit easier. Her own muscles loosenin', which of course also meant all them aches and pains came roarin' on back, reminding her just how tired she was.

Real tired and real hurting.

She wanted nothing more than to lean back in that rock-hard seat and close her eyes all the way to Mrs. Allen's.

She didn't get the chance, though.

Not when Jack glanced back at her, his eyes gleamin' something fierce and bright—

And a worry in them that Cat could see, clear as day.

A worry that she, herself, suddenly felt. Almost like someone had gone and lit a stick of dynamite right under her boots. A sense, an instinct really, of the same sort that her pa had taught her out riding the range, knowing when to turn and ride the horse hard for higher ground, gettin' far away from those dried river beds even when there was barely a crackle of electricity on the air. The kind that just caused her hairs to stand on end.

He'd taught her all that, and just like back then, the sense didn't fail her and whatever relaxin' feeling she'd had moments before simply up and galloped right on off.

Vanished.

Just like that.

And just like that, just with that one look in Jack's eyes, Cat felt herself gettin' sucked down into some other story, a bigger and deeper one than she'd first signed onto. Had promised. Just like Norma and her smile, 'cept now, this time, it was about a mother...

A mother missing her smile and her son.

And so much more, apparently. So much more indeed.

CHAPTER TWENTY-SIX

Cat slowly sat up in her seat, careful to keep from jostling the hack more than necessary or makin' the kind of noise that would instantly awaken an unsettled, uneasy boy. Not an easy thing to do, seein' as how those wheels seemed to find all them biggest bits to roll over, and the hard seat creaked in a protest all its own, as if determined to let the whole passing neighborhood know they was goin' on by.

"You heard something," Cat said, keeping her voice pitched low. "About the father."

"Aye, I did."

Cat's instincts again pointed her in that direction. Telling her straight, telling her true, that all this—including that look now in Jack's eyes—tied right back to Lou Blonberg.

Lou and *not* Evie.

Not like Cat had doubted her, but still having all the information, all them bits and pieces that fit together just so and in which way, was important. It was somethin' her life in the streets, of walking in this shadow world, had taught her.

Jack bit down hard on his cigar before puffing out another white cloud. He gave a hard shake of his head.

"Christ almighty, Cat, first damn day you're outside and you've somehow stumbled into this mess."

Cat's stomach did a slow, uneasy roll while her mind did its best to piece together everything she'd heard from Dusty and Evie both, but not finding anything that would warrant *that* look in Jack. It was the same kinda look he'd given her when he'd hauled her ass up, pink, frilly dress and all, out of those tunnels near the Gardens. It was a look, one that spoke plain and true, that she was crazy as all hell, but tied up in there was also a fair amount of admiration.

Very few would care to stop and help someone like Norma. Or like Evie and her kids. None at all, in fact.

Except for her, and Dusty, of course.

Cat took in a deep breath.

She did her best to center herself, to separate herself even from all them aches and pains and the way the air here just made her want to start coughing. Tried her best to see the larger puzzle, the larger story—

And not yet seeing nothin' useful.

Instead, it was all just a feeling she had, that somethin' wasn't sitting right.

Something important and just slightly out of place. Or missing, even.

"You got an idea what kinda mess the family's in?" Cat asked.

"Well, there's the expected amount of trouble that comes from a husband postin' a classified as he did."

"*And...?* There's got to be more to the story, Jack, otherwise you wouldn't have said nothin'."

Jack chewed on the cigar some. He worked the reins with one hand, easy like, unconcerned, and Cat wasn't entirely sure he was gonna to answer...

"Do *you* know what it is you're dealing with?" Jack finally asked.

"I offered to help a mother find her missing son."

"Uh-huh. Just a simple job, right? Just you comin' in and helpin' out. Tryin' to talk some sense into the lad before truth decides to grab hold of him hard and shake him some? Simple. Straight forward."

"That was the plan."

"Just like you finding out why someone up and killed a prostitute was a simple job. Go in, find some answers." Jack puffed at her again, sending a big cloud of white smoke in her direction—and at her shoulder. "Look where that got you."

Cat waved that smoke away, lettin' it meld right in with the black and sulfur clouds turnin' her eyes red and making them burn something fierce.

She glanced at Peter, not sure why she suddenly needed to...

But he kept on sleeping, those eyelids of his lookin' so heavy like it'd take some great effort to pry them open. Still, she didn't trust it, didn't trust that hearin' the name of his parents or his last name wouldn't snap him back to the land of the livin'.

They both needed to be careful here.

Real careful.

Her, especially, because she didn't actually want another repeat of this business with Norma. She'd rather not face down someone quite intent on killin' her again, and certainly not anytime soon. Not until she could hold her own somewhat better.

Still, she'd already given her word and that was somethin' she'd never go back on.

Never again, anyway.

"You gonna tell me more," Cat asked, "or just leave it at that? Is there a story you mighta heard that would help me out some?"

A mess that had started with a newspaper... one given to her and to Evie as well by Dusty...

Cat felt another piece to this puzzle draw closer to the whole, this puzzle that was the Blonberg family, Evie and Lou and their two kids. This piece, though, it didn't fit anywhere that she could see. Dusty. As if he weren't the right shape or size, not quite fittin' as it should. But then, he'd told her himself that Peter's story hit a bit too close to home...

And she wondered again just *how* close it was hittin'...

And there it was, that tingle along her senses, right there dancin' like spider legs across the back of her neck.

Jack tipped his hat back a bit with his knuckles, still smoking that cigar in one hand and easily handling his team with the other.

"Wish I could tell you more, but it's just a feelin' I got, sitting right there in my innards. And my innards aren't so happy right now, and I promise it's got nothin' at all to do with my rheumatism."

Cat let out 'a breath.

It wasn't the answer she'd wanted. A straightforward one would have been more to her liking, but then she didn't exactly choose this life 'cause she'd wanted an easy one. She'd wanted to help those who were down on their luck and had no way of pullin' themselves back out again.

She closed her eyes a moment, rememberin' how Evie had looked in Mrs. Allen's sitting room. Those eyes and how they'd swum with all those tears and sorrow and a knowledge of what was to come. And despite it all, all Evie had asked for was Peter.

To bring Peter home.

Now sure enough, Evie *had* told Cat she wasn't interested in her husband no more, that she didn't want Cat to go digging up Lou's business or bringing him back by the ears as he rightly deserved. But Cat had learned over the years, surviving and whatnot, that the more information one had, the better off a chance you had at surviving.

Breathing was the key here, and making sure one kept on breathing the biggest key of all.

So contrary to Evie's wishes, Cat asked if Jack knew anythin' about Lou.

"Course I know 'bout him," Jack said. "He's quite the sight. Can't miss him. Can't mistake him, either. He's already gone and skipped town, too."

"You sure?"

"Drove him myself just this mornin' in fact, if you can believe it." Jack shook his head, his goatee shaking a bit as well. "The odds I'm tellin' ya, or maybe it's just my gift for pickin' up the likes such as you."

Cat was pretty darn sure it was the latter.

Jack was drawn to those with stories like a moth to roarin' bright flame, mostly so he could go and retell those stories to every soul who'd listen. She said as much to him, and in return he gave her a big, yellow-toothed grin.

Just for a moment the rest of her worries fell away, or lessened, anyway.

Enough that she was able to enjoy this moment here, the feelin' of rightness and home, of sitting in Jack's hack and riding off into that smoky darkness. My, how she'd missed his company this past week. And while a part of her wanted to know all he'd heard about Daly and Nadeau, especially their obvious (and deserved) dislike of her, she didn't. Instead, she kept the focus on where it needed to be.

On her promise to Evie.

And now, now to Peter.

Cause there was just something about all this...

Specially now with what Jack was tellin' her, about the way Lou had looked as he'd stumbled into the hack, even managin' to miss on that little step there and nearly face-plant in the undercarriage...

Something, something about Lou's story and Evie's just wasn't sittin' right, wasn't makin' sense. And that itch there, that spider doing it's dancin' across her back, kept on going. Soft and persistent like and keeping her from relaxing and moving on. Something... Maybe it had even been something Evie had said or the way Rose had lost her dancing and the light in her eyes, or those ladies who'd gotten to gossipin' about the family or the way Peter had looked at his mother before runnin' off into that darkness. Whatever it was, Cat didn't know the reason exactly, but she'd learned to trust her instincts.

Even if she, herself, wasn't back to normal just yet.

And maybe never would be again.

Jack glanced back at Cat, slowin' his team even more, sending another two puffs of that great white smoke into the air.

And right in her direction.

Cat closed her eyes a moment to keep from feeling the sudden burn from that smoke, somehow even managed to keep her breath even and calm. "Lou say where he was headin'?"

"He did."

"And...?"

"*Helena.*"

It was not a kind way Jack spoke the name, either. In fact, it was probably the first time Cat had heard anything at all like anger from him. She tilted her head and got an even closer look at Jack, how his eyes kept darting from her and then to Peter, as if barely paying any attention at all to the road.

And Jack being Jack, didn't miss it for a second.

"I drive the likes of him from time to time," he said. "The one part of drivin' folks that don't sit right with me, them pickin' up and runnin' out on their families, leaving town but leaving the family behind. It ain't right and ain't my place to shove 'em straight into a pile of horseshit as they deserve, much to my sorrow."

Jack lifted his whip and gave a good crack in the air.

Peter somehow kept on sleeping.

Cat paused though, and wondered if maybe those lines about his forehead were lookin' a bit more creased than before... but no, his breath was stayin' even and calm. Maybe it was just her being tried and all, maybe it was just her being out of practice. Another sign she just wasn't cut out for this life no more, thinkin' she could do somethin' like bring justice when it was clear as night that this kid here wanted nothing from her. And certainly would feel the same in the morning when he learned the real reason Cat had gone huntin' after him in the black of winter.

Jack, though, he kept on going—both driving the team and his story.

"They all tend to do that, you know. Leave." Jack went on, voice gettin' a tad bit louder. "Specially when they feel like they got some big opportunity and the like, or they be coming up into the world."

"And was he?" Cat was careful not to mention Lou's name. "Coming up in the world?"

"No idea, but he said he was right done with Butte. Had himself this big opportunity, go on over to Helena and give their mines a shot—which is a silly thing since everyone knows *Butte* is where the copper is. Still, he kept goin' on about how all he had to do was get on the train and all would be right. He'd get himself signed on as hoist engineer before long and he'd show them all." Jack shrugged. "Something about all the mines being against him. Not sure what he meant, cause that's usually not the case. He also wasn't too keen on elaborating, either, though I've got my hunch."

"What do you mean?"

"Well, I don't know the exact details. Even if a man gets deep into his cups there are certain stories, certain memories a fellow isn't interested in remembering. Those, you know, are usually the very ones he was aiming to forget. What I can tell you rightly is that drivin' around in Butte for awhile, which I've been doing, you tend to pick up some things and how those big mining companies work. There are lots of shift bosses and foreman who tolerant shenanigans, and some things... well, they just don't tolerate."

"Drinking, you mean. Drinking on the job."

"That's my guess."

"And this morning, how much do you think he'd been drinking?"

Jack glanced back again, his eyes narrowed and bright—with anger.

"I picked him up early before the sun had warmed the air, not that we've seen the thing in a month, but Lou was already well into his cups. Maybe still was from the night before, I'm guessin'."

Cat let out a sigh, not surprised in the least.

It sure fit the description that Evie had given her.

So... Lou had lost his job at the Spectacular Mine, possibly because of drinking in some form or another, or a reason for his firing. Evie, herself, had said she'd thought as much though she didn't give details—Cat had a hunch she hadn't *known* the details. And then Lou couldn't keep himself another job, so Evie did what she could to pick up work while still caring for the two kids, 'specially Rose, and yeah... yeah Cat could see why Evie would know exactly where her life was now gonna lead. Hell, Evie had been trying to make ends meet for some time and that hadn't gone so well. She must have known, deep down, what was coming.

"He say anything else?" Cat asked.

"A bit. About the classified, mostly. How he had to write it and tie up his loose ends here. Wife and kids being the loose ends, of course."

Jack spit into the darkness.

Then they promptly hit some good-sized bump or rock or hell even a body, not like one could see the difference in this smoke. Cat got sent off her rear then slammed back down again. Hard, too. She was fair certain it was now just as bruised as the rest of her.

She glanced at Peter.

No movement, no sign or stirring that she could see, and yet...

"But I'm telling you," Jack said, "there's more to Lou's story than an unfaithful wife and it's not sitting right with me. Not sitting right at all."

"Jack," she whispered in warning.

"Kid's sleeping, as he well should before he goes and wakes back up into this nightmare, believin' his ma was the unfaithful one in the marriage."

"I never once believed she was," Cat said.

"Rightly so. And I know for a fact 'cause the mister went and told me so. He was the one who hadn't kept the marriage vows, though that's certainly no surprise in this town."

Jack, of course, being polite enough to not point out that was the very life Cat herself had come from.

Still... only part of it made sense.

Lou writes the classified and publishes it in one of the many papers, and in the eyes of the town, gives himself a free ticket out'a the marriage and out'a town. But admitting to it? *That* didn't make sense. Even if the man had been drinking as much as Jack said he'd been, which Cat had no reason at all to doubt, it was still the type of thing a man would keep quiet about. Especially since the classified about Evie *was* burnin' up the papers. Or maybe there was something else burning through him, makin' him mad, makin' him do dishonorable things like leaving his family.

Cat tipped her hat back a bit, thinkin' hard, thinkin' on everything she knew of the family and all them details she hadn't yet learned or figured out...

Something was certainly not makin' sense.

Something was missing.

And nothing Jack had said gave her that missing piece, just... just more questions. And Jack, just like her, was havin' this feeling that she was walking into some mess bigger than any of them knew or understood.

Jack gave a final puff of his cigar before pressing the end against the side of his hack. He went and gave the whip another cracking, urging the horses to pick up speed and just by the sound alone, they got themselves movin'.

"You know who'd be interested to hear all this," Jack rumbled, "a good ear to talk it all over with, don't ya?"

Cat did.

Exactly who, in fact, Jack was referring to.

"No," she said instead.

"Your favorite officer. Officer Blake, well, he's got himself a good mind for this kinda detective work, you know, the kinda stuff most good folk don't see or care about."

"Blake's too busy doin' his own real detecting work to muddle with the likes of us."

"You sure about that? Sure he wouldn't mind you stoppin' by?"

"Yes."

Jack shrugged. "Just sayin', is all. He'd seemed mighty interested in the Blonbergs—"

"*Jack*—"

"Not that he would say much to me, man's got a tighter grip on his wallet than those copper kings when it comes to trading information."

Which wasn't true in the slightest. Word around town was Daly and Clark were goin' head-to-head on a spendin' spree to win the folks over and vote Clark in for senator. Yet another bit of a mess she'd accidentally walked into.

And this one, this one right here with Blake was one she wasn't *gonna* walk into. No matter how much Jack or Mrs. Allen pushed her.

"Blake's made his feelings quite clear," Cat said. "And I'm done makin' *mine* clear."

"Sure thing, Miss Cat. Just thought you'd be interested in knowing—"

"Which I'm not—"

"That he went and put in a long day at work, you know, 'specially on a case he'd officially turned down and all, seein', too, as how he'd gone and paid a visit to the man in question's previous employer. You know, the one that went and started this whole mess."

And like that, Cat felt the breath whoosh out of her body.

"I got a good look of Blake afterwards, you know." Jack just kept right on going, as if not noticing Cat's sudden, shocked silence. Or the way her mouth kept opening and closing. "It was like he'd found somethin' hard and rotten to chew on, like maybe the foreman or shift boss or someone at the Big S had something to say 'bout your kid's pa there."

Cat shook her head. "They wouldn't. Wouldn't remember one of the thousands they've got working for them."

"Except I'm tellin' ya, this time, well... this time I think they did and I'd wager Blake found somethin' out. Somethin' interesting."

Course, Cat didn't get much of a chance to say anything 'cause right then Jack went and pulled the hack to a stop—and right in front of Mrs. Allen's, no less.

All of which clearly had been part of his plan.

"A visit might well be in order." Jack swung his arm on the back of his seat and gave her another yellowed, toothy grin. "Just sayin'."

CHAPTER TWENTY-SEVEN

P eter heard every word.

Every single one...

And didn't move one muscle. Not even a twitch or grimace, not even when they was talkin' about his pa and his mother like... like this Cat and Fat Jack had been knowin' details about them that not even Peter had known—

Peter forced the breath out of his lungs as calm and even as he could.

Yet despite all his practice and experience, it still took a hell lot of effort to *not* bunch his hands into fists or jump right on up to his feet and demand answers. Demand the truth and every single painstaking inch of it.

He didn't, though.

He stayed calm and quiet, listening to every word... or at least as much as he could hear over that constant crunch and rolling of wheels over gravel. The way, too, his shivers kept on going. It was so cold out he was havin' a hard time even hearing straight.

Thankfully, though, Fat Jack started talkin' even louder while this Cowboy Cat was a hell of a lot more mindful, as if she didn't quite trust that Peter was asleep. But she couldn't know. Peter gave nothing away, and he was *real* good at pretend sleeping. It was one of the ways he'd learned to keep himself and Rose safe when his pa finally got home on those really bad nights, staying up late and drinkin' hard. When he'd look into their little room and their too-small bed and he'd stand there for a spell, watchin' Peter breath in and out, and Peter not givin' anything away. Nothing at all.

Still, this Cat kept her words quiet like, to the point where Peter almost couldn't hear...

Which was all right cause he'd heard enough.

More than enough.

It was why, too, he stayed right there, pretending to sleep as that hack bounced down the streets, going to God knows where, if they were takin' him to this Mrs. Allen's or some place else entirely. But the longer he stayed, the more he'd learn, and right now he needed to learn, needed to understand real clear what was goin' on...

And why his pa had done what he did.

A thought that nearly got Peter bunching his fists up again and he had to focus, focus real hard, on staying calm.

Which was why he was so damn grateful when the hack finally stopped and he could finally stop pretending.

And sure, the stop was all sudden like, just about sending him flying right off his seat and onto the carriage floor. It also meant that he finally got to jerk around and move those muscles that were tensing and tightening, wanting nothing more than to just turn and *run...*

Except he'd already done that.

He'd done the running. Had charged full head-on into that blackness and smoke with not a coin to his name and no safe place to huddle through the night. Some rocks and thinned-out tin boards under a rotting bridge did not count as place to stay. Certainly not safe. It wasn't like the side hill had been the actual forts and tunnels and hidey holes he and Bugsy and the other boys had made. Not in the real world where him sleepin' outside in the cold would surely have meant his death if this, this Cowboy Cat hadn't found him—

If his *mother* hadn't sent for her.

Cat, who turned and looked at Peter right then as he rolled off that seat onto the dusty, dirty floor of the carriage. Those brown eyes of hers seein' a whole lot more than Peter wanted her to as if she could see the hidden bits of anger still inside him, clawing like little fire ants just beneath his skin. It's what his pa had felt like to Peter every day coming home from the mines, a fire in him that was smoldering good and hot but hadn't yet lit to flames. Something Peter could always see no matter how much his pa had tried to hide it.

"You all right?" Cat asked.

Peter managed a nod despite the fire ants. And his stomach thankfully took over and grumbled something loud and quiet fierce.

No translation was needed.

"Fair enough," Cat said.

She jumped down from the hack, landing soft like with her two cowboy boots as if she'd done such a thing every day of her life. As if wearing dresses and aprons and the like had simply never been a thing for her. Maybe they hadn't been.

Peter glanced around, doin' his best to get his bearings, of where they were, what side of town they were even on, but all Peter got was burning eyes from the smoke and some kinda heavy, darker shapes in the distance. Not one street lantern or light from any nearby houses managed to burn through that smoke lighting a beacon home.

Nothing at all.

They could be standing in the middle of some desert with just this one house, and that was all.

A house that from what he could see looked invitin' enough. A simple house, least two stories (he couldn't see anything higher), and a porch with one of those swings out front. He'd always liked those, had always wanted one, but his pa had grumbled something fierce when Peter, the one or two times, had been brave enough to ask for one.

They never got one, of course.

There was a light comin' out from the inside, warm and cozy even with this smoke doin' its best to swallow it hole.

All the while Cowboy Cat stood there watching him. Her eyebrows went and lifted up towards that wide-brimmed hat of hers.

"You coming?" she asked. "No skin off my teeth if you decide you've another place to go. Long as you promise it's not out under that bridge."

She didn't move, though, and neither did Fat Jack who leaned across his seat and peered down at Peter.

"Well?" Jack grumbled. "I can drop you anywhere off you like, though I can guarantee you'll be missin' out on the most excellent pie in all of Butte. 'Cept maybe what your own mother made."

Cat, he noticed, shot Jack a glare.

Jack ignored it.

Peter, though, didn't.

Thinkin' bout his mother right now wasn't a good idea. Just the thought of her and her pie, the way she'd pour on the extra cinnamon cause she knew how much he loved it so. All that, it was just catchin' there, right in his throat. A great big ol' sob like the ones Susan Hoy would let loose whenever Peter or Bugsy sprinkled pepper on her desk or snarled cobwebs in her hair.

Peter, though, he didn't let that sob free.

Instead, he swallowed and focused on his anger, his own brand of fire ants.

Still though, this Cat and Fat Jack, they were givin' him a choice.

This one, right here, to go in that house or not... even after everything they'd said. Knowin' all that stuff they had about his pa, stuff that Peter hadn't ever heard about but... but nothing they'd said so far didn't sit wrong with him. Not really. In fact, it'd all felt right, had sounded true to him. It just fit the man he'd known for most of his life and certainly recently, too.

And this Cat here, she was doin' all this... cause his mother had asked.

There was that damn sob again, and Peter clamped down tight on it, so hard, so quick, might as well forget breathing.

'Cause he wasn't gonna cry, damn it.

'Specially how this might not actually be his mother's fault. Cause it had to be.

Had to.

Peter didn't have no one else he could yell or blame or rail against.

Regardless, though, he wasn't about to trust these two. Certainly not when this Cat hadn't said a word about his mother.

Except... Peter *was* hungry and cold and tired... and fire ants or not, he needed a place to stay.

And maybe here, maybe he'd find some answers.

If he even wanted them... he still... just wasn't so sure. Wasn't sure about anything, really, except the cold and hungry part. And... and hurting. He was hurting real bad on the inside and Peter, unlike his pa, was man enough to admit it.

At least to himself, anyway.

"I'll stay," Peter said. "For a bit."

Cat was watchin' him again, real close like, with those all-seein' eyes of hers. It was so hard *not* to shuffle his thin, frozen shoes on the bottom of the carriage.

"I meant what I said, Peter." She nodded to him. "Stay if you like or not, it's up to you. All I'm askin' is for you to listen. Don't have to be for long, either. But if you do, and just for a bit, I'd appreciate it."

"I ain't makin' no promises."

Not when there was all that stuff that he knew that *she* didn't, but so long as he did, he had some power in this game. Had something, anyway, even if he wasn't quite sure what.

Peter got down off the hack, which wasn't easy seein' as how stiff his whole body was all the way from his muscles to them bones. Stiff and sore and tired, real tired. Like every bit of movement felt awkward and uneven. Nothing at all like his usual self.

Still, he wasn't no coward and he certainly wasn't a sissy like Susan Hoy. So he jumped down, just as Cat had. But unlike her, his shoes went and slipped a bit on a patch of black ice, one he hadn't seen.

And his whole body started moving one way while his feet went another.

Peter scrambled right quick, twistin' this way and that, but it was like his whole body was just done and didn't have it in him no more to keep himself upright. And then he was falling, face first, right towards Jack's front wheel—

The one he didn't hit.

Cat's arm was right there, holding onto his arm hard. Tight, too, with a strength and grip he'd never seen in a woman before, certainly in no girl. She held him there a moment, steadying him, while Peter's mind tried to even pick up on what the hell had just happened.

Just movement. Just reaction.

Faster, too, than Peter had ever seen. Like Cat's left arm simply flew out towards him without any thought or mind at all.

But the second she touched him, though, keeping his head from hitting real hard on that side curve of the wheel there, her eyes squeezed hard and tight.

And they still were.

She let loose some kind of choked cry—though was nothing at all like Susan Hoy.

Peter watched Cat swallow, then swallow again, all the while keeping her eyes still closed as a shudder then another rippled through her body. Peter, quick as he could, got his feet under him and then she immediately let him go. This time, though, it wasn't as fast and there was no doubt at all that she was hurting. Hurtin' real bad, too.

Still, she'd not only caught him, saving him from his own real hurt, she'd let him go without him him asking her to. Both something he thought he'd never seen again in adult, certainly not after today.

"You're hurt," Peter said.

"Injured. My last foray from helpin' some folks didn't end well. Least as well as my body would have liked."

Cat rubbed at her shoulder, though the very touch seemed to cause her pain. She squeezed her eyes shut again and inhaled sharply—which she promptly coughed out again. Meant, too, that she hadn't been to Butte long if she wasn't used to the smoke.

Still, though, she was trying to hide the hurt... which wasn't much different than him, really.

"I'm guessin' I'm hurting more than the Doc's gonna like, too," she said. "Fact, between him and Mrs. Allen, they'll have my head come morning. Well, least your head's safe so some good came from it."

Jack, who'd been sitting there on his hack the whole time, was also glaring hard at Cat as if he had some say on the matter but was holding his tongue.

Cat, though, she waved Jack and his look—with her right arm, Peter noticed.

"Fool of a woman. Keep this up and you really won't get to see that sun of yours, 'specially if get tangled in this mess."

"I'm already tangled, Jack."

He shoved his hat down harder on his head, giving Peter a hard glare then back to Cat. "Don't I know it. You just remember what I said about Blake. He'll hear you out and yeah, Cat, you're gonna need the help. Don't even bother denyin' it."

She didn't, though she would have liked to.

Cause Jack took off right then, pulling out his whip and lettin' that thing snap hard in that smoky, black air. Then he was gone. Just went and disappeared into that smoke like the hack, horses, and Jack was a bunch of specters headin' right back to where they came from.

Hell, most likely.

Certainly felt like it.

Peter didn't move for a time. Just stood there, starin' off into that darkness. He still couldn't see the houses across the street, though maybe he glimpsed a lantern or two. But even that felt like something his mind went and made up, as if those lights there couldn't actually be real.

He turned towards Cat. Part of him still not sure what to do 'cause he'd never met someone like her before. She'd gone into that black winter to find him, all cause his mother had asked. Then she'd gone and hurt herself to keep Peter from hitting his head.

A kid she didn't know before today, and one she still didn't.

All the while, Cat just waited on him to make up his mind. If her shoulder there was still hurting, she didn't show it. Nor did she show if the cold was gettin' to her, either.

Peter, though, he was freezing and just about numb everywhere else. But like her, he certainly wasn't about to show it, either.

"The pie better be good," Peter finally said. His way of saying yeah, he'd go inside, if only for a little while.

Cat grinned at him, which was her answer, and the one part of him expected.

What he didn't expect was what Cat said next:

"Sure is. Your sister certainly thought so."

CHAPTER TWENTY-EIGHT

Peter froze.

He stood there, right there near the entrance of that boarding house, the one he could barely see through all that smoke. There was a few dim glows of light from the inside, pushing their way through the blackness but not gettin' too far. Far enough, though, to see Cowboy Cat standing there with one arm on her hip while the other, the left one, was cradled softly to her side as if it still hurt.

He saw the porch fine, too, and them wooden steps leading up it. And that swing there creaking just a bit, like there really was some cool, biting breeze even though he couldn't feel a damn thing.

Actually, Peter couldn't feel much of anythin', really, unless you counted that rushin' in his ears. The pounding of his heart.

And him, not be able to move a damn muscle.

Hearing about his sister was the very last thing he'd expected. But then... he should have... certainly if Cat had met his mother and his mother had asked her to come find him so of *course* she would 'a met his sister.

He wanted to swear at himself for missin' something so obvious, then swear right on over again 'cause the whole time he'd thought she believed he was sleeping.

And he'd missed it.

Cat gave him a look again, tilting her head to the side like, like she was just watching him and just curious.

Seeing everything, he figured. Which he wasn't about to underestimate again.

If there was an 'again.'

"You thought I didn't notice," she said, "pretending you was asleep. Don't get all hard on yourself. I didn't, for a time. Which was good. Real good. Like you've had some good practice there."

Peter said nothing. He wasn't about to admit the reason for all that practice—which hadn't actually done a thing for him right now.

"You've got a good head on your shoulders, Peter, even with what's all been goin' on."

"You don't know me at all."

"I don't, but I'd like to."

Again, he said nothing. Cause, in truth, he didn't know what to say. Or what to do. Before he'd had the upper hand. Maybe not much of one, but it was somethin'. Something more than he'd had once his pa's classified hit the paper. And the town gossip. He coulda walked into that boarding house with a few aces up his sleeves, bits of information that he could have, and would have, used to his advantage if the chance came up. Now, though, now he was just some kid with nowhere else to go—

Which meant Peter started feeling those fire ants again. Crawling all up around his arms there. Poking there. Desperate to come out. Angry. Resentful. Each and every bit he'd seen in his pa and had sworn he'd never feel himself...

Now... now all he had to do was breathe *out*, and they'd come. Just like the anger, the red hot flashes of fire, a world that was nothin' but red, just like he knew his pa had lived every day of his life. Or, at least every day that Peter was a part of it—

He'd turn into that monster.

He'd turn into his pa.

Cat saw all this. No doubt about it. Saw those flashes of his pa in him and instead of tellin' him to get on out, something that Bugsy's mom had done only twice when she saw those fire ants comin', Cat, however, didn't. Instead, she went and turned on her heels and started walking towards that front porch with the big porch swing hanging there, just so.

Her boots smackin' hard on the wooden steps, and he imagined clumps of frozen mud came off her heels.

She opened that door, turnin' on the knob and using no key that he could see, as if the whole thing was left unlocked all day and all night. She walked inside.

And left the door open for him to follow. Or not to.

His choice, just like she'd promised.

But that meant Peter *did* have to make a choice. To go inside and hear her out, as she asked, or not.

He took in a deep breath, feeling that smoke fill up in his chest all the way to his nose, stirrin' those fire ants under his skin, swirling around the ones in his belly. Then he let it back out again.

Just the breath and not the fire ants.

'Cause Peter had made a promise to himself, too. And to Rose.

He *wasn't* his pa and never would be. Not after what his pa had done. Done to Peter and Rose and their mother. Not after leavin' them as he did, startin' over a whole new life. And sure those ants were still there, he couldn't seem to even think of his mother without wanting to grind his teeth and scream and cry...

But they stayed inside him. Just like those tears.

'Cause he wasn't Susan Hoy, either.

Still, just to be sure, Peter wiped hard at his eyes. Rubbed them until he knew they were red and didn't care at all 'cause he was so damn tired and hungry and... just plan cold. Then he marched after Cat and walked into that house.

He tried closing the door gently behind him as his mother had always insisted on manners... except he couldn't. It got stuck there, right on that jamb, and it wouldn't budge no matter how gentle he tried to be, which just stirred those ants up all the more 'cause he was just plain tired of everythin' not going his way—

"There's no use." Cat stood there near the entry way on the most polished wood floors Peter had ever seen. "The thing's busted. Go ahead and give it a good slam. It'll let the others know we're home, too."

Peter couldn't see why *that'd* be a good thing, but he did as he was asked. For once. Meanwhile, Cat shed off her hat, then her coat, before hanging 'em up on the hat stand. Peter slowly, carefully, did the same. He still wasn't sure what he was doin' in here, wasn't sure what the heck he was actually gonna do now... now that she knew he hadn't been sleeping.

Ash and soot floated off them both, coating that nice floor with a sheen of black dust and ash. Hell everythin' about the house looked nice even from where he stood at the entryway. A dim, welcome light despite that it was gettin' late as if someone had actually kept them turned on purpose, knowin' that they was gonna be coming home. The lamps seemed lit from both a mix of gas and electric, which had his mouth droppin' a bit.

Peter didn't know of anyone who had themselves an electric light —certainly not one that *worked*.

He couldn't even imagine stayin' the night in a place like this. Which when Cat led him to the sitting room, only made that ache in his chest startin' to pound even fiercer. And he was aching. Aching real hard and he hadn't even known it, hadn't even realized it until he stood there in a room with soft couches and chairs. Quilts drappin' off those armrests like they'd been regularly used. A fire, too, in the corner with its glowing red and orange light. Some piece of wood gave a quiet pop, sending a few embers out into the air before they fizzled away.

All of it, the whole place here, eased some of that tension and worry in his heart. A little, anyway. It'd been there from the moment he'd started hearin' those whispers in school and the faces of those who'd glanced his way then quickly look away again.

Everythin' 'bout his life felt turned upside down and twisted inside out, but this place here... this was the kinda place he'd always dreamed of havin', a place he'd wanted to call home and knowin' he never could. Not when he had a pa who'd been out'a work for too long. With those chairs he refused to fit that could barely stand upright and a front door that didn't close right.

Well, apparently this one here didn't, either, though this one felt like it was done on purpose. Hell, everything *here* though felt right. Felt like it was meant to be in the exact way that it was.

And...

Peter knew this was a kinda place he'd still never have. Never get to call home. Not with his mother being known throughout town as a fallen lady, as someone who'd forsaken her vows on marriage. Cause Peter wasn't dumb. He knew darn well what his pa's classified meant.

Which meant, too, that he had no business at all standing here. Even if Cat had been a fallen lady, which about admitting herself, that same truth didn't apply to Peter or his mother or Rose.

Cat said nothing this whole time as she slowly entered the room, walkin' inside like it was a place she actually belonged and called home. It was like she was lettin' Peter soak in the place as if she knew darn well what it meant to him, as if she'd been in his same shoes once before.

He doubted it.

Doubted it very much.

And just the thought of her thinkin' she understood made those ants come crawling back.

Cause she *couldn't* understand. Couldn't know what it meant to be standing here in a place like this and know it'd never be his. That soft rug there he could practically *feel* through his scuffed, worn-thin shoes. A rug that trailed along that wood floor, perfectly clean, too, except from where Cat seemed to walk—or stomp—and the ash that kept floating down off her.

Cat paused, glancin' down behind her as if either seeing or sensing Peter's gaze.

She shook her head, that long braid of hers flopping slightly at her back. "Chin's gonna give me an earful."

She shot Peter a grin.

"Good thing I can't understand a word of it."

It was the smile that did him in.

A smile, a bit of joy there, that hurt more than anythin' else.

Cause it was kindness. Pure and simple kindness.

Peter had no doubt in that moment why his mother had come here, why she'd trusted in this woman here. But also, too, in that moment Peter knew he couldn't relax, couldn't ease that ache in him until he got some answers.

Like his sister, Rose, and what she'd been doing here.

And... and what his mother had promised.

Cat must have seen all this on his face, as if his face were some fancy photograph of all he was feelin' inside, because she nodded at him and waved her hand towards those nice chairs—chairs Peter and no one he knew had any business actually sitting in.

"You've got questions," she said, "hell, probably a whole trainload of 'em. I was hopin' to give you a good night's rest but then I don't think sleeping will be much on your mind tonight."

"No."

"Food?"

"It can wait."

"All right. If you say so. Sit yourself down. I'll tell Mrs. Allen to heat somethin' up and bring it out later. You let me know if you change your mind."

Peter noticed she hadn't said 'when' like his mother would have or Bugsy's mom or anyone else. Instead, Cat had said 'if,' like she was actually respectin' his wishes.

And because of that, and with her leaving the room all quiet like, and with that warm, glowing fire right there in the corner and those quilts tossed as they'd been on that couch as if there wasn't no order or tidiness about them cause they were meant to be wrapped around a body just so like. Cause of all that...

Peter finally felt the tears comin.

And this time, this time he didn't stop them.

This time he cried, knowin' it was finally safe enough to do so and not havin' one clue, either, that this was the exact place his mother had cried earlier.

CHAPTER TWENTY-NINE

Cat was exhausted through and through.

She leaned against that wood table there, the one in the kitchen Mrs. Allen like to use for cutting and dicing as well as rollin' out all that dough she made those pies with. In fact, flour still dusted some parts of that surface, as if she or Chin hadn't paid much attention or care this day when it came to keepin' the kitchen spotless—which was quite unusual for them. So, too, was the fact that neither of them were here yet, already waitin' for Cat and heatin' up that food like she'd promised Peter.

Which... wasn't so bad.

Cat closed her eyes a moment and rubbed her forehead, hopin' it'd ease that ache she was beginning to feel all over. Specially after she'd gone and used her bad arm to keep Peter from finding his way to an early grave.

Christ, she was tired.

Mostly, though, cause nothing in her day had actually prepared her for finally facing Peter, for talking with him and seeing all that hurt and anger, plenty of both, too. And also the way they both swirled up inside him.

Both of which she'd recognized in herself.

No wonder why Dusty hadn't wanted anywhere near him. It wasn't just about Peter and keepin' him from running out into that darkness when they got to that side hill Peter called refuge, it was for Dusty, too. Keeping himself sane, keeping himself level on that narrow edge of a knife he constantly balanced on.

An edge that if she were on it, which in some ways she was, she'd just go and topple right on over.

Face first, too, more than likely.

Truthfully, Cat would have gone for a nice shot of whiskey about now, but not the brightest idea considering the circumstance, especially, too, with how Peter would react to another adult figure indulging in drink right in front of him. Besides, a dull mind wasn't gonna see her through this and it certainly wasn't gonna dull the pain she was feeling right then, creeping up and out of her past. She couldn't help it, either. Couldn't help but see her own ma's narrowed eyes, disappointment shining straight through, as Cat came stumbling into their home. Bruises about her knees, elbows good and skinned, a shiner right there on her left cheek, all from yet another tussle she'd gotten herself into. A regular occurrence for Cat, but never for Alice.

The situation, it was different than Peter's, yet in many ways the same.

Parents and the disappointments they saw in you for just goin' and being yourself. Unable to measure up to some vision they'd had in their heads or just plain disgusted with the way you went and turned out.

Cat had a feeling that was exactly how Peter's pa had seen him.

Damn, she would have liked to dull this sudden pain sprouting in her chest, right there, right at her heart's center, even if just a little bit. But... the whiskey and all those memories, they'd have to keep. After all, *she* had promises of her own to keep.

To Evie and Peter... and Dusty, too.

Dusty, most of all. The kid who kept on believing in her when it felt like she'd nothing much left to believe in.

One of the side doors leading to the kitchen creaked open, the hinges there protesting a bit, as Mrs. Allen finally joined Cat. She was huddled up in a night robe and a nice, warm, shawl thing wrapped around herself good and tight. Her hair, like always, was still tied back in a neat and orderly bun, as if she didn't dare let it loose even while she slept. She closed the door, nice and quiet like. Everything about her and her movements, as usual, were nice and quiet and gentle as if she were one of those rarified breeds of women all them mothers dreamed of their little girls becoming...

However, there wasn't a damn thing gentle about the look Mrs. Allen went and shot Cat right then.

No siree.

"I was expecting you hours ago." Mrs. Allen gave a hard and pointed look at Cat's shoulder—and how she was cradling it against her body. "And *not* in this state."

Cat certainly wasn't about to argue with that. She knew she looked a mess. Hell, she *felt* a mess. Like someone had gone and pulled her from the inside out, stretching her whole being this way and that, twisting and turning, too, until she had nothing to left to give, her body nothing else to *give*.

"It... wasn't part of the plan," Cat said.

"It never is."

Mrs. Allen crossed her arms, careful to keep her shawl from slippin', and wow did it look so cozy, too. What Cat wouldn't give to be out of her pants and boots right now and wearin' something she could just float away in... like right into sleep. Since that wasn't quite an option yet, Cat managed to stand away from that table, and even more amazing, didn't just topple on over when she did so. Maybe her body had some bit more left to give—

Though not much. Not much, indeed.

She could feel it. And there was that matter, too, of making her own promise to Mrs. Allen earlier, that she *would* listen when her body said no... and she hadn't done that. In fact, she still wasn't doing that 'cause she was standing here in this kitchen instead of being in bed and sleepin' soundly as she so desperately needed.

Well... her body was gettin' pretty sick and tired of waiting for Cat. It was tellin' her, pretty darn loud and clear, that time was just about up.

Except... except there was Peter in the other room and—

Cat hadn't realized she'd spoken aloud until Mrs. Allen started nodding that head of hers, all sage like and all knowing.

"Yes," Mrs. Allen said. "I know he's here. Dusty send word straight away."

Cat merely blinked. "How the hell does he keep on gettin' news before me like this? First with Fat Jack pullin' up in his hack before I even think of callin' for him, and now again with you. *I* didn't even know if I could keep Peter from runnin' off right up until the moment he decided not to."

"I suppose Dusty's got more faith in you than yourself."

"No argument there."

Except it seemed pretty clear that Mrs. Allen was damn interested in having an argument, just not about Dusty and Cat's lack of belief. What Cat wanted to do was finish what was needed of her, getting Peter a plateful of food and somehow getting herself up those stairs and into bed... except Mrs. Allen didn't seem inclined to help Cat none.

In fact, she stayed right put, keeping her arms crossed and glaring at Cat.

To which Cat sighed, knowin' darn well with even their short-term association that Mrs. Allen wasn't gonna do anything until she had her say. Which, in reality, Cat was just too tired to hear at this moment, anyway.

Cat sighed, feeling the soreness and ache humming and thrumming through her entire body. "Look. I know all of what you're dyin' to say right now and truthfully, you're not wrong, either. I made some choices today to keep on going and find Peter, bring him home, even when I knew was falling-down tired."

"You went out again. Even after you spoke with Mrs. Nadeau."

"Yeah, yeah I did."

"And not only that, you went and walked up nearly the whole hill of Butte in your condition. Your *healing* condition. On your first day out, no less."

"That's about right."

Cat decided to mention about the hack she'd *wanted* to hire, figurin' there was simply no point when Mrs. Allen had her mind set on being right-plain mad at the moment.

Deservedly so, of course.

Mrs. Allen dropped her hands to her hips and gripped her fingers there like she wanted to grip Cat round the neck and squeeze. Squeeze real, real hard.

Yep. No question 'bout it. Mrs. Allen was darn hopin' mad.

"And you've gone and injured yourself again."

"I did," Cat answered.

Cat didn't bother with the reason or an apology. It'd only sound like an excuse at this point even if she'd done it to keep Peter from knocking his head hard. Instead, she steeled her nerve for what she knew was comin', a real, real good tongue-lashing of the kind even her ma would be right envious of...

Except... Mrs. Allen didn't.

Instead, she hugged Cat. Hugged her hard and didn't let go.

CHAPTER THIRTY

Cat stood there in the quiet, dimly lit kitchen. Her arms frozen at her sides, the left side aching somethin' fierce while the right one was just in too much shock to move or do much else.

"You're not alone out here anymore."

Cat didn't move. In that moment, just wasn't sure she could.

Or wanted to.

"You've got people who care about you," Mrs. Allen whispered. "So please, please go and take more care."

Cat still didn't move. Shocked by Mrs. Allen's warm, gentle arms around her. Shocked, too, by the words—and the conviction—of what she'd just said. Not one hint of doubt. Instead just complete confidence... as someone who'd walked down this similar path, not only survived it but went and made a whole new kinda life for herself.

Then, after a few more breaths where the world seemed to slow, Mrs. Allen pulled away. "Hard to believe, right?"

Cat said nothing.

Mrs. Allen gave her a smile.

It was just a little one with the wrinkles at her mouth there pullin' just a bit, as if those lines and crinkled skin were all the reminder necessary of a life and a time where her life hadn't been so simple.

And never easy.

"People," Mrs. Allen said, "somehow still find a way to care about you even after everything you've done, after everything you've been." She gave a slow shake of her head. "It took me a long, long while to come to terms with that, too, and accept it. You will as well. In time."

Cat doubted that, doubted it very much.

Mostly, though, she doubted the ghosts following her, those like Alice and her ma, would ever leave her long enough to find any measure of peace—let alone accept it.

Just didn't seem like somethin' that was meant for her, and certainly not something to believe in. Belief, however, it seemed to be something that Mrs. Allen, right along with Dusty, had no problem doing and trusting in, certainly when it came to Cat.

Mrs. Allen said nothing more on this. Instead, she went to work doin' what she did best: fixin' a grand ol' plate of food that would make even a high-brow lady like Mrs. Nadeau drool in delight over.

Mrs. Allen went to the cupboard and started opening some, the hinges there creaking just a bit just as that door had, as if they, too, needed a slight touchin' of oil to truly be silent on this still, quiet night. A night filled with not a single hoot of an owl or the high-pitched squeak of a bat callin' out for dinner, a night that had nothing but ash and smoke livin' in the air like they owned the place.

Mrs. Allen pulled out a plate and a fork, setting them up nice and pretty on a tray that Cat had grown quite familiar with this past week. The porcelain clinked a bit, but not overly loud. Instead it was a gentle reminder of the gentle life that Cat was still, somehow, apart of... even though she'd just spent her day followin' after another mother and then searchin' for her missing son, a mother who was about to walk, full-knowing, into the shadow life.

Mrs. Allen pulled down both a saucer and cup. This time, though, the clink was a bit harder, as if a bit of anger or frustration was slippin' free of her usual control.

"I saw from upstairs," Mrs. Allen said, "what you went and did for Peter, and I'm not angry at you for saving him from that hard fall. Far from it. I'm just mad you got yourself hurt again."

"It's part of the job."

Mrs. Allen paused. Not just her movements, but like her whole being. Even, even her breath.

"It doesn't have to be, you know. Your job."

"I know."

And... Cat did. And yet, despite how she'd felt that morning, unsure, uncertain, both tempted and fearful that she wasn't actually cut out for this life, to simply hang up her hat and gun and walk away into that sunset... she also knew she couldn't.

It wasn't just about her ghosts, either, or that promise to Alice.

It was about Cat.

The real, simple truth of the matter was she simply couldn't live with herself if she'd gone and walked away from Peter and Evie and Rose. If she'd done like those other mothers had done today, Flossie and Marybell and all their like, turnin' up their noses and backs as if somethin' so terrible could never happen to them, good Christian ladies that they were—

She couldn't.

Simply couldn't live with herself or her soul after doin' something like that.

"It's my job," Cat said simply, "and you know why I'm doing it."

Mrs. Allen nodded. She certainly understood all about those ghosts.

"Besides," Cat said, "someone needs to do it."

"I just wish that someone didn't have to go about and keep on reinjuring herself unnecessarily."

Cat thought back to Peter, there on that couch in the sitting room. The sorrow and anger that seemed to be livin' in his eyes as the whole world he knew went and turned against him. Peter, who probably wouldn't have lived through the night if Cat hadn't come after him, if his mother hadn't asked a fallen lady like Cat for help in the first place.

"It was necessary."

Cat came forward and started helpin' Mrs. Allen put out some food for Peter. Mrs. Allen watched her close like, those gray eyes missing nothing, to the point even reminding Cat of how Mrs. Allen would have looked back during her former days as a madam. A shrewd, calculating mind, one that saw everything and anything. And apparently saw Cat for who she was, too, and probably more, underneath all that ash and soot.

Mrs. Allen said nothing to this, simply accepted the help.

They worked in silence for a bit, and despite all that aches and pain and the way Cat's body just got more and more sluggish, she felt at peace. She wasn't certain or anything, not even confident, but it all felt right, though, and to her, that was the exact place she needed to start, simply needed to be right now.

There was so much to say, so much she'd learned about Evie and especially about Lou, all those questions to this puzzle that weren't adding up or making sense, but right then the only thing that mattered was the silence.

And the company... of not being alone anymore.

Or feeling alone.

Like Peter out there on that couch.

Still, this feeling, it went and held close to Cat's heart. Regardless of what the next day or week or month would bring for her, she'd remember this moment...

Course, it didn't last... it couldn't. Because Peter *was* there, right in that room beside the kitchen, finally lettin' out some of those tears and maybe even loosin' some of the fire she'd seen him wrestling with.

Peter needed her.

Evie needed her.

Here Cat was once again called on to do this job, but unlike last time with Norma, she wasn't her usual self. She wasn't sure or confident or even whole of body. And... she didn't have a clue in hell just how she was gonna go 'bout doing it and here all these folks were trusting in her, expecting that she go and do something... and not make a right mess of things.

"Dusty home yet?" Cat asked.

Mrs. Allen shook her head. "He won't be either, not tonight, anyway."

Cat let out a breath. Damn, she could 'a used his advice about now. He'd walked this life same as Peter. If there was someone could tell her the *right* things to say, it would have been Dusty.

Then again, if he'd thought it would have helped, he'd have already told her.

"I was hopin'..." Cat started, then shook her head. "Well, I had a feeling Dusty would be staying away."

"It's for the best, at least for now. Him being here would just confuse Peter more, and if you want to get through to him, you'll need to do it fast."

"You think?"

"I do. I've seen it before. More times than I want to think about."

"What do you think's gonna happen?"

Mrs. Allen, a true artist in there in her cozy little kitchen, went and sliced off a piece of pie, easily sliding it onto that plate—all in one piece and not breaking in half or in bunches as Cat would have likely done.

"Peter will believe them," Mrs. Allen said. "The town. The newspapers. Everything they're saying about his mother, he'll believe. It will fester in his little soul, settling cold and hard, leaving behind a colder, harder being. And those bits of his father—you saw it, I know you did—that will be the fire that keeps sparking and burning and *not* the boy crying there on my couch. We can't have that, Cat. We just can't. It doesn't ever end well."

That Cat understood all too well.

"You know the father?"

Mrs. Allen shook her head. "Nothing but what Evie shared. But I could see it clear, straight from my window, a whole lot of anger in a boy so young. Too much."

Cat agreed.

And yet, she also wasn't sure what Mrs. Allen or Dusty or even Evie was expectin' her to do about it, about convincing Peter to let go of all those voices, the town's and whatnot, and listen to his mother.

Heck, listen to what Cat had to say.

She said as much to Mrs. Allen, who sighed mightily and carrying more weight than the situation warranted.

Which meant Mrs. Allen had quite a few stories of her own, including why, exactly, she was so quick to open her home up to a wayward boy like Peter and his distressed mother.

"I know," Mrs. Allen said. "I know. None of us are being clear here, giving you anything in the way of good advice because, frankly, we ourselves don't know. How *can* you reach a young boy whose whole world just got flipped on its head and twisted inside out? The woman he loved as his mother and the vile words now being said about her? How can you get him to listen and love and trust again? How can he when the rest of the world won't let him?"

"The truth's a mighty powerful thing. He knows his father's no great man. What if I find out what happened, exactly, and tell him that? Tell him what he did?"

"It won't matter."

"It should. It's the truth."

The truth was something Cat tried hard as hell to live. And to live up to, too. It had to mean something even for a kid like Peter.

But again Mrs. Allen was shaking her head. A strand of hair dared to slip free of its place. It dangled right there across her cheek.

"I wish I knew the answer to that, dear. I so desperately wish I knew how you could help him."

"All I know is the ugliness of this life. That ain't gonna be enough to convince anyone of anything."

Certainly not a boy hurtin' for his mother.

Because all the rest of it, all those bits and pieces that went and made up a family, like love and this home right here, Mrs. Allen's, it simply wasn't something Cat had known or felt in a long, long time... and... if she were honest with herself, maybe never at all.

Certainly not the kind of love Evie held for her two kids. Cat's pa... he loved Cat in his own way, but even that didn't come close to the hurt shinin' out of Evie's eyes when Peter went and ran away from her.

"All I know," she said again, "is the ugliness. The darkness."

A darkness that ate away at a soul until there was nothing left but that darkness... and the slim, silver strands of hope until even those, too, faded.

Cat leaned against the table, feeling her whole body sagging and growing heavy. "It's not much to offer. It ain't much at all."

"Maybe. And maybe it'll be enough."

Cat... didn't believe it. Couldn't, not when she, herself, was fighting her own bits of darkness and that loss of hope, of following through with this new life she was darin' to even try.

Mrs. Allen was still working on that plate of food, moving bits and pieces around. Piling on yet another slice of ham, then another two on top of that. Grabbed a basketful of bread and wrapped it up all nice and neat in a bit of cloth. She tucked back in a bit of apple that had slid free of the pie and she did it so careful like, too, setting it back together so nice and neat, as if that small act alone, of care and beauty and presentation, could fix all them problems in the world. Maybe that was the only way Mrs. Allen had found to cope with her own ghosts. The love and care she put into this home here, the small acts of kindness like delivering those letters to other girls so their families and friends wouldn't learn the ugly truth about their profession as was now happenin' to Evie.

That and feeding young, stray boys like Peter. Like Dusty. Like Cat. Letting them all stay under her roof and that part, there, that was starting to feel more.

More like family.

And, as if reading Cat's mind, Mrs. Allen started talking about family... but Peter's family, reminding Cat that she did have a job to do and it was not at all going back and digging up her past.

"You've got a bit of time, though," Mrs. Allen said, "because of the sister. Adorable button, she is. That'll help. Just hearing her talk about Peter, I know for a fact he cares for her greatly. He'll listen to you, if only for Rose's sake, but it won't be enough if you don't act fast."

Finally satisfied with the plate of food and the arrangement, Mrs. Allen pulled out a cloth napkin from the cupboard and began arranging that, too. Which was also when Cat finally noticed the little details she'd been seeing this whole time but not putting them together in their proper order. Or in the story they'd been telling her this whole time.

God, she must be exhausted.

Either that, or she really was wrong about this calling of hers.

"You're stalling," Cat said. "You don't want to go back out there."

Mrs. Allen paused in the act of folding that napkin there into some elaborate, flowerlike shape. She sighed before letting her hands fall to her side.

The napkin she left where it lay. Half folded.

"No, no I don't. I don't like staring at reminders of my own failures and mistakes."

And while Cat may have been a bit on the slower side putting this piece together, she was understanding it now. "Because you've been the cause of breaking up families before, back when you were a madam."

"Much to my great sorrow. Yes. I've seen mothers lose their kids. I stood back and watched and did nothing at all, or too little to support them as they tried to walk this duel life of fallen lady and... and mother. Back then, I'd been just as trapped as they were, just as Evie is now, but that still... still doesn't make it right. Or hurt any less."

"Especially after you went and had kids of your own."

Mrs. Allen closed her eyes tight. Watched as a shudder shivered through the older woman.

Great big looming ghosts, indeed.

They all had them. Hell, Cat would be surprised if anyone escaped this life without any. Or a whole army following behind them.

Still, she could only understand what Mrs. Allen and Evie were feeling to a point. She knew what that life was like but she'd never been a mother, nor planned to, either. She'd no idea what the depths these two other women were feeling. For Mrs. Allen, it was loss and regret. For Evie, the coming loss of innocence and so much more.

Like her son, if Cat couldn't reach him, if she couldn't help him understand and see the truth exactly as it was.

Mrs. Allen seemed to pull herself away from whatever ghost from her past held her, because when she opened her gray eyes they were clear of any tears—and sharp.

Angry, too.

"I'll do what I can for Evie tomorrow," Mrs. Allen said. "Ask some of the girls for help. I've got a few letters to deliver; that should make my presence less worrisome for the Nadeau family."

It was a good idea.

So, too, was that other thing that Jack had mentioned to Cat earlier... or truthfully, more than a few things. Something that she really should mention to Mrs. Allen while they had this quiet moment.

Much as she didn't want to.

"I might have got a lead." Or two. "You saw that Jack gave us the ride, well, turns out he gave one to Lou earlier and learned a few things."

"Oh?"

Cat gripped that table hard, as if suddenly needing it to keep herself upright.

Maybe she did.

"Specifically," she said, "that I'm walking into another mess."

Mrs. Allen straightened. Her shoulders going back, slow and straight, and her mouth forming a small, pinched line.

"He can't say how or why," Cat said.

"But he's worried."

"He is."

Mrs. Allen's mouth stayed right there in that pinched line before she seemed to force a breath down her throat, then another for good measure. "I think he's right and I think you need to be careful. Real careful. When it comes to the mines and the men who work there..." Mrs. Allen shook her head. "They're a close-knit bunch. A fellowship, of sorts, and it's real and it's powerful. You go sticking your nose and askin' the wrong people the wrong questions—"

"You mean the right people."

"Maybe I do, but I doubt you'll be getting the kind of answers you think. Certainly not ones you need."

"He was fired, Mrs. Allen, and from what it sounds like, for drinking on the job."

There was a look in Mrs. Allen's eyes.

"I'm telling you, Cat, in this town, nothing is ever simple and it's certainly not straightforward. And when you've got the kind of father who skips town and leaves his kids behind? All I'm saying is: be careful. For Evie, the Spectacular might be all in the past, but it doesn't sound like it was for Lou and it probably wasn't for those on his crew. But... but that's not what you've been biting your tongue about, is it? Hoping I was gonna just go and forget asking you about it?"

Cat let out a breath of her own.

Damn it.

There was a reason why Mrs. Allen had been one of the most successful madams and business woman of Butte—even with her colored, eventful past hanging over her.

"You saw me right through," Cat said.

"I sure did. And since the only person you're not wanting to speak of or see these days is my nephew, why don't you just cut to the chase and tell me what on earth Jack knows about Christopher. I was under the impression, from Evie, that the police involvement was quite clear on this matter."

"She was." Cat managed to swallow. "Blake, apparently, wasn't."

So then, Cat went and told Mrs. Allen how Blake visited the Spectacular Mine and, according to Jack, where Blake *must* have learned something important there about Lou, enough that Jack thought it a good idea for Cat to pay him a visit. Though Cat was under no illusion it wasn't the *only* reason Jack thought she could go talk with him.

"He's probably right, you know." Mrs. Allen sighed yet again, this one somehow deeper and more weighty than the last. "That you should talk with him."

Apparently Mrs. Allen's ghosts didn't extend just to fallen ladies and their families, but her own as well.

Cat, of course, didn't ask for details.

"I know you and my nephew aren't on the best of terms," Mrs. Allen said.

"Blake's made his opinion of me quite clear."

Even after everything they'd been through with Norma. Even after they'd come so far in trusting each other, in him trusting *her.*

But all that, well, it just straight up didn't matter. Cat had been a prostitute and that's the only story that mattered.

"I know, I know." Mrs. Allen nodded. "What you two have is complicated—"

"There's nothing between us."

"There darn well is and you know it. Do you honestly believe that no one notices the way you both go and look at each other? Or glare? All I'm saying is if you *do* want to help Evie, than you owe it to her to talk with him. That's all you have to do. Talk. You don't have to work together like you did lookin' for the truth about Norma, and please not as partners goin' into that hell of a place Grace has turned my parlor home into. All you've got to do is talk. Find out what he knows."

Cat really, really hated when Mrs. Allen was right.

Especially when it involved Blake.

"I'll talk with him," Cat finally said. If you could count her grumbling as 'talking.' "But I've got Peter to deal with first."

And she still hadn't a clue how she was gonna do that.

As if knowing this, Mrs. Allen reached out and touched Cat's shoulder. Gently and lovingly.

"You'll figure something out, Cat, I know you will."

"You don't know me at all."

"I know more than enough. And I know that you won't give up on him. Or on yourself. That's all anyone in this life can ask for."

Cat said nothing more and neither did Mrs. Allen.

Truth was, there wasn't a whole much else to say but to see where the chips of fate landed and go from there. All she could do was keep her eyes and ears open, see and hear everything she could.

That and do her best.

When they got back out to the sitting room, Peter's tray of food in hand, they found him fast asleep on the couch. His face red and stained from drying tears and that quilt wrapped around him so tight it was like he had such a grip that not even death could pull it from him. But his face, though, it was finally at ease.

Finally relaxed.

It'd been exactly what he'd needed, the time and space to simply be a lost little boy. And... much as she was doubting herself these days, Cat *had* been right. At least about this, anyway.

Sure Peter had a long, long ways to go to lookin' happy or even certainly content, but at ease... well, that was a good place to start.

All she had to do was look within herself to know it.

Cat pulled out another quilt, being careful to only use her good arm, and draped it over him. Sure it was warm enough in the house, certainly warmer than outside under that rotting bridge where she'd found him, but the fire was down to a few glowing logs and she'd this feeling that his whole soul was feeling a deep kinda cold. Even in here.

Then they let him sleep.

Cat managed to get herself up those stairs before passin' out on her own feather-soft bed. She didn't even remember her head hittin' the pillow, let alone unstrapping her holster and laying her gun down by the stand there, always within reach. Nor did she remember pullin' off her boots and dropping them right there at the foot of the bed.

In fact, if she dreamed that night, she didn't know it. And was glad, too, because for once the dreams, and her ghosts, let her be.

CHAPTER THIRTY-ONE

Under normal circumstances, Cat wouldn't have woken for hours. Truly. Her body knew what it needed and that was rest and healing, no question 'bout it. And any person with half a working brain knew the best way to get all them healing done was by sleeping.

Sleeping long.

Sleeping hard.

But apparently not Cat this time, even though her body clear as hell needed it. Couldn't cause there was this worry just sittin' there, right at the edge of her consciousness. It was almost as if she knew intuitively that she couldn't stay sleeping for all those long hours. Not when Peter was downstairs and that door so easy to slip through and he'd never be seen from again.

So when the sun started creepin' up there in that sky—even though Cat couldn't actually see it—she felt it. And as she felt it, her mind stirred and she came slowly to...

And found herself sore as all hell.

So sore she wasn't exactly sure at first she could even get herself out'a bed. She even thought about callin' out for Mrs. Allen or Chin or Dusty—if Dusty had even come home last night, which she doubted, especially given the circumstances of just *who* was sleeping under the roof last night.

Peter.

It was that thought alone that got Cat sitting up in bed, though inching was more like. Still, she got herself moving and tossed off the wrinkled, ash-coated pair of blue jeans and blouse she'd worn all day yesterday. Got herself out a clean pair from that chest in the corner. Even her scarf was in a sad lookin' sort of state, in need of a good long washing, and she thought about handing it over to Chin to get cleaned.

But then, after a moment's thought, Cat decided against it. Had this feeling, right there in her gut, that today of all days she'd need the reminder. She'd need Alice and her ghost if she had any chance in hell of gettin' through to Peter, to reaching him, helpin' him understand.

Maybe... maybe she wasn't on some impossible of task of askin' a kid to forgive his mother, and all the rumors now flying out about her.

Ones that were about to become accurate.

Somehow Cat got herself dressed and marginally presentable, though it took longer than normal. She moved slow, though. Real slow... and swore quite a bit while she was at it.

Which was understandable, really.

Every movement, every turn and bend, especially when she needed to tug her boots on, oh my, did that hurt. Hell, she didn't even bother with her hair. Just left it there as it wanted, hanging loose down her back and gettin' in her way, especially in front of her eyes. There was just no way she was gonna get that thing braided when simply moving her left arm made tears just about spring to her eyes.

Still, Cat was dressed and got herself down those creaking, squeaking stairs. All the while, her heart pounding hard in her chest. She felt the lateness of the hour like it was a part of her. Felt her own growing frustration when on any other day, a normal day when she hadn't gotten smacked by some big-ass piece of wood that near crushed her left shoulder there, she'd have been downstairs in moments. She'd be sitting right there by Peter's bed, or couch in this case, waitin' for the kid to get up.

Instead, she'd be too late.

He'd be awake and gone just as she'd feared, and her own injuries had kept her from stopping it from happening. More proof that Dusty and all the rest were wrong about her, that maybe she should find some other profession, some other means of helpin' those out who had no one else to turn to...

Cat finally got herself downstairs, wincing and groaning from the effort of simply moving, all those thoughts and doubts smacking hard, right into the heels of her boots, and she near about fell over when she got to the bottom of those stairs, turned—

And saw Peter.

Peter, who was still sitting right there on the couch where she'd left him the night before, the very place his own mother had cried on Cat's shoulder.

And even more of a shocker, the kid was awake, too.

The quilt was now wrapped about Peter's legs, as if he were needing the extra warmth, while the one Cat had placed on him was now bunched up to the side. There was a plateful of food on that table there as well, lookin' mighty similar to the one she and Mrs. Allen had prepared.

And not only was Peter still there, shoveling large helpings of food down his throat like the food itself were air and not the other way round, but he also wasn't alone, either.

He was talking... with Mrs. Allen.

That's right. Mrs. Allen was there as well, sitting at her usual spot, her voice humming along as she told some narrative and was actually gettin' an occasional glance up and smile from Peter. Perhaps the stories were of her own kids, grown now and far, far from Butte, or maybe they were just stories about some folks who'd stayed in the boarding home over these years. Tales of the kinds of characters who'd stopped by for a spell.

Cat was under no illusion whether or not she'd be one of them.

Still, regardless of the subject matter, it sure did the job of gettin' Peter to relax. His shoulders seeming to loosen with each word of Mrs. Allen's riveting voice, letting loose this flare for the dramatic that surprised Cat. Hell, it made her want to stand right there for a bit, leaning against that staircase banister and just listen in.

As if she didn't have nothin' better to do with her day.

Mrs. Allen looked transformed from last night. Gone was her comfortable night gown and shawl, and those few strands of hair that had actually slipped free of its expected place. Nor was she wearing her usual flour-covered apron or the simple dresses. Instead, she looked... rather put together, actually. Hair carefully pulled back in yet another bun though not a single strand out of place or slippin' free —as if the darn things didn't dare.

There wasn't one one hint, either, least none that Cat could see, of the worry and anger she'd worn last night when Cat had finally stumbled home, sore and hurtin' and tired. In fact, for all intents and purposes, Mrs. Allen looked like she was goin' out. All prim and proper like, the perfect image of a matronly woman... the very one that the civilized world demanded in their ladies and that Cat wouldn't be caught dead in.

... unless, of course, the situation called for it.

Mrs. Allen paused in her narrative right then and turned, looking right at Cat, who was still standing there in that small space between sitting room and entryway. Mrs. Allen said not a word, but then she didn't need to. The look itself said a great deal.

And Cat knew, instantly, why Mrs. Allen was here.

She'd known Cat wouldn't awaken at her usual, crisp and early hour or that she would dress herself in a timely fashion. She musta known last night before Cat's head had even hit the pillow that she wouldn't be there when Peter awoke. So, Mrs. Allen had taken it upon herself to keep an eye on their reluctant charge while Cat got in what sleep she could.

Cat was ever so darn grateful.

To think after everything they'd done last night, her and Dusty and hiking all over that hill in the cold, all of it coulda been for naught if Mrs. Allen hadn't been there.

Cat nodded her thanks and Mrs. Allen nodded back.

During this whole exchange, the pause in Mrs. Allen's stories and her attention turning to the entryway, Peter didn't once look up or acknowledge Cat. His whole attention there was on eating that slice of ham as if his whole life depended on how much he could eat in as short a time as possible. There, too, was that basketful of bread, half-gone.

And the slice of apple pie, to no surprise, was completely gone.

None of this surprised Cat, either 'bout the pie or his feelings towards her.

He might'a fallen asleep last night, but they'd not finished their conversation. Far, far from it. And he was telling her, quite clearly in fact, that he fully intended it to continue.

Cat being her usual observant self didn't miss one sign of it.

Like the way his shoulders, which moments before had been so relaxed and at ease, suddenly bunched together so tight it looked like the muscles there were a coiled rope. Clearly, Peter still had quite a bit he wanted to say—

No, *needed* to say.

Again, she didn't blame him.

Cat was some stranger after all, a strange woman wearing the kinda clothes that didn't bother leaving the truth to the imagination, and he knew, rightly, what her former occupation had been. The very one his mother was now having to walk into, and this someone, too, who his mother had chosen to go out into the town and find him. Bring him home.

Yeah, no surprise indeed that he was feeling a might bit pissed.

Well, hell, might a' as well get this over with.

Cat entered the room, the heels of her boots tapping on that polished floor which had not one speck of the ash she'd left behind from the night before. Chin, clearly, had been hard at work, probably before the sun had even risen.

Cat pulled out a chair, giving Peter as much space as she could. Even from here, she could feel his anger coiling tight 'round him, bunching together just like his shoulders were now doing. He held that fork there so tight the slice of ham started shaking, even lookin' like it was gonna slide right on off.

Lots of anger there.

Deservedly so, too.

Still, anger or not, Cat was just so relieved to be seein' him. Even if she was sore and hurting, even if she wasn't awake yet and probably wouldn't be for a good hour or two. Even if... no, *when* Peter went and turned that anger on her.

Cause what mattered most was that Peter was still here.

It meant they all had some hope. Meant that he was willing to listen and that, right there, was all she'd ever asked of him. Just listen and hear what his mother's story was now gonna be.

A mother who was gonna do just about everything she could for her two children, make no mistake.

Cat leaned back in the chair, slowly crossing her ankles and wincing at the sharp pain that shot right on through her. Damn she was hurtin' and in just about every way possible, too.

Peter still didn't look at her.

Mrs. Allen, on the other hand, didn't miss a thing. She picked up her little tea cup and stirred the small spoon, those gray eyes of hers never once leavin' Cat.

"I've sent for Doctor Griffin."

Cat swore, softly. "That's not necessary. I just need—"

"To relax and heal. To rest and take it easy, which I believe was what you promised before your little outing yesterday. The one that turned into several outings and you being gone for all hours of the day. Since it wasn't possible for you to keep your promise, then I *will* do what I can. If that means having the good doctor examine you again, so be it."

There wasn't a thing to argue when Mrs. Allen was *that* clear. And that worried her. Cause somehow, despite all the trouble Cat kept tangling herself into, Mrs. Allen was still seein' Cat as something like family.

And... Cat was, too.

Even if she didn't deserve it.

So she grumbled 'bout seein' the doc again. She was certainly entitled to that at least, but she'd accepted Mrs. Allen's wishes.

"Good. He'll be by in a short while. You *will* be here, right?"

Cat gave another glance at Peter who was still so focused on that plate of food. "I'm planning on it."

Mrs. Allen accepted this, along with what was left unsaid—whether or not she'd be here depended on Peter.

"Well, then..."

Mrs. Allen stood from the chair, her dress falling about her just so, like she were some great and graceful lady and nothing at all like the boarding house owner she actually was. It was interesting to see how, in such small ways, the truth about Mrs. Allen's past, walking among those upper echelons of society, those great men with all their great wealth, slipped through. It was like such mannerisms were simply part of who she was, even if it had been twenty or more (or less) years ago that Mrs. Allen had catered to those great men, showcasing the best and most beautiful ladies in all of Butte to be their companions for the evening—or whenever suited them best.

Peter was watching all this, too, as if he was startin' to catch glimpses of what was so clear to Cat.

"It seems best for me to be on my way now," Mrs. Allen said. "You both have a bit to talk about and I have my own errands to run."

"Errands."

It was Peter who spoke.

His voice croaked a bit, as if he hadn't yet used it this morning and was still warming up the sound there in his throat.

He cleared his throat and tried again.

"You mean, about my mother."

Mrs. Allen looked right at him, her cool, clear gaze. "Yes. About your mother. She needs help during this difficult time. Any help and from any avenue that it is given."

"Like her."

He didn't nod at Cat, but then, he sure as heck didn't need to.

"Considering this woman here, including her friends, are about the only people in all of Butte who care what happens to your family, you, your sister, your mother, yes. Yes, a woman exactly like her. Someone who, despite life's circumstances and quite cruel sense of humor, still has a heart."

Peter clutched that fork even tighter. "I know who she is. I know what she was."

"Good. That's a good place to start. And maybe you'll get some idea of just what your mother is about to sacrifice to keep you and your baby sister safe and well."

Peter said nothing to this, though Cat noticed his eyes going wide at the mention of his sister—shock or shame, though, she wasn't yet sure.

She'd find out, though.

After she got herself a mugful of coffee. God, did she need it right then. This was certainly not the best way to start the morning. Her mind was still fogged up from sleep and the aches and soreness still hugging her close.

But then, Mrs. Allen had apparently planned for everything because she informed Cat that Chin was coming with her coffee and for Peter, another plate of food.

"I'm not hungry no more," Peter said, chin tilted up in that defiant way all kids seem to have come equipped with.

"Then you may choose not to eat it. Still, it will be there. Just as your mother will be, if and when you decide to speak with her."

"I'm not ever gonna speak with her again."

Mrs. Allen tugged her delicate gloves on. First one hand, then the other.

"Your choice," she said. "It is *always* your choice. And as such, you are welcome to stay here until you figure out what that choice will be. And Cat—"

Mrs. Allen turned that sharp gray gaze on her. The kind of gaze that made Cat want to squirm in her seat as if she were the kid and not a grown adult herself.

"Do try to *not* injure yourself today. I would see it as a great favor."

And with that Mrs. Allen left the home, donning her coat and hat, gathering up those letters from the small table beside Cat even as Chin arrived with the promised coffee and food, muttering the whole time to Cat in a language Cat was sure was English but she couldn't understand work a lick. Still, she happily accepted the coffee and gave her thanks, though Chin's reply sounded a bit dark and angry (probably 'bout all that floor polishin' he had to go and do first thing that morning).

And just as he had promised Mrs. Allen, Peter didn't touch the food.

However, he did finally look at Cat.

The look he sent her was just as angry as his body's reaction had been. And telling her rightly, too, just how hard and difficult the task she had before her was gonna be.

Great. Just great.

At least, though, at least she had her coffee. That was something. She'd start with that.

Start with something simple and small, like how Peter was still sitting there, still willing to listen.

For now.

CHAPTER THIRTY-TWO

P eter crossed his arms and glared at Cat as hard as he could.

Everything from last night came rushing back. All those thoughts and feelings, the ones he'd just been too darn tired and cold and hungry to deal with, slamming into him like a heavy-loaded train of copper ore or the like. The bumping ride in Fat Jack's hack while Peter had pretended to be asleep as he heard everything they'd gone and said about his pa.

Everything.

How his pa had straight taken off. Hitched a ride right out'a town to Helena without so much a backward glance or care. Not for Rose, certainly not for Peter. All the while, his pa and his classified doing their very best to tear their mother right down, ripping away any hope or chance of their family surviving, and him not caring one whit, not one whit at all—

Peter breathed.

A long, slow inhale.

Then he let it out again.

He kept focusing on the breathing. Focused on keeping himself as calm as he could. Which was just about impossible right then 'cause all of it, my God, it was stirring and swirling in him. Refusing to be ignored any longer. Refusing to stay quiet and hidden as everything and everyone 'round seemed to want him to do. Like his teacher, Big Eyes Bertha. Like Bugsy. Like all those mothers who'd stared at him right outside the schoolhouse with those cracked, wooden doorsteps...

They'd all gone and done just that. Whispered. Talked as if he and his family no longer mattered.

But this Cowboy Cat, she hadn't.

Nor was she doin' it right this moment, either, which made it even harder for Peter to understand, to sort through his feelings let alone tellin' which way was up and which was done.

Cat sat across from him at that table that suddenly seemed too small, too close. A woman who looked nothing at all like his mother, nothing at all like those ladies 'round his neighborhood with their heavy skirts and aprons that always seemed to be stained from some food or smudge of dirt from when they'd gone and wiped off their kids. Cowboy Cat in her jeans and blouse and that revolver there hanging off her hip like she'd gone and been born with it...

She said not a word to him.

Just, just watched him, studied him and the like.

But then, she didn't need to say a word, either, cause just her presence there, it was like she was the spark. The spark for that dynamite that was livin' inside Peter. The one his pa and his legacy had left in him and was now practically boiling over.

Peter had felt it from the moment he'd heard Cat and heard boots smacking hard down those stairs. For awhile, when it had just been him and this Mrs. Allen, he'd almost been able to pretend, to forget even for a moment that yesterday had happened. Like maybe it'd all been some mistake or nightmare. That maybe he really was staying over at some friend's house and life was all simple and easy, and there was this plateful of warmed-up food, and everything was all good and perfect.

Except... it wasn't.

And Cat's presence, she'd gone and reminded Peter of all that to the point where forgetting just wasn't possible. Not anymore. It was like everything he'd pushed aside so he could actually sleep, so he could get that plateful of food into his belly and have it stay there, to not hurl it right back up again...

All of it just came alive again.

Sizzled. Sparked.

Like, this whole time it'd just been waiting, desperate almost, to be ignited and he'd been a right fool to forget that it was there—

Even for a second.

The smell of that sliced ham and apple pie hung in the air. Made his stomach growl and his mouth water, but he didn't make one move to eat it. Just couldn't risk it. He had to be ready.

To run. Again.

He couldn't let that monster in him out, yet didn't know how, either, to keep it safe and locked away. Not after everything he'd heard last night and everything he still... desperately... needed to understand.

All Cat had to do was push him, even a little bit, and she would have ignited that whole lot inside him. It's what all those other mothers woulda done, or even his teacher. Cluckin' with their tongues right along with their narrowed, nasty-looking eyes all their thoughts and opinions so gosh darn loud and clear they didn't actually have to speak a single word...

Maybe Cat kept quiet cause she understood. Understood just how close he was to the fire in him, to all those angry ants that just seemed to want to eat him alive, tearing him apart from the inside out.

And still, Cat said nothing.

Just went and leaned back in her chair, watching him with eyes that saw everything. She took first one sip of coffee, than another. Closed her eyes a moment, too, as if savoring the taste, which Peter couldn't understand none cause coffee had always tasted like black sludge to him. But then that moment, too, passed and Cat was back and looking at him. Seeing through him, seeing everything—

Like he was some kid and he couldn't even begin to understand the kinds of things she'd seen and done.

Except Peter wasn't no kid no more.

He wasn't.

He wasn't crying—at least anymore. And no one had seen, which meant it didn't count. And sure, he wanted that Mrs. Allen to come back, to sit back down and tell him all those stories of the sort of happy times Peter hadn't really ever known, but that didn't make him a kid or anything.

And what Peter really *didn't* want—

Was Cat.

Cat, sitting there across from him and sipping her coffee. Cat, with that gaze of hers which clearly flicked to his arms as if she could *see* those fire ants right there, right now, crawling just under his skin. Cat, who seemed to know that Peter couldn't go on pretending or ignoring the truths in front of him any longer about his pa and his mother. As if Cat's whole purpose here was to make Peter go and face this, to deal with it and his mother...

When all Peter wanted, more than anything, was just to forget and run. Run far and wide and never, ever come back...

Just as his pa had done.

That thought alone, it made those fire ants in him just so angry, so desperate to come out. Getting ever so closer to that cluster of dynamite... that one there... just a few inches away from that tangled cluster of fuses...

So close.

And by damn, it was like Cat's presence, that gaze of hers, was almost enough from him to really feel that spark, to feel that flame just dancing out, reaching almost, to those fuses.

All he had to do was let it.

He knew why, too, knew why she was suddenly having this affect on him, a woman he'd never met before last night, a woman who'd technically done him no wrong, and in fact did the opposite. She'd gone out into the black winter to find him at his mother's request and brought him here where he'd had a safe, warm night's rest and an even warmer plate of food in his belly.

Peter glanced at her shoulder, which he noticed she was favoring. She kept it cradled against her body, easy like, so as not to draw attention to it, but Peter saw easily enough. Remembered, too, the kind of pain it'd brought her last night when she'd gone and saved him from a right hard fall. She hadn't need to, but she'd done it.

Which made it all the more frustrating that he was feeling this way, feeling those ants crawling under his skin like that.

He needed someone to be angry at. Someone to blame.

Desperately.

Because she was a whore.

A prostitute.

Just like his mother was gonna be.

And everything that had happened, all of it, suddenly felt so easy to put on Cat, to blame her—and all those women just like her. Those women that Fat Jack had talked about last night when he'd thought Peter was sleeping in his hack, the women his pa had visited instead of coming home and being with his family, with Peter's mother—

His mother.

Suddenly, it was too much.

All of it.

And knowing... knowing this Cat, this woman here, had been the one his mother had chosen to send after Peter. Not Bugsy's pa or even some police officer.

Her.

It was like his mother had already gone and given up, had just accepted what her life was gonna be now and that was all that mattered. Wasn't fightin' no more, wasn't trying to clear her name or anything, just, just accepting it just so, and that was it.

Cat kept on watching Peter and sipping her coffee.

That was all.

This time, though, she didn't once take her eyes off him, almost as if she knew darn well what she was seein'. And knew, too, how close Peter was to lettin' it all lose.

Lettin' that dynamite sizzle.

Spark. Explode.

Peter's fingers itched. Twitched. His hand... mere inches away from his plateful of food. He could fling the whole thing across the table at Cat, even. He knew how it was done.

Hell, he'd seen his pa do it enough times. It was an art form all its own, and Peter knew how.

It'd be so easy, too—

Cat slowly put her mug on that table. Her eyes never once leavin' his.

Watching him. Studying him.

Testing him.

Peter felt it with every inch of his being. And how could he not? How, when that mug of steaming hot coffee was right there and in such easy reach of Peter?

All he had to do was reach out, take it, and let all that anger out, let loose those ants crawling right under his skin. Everything then would finally fall into place. Everything would finally be right and maybe he'd even know what the heck to do. 'Cause it was all their fault, right? People like Cat. Like all those women who walked this life, just like his mother was now gonna do.

It was Peter's choice... just as Mrs. Allen had told him.

His.

CHAPTER THIRTY-THREE

———

Peter didn't move for a long, long while...

And neither did Cat.

Instead, he watched the steam slippin' off her coffee. How it curled down that cup's handle until finally disappearing around that nice table cloth, the one that had no stains or mendings.

Perfect, just like everything in this house.

And that right there, that little thought, that little detail, it got to coiling inside Peter. Coiling tight in his belly. A reminder that everything he and Rose had never had, like this beautiful house with all that lace and all that warmth, they now never would. Couldn't cause of who his mother was and who everyone in town now knew her to be.

He closed his hand into a fist and squeezed.

Cat watched.

Peter just sat there and squeezed.

Truth was, he didn't trust himself to move, not when he was this angry. Not when Cat's mug was there, too, right next to him, right along with that that red haze he'd seen his pa livin' in almost every day for a year or more now. The haze... which was now so very close to Peter.

All he had to do was reach out and let it all in.

So instead he sat there, stubborn like, unable to move and unable to make a decision, or even trust what he was gonna do next—

Just like his pa.

Which, of course, just got those fire ants in Peter bitin' even harder. Burning even brighter.

Cat's brown eyes, he was sure they saw straight through his soul, didn't miss anything. He just couldn't believe that she didn't even need to say anything for him to start feeling this way, getting so close to losing his control, of becoming exactly the kinda man his pa was—

Peter dug his fingers harder into his palms, the nails biting hard into his skin, just like those fire ants were now doing.

He... he could leave. He didn't have to stay. Didn't have to sit here with this woman watching him and studying him so, calling up all these thoughts and feelings in him that he wanted no part of. None.

He could just get up and walk away. Leave. Right now. There was nothing, and no one, stopping him.

Maybe, maybe he *would*.

Who the hell cared about the promise he'd made last night to Cat? Or any kind of promise at all? It wasn't like his pa had ever kept them. Or his mother. How many times had she promised Peter? Promised to keep him and Rose safe, that his pa was gonna get better and he'd have another job real soon and this time, well, this time he'd keep the darn thing—except now, now what had happened. To him? To them?

So, no—there wasn't anything keeping Peter here.

Nothing, nothing at all.

And besides, he certainly didn't want or *need* to hear whatever it was his mother had to say, whatever message she'd asked Cat to deliver to him. After all, *she'd* just gone and given up. *She'd* stopped fighting.

Peter was done, totally done, with letting his mother have a say in his life. Hell, she'd lost that right when his pa had gone and told all of Butte what he had.

And... if he got up and left now... that meant the anger in him wasn't gonna come out, that it wasn't gonna swallow him whole.

Not yet, anyway.

Peter took in a deep breath. Let it out again, slowly. "I'm not gonna be here much longer."

He kept his words strong, determined.

Angry.

Every inch of him sounding and feeling exactly like his pa. Peter's stomach churned. Felt for a moment that he really was gonna hurl up all that food he'd eaten.

He didn't, though.

And even if he might'a sounded like his pa, his words weren't slurin' none. Which meant he wasn't his pa.

Not yet.

Not ever.

... right?

Cat lifted a hand to her chin and studied him with that same damn intensity she'd done since he'd first laid eyes on her, and this morning, too, when she'd come downstairs.

"I see."

That was all she said.

Which really didn't help with those fire ants burning inside him. Not one bit.

"Fine, then." Peter stood. Hard and fast enough that those feet of the couch went and scrapped back a few inches on that polished floor. "I'm leaving now."

Cat, no surprise, stayed seated..

"Of course, you are," she said. "Cause you've got all those places to go, right?"

Her words... they should'a been like dynamite.

Should have set him off, all those sparks and all that fire, all of which had been building this whole time as her gaze had stayed on him, calm like, seeing right through him...

This, this right here, was his chance.

His chance to finally let it all go. To rail and scream and kick. To let all that anger out, the same anger that had been burning inside him since he sat there in the school room yesterday, hearing all those whispers, feeling so damn trapped. Unable to fight back. Unable to defend his mother, 'specially in front of all their neighbors. Unable to do anything, but... but run.

And now here he was. He could stand up and say something. Do something, *anything*, even if it meant turnin' into his pa, but at least then the anger wouldn't be a part of him no more...

Except that explosion, it didn't happen.

No loud, deafening crack. No sudden bright light seconds before that earth-shattering boom as all that dynamite in him went and lit up, blazing straight through that smoky-black sky outside...

None of it happened.

Instead, his anger slowly dissolved away. Bit by bit, as if those fire ants were quietly laying down and sinking deeper into his inside him. They weren't squirming no more and weren't biting, either. Just simply faded away.

Oh, they were still there, he wasn't that much a fool to go thinking otherwise, but they weren't so close to the surface no more. Weren't taking over his thoughts, weren't pushing him to act in a way that wasn't him.

And like hell if Peter knew why, either. In fact, he hadn't one ounce of understanding... why.

Cat leaned back further in her chair. She crossed her legs and shifted that gun at her hip so it wasn't digging into her side or something.

"I get it, Peter," she said. "Get everything that you're going through, everything you're thinking. You're mad and confused as all hell, and you want more than anything to let it all out. You've got every darn right to feel that way."

Peter tried to swallow, though it didn't seem to work so well. He could go and deny everything she'd just said, could dig his heels into that ground... but... he wasn't a fool so what was the use acting like one right now?

"I don't... don't feel angry," he said. "Not anymore."

"That's good."

"I don't understand," he said. "Why? Why... why don't I..."

He couldn't even finish the sentence. Askin'... asking why he *wasn't* angry when he shoulda been, like maybe he wasn't strong enough or man enough to feel the right kinda way in a situation like this or—

"What it means," Cat said, "is that you're not your pa."

"I don't, don't understand."

"I know. I know. Will you sit? Will you listen?"

Cat gestured to his spot on the couch, silently asking him to join her, but Peter remained standing. It felt, right then, that was about the only thing in his control. But instead of getting mad like maybe his pa woulda done or making some little comment like all those mothers he knew, Cat just nodded at Peter, accepting his choice.

That, right there, nearly had him sitting back down on the couch in shock, more than anything.

Somehow, though, he kept on standing.

"I don't know your pa's story," Cat said. "I don't know how he got to be the way he was, what set him down that path, or if he was always that man to begin with. I might never know, and you, or your mother, you might never know, either. But what I *do* know is that he was angry and he was hurtin'. Somehow. In some way. I'm guessin', too, that's pretty much all you saw these past few years. You saw his anger, lived with it, and it became a part of you. Didn't matter how much you promised yourself otherwise, it's there, sleeping right beneath the surface. It's a part of you, or could be, but but it ain't you. Unless, of course, you decide it is. Your choice."

There it came again, that word:

Choice.

Peter wasn't at all familiar with having choices. Or... what even to do with them.

And Cat somehow seemed to understand that. Certainly in a way that he couldn't, not yet, maybe not ever.

She gave him another nod, a real understanding one, too.

"And," she said, "I truly *am* sorry for what he did. Your pa, what he's gone and put you and your family through. This kinda situation... there's just no good outcome. You can either run. You can get angry. You can't get even. Don't matter how much you may want to, you just can't. The only real choice he's about left for any of you is becoming just like him."

Which was exactly how Peter felt, and the one thing he didn't ever want to have happen.

Those little ants, with just that thought alone, started coming back. Poking their heads out and looking around, thinking about maybe gettin' their fire goin' again. Almost as if this feeling of being trapped, of having no choices and no way out, *was* their reason for gettin' all riled up again.

Peter wasn't gonna let 'em, not when he was finally getting some answers. Straight ones for a change.

Peter had never known how desperately he'd needed them before now.

So, he took in a deep breath and let it out again. As he did, those fire ants calmed themselves and went dormant. Least as much as they could, anyway.

At that, Cat gave him a small half-smile, as if she could *see* beneath his skin, see those ants there just waiting to be let loose.

Maybe... maybe she did. Maybe she really did understand the way she was claimin' to.

"And that's what I mean," Cat said. "You don't want to be like him and you're trying like hell to keep from turnin' into him."

"Except you're saying none of it matters. That there's nothing I can do now, that there's nothing my mother—"

Peter cut himself off.

Just, just couldn't say the rest.

Aloud.

As if speaking that truth, at least in that moment here where truth seemed to become real. Almost, almost as if Cat's honesty was givin' him some kind of power that he hadn't realized he'd had before. And saying it, speaking that word right here, right now, would make it all real. And once it became real, it couldn't ever be changed again.

Not ever.

He didn't *want* his mother to become a whore.

He wanted her...

He wanted her to still be his mother.

Cat leaned across the table a bit, her blond hair fallin' over her shoulder a bit and nearly spilling into her still-steaming mug of coffee. She frowned at it before tossing it back over her shoulder like she was annoyed with it or something. It certainly wasn't the kinda look Peter had experience with, not when it came to girls and their long hair, usually so cared for that he couldn't *not* go and mess with it, puttin' in sticks or pepper and the like.

Cat rested her hands on her knees and those brown eyes of hers, so intense that every inch of him wanted to squirm away—but didn't.

She looked right at him and it was like she knew what he was thinking. "She will always be your mother. And that's why she sent me to find you. She doesn't care about your pa, about where he went or why he went about ruinin' her name and her reputation as he did. All she cares about is you."

Peter's mouth went dry.

He couldn't speak even if he'd wanted to, even if he'd known what to say.

"You," Cat said again, "and your sister."

Peter slowly sank back into that couch. The quilt from last night pressing up against his legs, the smells from that apple pie and the sliced ham remindin' him he did, indeed, have a full belly.

All thanks to this woman.

Thanks to his mother, who'd sent Cat after him. Not Bugsy's

mother or any of the others, not even some officer. This woman here, who'd lived that life, who'd walked it. And now here she was, the only one reaching out to help them now.

In that moment, Peter believed them both. Believed Cat. Believed his mother. He just... just didn't know how to trust that no more.

In belief. In hope.

And he wasn't sure he ever could again.

CHAPTER THIRTY-FOUR

Cat immediately saw the change in Peter. His brown hair tangled and hanging down over his eyes, almost like he was trying to hide them from her even though he couldn't.

Not completely, anyway.

Cat saw how his eyes widened in just that way, one showing both pain and hope and everything else in between. A single look, that's all it took, for her to see. And also, too, the way his eyes were watering there, just at the corners.

Relief. Love. Fear.

All those emotions and probably a heck of a lot more, swirling right there inside this kid. A kid who was hurting with every inch and fiber of his being. A kid who shouldn't have to think or feel such heavy things, but had to now because that was the way life worked.

It was exactly the kinda world they lived in.

A world where one good woman doing her best as a wife and a mother had everything taken away by one damning classified. And, of course, not a one person turning to look at the character of the person doing the writing to begin with—a person who everyone, from family to friends, knew exactly what *his* character was. Didn't matter, of course. Never did. It was one of the many things Cat hated so much about this world. And truthfully, one of the reasons she couldn't ever turn away from people like Evie or her family.

Even if Cat still wasn't herself. Even if she wasn't as whole or confident, her body and mind hurtin' in ways she'd thought herself tested by in the past, and yet hadn't ever really been before. Cause... cause she hadn't ever had something so worth fighting for. Fightin' and quite possibly losing.

Failing at.

Hell, she might not ever be that person again, like when she'd first stepped off that train into Butte. But then, it also didn't matter cause she couldn't turn away from them, Evie and her family. Couldn't live with herself if she had.

She had a lot to thank Dusty for next time she saw him.

If she did. If he just didn't go and disappear into those shadows like a part of her deep down feared that he would.

His choice, though.

Just like this here was Peter's. Peter's choice to hold onto his legacy, the anger and bitterness that his father had left him, or let it go. Let it be. Which he had. Oh, it was still there, but Peter was workin' hard on not letting it control him. Maybe that meant she wasn't quite as clueless in this venture as she'd first thought... even if it still felt like she was fumbling a bit around in the dark.

Peter rubbed at his eyes, dissolving any sign of the hurtin', crying boy he'd been just mere moments ago. He looked at her, straight and level, and... determined. Like a kid who was standing there, arms crossed, feet digging into that sand, almost daring her to prove it.

Prove herself.

Cat knew without a doubt, especially with her insides tingling and the hairs on the back of her neck raising, she'd a long, long way to go yet before she kept that promise to Evie.

Peter hadn't forgiven his mother.

Until he did, he wasn't ever gonna accept what this new life would be like. In that moment, too, Cat understood just *why* Dusty had been so adamant about staying away—and why he'd pushed so hard for Cat to help this family in the first place. Sure, Peter might not be as angry as earlier, but there was still so much that could go wrong. Still so much that could get in the way of moving forward and forgiving his mother. Regret, resentment, bitterness, you name it. Each and every one of those feelings powerful and strong enough to trip Peter up and send him down another path.

A path like the one Dusty had taken.

Or... or Cat, herself, if she were being honest.

Out of them all them paths, out of all them choices, there was only one, small and narrow as it was, to gettin' Peter back to his family again.

Back to his mother.

Cat hadn't realized until this moment just how careful she needed to be here. Getting Peter to follow her to Mrs. Allen's last night, out of the cold and an early grave, of staying 'till morning and getting a bellyful of warm food... that, that had been the easy part.

Now came the real challenge.

And she still hadn't a clue where to start.

Except... except of what she'd told Mrs. Allen last night.

Cat knew the darkness of this life.

Maybe that there *was* the right place to start.

She felt that shift in her, that knowing feeling that happened when her instincts came alive, when they pointed her where to go. The tingling in her belly. The swirl and knowingness of putting your boots onto the right path and walking forward through the brush, brambles, and all.

Yes. She knew what she needed to do.

And where to go.

She had to show Peter exactly what his new life was gonna look like, shadows, cobwebs, and all. Didn't matter that he was angry about it, that he didn't want it. This life, it was his now whether he wanted it or not. And all that stuff his mother and those in his neighborhood, those Marybells and Flossies with their narrowed, pinched mouths, with their aprons and bonnets and Sunday dinners, each of them who were hiding their own secrets and make no mistake, 'cept each of them never once dared lettin' their kids know about the real truth, the hard truth, the ugly truth. The truth of all their lives, *all* of them... and the underside that lived beneath it.

Copper kings didn't become kings out of kindness or charity or the constant buying of drinks when one was attemptin' to win some Senate race (or disfavoring the other fellow runnin' for it).

Cat grabbed her coffee again and sipped. A plan, an idea taking hold, taking shape in her mind. The coffee had already cooled down from when Chin had first brought it, but right then she didn't care. Just the taste was enough to fill her insides with the kinda warmth she was gonna need for what she needed to do next.

Peter, who was still standing, watched her with a new kinda wariness—and hope.

That was there, too.

Hope.

And it meant that just maybe Cat had a chance here. Course, it still didn't make it any easier to not become paralyzed in fear that she might go and mess up this kid's future somethin' good, that maybe despite everything she tried he *would* end up becoming a kid just like Dusty.

She sure as hell hoped not. Wouldn't wish that kinda hard life on anyone—and Dusty most of all.

Choices. All this here was about choices.

Cat took one last sip, savoring it, promising her body she'd give it the rest it deserved but later, later when it was safe, when this kid was safe and back with his family... and his mother. Then she set the cup down and stood. Cat felt the heaviness of her gun and holster hanging there, reminding her of all those promises she'd made.

To Evie.

To Dusty.

To Cat's own sister, Alice.

Felt each and every one of those promises, though not like chains wrapped around her, but just... just heavy. And maybe that there was the truth of when something actually mattered to you.

Peter and his family, they mattered to Cat.

In just the brief time she'd known them, they mattered. And she was gonna help them, make no mistake, regardless of where it might —and would—take her.

Like staring right down into her own past and family, one she'd rather keep buried and hidden there where she'd left it.

Cat took in a deep breath, feeling her insides settle and calm, just like her pa had taught her a lifetime ago when he'd taught her how to use the rifle. A lifetime and a whole lot'a pain ago.

"Come on, kid," Cat said, waving him after her.

Peter didn't move. Instead, he looked right at her arm.

The injured one.

"What about the doctor?" he asked.

Cat swore softly. Oh man, was Mrs. Allen gonna be mad at her, probably Doc Griffin, too, once Chin (or Mrs. Allen) went and told him what had happened to Cat last night. He'd be right furious to hear that she'd gone and strained the healing muscles and bones and whatnot. Hell, Cat could very well guess but *what* the doc's prescription was gonna be next.

More rest. More sitting down with her feet up. More of her questioning just about everything she was doing and everything she was.

Well, there wasn't a whole lot she could do about hurtin' herself again. She had things to do, after all, and a family to help. Besides, it wasn't like she'd exactly promised that she'd be here...

Only that she'd try.

Cat shrugged. "The doc knows where to find me, and it's not like I don't know what he's gonna say."

Peter gave her the kinda look she knew well—from Dusty. "Mrs. Allen will be mad."

"Yep, that she will. Not a whole lot I can do about that."

Cat made her way to the front door, grabbing her coat and carefully putting it on, doin' her best to *not* wince while she did so. Her hair fell over her shoulder, getting in the way and makin' the whole process a hell of a lot slower. She really shoulda asked Mrs. Allen to braid it before she left. Or Chin.

No time, though.

But at least she'd managed the buttons on her coat well enough. Even though it was hurtin' like hell, least she could do it. That was something. Something indeed, and right now she would take all the small favors she could come by.

She grabbed her wide-brimmed hat and slapped it on her head. "Besides, you and I got some things to do."

"Why? Why should I?"

"Well, leavin' things as we did isn't gonna help you none and sure isn't gonna help you decide what to do next. I told you your pa didn't leave you a whole lot'a options, and he didn't, but that still doesn't mean you don't have some choices in there."

"What kind of choices?"

"You gonna come with me and find out?"

Peter eyed her for a long, long moment. "Where would we go?"

"Where do you think?"

Cat met his gaze and held it, and right then and there made a similar promise as the one she'd made to his mother.

"I'm gonna show you the truth," she said. "All of it."

CHAPTER THIRTY-FIVE

Evie woke with her eyes crusting and feeling like they'd been glued shut. Her arm was both numb and tingling from how she'd laid on it all night, tucked up close as she had been to Rose, as close as she could in that narrow bed.

Her mind was sluggish and dull, but not so dull that she couldn't remember... remember those words Lou had written in that classified, along with the unwritten ones right beside it...

Evie pulled Rose closer to her.

It wasn't enough, though, to help her forget. Forget Lou's words. Forget the implications. Forget this bed, either, their *family* bed.

Or so she'd thought.

She buried her face in her daughter's hair, those pigtails that were somehow still holding together, though more than a few strands had slipped free and dangled both down her daughter's back and the front of her shoulders.

Evie needed to feel Rose right then, safe and close, just as she'd needed her close all night long. As if with her one arm around Rose's middle was the only way she knew how to keep her little one safe from this terrible, cruel world.

The one that'd turned on them and without so much a warning, either.

She squeezed her eyes shut, wishing with all her being that she could just go on sleeping, go on living in what small bit of oblivion that she could find for herself...

Except she couldn't.

Not now. Not ever. Not when her children still needed her, when Peter...

Peter.

The very thought of him was enough where she nearly sprang up and out of her bed. Her heart, beating so hard felt like it was going to leap out of her chest and straight up into her throat.

Evie pressed her hand there, right above her breasts. Fingers shaking, terribly so.

Peter.

He wasn't here. He hadn't come home.

She knew this, knew for a fact without even having to check in the small room he and Rose shared. He wasn't there, wasn't twisting about in those quilts in the way he always liked, as if his body simply didn't know how to stay still and quiet even when sleeping.

His bed, she knew, was empty.

The quilts, they'd be still untouched, nice and neat from when she'd gone and folded them after he'd left for school yesterday, walking with his friends and other children in that wintery blackness.

Evie had spent all night with half an ear to the door, always twitching, practically waking at every sound that could possibly mean her son was coming home. It hadn't mattered that both her body and mind desperately needed every bit of peace sleep she could find, could steal away. The truth was, she couldn't sleep knowing he was still out there. Knowing that he...

He might not ever come home.

Evie's hand trembled against her chest.

Her thoughts were a mess of confusion and hurt and a longing so intense she didn't know what to do, didn't even know how to think straight. Wasn't even sure she could get up out of bed and keep on standing. Just, just the very thought of him, out there, alone—

Evie forced herself to take a breath.

Then another.

Slowly, the trembling in her hand quieted and she lowered it. Only to glance over at Rose...

Who lay there unmoving and perfectly still.

Too still.

Too quiet.

Evie's breath caught. It caught right there, good and tight, in her throat.

She reached a hand out. The same one. Fingers shaking all over again, but this time stronger. Much stronger. Barely able to breathe, barely able to think of the possibility. It was all just a chorus in her head, a single word that kept on repeating, kept on escalating and growing...

No, no, no...

Still, no movement.

Evie lay her hand on Rose's chest and held her own breath.

There.

Evie's own breath left her body in one giant rush.

Thank God.

And no, it wasn't her imagination for there, there it was again. A slight inhale of Rose's chest, so deep the movement itself appeared almost still.

One breath. Then out again.

A second time, in and then out.

Slow and methodical. Rhythmic, almost, like the kind of breath that only came when a person was in the deepest of sleep—

Rose was safe and well and sleeping peacefully. Finally, finally sleeping.

Evie swallowed a sob, unsure how much of this she could take. Of her, her imagination running wild as it was. How foolish she was acting, thinking her daughter... her daughter...? Dear God, she couldn't even think the words in her head.

Foolish. Childish, even.

Clearly she was a jumbled mess and now, now making up all these nightmares, all these flights of horror as if she didn't have enough difficulty before.

She *was* being silly. In fact, she hadn't once left Rose's side all night. Hadn't dared to move, even. Clearly, she was exhausted. Worn through in both body and mind, certainly in soul.

The truth was neither she nor Rose had slept well last night. They'd both equally tossed and turned, as if all the fears and worries and the dark cloud that was now their future fell over them like a tight, suffocating blanket, one that refused to let go.

Now, at least, Rose was sleeping.

That was something. Some small, precious gift, and right now, Evie would take just about anything.

She got off the bed, slow like so as not to wake Rose. And thank goodness, Rose didn't stir. She merely turned over to her side, her back now facing Evie while Evie draped the thinning quilt around her.

Evie's own long, dark hair was a tangled and knotted mess, having slipped free of its pins some time during the night. She hadn't bothered letting it down or changing into her nightgown last night. Hadn't, in fact, found much reason to care. So her dress now looked about the same state as her hair, covered in ash so thick and stained, wrinkles a plenty and so deep she doubted even her nana—if the woman were still alive and if she would consent to being in the same room as Evie, and given what the classified had said about her Evie knew, most certainly she would *not*—still, even this dress was beyond even her nana's ability.

What could she even do about it? It wasn't like Evie could replace it anytime soon, certainly not now with their change in circumstances.

And while she did look quite the disaster, it... it wasn't just that. She felt like a disaster on the inside.

Evie gently touched her forehead and the constant throbbing there, right behind her temples.

She felt... dizzy, almost. Confused. As if everything from yesterday, all those emotions and fears and the unyielding, unwelcome road which lay before her, had gone and twisted her head and thoughts inside and out.

And, too, there was this constant pounding.

A headache so intense she it remembered her from those long ago days when Rose was an infant and keeping Evie up at all hours of the day and night, her body and mind so desperately wishing and needing sleep and never able to get it.

Evie didn't know how long she'd slept or even what day it was. And there certainly was no sunlight slipping past that curtain to help inform her, a curtain whose fabric was so thin you could almost see your own reflection shining through.

Evie lowered her hand, yet the pounding for some strange reason didn't stop or ease none...

If anything, it got louder.

More, more intense.

Which was when she realized this particular pounding wasn't coming from her head, but from the front door.

Peter...?

Evie's thoughts immediately flew to her son, but before she could even take one springing step forward, she stopped herself—and the hope.

No, it wouldn't be Peter.

He wouldn't knock. He would just enter, slamming that broken door behind him and stomp in as hard as he could. Determined, almost, to drop off whatever black muck had collected along the bottom of his shoes right then and there, and expecting Evie to clean it up after him as she always did, both from him and Lou.

So, no. This, this wasn't Peter.

Evie took a slow, steadying breath. It didn't help to quell this new shaking, the one she felt coming straight from her soul. One which began the very second she thought of her son—

And wouldn't ever let go.

Not ever. Until she at least knew he was safe. Maybe, maybe then...

The pounding continued. It echoed through their small home, even caused the thin curtain to shake a bit.

There was no more time for inaction or silly, confused thoughts. No more time to indulge in fears and feelings that couldn't ever exist when the light of day hit (even if one couldn't exactly see the sun).

Evie glanced down at herself, at the mess she looked, completely un-presentable to whoever this visitor was, but then she looked at Rose. Rose who, somehow, was still sleeping.

Evie couldn't stand the thought of her dearest daughter waking, and there was simply was nothing she could do to make herself more presentable.

So be it. It wasn't like her reputation could get much worse.

Evie left her small room, closing the door behind herself as quietly and quickly as possible, and made her way to the front door of their cold home. So cold, in fact, that sometime during the night the temperature had dropped low enough that her breath was now puffing in a white mist.

She shivered, already missing Rose's warmth, and grabbed a shawl from its post and wrapped it around her. She didn't allow her thoughts, even for a moment, to linger on the shawl, to think on her nana who'd made it for Evie as a wedding present all those years ago.

There was no time for sadness or regret or family long lost to her.

Evie tucked some wayward strands of hair behind her ears and breathed in.

The pounding got louder.

She refused to let it unsettle her as her thoughts sprang this way and that, trying to guess who might actually be calling on her, especially given the entire town knew of Lou's classified. Perhaps,

perhaps she'd been mistaken about Marybell, or maybe even the Reverend Jacobs. Perhaps what she'd seen of them yesterday, of their cold disdain and how they'd turned away without so much a kind word, had simply been a momentarily lapse. Perhaps they were, indeed, still good friends and confidants as she'd always believed them to be.

Evie turned the knob, which squeaked from old use and opened the door...

It was not Marybell or the Reverend Jacobs, not even Flossie and her narrowed, cruel eyes who'd never liked Evie though Evie hadn't a clue why.

It was the boy.

The one who'd given her the paper with Lou's classified. The one who knew Officer Blake and whose eyes, green and sharp and piercing, saw right through Evie. Haunted and sad eyes, ones that seemed to look right through her.

Dusty.

She would never, ever forget his name. His kindness towards her and then to Rose at Mrs. Allen's house, protecting her daughter in the only small way that he could. And the very same boy who'd brought Cowboy Cat into Evie's life, who now was Evie's only chance she of getting Peter back.

Dusty stood at the entrance to the door. He'd pulled off his dark news cap, which caused his hair there to spring up in just about every direction. It was dark, too, just like his cap, but she glimpsed a few shades of red underneath all that dust and ash. He just, just held that cap loose in his hand and with those ink-smudged fingers, not quite looking at her directly either like he had before.

Evie's heart caught in her chest again.

Had he, had he brought another classified?

My God, she could barely even think such a thing. Wasn't sure she could survive hearing another, another story about her. Another lie that might as well be listed as truth.

Dusty sucked in a deep breath and twisted that cap in his hands, only once, though. Just once. It was then that he went and looked at her.

It was enough to make Evie's stomach drop right down into her toes. Her mouth, suddenly going dry. Her whole being going still and quiet.

Peter.

This, this was about Peter.

Her son.

She didn't know what know Dusty had to say. Didn't want to know why he was here now or what he had to offer, except... except there was Peter. Out there somewhere alone. Hungry and cold, more than likely. And maybe... maybe not even...

No. She refused to think on it. Refused to believe, even for a moment.

Somehow, Evie found her breath. Somehow, she found the will to keep standing and not sink to that floor as her knees and whole body so desperately wanted her to do.

And she found her voice.

"You have news about my son."

CHAPTER THIRTY-SIX

Evie had prepared herself for the worst. Perhaps that was why she hadn't slept well. Perhaps that was the whole point of all those nightmares, both sleeping and the waking ones.

She and Dusty were sitting down at her table now, the one with the burns and knife gouges from Lou, which Dusty saw but went and sat down, saying nothing. Neither did she, for that matter. Truthfully, there was nothing much to say because Lou was gone and wasn't ever gonna come back.

Evie was sitting in the same broken chair as yesterday, uneven and even now threatening to spill her onto the floor. Strange to think that just yesterday morning she'd had no hope, no way or idea of moving forward, and it had been this boy here who'd delivered that damning news to her. Now here he was at her table as she offered what bread they had left.

Dusty shook his head. "No need to worry about me."

Evie held out the small basket to him. "Please. I insist after... after everything you've done for my family. It's the least I can do."

They looked at each other for a long, long moment, saying nothing, though just as deep and detailed a conversation was taking place.

It needed no words, just mere looks and simple understanding. Of her situation. Of his. Of how desperately she was trying to hold onto what was normal though they both knew offering what food she had was not the best choice.

But pride... even she had it.

And without a word, just holding up that basket of bread, the slices she'd purposefully saved for Peter yesterday, hungry as he always was gettin' home for school—a thought that made her hand and that basket of bread shake a bit. But Peter never got the chance to eat them, and Dusty was welcome to it. In fact, needed him to have it.

Course, he was telling her just the opposite.

Both of them pretty darn stubborn and determined, and yet, after a moment, with those green eyes of his never once leaving Evie's, he reached out and took a slice.

The smallest one, she noticed.

A compromise, and, and an acknowledge that she needed to serve her guests, even if she didn't have much to give.

It was just one small piece of her life, her purpose, that felt even remotely normal.

"Thank you," Dusty said.

Evie nodded, feeling that coiling tightness in her chest ease just a little bit. Not enough, though, not until she found out about Peter. Every inch of her seemed to be alive, to be quivering and shaking. She needed news of Peter, any news. Good or bad.

She just... just needed to know.

But somehow, her nana's teachings, her insistence on politeness and manners kept her from bursting out with all those questions. Instead Evie clasped her hands in her lap, smoothing out the wrinkles and smoke stains which left her hands a bit darker in some spots.

Dusty bit into the bread and wiped his mouth, crumbs spilling onto his lap. He glanced at the closed door to Evie's room. "Rose sleeping?"

"Yes. Finally."

"That's good. Real good. And you? You sleep much?"

"No."

Dusty just nodded even as he took another bite. While he seemed to have gotten his fair share of food, especially if he did in fact stay with Mrs. Allen's, which Evie had assumed by his familiarity with the place that he did, he sure was hungry.

It was that small detail that helped loosen more of the tension in her, the coils there constricting on her heart. Even after everything those piercing eyes of his had seen, he still was a boy. Even if, even if only in this small way.

And for some strange reason, it gave her hope.

For Peter.

Peter.

Evie closed her eyes. To hell with her nana, with social politeness and manners. Her son was out there. Somewhere.

"Please," she said, "do you have news about Peter?"

Dusty stopped eating and just looked at her a moment. And then, right there in his silence, she understood.

Dusty hadn't said anythin' for a reason. It'd... it'd all been a test.

For her.

The tension in Evie's heart, in her chest, came back and this time, this time it was something fierce and terrible to behold. Right along with all those thousands of questions running rampant inside her, each of them screaming to know... *why.*

"If you know anything about my son, I demand to know. At once."

And although Evie was demanding, she was also careful to keep her voice low to keep from waking Rose.

"Good." Peter took another bite. "That's real good. I'm glad."

"What could possibly be good?"

"You're mad, for starters. For another, you're willing to fight." He pointed the bread at her. "That, right there, you need and more than you know, too."

Evie's clenched her hands, grabbing hold of her dress and that wrinkled, dirty fabric. "You did this on purpose. You're *still* doing it on purpose. Keeping the truth from me."

"Yep." Dusty wiped his mouth. "Though not so much as keeping the truth from you as delayin' it. Again, sorry 'bout that. And sorry, too, to be calling on you so early again. I figured you'd want the news."

"Then *tell* me already." Evie nearly sprang up out of her half-broken chair. "Is Peter safe? Is he—is he with Cat? Did she find him?"

For a whole breath, one that felt like a whole lifetime had passed before she went and inhaled again, and all that while was Dusty, just sitting there, chewing on that bread.

Evie wanted to scream at him. To rail. To cry.

She... she didn't, though, because part of her began to understand... just why Dusty was doing this. Testing her. Pushing her. He was checking to see just how much finding Peter meant to her, how willing she was to fight and keep on fighting for her children, regardless of the outcome because they were *her*...

Evie's intuition, her mother's intuition, came alive.

It was almost as if... as if Dusty had already seen, maybe even experienced, many different outcomes. He wasn't doing this to be mean or callous, but instead pushing her to be ready—ready for what was to come.

Evie let go of her dress. She forced herself to smooth it out, nice and calm and even. Told herself, too, to keep on breathing.

If, if there'd been bad news, surely Dusty would have already said something.

She hoped.

"Is he...?"

But Evie couldn't even finish the thought, let alone the sentence.

"Peter's fine," Dusty said. "You're right. Cat found him and convinced him to come home with her. He went and spent the night at Mrs. Allen's."

A breath sucked into Evie's chest. Tears filled her eyes and fell, one after another.

"Oh, oh," she whispered. "Peter. He's all right? You're sure. I was so scared. Couldn't, couldn't even think—"

"He stayed until morning, at least, which I made sure of," Dusty said. "Cat will be talkin' with him and from there, well, we'll just see what happens."

Evie rose from the table. "Maybe, maybe I should go and, and..."

Dusty stood. He touched her arm.

Gently. Kindly.

"No. No, ma'am. I really don't think that's a good idea."

"But why on earth not? I'm, I'm his mother. Surely he'd want to—"

Evie cut herself off.

She looked right at this boy, the one who'd come to her yesterday carrying a newspaper with a classified that had forever changed her life and the lives of her children. This boy, barely older than Peter in age, yet much, much older if one went and actually *looked* into his eyes.

Green and piercing. Haunted and lonely.

So lonely.

And so very much older than Peter simply by manner of what he must have clearly seen in his too-young life... and what he'd clearly lived through.

So no, she wasn't going to insult him by saying she knew best. She didn't. Maybe, maybe never would again considering how she'd gone and made a mess of things; that she'd *allowed* Lou to make a mess of things. And all that, well, it hurt more anything she'd felt so far. Except... except the look Peter had given her right before he'd ran away.

More tears fell and she wiped them, one by one.

"It's because I am his mother, isn't it?" Evie asked. "That's why you don't want me to go to him."

"You're the only person he's got left."

Dusty glanced down at where his hand touched hers. "And the only one he can afford to be angry at right now. *And* you're his mother. He knows exactly the kinda life you're all goin' to walk into now, and it's the kinda life no kid should ever see. Or know about."

Neither of them looked at the closed door behind which Rose was now sleeping.

"But then," he said, "you don't exactly have the luxury of keeping this a secret anymore."

Dusty stepped away from Evie, letting go of her hand.

She knew, right to her heart, her mother's heart, that there was so much more than what Dusty was saying. Something... she'd a feeling... he didn't want to say. Maybe not ever. And she knew this *because* she was a mother. Knew right to the core of her being why he didn't want to speak of this, of why, even though he looked right at her, Dusty was still holding back parts of himself.

Almost like he was the one terrified... of her.

Evie wasn't his mother, but she didn't need to be to see this, to know it. In fact, that there was the very look Peter had had in eyes yesterday. Both Peter's and Dusty's eyes were filled with such anger and hurt, and all those unshed tears. Peter's had been fresh and full of fire, while Dusty's were older, dulled yet still there, certainly in this moment with the two of them standing in her small kitchen and that forgotten slice of bread on the table.

Yesterday Peter hadn't dared let those tears fall, not while everyone watched. Dusty, she knew, was more so. As if he couldn't be allowed to even show such a moment, to show those feelings even to himself.

Especially himself.

Evie let out a breath. My goodness. What, what had Lou done to them? What kinda path had he put them all on? The life he set their dear children on, to survive this new life or... or not?

She could barely think it. Yet there was Dusty, a living example of what Peter could become, of what he *would* turn into if she wasn't careful. If she didn't take some deep breaths and get control of herself. To think, clear as she could, anyway, and stop being so afraid all the time. She was a grown woman, an adult. She had the capacity and ability to make decisions for herself, to trust in her own counsel and those, those she trusted.

And yet... that fear just wouldn't leave her.

There *had* to be something she could do... wasn't there...? Something, anything at all, to better her life? Peter's?

Evie's legs shook and she gripped the table to keep from falling over.

Dusty cleared his throat and looked away, as if, as if he knew. He probably did.

He sat back down into the one good chair and started eating again... almost like he wanted to forget the whole conversation, including all those unspoken parts. Truthfully, Evie perhaps should have felt more afraid for Peter, more uncertain of what she needed to do next.

Instead, she felt the opposite.

Because despite the fear, there *was* something she understood.

Being a mother.

Evie lifted her head, still holding onto that table, and really looked at Dusty. In her mother's heart, she saw those parts there he was trying so damn hard to hide from her.

Long-buried feelings. Abandonment. Loneliness.

Oh, did she indeed understand all this.

But now, Cowboy Cat's part in all this, that still didn't quite add up. Not fully, anyway. Sure, Cat had explained yesterday, had allowed Evie to cry in her arms with kindness and understanding, including a refreshing lack of judgment, but even afterwards, Evie still didn't understand.

To Cat, Evie and her family were strangers.

That was simply how their world worked, functioned even. Yes, their story was a sad one, yet still they were strangers to each other; they owed each other nothing. And those, those that *should* have supported Evie, the reverend and Marybell, chose not to.

Dusty, on the other hand, wasn't a stranger.

Dusty had lived this story. Not this one exactly, but another one. Similar. Similar enough for him to know that *he* couldn't be the one to have found Peter.

Evie slowly sank back down into her own chair. Her dress falling about her again, dropping bits of ash to a floor she hadn't swept in what felt like a week but was only a day. She had this sense, another one, that spoke right to her mother's heart.

She breathed in, not feeling as afraid as she'd been upon waking up.

There was still so much she didn't know or even what the future would bring, but she felt a bit... calmer. Centered, even.

Dusty had found Peter. Not Cat.

Yet, yet Dusty had gone and asked Cat to speak with Peter. Not himself, nor Evie. But... but Cat.

Why?

She closed her eyes a moment. She knew the answer.

This was, after all, Dusty's story just as much as hers. Just as much as Peter's.

She opened her eyes and looked right at Dusty. "So who was it? Who found you?"

CHAPTER THIRTY-SEVEN

Cat wasn't much surprised that Peter chose to follow her. He could have left, going off on his own, or he could have stayed at Mrs. Allen's and finished that plateful of food.

Instead, he'd followed her.

Although to be fair, he did grab some of that bread, stuffing quite a bit of it into his coat pocket. A pocket, Cat noticed, that was in particular need of mending again. A small thread there hung so far down it brushed against the kid's thighs. Looked, too, like if you went and so much as tugged on it, and that whole thing would just flap on open.

Cat shook her head.

Poor Evie. The woman had more than enough to worry 'bout now besides mending pockets and stockings, yet she'd still need to find the time to do just that.

Cat was a might bit grateful that Peter hadn't questioned her further, hadn't peppered her with questions or dug his heels in as she might have expected. Instead, he just got his own hat and gloves on, all the while still chewing with his mouth near to bursting, and followed her outside.

Followed her right into that still black and ashy day.

A smoke which somehow seemed even stronger today, if that were possible. Just taking that first step, her boots banging onto Mrs. Allen's front porch, the wood there that creaked and groaned from the unexpected weight, and that smoke which went and smacked right into her. Like, it went and stole her breath straight away—as if she had anything left to give.

Her eyes, watering and tearing and burning, all in about one second flat.

Cat stood there a moment, near that swing that wasn't swinging cause there wasn't even an ounce of breeze stirrin' that air, and oh my, did she suddenly long for those open ranges. Her heart, missing something fierce, feeling how the wind liked to go and tug at her hair, tangling and knotting it as she rode a horse as fast and as hard to her heart's content. Part of her would have given anything to be back in Miles City or maybe... maybe even back home.

The other part knew better.

Cat slammed that part of her shut, just as hard as she went and slammed that front door the second Peter got outside. She left the porch without a word and walked towards the street, leaving all those thoughts and longings back there at Mrs. Allen's...

Where they were safe and hidden and couldn't do her no harm.

It wasn't like she had a home no more and it wasn't like she'd have one again, much as Mrs. Allen tried to convince her of the possibilities. All she needed was to remember back on Blake's face, and that there, was more than answer.

And proof.

Still, with Peter, he had a chance. That was what mattered now. Give him his chance, get him back to where he belonged and—

And the kid was still standing at the porch.

His shoulders a bit hunched, crumbs lining along a mouth that was now pulled in a thin, tight line. Second guessing, more than likely. Or maybe he just didn't want to leave the safety of Mrs. Allen's.

Their gazes met. He didn't look away.

"It's your choice," she said.

"Is that right? You're gonna tell me the truth?"

He went and looked at Cat in such a fierce way that he didn't need to say anything more for her to know exactly what he was askin' her to do.

The good. The bad. All those ugly parts in between. The parts that were gonna detail it all right out, about his mother and the life they were walkin' into.

"I will," Cat said. "I promise."

"Alrighty, then."

Peter got down off that porch, leaving the safety and security and warmth of Mrs. Allen's home and stayed right on the heel of Cat's boots. Stayed so close it was like he didn't quite trust she wasn't about to lose him along the way, or purposefully leave him behind.

Already without even realizing it, Peter was learning the ins and outs of this life. It was something his pa had unknowingly started teaching him, and as much as Cat or Evie wished otherwise, it was already happening.

Peter was already changing and nothing would stop that, not now.

Cat felt that she was toeing that narrow path of gettin' Peter back to his family. Somehow he hadn't gone and fell off onto one of them other paths, ones that were just waitin' to swallow a kid like him whole.

Though, quite possibly, fallin' off might very well happen, and soon—especially considering where they was heading.

No doubt if Dusty were here he'd have quite a few choice words to say about Cat's decision right then, and maybe he'd even be right, too.

Maybe. If he'd been here.

Which he wasn't.

All Cat could do was what she thought best for Peter and gettin' some answers, gettin' some real truth, well... let's just say her instincts were tingling right good and hard. This was exactly what she needed to be doing, though... even if the thought of just where they were goin' turned Cat's stomach into twistin', hard knots. The thought alone of stepping back into that world, all the lights and candles and dazzling beauty... and the real truth that slept just beneath the crystal chandelier, down below those floorboards...

No. She'd rather be going any other place than there.

Peter jogged to catch up with her until they were side by side. "What about that officer? The one that Fat Jack mentioned? He might be able to help out."

Correction. She'd go to almost any *other* place than the Gardens.

"Maybe later," she said.

Cat picked up her pace, and Peter, boy, was he right on her side. He matched her wide, lengthy strides in the way that kids did when they knew, darn well, they were being given the brush-off.

Which she was.

"Why not?" he asked. "Jack said the police officer had learned something about the Big S. I don't know the details, about why my pa got fired and all, but my mother seemed to think it was cause of his drinking. Easy enough to believe. *He* sure seemed like they did him wrong, though."

Cat didn't slow her pace. Not one bit.

"And let's see..." she said. "And your pa gettin' fired, is that what got him started on drinkin'? That first time he went and done something like that?"

Peter frowned, and Cat could have just gone and kicked herself.

She shouldn't have asked. Shouldn't have even brought it up, specially when they *both* knew the answer. It hadn't been fair to ask— and it was no surprise why she'd gone and done it.

Blake, again.

Even when he wasn't here, he was still somehow gettin' under her skin, gettin' into her head.

Damn it.

She thought she'd gone and left all that back at Mrs. Allen's. Just couldn't afford to be carrying it with her now... right along with all that confusion and feelings that went with it.

Went with *him*.

Cat heaved a sigh and got a chestful of smoke for her troubles. She coughed up some, her eyes burnin' all the while.

"Look, I'm sorry," she finally managed. "That wasn't called for, and while I don't know how your pa losing his job plays into this, I'm sure you're right. It does, in some way."

On that fact her instincts *were* tingling like crazy.

Those butterflies in her stomach, stirring and fluttering even as she thought back to her conversation with Jack—and all those questions neither of them had answers to. There was something here, something that played into all this, into what had happened with Evie and their family. Maybe even what was gonna happen next. All she had to do was concentrate, let her focus still in the way that she always did...

But try as she might, it just wouldn't come to her.

Damn it. She really did need to talk with Blake.

"So you're gonna talk to him, then?" Peter asked. "The police officer?"

Cat almost growled.

Didn't, though.

Course, Peter couldn't quite take the hint and went on pushing...

"You're gonna find out, right?" He asked. "Find out what that Fat Jack was talkin' about, about the opportunity my pa had in Helena and—"

"Right now," Cat said, cutting him off, "what I'm gonna do is look out for you."

"I don't need anyone lookin' out for me."

Right. Says the kid who nearly went and spent the night under a half-rotted bridge. Thankfully, this time Cat had a good enough hold on her tongue.

"I made a promise to your mother," she said instead. "I promised her to see you safe."

"I don't care about—"

"Yeah, yeah, I know. You don't care. But what you are is curious. You want answers. You don't want to go and get run over by a herd like what happened to you yesterday at school."

"Which this officer can give."

Maybe.

If Blake were feeling like even being in the same room as Cat.

Cat shook the thought off.

He would be there, if she asked it of him. Even if that was the last thing he wanted, either. But... he'd be there. Blake, in his own way, had made a promise to Evie, one which Jack had confirmed when he'd told her about Blake not dropping Evie's case. As an officer of the law, there wasn't a damn thing he could do to help her... and yet, he was trying to, anyway.

She'd deal with Blake, but on her terms... and without an audience.

"You're curious," Cat said to Peter. "You want some answers. We do that first and then, *then* I'll go talk with Officer Blake."

Now it was Peter's turn to suck in a breath, though he didn't cough like she had. But by God, she could see that stubbornness flashing back into his eyes. And right alongside it, that anger and fire that was his pa's legacy.

Cat waved him off.

"Just breathe, kid. Your pa isn't going anywhere and what he did, months ago, it ain't gonna go and hide itself in some hole while our backs are turned. The truth has a way of comin' out... no matter how much someone goes and tries to bury it."

Especially when you go and keep on digging, like Cat had a habit of doing.

"And that's what you do," he said. "You dig. Why? Why do you care 'bout what happens to me or my family?"

"Cause it's what I do. It's what I wish someone had done for me when I needed it most."

And no, no she wasn't gonna think one moment on Alice or her husband Stan, shivering and being in that bedroom with the rusty latch thrown down as tight as it could. The way the dust fell down from those rafters as he pounded—

Cat swore to herself.

"Look," she said to Peter, planting her feet firm and present in the here and now. The gravel crunched as she stepped off the boardwalk and onto the street. "Your mother asked that I find you. She wants you safe and she wants you home. And no, don't bother openin' your mouth, I know exactly what you're gonna say. Trust me. I ain't gonna force you home and neither is she. What we are gonna do, though, is cross this street here, hop in a hack, and take a long, close look at that life your mother is headin' into. The very one she and all them other mothers like her tried so damn hard to keep your noses clear of."

Peter blinked at her.

Cat watched as the anger, the frustration she'd seen flashing in those eyes moments before, dwindled. Not died, not completely.

Maybe, she hoped, what Peter was about to see and experience would finish the deed. Maybe, though, she wasn't holding her breath, either.

"What, what do you mean?" he asked.

"Trust me. It's better if I show you."

Cause what happened next, though, was up to Peter to decide. The least she could do was show him the truth, all the bright and shiny bits, and then those parts that not even she wanted to look at too closely.

Cat turned again and started walking through that smoke and swirling darkness. She called once more over her shoulder and said:

"Still your choice Peter. You can follow, or you can find your own way."

CHAPTER THIRTY-EIGHT

Dusty froze.

Right there, sitting at Evie's small table in her even smaller kitchen with his mouth open and ready to take another bite out of her bread, he just... just stopped.

There wasn't a sound coming from her home. Just, just stillness. Just the flickering of light from her lantern and that dull glow it cast about the place, making everything look even more shadowed, even more uncertain.

She was certain about this, though.

And what she saw.

Because for the briefest moment she glimpsed something in those green eyes of his. They were no longer piercing or all knowing, no longer the kid who'd spent years livin' off the streets and seein' the kinds of things that no adult, let alone a child, should ever see... but then, there it was. This slight shift, a flicker more like, but it was there.

And Evie saw it.

She saw *him*.

She saw the boy. The one hiding right there in the shadows. The one doing everything possible to remain there, to never step back into the light and the thousands of ways one could get hurt.

It was the real boy Dusty had been once.

The one whose family had somehow, in some way, broken his heart and trust all those years ago, who'd left him alone in this dark, unforgiving, cold world. That lost boy was still there, still inside him.

Somehow.

A lost little boy even after all this time. Still hurting. Still alone. And if her mother's intuition was correct, still scared.

Evie's heart nearly broke.

Then the moment was gone, quick as it came, and Dusty was back to being himself. He shrugged his shoulders, as if her question was so unimportant it didn't deem more of a response. And his eyes, they were distant like again, hooded and shadowed, not lettin' even a flicker of that boy out.

But... she'd seen it.

Evie took in another breath and forced the question out of her again, knowing it'd hurt him, knowing the memory it must have brought up. But... she needed to know.

Had to.

Now more than ever she understood just how fine a line her dearest Peter walked. She needed to know exactly why Dusty thought trusting in Cat this matter was the best choice. There was simply too much at stake.

"Who was it?" Evie asked again. "Who found you?"

Dusty slowly lowered the bread and put it there, right on the table beside the burned wood, a mark leftover from one of Lou's many outbursts.

His hand, though, stayed right on the bread.

"I don't see why the matter's much your concern."

"It is. A great deal, in fact. You're asking me to trust in you with my son. I need to know why I should give you that trust."

"Cause it's the smart thing to do."

"Is it?"

Dusty didn't say anything for a long moment. Just went on fingering his bread there on the table.

She waited for him.

He didn't look up, either, to meet her gaze.

"You sure someone found me?" he asked. "You sure I didn't *want* to maybe just run off cause my life back home wasn't so wonderful and great? That maybe it was nothin' at all like in those stories or what those preachers and rabbis and their like go on about? That maybe livin' in the streets was a better outcome for me so I decided, 'what the hell?' And hopped on the first rail I could that'd take me as far from them as could go?"

As he talked, he started breaking bits and pieces of the bread, crumbling like, in small, sad flakes. And he kept going, too, as if unlike her kids who had such found memories of her bread, of the smells lingering in their house for days after she'd baked it, for him, for Dusty, it wasn't so fond a memory.

Maybe, even, a painful one.

Evie wanted to reach out and touch his hand. She didn't, though, and kept hers in her lap.

Her comfort, she knew, wouldn't be a welcome one.

"You think," he said, still breaking up the bread, "that someone actually cared enough to find me in the first place?"

"I think," Evie said slowly, carefully, and not hiding one ounce of the sadness she felt for him, "that everything you said is true. All of it."

There was nothing now left of the bread.

Just, just broken bits.

Dusty's hand fell to his lap.

"You ran away," she said, "and you wanted to. It was the best choice for you, so you took it. You did hop on a rail that took you somewhere, and... and someone did find you."

"You're starting to sound a bit like Cat now, all them guesses you're makin' bout me."

"But they're wrong, are they? And they're not guesses, I simply know."

"Cause you got the gift like Cat does? Seeing all the pictures? All the pieces and puttin' 'em together?"

"Not at all. I'm a mother, is all. That's why I know everything you just told me was true. And someone *did* find you but they didn't bring you home, did they?"

Dusty gazed at her a long moment, silent, not saying one word, and Evie for sure thought he was closin' up even more on her, which she couldn't let happen. Not until she knew about Peter—

"Not from lack of trying," Dusty said, breaking the silence. "She tried like hell to convince me. Even bought me a ticket to take me right back to them."

"But you didn't go."

"Nope."

"Why?"

He shook his head. Lips pressed tight, as if he really didn't want to even think of that part of his life. "Cause there wasn't nothing at all there for me. I *knew* what was waiting for me, and why should I go back to that? Go back to being hungry and beaten and hungry again, maybe even the opposite order. On my own, all I had to rely on me was me. Going back home... it meant *they* were relyin' on me and kept much as they could for themselves."

Evie reached a hand and tucked a strand of hair behind her ears.

Her hand, she noticed, was shaking.

Probably because she could imagine, so very well, Lou in the center of Dusty's story.

"Who found you?" Evie asked for a third time.

"The only person who really cared about me, though not enough to stay, not that I blame her. Then or now."

It wasn't the mother, Evie knew.

Knew with that swelling right there in her chest, a kinda hurt she felt through and through. And yet... she also wasn't surprised by his answer either.

"My sister," he said. "It was my sister."

And with no prompting from Evie at all, Peter told her about his sister. Norma. A woman whose story, after a moment, tickled in the back of her mind, and she realized this was the very same woman who'd died not long ago. The woman who Cat had found justice for. Everything started settling in and making sense, but that wasn't the part Evie cared so much about.

It was Dusty's story she wanted—no, *needed* to hear.

And for whatever reason, he told her.

Told Evie how Norma had found him. How she'd heard from their parents that he'd run off, months after, actually, and Norma who'd dropped everything she was doin' and came after him. And the sight of her... it had taken him a full five minutes before Dusty was convinced it *was* his sister.

"All decked out in them pretty jewels. A dress so fine, too, I thought if I touched it the whole thing'd fall to pieces."

While Evie had done her best to keep Peter and Rose from learning some of those darker truths about this life, she knew more than enough to know what kinda woman Dusty's sister had become.

A working girl in one of the big parlor houses.

Evie had seen them more than enough, riding about town in their own finery and fur coats on the arms of those big, prominent men all those newspapers liked to tell of.

She could understand very well why seeing his sister would certainly not have convinced him to return home.

"And when you wouldn't return home?" Evie asked.

Dusty shrugged. "She couldn't just leave me. I think, maybe, she always knew it'd come to this cause she took me with her and introduced me to the kinds of folks that I could... get started. Earnin' my own money and such."

Evie wasn't about to ask what he meant, though. Sure, he sold papers. The ink stains on his fingers and how he knew about Lou's classified told her as much, but there was more a boy could do out there in Butte. More ways to earn a handsome coin or two. She also understood enough that those might be the only jobs left open to Peter now that... now that she was to become a whore herself.

"And... and Peter?" Evie asked. "Don't you, don't you think he might choose the same as you?"

Dusty looked at her, long and hard.

"I don't know, Mrs. Blonberg. That's up for Peter to decide."

Her whole body shook. Her hands so hard she clasped them in front of herself, burying them into the wrinkles and stained fabric of her dress.

"And Cat? What can she do that you can't? Or me, even?"

"She'll tell him the truth. All of it."

That wasn't enough for Evie. *Couldn't* be enough. Could never be good enough. There was too much on the line; this was her son, for cryin' out loud, and she wasn't about to leave his future to some, some truth—

Evie rose from her chair so fast the thing clattered behind her. Thought a moment about Rose and accidentally waking her, but then it passed quick as it came.

All her thoughts, all her heart went out to Peter and how she *needed* to go to him.

Now.

Evie opened her mouth, ready to tell Dusty just that, demand just that, when for the second time that morning someone knocked on her door.

No, she corrected.

Pounded on her door.

CHAPTER THIRTY-NINE

Cat left Mrs. Allen's quiet street with its mismatched boarding houses and single homes and three-floor mansions with them green growing things along the outside fences, which were somehow still alive given their living conditions, and headed deeper into that black smoke and ash.

Her eyes burnin', her lungs hurtin' even more.

Behind her, her ears strainin' to hear that telltale sign that she wasn't alone.

So far... nothing.

No Peter.

Hoped, too, he wouldn't be long in makin' up his mind because that smoke was so damn thick today it felt almost like an actual living, breathing being in its own right. One that was intent on makin' each and every one of them good and lost. If Cat hadn't known where she was heading, if she hadn't this map in her head, the one that started takin' shape the moment she'd stepped off that train, no doubt she'd have been lost in about two steps flat.

She didn't get lost, though.

And to her great relief, she wasn't walking alone, either.

Peter followed her.

It took a short while, just a few breaths, really, though it felt a lot longer than that. Then came the sound that she was strainin' real hard to hear: the soft sounds of thudding feet behind her. Those worn-out shoes of Peter's, unmistakable, and making their way over that crushed gravel and broken rock, both which were covered in frost and black muck and other things that was best not to look closely at.

But still, Peter came.

Cat let out yet another relieved sigh when she saw him. That thin coat of his buttoned up as far as it could go, his hat squashed so far down his head you could barely see his eyes—but see them she did, and they were burnin' bright. Real bright.

Bright and furious and determined.

It was a look she was gettin' to know real well. Like it or not, whether he realized it or not, Peter sure was gettin' prepared for this life... and what was coming.

"You're really gonna show me?" he asked. "You'll show me the truth?"

"To the best of my ability."

"All right, then. I'll tag along. For now."

"I never asked for nothin' more."

Peter glanced in the direction she'd been heading, and Cat followed his gaze. The crunch of wheels and hooves over that same gravel came slipping through that smoke. Voices callin' out, too, and in quite a few tones and languages, though they coulda been just too far off, too muffled to make out rightly.

Still, it all seemed to echo, fading in and out, and her not seein' one thing, either, even with her sharp eye sight. Not one person or wagon, almost as if there was a whole bunch of ghostly specters instead of real and breathing kinds of beings.

"Where we heading?" Peter asked, turning back to her.

"Grace's Gardens."

"Never heard of it."

Cat's eyebrows lifted.

That was disappointing. Real disappointing.

She had a real, real big job ahead of her. Evie and all those mothers on whatever street Peter had called home had done a grand job of keepin' this shadow life secret. Which meant they hadn't done one of them, not one, any favors in the long run.

"Come on." Cat gestured for Peter to follow. "Best get started on your education, then."

They hitched a ride with the first hack that stopped and one that didn't seem to mind Cat's manner of dress. Or lack of one, as the case might be. The driver wasn't Fat Jack, which meant this one gave Cat a long, calculating look—taking in her jeans, wide-brimmed hat, and lingered a bit longer on her gun—before spitting out something black out onto those streets and mouthin' something along the lines of:

"Hop her in."

Cat felt both relieved and disappointed that it wasn't Jack drivin' them around the hill this morning. The good news was that with traffic being a bit busy right now, certainly compared to last night, it was good they weren't spinning round corners on only one wheel, as Jack likened to do. And there *were* quite a few carts and wagons and foot traffic about, ones that you could hear only and not see worth a damn.

On the other hand, Cat could 'a used his thoughts about now, seein' if he'd learned anything knew about Lou and whatever business he'd gone and gotten himself tangled up in.

Course, that would also have meant Jack's uncanny gaze landing right on her as he again went and asked if she needed a lift to Blake's place.

Better for all intents and purposes that Jack wasn't their driver right then.

This driver wasn't of the talkative sort or maybe he didn't approve too much of the company he was drivin', which made for a silent yet bumpy drive to the Gardens. They seemed to hit every rock and dip those wheels could find, and she and Peter went bouncin' around like little dolls. Their bums smackin' hard into those hard wooden seats—and her shoulder smacking equally hard into that seat backing.

Either way, she was hurtin' and hurtin' pretty good by the time their driver went and pulled up to the familiar brick building. Hell, Cat had been so distracted, doin' her best from causing too much damage to her already damaged shoulder, that she hadn't much a chance to think on just what she was gonna say when they got to those doors.

Those heavy specially carved doors, all fancied-up and polished gleaming for the clientele that usually went through them. Those people with all them money and influence and a boatload of power.

Certainly not someone like her.

Which, considering what had happened the last time she'd gone through said doors... well, let's just say she wasn't exactly holding her breath on this particular outcome.

Still, it was an important place to go for Peter, especially if she had any chance of getting through to Peter, of getting him back to his mother.

She needed to start somewhere, and this here, it was the place to start. Start pulling back on that curtain to the shadow world—or more like ripping the whole thing down.

Cat sure hoped Dusty would forgive her for bringing Peter here. She had this tingling, though, right there along her senses, that maybe Dusty already knew. If there was one place Peter could fall right on off the edge, it was here. Here where all that dazzling sparkle and beauty lived. A perfect trap for a kid whose idea of luxury was hot basket of bread and a warm place to curl up and sleep, without the cold slipping in between threadbare quilts.

Despite all that, despite the risks and fears that shivered and tingled all the way up and down Cat's skin, she also knew, without a doubt, this here was the place they needed to be...

That Peter needed to be.

Cat paid the driver and they hopped on down from the hack, with Peter not slippin' on any ice this time, as if he was purposefully takin' more care. To which she was mighty grateful. Lord, moving her shoulder the slightest bit went and sent a wave of agony right through her, one that she felt from her teeth to her toes.

"You all right?" Peter asked.

"Been better."

Which wasn't a lie, not at all.

Though, in all fairness, she wasn't exactly sure if she was talkin' about her shoulder... or walkin' up to the Gardens and knocking on those grand ol' doors. Especially when this place here brought up a whole lot'a memories... ones that Cat wasn't exactly ready to deal with.

Or ever would be.

Like the memory of her and Blake walkin' inside, arm in arm, with him decked out in the finest suit and tie and hat money could buy—borrowed, of course—and she, well, she went and looked the part that was called for. All darned up in the kinds of finery that would allow a lady entrance to the Gardens without question or hesitation. Pink layered and ruffled dress, jewels sparkling all about her person, hair twisted up in curls and ribbons by Chin's somehow expert hands. She'd looked every part like some princess of old.

And breathing 'bout as well as a princess, too.

Which meant barely breathing at all, certainly the way that corset had gone and done its darn best for her to faint whenever she took too big a step.

Cat closed her eyes a moment, feeling the burn from both the smoke and something else.

Something that felt an awful bit like tears.

Down there, down in the basement of the Gardens, in those cribs where the only light that touched the place came from those hanging, blinking, naked light bulbs. The only sounds came from the creaking, shifting floorboards of those elegant rooms up top and the usual, beautiful notes of the piano being played, either due to some grand party or fine guests. Those sounds, all of which filtered down to the cribs until they became muffled and warped, to the point where the notes themselves changed. Became sorrowful and trapped, just like the girls who lived there.

And it was down there, where Cat had fallen.

Her right hand crept to her shoulder but didn't touch. Her gloved fingers mere inches away from where Mr. Rippi had swung that monstrous log of wood at her, aiming for her head and gettin' Cat's shoulder instead.

She'd fallen and lost more than the use of her left arm. Much more.

The kind of injury, too, that one couldn't see from the outside.

Peter was watching her.

Maybe, maybe he could see it... maybe 'cause, like her, he was livin' in it.

"So," Peter, taking a good, hard look at her shoulder. "This where you got hurt?"

"Yeah. Yeah it is."

"Why'd you come here?"

"It's where the job led me."

"You mean, a job like me."

"Sorta. Only... only the person I came here for wasn't among the living no more. I was trying to find answers, trying to find her what justice I could, even if it'd be only be the truth to those who still cared 'bout her. So yeah, yeah the job brought me here."

Peter turned to Grace's Gardens, taking in that large, sprawling, two-story brick building. Like all the others in Butte, the Gardens weren't free of those black stains, either, the smoke and ash leavin' its mark. Yet somehow, despite all that, the building looked and felt different than all the others... lighter, almost. It was as if the beauty hidden in there was so great not even those brick walls simply could contain it.

She watched Peter and got a sense that he felt it, too—and didn't know what the heck to make of it.

After all, his education on matters of the shadow world had been pretty hard and narrow, and already he was losin' his grasp on that.

Cat saw it.

Saw the discomfort settling into him, the way his shoulders got to pulling back, the tightenin' right there at the corners of his mouth.

There were no sounds slippin' past the Garden's glass windows with them fancy, lacy curtains. No delicate notes being played on the piano and no delicate, ladylike voices, either. Too early for both. More than likely, the whole house was still sleepin' and sleeping hard, considering the hours those girls kept.

Maybe a maid or two would be up.

Hopefully someone sympathetic enough to Cat's cause they'd let her in without the madam being the wiser.

"You find who did it?" Peter asked.

"I did. The guy who did the deed and then another, the one who was profiting from her death."

"Sounds like a right mess."

"It was. Still is."

"Yeah?"

"It was hard, real hard, especially on her brother."

Peter's attention shot back to Cat. "Brother?"

"Yep. He's about your age, give or take."

"He's still around? Another person you're trying to help out? Make a job out 'a, like me?"

And just like that, Cat watched as that anger seemed to come hurtling right through Peter again. It was there, flashin' hard in his eyes, as if the very idea of her helpin' him out, of him being some charity case, was enough to bring it all roaring back again.

My God, was it exhausting, just watchin' him. Just being near him while he went through the whole range of emotions all over again. Were all kids like this? Just boys? Or just maybe when their whole world gone spun upside down and couldn't do a damn thing to stop it?

Cat snorted.

"If you think that," she said, "you've got a whole hell of a lot to learn if you think you're gonna survive out here."

She stepped in front of Peter, making sure she had his full attention. She did.

"Truth is," she said, "it was the other way around. Dusty found me."

"Whatever."

Peter stepped back, getting some space between them, stuffing his hands into his pockets, making one of those bread slices nearly tumble on out.

"And this place," he said, "this was where his sister worked? Should I be surprised you're good friends with someone like that?"

Cat deliberately ignored that last. Barely.

"Norma was her name, and yeah, she worked here. For a time. I never knew her in life; you'd have to ask Mrs. Allen 'bout her."

"And why would Mrs. Allen know—"

"Cause she was a former whore, herself."

There was only so much patience could do for a person. And hell, maybe just being so close to the Gardens and all them lovely feelings were doin' a lively jig through her right then and there, cause Cat was well and done being nice.

Peter's brown eyes, they went wide.

Real wide.

And his anger, it drained away leavin' behind one thin, pale face.

Cat didn't care right then. She was far, far from being done.

She planted her hands on her hips, which caused her left shoulder to pull a bit, but hey, she was mad and it certainly didn't feel too bad right then.

Anger was good for something, after all.

"Yes, Mrs. Allen," Cat said, right good and clear. "The same lady who sat with you all morning, tellin' you tales about her kids and her nephew. The same lady who made that pie you just about devoured and that bread there—yeah, those ones stickin' out of your pockets. She was a whore. Got a past, same as I. But she was also the very madam of this place right here, before she went and sold it."

Peter's mouth dropped open. "But... but..."

"If I were you," Cat said, cold and quiet, "I'd be mighty careful with your words, especially before you go and start judging people. Certainly before you know the whole story."

She took a step closer to him and lowered her head until they were just about eye level.

"After all, ain't that how you and your family got into this situation?"

Peter closed off.

Hard. Fast.

Watched as Peter's anger literally flared right up in him again, like it really were a living, breathing thing, ready and willing to lash out at whoever it come.

She knew this would happen, knew if she pushed it would all come roaring right back up. But she knew, too, that all this was needing to be said. Straight out. Loud and clear, not tipped-toed or danced around.

Peter *needed* to understand.

Even still, wasn't easy to watch. Wasn't easy how her own memories took it upon themselves to bring what Cat had longed to forget. Seein' that same look in Stan, in his narrowed eyes just about every time his gaze landed on Cat—

Cat turned on her heels and walked away.

She wasn't about to give Peter or her memories exactly what they was needin', exactly what they was hopin' for to keep that flaming bonfire alive and going strong.

Not today. Not from her.

Then, she did the next hard thing... she let go of her own anger. Let go of her own frustrations, her own hurt that Peter's words had caused without him understanding one whit of their meaning or significance or just how deep such simple words cut.

Cat faced the Gardens where quite a few of her own fears and difficulties lie and were now stirring and waking up. The place which was very much a living reminder of what she'd lost... and who she might never be again.

After a moment, Peter came up beside her.

She didn't look at him.

Not yet.

"Peter," she said. "Until you learn that not everything in our world is black and white, you ain't gonna survive. My friend, Dusty, he learned. Learned the hard way and it cost him, cost him probably more than you or I or anyone else will know. And for that same reason, he doesn't want to see the same happen to you."

"He told you about me? About my mother?"

"He's the one that put that paper in your mother's hand so she wouldn't be surprised when all her 'friends,' so-called as they were, went and turned on her. Which they did. And you saw it firsthand, just like your own friends did to you."

Cat turned to him then, dropping her hands to her side, hopin' and prayin' that Peter was a smart enough kid to listen and not fall off that edge first chance he got, first moment the truth got to hard to carry.

He didn't, though.

Instead, Peter nodded.

"You think my mother's gonna work here?"

"No, Peter. Not your mother. This is the kinda place, well, it's... nothing at all like you've been told. It's where the real powerful men go, with lots of money and a desperate need to spend it. The girls who work here... the special ones... livin' a life of elegance and beauty. So no, it ain't a place for your mother. She's well into her years, her life hasn't been easy and it shows, bearin' two kids on top of it. No, it ain't a place for her."

"Then why are we here?"

"Cause if I'm gonna do this right, then you've got to see the whole picture. The real pretty parts, and the ugly-as-sin parts."

Peter looked at her a long moment, and she knew why. He couldn't even seem to fathom that there'd be *any* pretty parts... even though... there was that question there in his eyes, as if he still sensed this building *was* different from all the others...

And just couldn't put his finger on why.

Yet, anyway.

"You've heard about any of these parlor houses?" Cat asked. "Any at all? The Dumas? The Windsor?"

He shook his head.

Wonderful.

"Well, let's see if we can't go and change all that."

Cat nodded toward the building with all that nice, red brick and those stairs leading right up to those fancy doors. She walked right up to them, her insides tingling like crazy, her instincts warning her—reminding her—just what the hell had happened last time she was here.

Cat ignored all that and slammed the big, brass knocker hard as she could. Sent the vibrations running through her whole body, her whole being, really.

Part of her wishin' no one would answer and the other part daring anyone not to.

Yet when the door opened with a slight creak and groan of those hinges, Cat wasn't surprised by the person who stood there. That it was Madam Grace herself who answered it.

As if... as if she'd been expecting Cat.

CHAPTER FORTY

Now, Grace's Gardens wasn't the kind of place where the lady of the house, or in this case the madam, went and opened the doors.

My God, the woman had a whole herd of butlers and the like to do such duties for her. Just like she had maids, colored ones all (least to Cat's knowledge) who went and served out the tea and coffee, who made the breakfasts and noon meals and whatever dinnertime feasts their guests were requiring at any given moment.

Yet, there she was.

Madam Grace, the very lady herself.

Grace, who stood there beside that ornate door with them designs of roses and springtime flowers. The hinges protesting a bit, unlike the utter silence Cat remembered from last time, like they hadn't been tended to since that grand ol' dinner party... which turned into a police raid.

Grace remained there, right at the entryway to her kingdom with all kinds of light and beauty slippin' around either side of her. She was as still as a statue, but those eyes of hers, severe and gray, left not one bit to the imagination. Especially when they landed right hard on Cat...

And stayed there.

So much for hopin' she could walk on in and keep her visit a secret from the madam.

Peter climbed up the steps until he stood beside Cat and looked at Grace... which was when his whole mouth just about dropped open.

Cat didn't much blame him.

Regardless of what she'd just told him, trying to prepare him for what he was about to see... when it came to actually seein' a place like the Gardens and makin' that fit into your world view... well, those were two different things entirely.

Far as Cat figured, seeing was believing and all that...

Though she was equally sure this was not a sight Peter had ever expected.

Far, far from it.

Especially a woman like Grace.

See, Grace was the type of woman that could have easily lived right there in his neighborhood, a woman who would have been right at home livin' beside their house or maybe even three doors down. In fact, she coulda been anyone, really. An aging aunt. A mother who'd long since left behind those child-bearing years. Clearly, though, a woman who now toed that line between just past her prime and being well and good put to pasture.

Grace fit the part, the role as it were, just perfectly.

'Specially if you went by the manner of dress she seemed to liken. That deep gray, nearly black, with its strict neckline that just 'bout buttoned all the way up to the chin. A dress that was completely at odds with the style and manner of those other girls boarding in the Gardens and what they were required to wear.

Not Madam Grace, though.

And there wasn't one hint of color about her person, either— unless you went and counted that shining silver hanging off her ears and that fist-sized brooch clasped right on her chest. The brooch which was different than the one she'd worn previously, though no less small—or costly.

Cat watched Peter a moment, could practically see those pieces there falling into their rightful places. Almost like a giant puzzle that was slowly taking shape, and he was seein' the exact shade and tone and colors of the hidden image. An image Peter hadn't expected and one, too, that shocked him silly.

Madam Grace was a matron in her own right, except by name... and profession.

That there was the piece that Peter was finally beginning to understand...

The beautiful, dazzling side of this profession.

Grace, whose entire job was catering to the great men who did business on the hill. Copper Kings and railroad tycoons, businessmen and bankers, princes from far off countries who came to play and enjoy life to its fullest in a place like Butte where there weren't many rules—certainly to a crowd such as theirs. All the while, there was Grace, a woman who insured such men had their needs met and they who, in turn, paid Grace with money and respect.

It was an all around winning situation for Grace and for those girls working under her...

It was a downward spiral into darkness. A trap made of glittering gold and jewels and dazzling lights. A trap you never realized you were in until you found yourself at the very bottom of that dark pit. No way out. No hope at all of climbing back out again.

A lesson Dusty's sister, Norma, had learned firsthand.

"Your mother really never told you about these places, did she?" Cat asked, keeping her voice low and respectful, but not a whisper.

She wanted Grace to hear. Wanted Grace to understand the exact nature of them calling on her.

Peter closed his mouth.

Then after a moment, he shook his head.

"And," Cat said, gently, kindly, "I'm guessin' none of your other friends knew much about them, either. Never talked about it with you. Never saw these great ladies riding about Butte...?"

"I... I... didn't. We didn't. It wasn't the places we usually played."

Damn.

Evie really had done one fine job, her and all those mothers. How *had* they done it? Kids talked. Kids saw the boundaries of their life and purposefully went beyond it. Just like how they spent their days playin' in places like the side hill or mine yards. And, as a matter of course, tinkerin' with whatever it was they found, blasting caps included.

Cat shivered, though she wasn't exactly sure it were from the cold, the conversation, or that gaze of steel Grace was sending Cat's way.

But shiver she did.

There had to be older boys, right? Older boys in the group. *They'd* surely have known. And maybe they had. Maybe they'd just all thought it best not to say anything.

Cat sure didn't know, and wouldn't ever know just by guessing... which wasn't the thing to do now when she had a whole bunch of unpleasantness glaring down at her. Grace's eyes, severe and unforgiving, pretty much demanding an answer of what the hell Cat was doin' here. And while it felt like long minutes had passed, it was only a mater of seconds.

Just a few breaths, really.

It was one of those things Cat did, where time seem to slow as her mind went and noticed all them details, and then went and put them together, one by one.

Least, it used to be.

Now with Grace shifting on her feet and planting one hand on her hip, in a not-so-subtle gesture, Cat wondered if it was another of her gifts she'd lost since her injury. But Grace kept on waiting and glaring for Cat to speak her peace—and then be gone.

Cat took in a deep breath. Might as well get the unpleasantness over with.

"Madam." She tipped her hat to Grace.

"Why Miss Cat," Grace said. "Or today are we going by another name, hmm? Cowboy Cat? No? How about... Miss Justice? Is that more in line with your current profession, your current reason for darkening my doorstep?"

"You know it wasn't me who picked the name."

There was no need to point out which one. They both knew.

"Yet," Grace said, "you wear it. You claim it."

"I try to."

Grace's gaze stayed right on Cat. Not one hint of softness or kindness about her person, nor in her voice or manner...

Though, to be fair, Cat hadn't exactly been expecting any.

To say her relationship with Grace was complicated was a... mild bit of an understatement. After all, Cat had entered the Gardens in a bit of disguise, certainly for her, and had purposefully gone to confront some of Grace's patrons, the big and powerful types.

You know, type who only fools went and kicked.

Well, Cat either was either a fool or just went by some other name entirely, cause she went and did just that. Kicked as hard as she damn well could, and wearing heels and a corset, no less.

But at the end of the day, despite Grace's financial ties to the Nadeau family and that great debt she owed them, Grace *had* helped Cat. She'd gone and warned Cat that one of her girls, Abigail, was missing and so was her client. One of those very men tied up in the death of Dusty's sister, Norma.

Cat and Grace had both understood the danger for Abigail—and that no one other than themselves would give a shit.

So Cat had acted. She'd rushed after Abigail, and Grace had acted as well in her own small way—including when the police finally arrived and Cat was nowhere to be found... though, a freshly dead body down in those cribs *was* found.

Despite how it'd ended, the two women working somewhat together, clearly they weren't about to be friends. Certainly not soon, judging by that growing amount of steel Grace was sending Cat's way.

"I had hoped," Grace said, "that after your last visit I'd made myself quite clear."

Grace's mouth twisted into an even harder line, if that were even possible. "But it seems I hadn't, or perhaps my manner and speech was not clear enough for the likes of you. So I shall say it yet again and with a great deal of clarity so there is no misunderstanding this time."

She leaned in closer to Cat, and all those unpleasant feelings and tension sparked like fireworks between their two persons.

"*You* are not welcome here."

Cat nodded. "I heard you first time around. If I recall, that was also right before your most popular flower went and got herself snatched by one of your very own clients."

"Abigail." Grace's face darkened. Her thin lips tightening. "An event that wouldn't have happened if not for your presence."

"Right. Because he would 'a been a right gentleman otherwise. As if he or any man who comes walkin' in through those doors cares one whit what happens to a whore."

Grace's face just about turned to stone.

It was a crude term and one never used by the girls—or the men— who frequented such a place. Though at the end of the day, regardless of what you called these girls, by this name or some other, didn't change the truth. Not one bit. Those men, including Madam Grace, by the very nature of their transactions, saw and treated them exactly as they were.

Nothing but flesh, beautiful and entertaining as it was, and always for a price.

A butt-ugly truth it was, regardless of how you went and dressed it up some, dazzling and glittering and bright. Truth was truth.

Now it was Cat's turn to lean in.

"No one cares what happens to a whore. Especially one like Norma, who went and tried to better her lot in life. Met the right people. Heard the wrong sorts of secrets about the wrong sorts of people. Found herself in a right foul place, in more than one way. And the end her story? Dead. No one but her brother and some former madam caring. Everyone else? Trying to sweep it all nice and tidy under some rug. For favors."

Cat's gaze narrowed on Grace and didn't look away none, either.

"For money."

From the corner of her eye, Cat watched as Peter's face went pale. So pale the flaking, falling bits of ash looked like black pockmarks on his skin.

And truthfully, Grace didn't look much better, either. She took in a deep breath, swallowin' some emotion that she was trying real hard to keep Cat from seeing...

But failed at it.

Pain, sadness, and something more...

Something very close to regret.

"It is... unfortunate," Grace managed. "What happened with Norma. Unfortunate. But she understood the risks. They all do."

"Not all of them, and that's why I'm here."

Cat gestured to Peter. He came a bit closer and she touched his shoulder. She kept her hand there a moment longer than necessary, as if needing to reassure them both of exactly what the hell they were doin' here and the price willing to pay to see such a place as the Gardens.

Dazzling.

Beautiful.

Deadly, in more than one way.

For Cat, it was takin' all her will, all her control, to not start shaking like a leaf. Standing there, right at the entrance to this house, and all them memories wanting to crawl all over her, pull her back down into those cribs below...

And even Grace herself pulled up those memories, even if she didn't mean to. They were still to new for Cat, too new to be healed, and there was no chance in hell of forgetting them.

Not in this lifetime.

"Look," Cat said, "can we go inside? Talk this over? If not, just send us on our way and we'll be out of your hair."

Grace's brows lifted, nearly touching the handful of curling gray strands that had slipped free of that tight bun.

"And..." she murmured, "you'd never return?"

It wasn't exactly the kind of promise Cat could keep; hell, it wasn't like she'd expected to be standing here, right on the doorsteps of the Gardens, today or anytime soon. Yet, here she was.

And still...

She had that promise to Evie... and to Peter. Like hell did she want him ending up on the streets like Dusty, a master of the shadow world with no real family and no real home, either. While it was all still in her power, she just couldn't let that happen.

"I promise," Cat said. "I'll stay out of your business."

"Unless your business brings you to mine? Like Norma did?"

Cat said nothing.

Grace waved her away. "Oh, don't bother. We both know you couldn't keep such a promise, not doing this... this work you're attempting to do. And, well, I can't rightly say I want you gone, either. You're one of the few people in this town not bought off by some, we'll say, much larger entities."

Cat found herself staring, not bothering to hide one inch of shock.

Grace sniffed. "Don't look so surprised, dear. This is merely a business transaction."

"It is?"

"Of course it is. There may well come a time when I need *your* help and I suspect, now that we've changed the relationship of our association, you will at least hear me out. In such a circumstance, of course."

Why on earth a woman like Grace, a madam and well respected in her own right, would ever need a person like Cat's help—but, for the right reasons, Cat probably would.

"All right," Cat agreed.

"Excellent."

And then Cat got yet another shock of the day. This wasn't at all something she was familiar with. Being surprised. Finding herself caught flat footed and unawares. Proving, once again, that she still wasn't up to her usual abilities. Her ability to see all those details, putting them together, knowing what was going to happen moments before they actually did.

Once again, she'd missed it.

Missed the signs.

Especially as Madam Grace turned to Peter, putting all her focus on that boy who'd just about lost his whole world and family. And there, clear as day, was a softening of Grace's eyes. A warmth and kindness of the kind that Cat had never believed possible from such a cold, calculating woman. A woman who'd *needed* to be to survive in her world and the role she played.

"Peter Blonberg," Grace said. "I've been expecting you."

That's when it hit Cat.

Grace hadn't necessarily been waiting for Cat. She'd been waiting for Peter. Or more importantly, sure she'd known that Cat would bring him here, but Peter... this whole time Peter had been the reason Grace had opened that front door in the first place.

Not Cat.

But, how...?

And then, Cat knew. Saw that one little piece, that tiny detail, she'd missed early.

Of course.

"Dusty," Cat whispered. "Dusty told you we were coming."

CHAPTER FORTY-ONE

Evie had no idea who it was, pounding on her front door.

But Dusty clearly did.

He reacted almost immediately to that first slam of fist on wood. Jumping up from his seat at the table, having his chair clatter behind him same as Evie's had done moments before.

There wasn't one inch of vulnerability shining out of his eyes, not one sign of that lost, hurting boy she'd coaxed into telling... at least part of... his story. That boy was gone. Replaced by the kid who'd learned to survive on the streets and who apparently did quite well at it.

The pounding on her front door was relentless, too.

So hard and fierce that it shook her poor, small home. Dust and ash drifted down from those rafters above until they settled on the table, on the bread left out there in the basket, on her.

All the while she simply stood there, blinking, trying to think, to even understand.

Who...?

Her very first thought, and the terror that followed it, was Lou.

Evie half-turned to the door, feeling her face goin' white, pale as

"

her porcelain kitchen sink. It, it couldn't be Lou. He was gone. Gone. Had no reason to return, not after what he'd done.

But, if he had... and if was fillin' with drink as was his norm—

"Rose," Evie strangled out of her. Fear, clasping so tight it was like she could barely breath but for that sudden, fierce determine to protect her child.

"It's not Lou," Dusty said.

"How..."

He didn't bother answering. Instead, he quickly ducked to the window, slapped on his dark news cap and pulling it so low it nearly covered his eyes. Then he peeked out one of her windows.

"Like I thought," he whispered, "not Lou."

Dusty ducked back so swift and silent not even her curtain stirred. As if hadn't been there to start with.

"Though, I don't rightly know if it'd be better for you if it was."

"Wha—what?"

The shock was wearing off and fast, especially when her bedroom door opened there stood Rose. Rose, still wearing her clothes from yesterday. Rubbing the sleep from her eyes with her chubby hands. Her twin braids falling across her chest, least what strands had remained there instead of slipping free.

"Mama?" Rose asked. "What's going on? Is Papa home?"

Evie's heart twisted hard, real hard.

That was all she had time for. All she had time to feel.

"No, dearest." Evie moved to Dusty, grabbing his shoulder. "Tell me. Now."

"Your friendly neighborhood preacher. Who *else* you'd think be brave enough to go pounding on your door? You, now a known fallen lady?"

If Evie thought she was feeling faint and pale before, that was nothing compared to how she felt now.

"The, the Reverend...?"

She reached up and touched her hair... which was still in complete disarray from the evening before, from sleeping in the clothes she'd gone out in and not bothering to wash up one speck of dust afterward, either.

The pounding didn't stop.

If anything, it increased.

"Evelyn Blonberg!"

Reverend Jacobs called out her name, his booming voice so clear the entire neighborhood surely could hear it. His had been a voice she'd taken such heart in. Listening to his sermons every Sunday, sitting there on those hard, wooden benches with her children pressed on either side of her. Sometimes Lou was there. In more recent times, he hadn't been. And yet, it had been Reverend Jacobs' kind voice and kinder eyes that had given her such strength, the courage to not give in and continue on. As if she worked even harder, did the work that God and his angels had called upon her to do, she could reach Lou, could support her small family in the way they'd needed.

She'd trusted in him, in Reverend Jacobs.

Evie's eyes closed a moment, remembering yesterday evening as her hack had pulled up to their home. She was helping Rose out, who'd been so exhausted she was practically limp in Evie's arms, when the Reverend Jacobs had driven by. Jacobs, who'd leaned out his window, making sure his eyes had met hers...

And the look he'd sent her way...

Evie shuddered.

How could she think, even for a moment, that he *wouldn't* be now pounding on her door? Perhaps, perhaps others wouldn't have done so, reverends and priest from other religions and neighborhoods, but not Jacobs. Jacobs, who'd always been so passionate and filled with such righteous belief against the sins living right beside them, here in Butte...

And her, now.

Living right beside all the rest of them.

"Oh, God." She covered her mouth, as if that could keep the words and her shock from escaping.

Dusty gave her a sad look, one that said simply: I'm sorry.

So was she.

Very sorry, indeed.

The pounding paused long enough for Reverend Jacobs to yell, "I know you're in there, Evelyn. I demand an audience with you."

She wasn't ready for this. Couldn't, couldn't do this...

My God, not as she was.

Her hands fluttered about her, touching her face and then her hair again. The state she was in, the absolute and complete mess. The stains from the smoke and ash, all the wrinkles.

This, this was unacceptable!

And more, she needed every inch of armor she had in her possession to stand there and be the object of his confrontation. His admonishments and the sinful ways he'd surely throw at her like the stones they were meant to be.

Except she had no time and no choice.

He was there, now, right at her front door. And even more important, there was Rose... whose small lips trembled.

What, what was she going to do? There was no possible way she could present herself to someone like the reverend, a pillar of their small neighborhood. He'd probably assume she'd already had some fellow spending the night, already earning her coin and right there in her home, right in their small community.

Her gaze shot to Dusty.

Had he seen Dusty come in? Could Jacobs honestly think that, that she would lay with a boy barely older than her son—?

Dear God.

But then no, it didn't matter what Jacobs believed as truth. Any kind of belief, any kind of statement, whether false or not, was enough. Lou had proved that to her. Had shown her just how clearly her voice did not matter.

All that mattered was the perception of men and what they deemed it to be.

"Evelyn!"

More pounding.

Or perhaps that was merely her heart.

Dusty looked at her, eyebrows rising high to his cap. "Well? What do you wanna do?"

Run away. Hide under the bed. Close her eyes and pretend like it was all just going to go away.

And for some reason, right then and there, Evie's mind took her back to yesterday. Yesterday outside of Peter's school, how all those others like Marybell and Flossie had turned away from her, turned up their noses so hard and fast like the very sight of her was enough to taint their whole house, even them with their bits of hidden shame and secrets who'd dare go and cast judgment on her...

But then Evie remembered the feeling of another's arms around her. Holding her there, stroking her back while she'd let out all those emotions riding through her, sobs that had wracked through her so hard she felt it right to her soul.

Cat.

Cat, who'd not given one inch of judgment or condemnation, but instead truth and comfort. And in that moment, there on Mrs. Allen's couch, Cat had shared a bit of her own strength. Maybe she hadn't known it, maybe she had. But shared it she did—with a woman the likes of Evie, who'd just gone and lost about everything that mattered.

Except... except she hadn't.

"Mama?" Rose's mouth kept on trembling. Her brown eyes so wide with fear.

Evie did not look away from her daughter's eyes.

Strength.

How much strength did she have? And then... what could she do with that strength? What choice or options did she even have?

Not many.

And... with the way Jacobs was pounding on her door, any moment the whole thing would just collapse inward. So, no real choice, not really. The only one left to her was to fall... and fall even further, and it sure was a long, long way down to that bottom of the pit.

But at least she could fall with strength.

Evie went to Rose, tucking a hair behind her little girl's ear before kissing her gently on the forehead. She turned to Dusty. "Take Rose. Go into my room and wait there. If need be, there'll be enough room for you both to slip out the window. Lou never got to fixing it like I'd asked."

Dusty's eyes landed right on hers. Still. Purposeful. Intent. Not one hint of the boy he'd been previously.

"You think it's gonna come to that?" Dusty asked.

"I have no idea and, and I don't care much. All I care about is you, and you keeping her safe. Staying right beside her. Can you do that?"

"I can."

"Good. Good."

Already Evie was moving towards the door, slipping her shawl back on from where it had fallen to the ground. This time, though, it wasn't to ward off the chill. Armor. Pure and simple armor.

Dusty touched her shoulder. "You know what's gonna happen."

"I do."

"I don't have anyone near in case... in case you're needing help."

And Cat, Cat was with Peter.

Evie smiled, a small one, but it was there. "I'll be all right."

"Okay, then. We'll be waiting."

Then Dusty took Rose by the hand and led her into Evie's room, closing the door behind them, though leaving a crack open to better hear. Or maybe see just who was comin' in.

No, Evie would not think of that.

Rose was safe. Peter was safe.

That was all that mattered.

Jacobs kept pounding, but Evie's heart suddenly seemed to grow quieter, more still. It no longer pounded in time his fist on her door. Instead, a cold determination, a steel, made its way through her, and she hoped it was part of that strength she'd seen in Cowboy Cat's gaze, the one when their gazes had met across the schoolhouse yard and then later in Mrs. Allen's. Regardless where it came from, it settled there, right in Evie's spine. She straightened her shoulders, adjusted her shawl, and made her way to that door.

There was nothing for it.

Nothing she could do to stop this, nothing she could do to change this fate. All she could do now was meet it.

So, Evie did...

By opening the door.

CHAPTER FORTY-TWO

O f course, Dusty told me." Grace opened the front door wider to Cat, those hinges creaking and protesting a bit more. A sound that definitely hadn't been there last week.

"I'd daresay," Grace went on, "that Dusty knows you better than you know yourself. Though that doesn't seem hard to do."

"I won't argue with that," Cat mumbled as she followed Grace inside.

While the place hadn't exactly changed since the last time Cat had been there, somehow there was this feeling tugging right there at the back of her senses. A feeling of... different.

Cat stood there wearing her jeans and boots and tilted back her hat so she could get a better view of the place. The crystal chandelier still there, hanging above her. Bright and dazzling, but not nearly as much as last time. Which made sense. After all, there weren't nearly as many lights on, gas light and electric, candles, too, in about every corner of the large receiving hall and all of which had been lit up a point where it seemed every one of those clear crystals came alive with this prism of colors.

Now there was just one or two on, enough to push off some of the shadows and the darkness from the outside... one that seemed to follow right on her heels.

The chandelier and it crystals just... there.

The feeling of different wouldn't leave Cat, either.

Yet even still, there was no denying this place and what it was, it being a threshold into a whole other world, one that Cat herself would never fit in or belong to—nor did she want to.

There were a few couches to the side and elegant sitting chairs with wooden, carved feet of some legendary creature of the oldest, far-off tales. A perfect place to speak with a guest or several, sitting there amongst luxury and beauty. Even the walls said beautiful, as they'd been darned up and decorated with a style of carving that Cat didn't know the name of and didn't much care, either. It was expensive, though, and only the rich bothered with 'em. The rest of the folks in Butte... well, they had a hard enough time getting a single roof over their heads and sturdy walls to keep back that cold, biting wind.

Cat heard a gasping sorta noise behind her, and it took no imagination to know who it was coming from.

Peter, of course.

Peter, still standing there on that brick porch as if his own shoes were stuck right to them. That mouth of his hanging so darn wide she'd have been worried about a fly or two buzzing inside if there were any flies around, as if they could survive the cold or that suffocating smoke.

Cat went back to him, and the kid didn't even acknowledge her presence. His gaze was absolutely fixed on the inside of the Gardens.

"You haven't even seen the ballroom yet."

"Uhh..."

He still didn't look at her.

Cat gave his arm a good tug—then wished like hell she hadn't.

Man, did that hurt.

Didn't matter that she'd used her good arm cause as apparently one side of the body was constantly connected to the other. She got to clenching her teeth good and squinting her eyes shut until that rolling wave of pain finished it course.

To which, no surprise, Grace saw. Those gray eyes of hers, narrowing just slightly, and her mouth pinching even more at the corners.

Of course, Grace saw.

A woman like her, a woman who needed to keep herself on top of this kinda place of business *needed* to be aware. Constantly aware, constantly vigilant. It was probably how she'd known about the trouble Norma was in before Norma herself.

"Your... injury?" Grace asked.

"Yep." There wasn't no reason denying it. "Courtesy of Mr. Rippi."

"Then, it's good he's dead."

Cat tipped her hat up a bit. "That right?"

"Yes. Of course."

Uh-huh. But she didn't bring up those... others who'd had a hand in this business and Norma's death.

Cat turned her attention back to Peter.

"Peter." She gently tugged on his coat, then again when that didn't do the trick.

Finally he seemed to come back to himself, his gaze landing on her.

"Come on," she whispered.

"But this... this..."

So he was fully awake and fully aware of just where they were.

"Yes," Cat said. "This *is* a house of ill repute. The very same place those families and your preachers and church warned you about. Yet it's nothing at all like the kind your mother told you about, is it?"

He shook his head.

"Come on." She nodded towards the door.

"But, but I can't—"

Peter, lookin' real worried, started backing up a step, then another.

Cat reached out and grabbed his coat again before he took one last step—one that would have 'em tumbling right down those stairs.

She ignored that flash and pull of pain. Managed, too, to even swallow the curse that was right there on her lips.

But she was also losin' her patience.

"Seeing as where your mother's 'bout to end up," she said, "I think we can skip this particularly worry. Your reputation's been trodden by a herd of buffalo. If someone were to see you, which they can't in this unrelenting darkness, it's not gonna change a damn thing."

Peter looked at her.

Really, really looked at her.

Those brown eyes of his, wide and fearful, and Cat saw a scared little boy... right along with that knife's edge he was walking.

One wrong move and he'd fall.

God, she hoped she was making the right call.

"Come on," Cat whispered again. Soft and gentle like, she pulled up from some long lost memory where her own ma had done the same once for her, a hell of a long time ago. The kindness, the understanding, the support over tears that Cat hadn't dare shed at the time. Or ever.

"You need the truth. All of it."

It took Dusty another moment, those eyes watching her, before her nodded and the two went inside.

Madam Grace closed the door, the latch clickin' shut. It was something a butler or maid surely would have done—should have done. Except they weren't. It was Grace in all her fine silk of grays and that silver hanging off her like they were some queen's jewelry.

Grace who turned to them both and said:

"Yes. He does need the truth. That's why I'm allowing your presence here. Both of you."

Cat had lost track of how many surprises she'd been handed this morning alone. And maybe if she'd been more herself, this time it wouldn't have knocked her over the head in surprise. But it both did... and didn't.

Dusty had told Grace they were coming. Dusty had guessed this was where Cat would take Peter first. And for whatever reason Cat still didn't understand and had a good feeling she never would, less Grace decided to tell her, Grace had agreed to let them in.

And meet them in person.

Cat could almost see Grace's own ghosts hanging off her. Probably lots of young ladies, some beautiful, some still young but looking ancient, falling close behind her. Grace's ghosts, her regrets and those she'd hurt or let down over the years, the reason she'd opened that door.

Cat could almost see them, though not quite, cause she recognized that look in the other woman's eyes. It was a look Cat had seen in her own eyes whenever she went and looked into a mirror, and her own ghosts, like Alice, who were always right there. Always nearby.

Cat swept off her hat, causin' bits of ash to float to the floor... a floor that had a few smudges of black. Ash maybe, maybe even a stain.

She looked at Grace, her mind thinking, putting it all together.

And while part of her job was guessin' about a person, seeing all them details and putting together a clear picture, she also wasn't trusting in that. At least not fully anymore.

Which meant she had to go and rely on the other half of her skills: directness.

"Why are you doing this?" Cat asked. "Why are you letting us in?"

"I've told you enough. I'm not doing it for you. I'm doing it for him." Grace nodded towards Peter.

"He's just some kid."

"A good enough reason for *you* to help him. Why not me?"

Because, Cat wanted to say, you aren't me.

She didn't need to say it, though. They both knew what she was thinking.

Grace huffed in a very unlady like way, as if Cat's presence were bringing out the worst in her manners.

"My reasons are personal ones. Ones that have nothing at all to do with you, this boy, or his family, so no, I will not reveal them to you. Do you wish your tour of the Gardens or would you rather leave? My girls are still sleeping and I'd prefer to get this over with while they are."

Keeping witnesses to just the one: Grace.

Was that why there were no servants about? Possibly. But then even that didn't feel quite right, didn't quite fit with the woman Cat had met last week, the queen of her domain and all those players on her board, and all her flowers that worked for her, hers and only hers to control.

"We'll take the tour," Cat said. "Then we'll be out of your hair."

"I sincerely doubt that."

Yet despite her obvious distaste for Cat's presence, she waved them to follow her, and they did.

CHAPTER FORTY-THREE

Grace said very little as she led them through the Gardens, opening doors as she led them from one receiving room to another. Each was small and intimate, closed off as it were, except for the windows near the doors. Windows which allowed the clients to move freely, see freely. To examine the wares and decide which might to be to their taste. These rooms, too, Cat noticed, looked as if they could be expanded into a single large room.

She shook her head.

Who on earth needed more than one ballroom was beyond her. One sure seemed plenty.

Grace didn't pause much, simply kept on going, her movements sure and graceful. Her heavy gray dress with all its fine silk swooshing behind her, the delicate little heels of her shoes tapping nice and light on those wooden floors. Cat's boots, of course, made a decided thump-tuck, and there weren't nothin' dainty about it.

Peter's, on the other hand, as worn out as they were, made not one noise. Just silent...

As was the rest of him.

He hadn't mumbled one peep, hadn't made one comment since

following Cat inside except for a kinda choking sound every once in awhile. His eyes gettin' bigger, growin' even rounder with each exhale. He stumbled about in circles, trying to see everything, maybe even trying to see nothing at all after a time. Like maybe his mind was simply shuttin' down and closing up shop.

Truth was, Cat hadn't expected him to say much of anything let alone processin' just what he was seein'...

And how the heck a place like this was, in fact, a house of ill repute.

Cat *knew* what kids like him thought, all those ideas in their heads 'bout the kinda life a fallen woman *should* live and what it *should* be like. In most circumstances, it certainly was true. In fact, the truth was probably a hundred times worse than Peter's own imaginings.

But then the opposite was also true.

The Gardens truly were that other side of the coin. The shiny, sparkling side that those mothers probably went to the greatest lengths to ensure their younglings *didn't* find out about. That perhaps, maybe, this life wasn't so bad after all. All the fine clothes those girls got to wear, the glittering jewels and cascading hair, the hot meals and a person never knowing an inch of cold or hunger... least, not while one worked in the Gardens, anyway.

Good Christian mothers and all, they certainly wouldn't want their girls seein' just how much they could obtain, rising above their family status, reaching higher than anyone thought possible... if, of course, they were darn lucky with that dice roll to begin with.

And if they remained lucky.

Which no one did. Not in the end.

The happiest ending was someone like Mrs. Allen, though even she was certainly the exception rather than rule, seein' as how she kept on living in Butte even with everyone knowin' her... colored reputation. But still, Mrs. Allen had done the nigh impossible, gettin' herself enough money saved and starting over.

New life. New family. The best of all outcomes, really.

Cat tilted back her head, seein' past the brim of her hat, and truly looked at the Gardens. Didn't matter that the rooms were only dimly lit right then, shuttered for the night, or the morning as the case were, one simply couldn't deny the presence in the Gardens.

Or the desire.

No, it certainly wasn't hard to imagine just why those mothers had been so damn afraid.

Just one look at these elegant rooms, dimly lit or not, with them crystals glintin' about the place and those nice upholstered couches and chairs, the silver trays and waiting champagne flutes.

All this, too, was why Cat had needed Peter to see it. And to see it first.

Grace opened the doors to the ballroom, the hinges groanin' just a bit from the effort.

Cat stood there a moment, her good hand gently brushing against the grip of her gun. Not in threat but in reassurance. She'd gone through these very doors herself with Blake on her arm. Or hers on his, dependin' on how one looked at it.

"The ballroom," Grace said, "which I know you're quite familiar with, Cat. Please, be my guest. This time, of course."

Grace waved them inside.

Cat, though, didn't move a moment. Just... just stood there.

She'd known it wouldn't be easy coming here, but knew that what she wanted really didn't matter.

"Of course," Cat said, nodding to Grace. Understood both the kindly gesture... and the warning.

Then she went into the ballroom, to a place she'd secretly been hoping to never step inside again. Peter followed behind her and what he saw... well, this time, it was definitely of the choking sound variety. But seeing as how he wasn't choking, Cat left him to his shock... and focused on keepin' her own self from falling to pieces.

Beauty everywhere you looked.

Fine drapes and curtains. The sleek, black piano resting in a place of prominence in the center of the room, simply sitting there, its keys still, not one note or breath coming from its grand body, as if it, too, were sleeping just like the rest of the house. The piano stood in a place where all eyes would naturally be drawn to it even as men selected their ladies, who hung off their arms in both delight and elegance and just a hint of promise in their eyes.

Really, it was the complete picture of perfection, brilliance, and beauty.

And Cat absolutely hated it.

Hated how her stomach started turning and churning in knots, as if standing there, right smack dab in the middle of that room, was more than enough to trigger a whole wave of memories and feelings—and not a one of them was she interested in dealing with right at that moment.

Or ever.

As if she got that luxury.

She knew better, knew firsthand the price of ignoring something as powerful as what had happened to her here.

Cat let out a breath. Felt herself slowly pull in another one.

Then again. And finally, another. Kept going, kept breathing until she felt herself centering again.

Oh, all those emotions, all them feelings?

They didn't go away none. Nope. They were right there. Right smack in her face, but they weren't controlling her, either.

Mostly cause she wasn't denyin' them.

Cat turned a slow circle where she stood. Her gaze sliding past Peter, past Madam Grace, who was studying Cat with that kinda intensity that told her straight out, this whole allowing Cat inside had been part of *her* plan, of *her* purpose.

As if Cat would have expected anything from less from a mind like Madam Grace's.

So be it.

Cat wasn't about to deny what she was feeling, her uncertainly, her hesitation, wasn't about to deny what had happened here...

Even if both her hands were shaking, even if her shoulder was flaring up all over again like Rippi had gone and taken another swing at her with that big-ass piece of wood he was tottin'.

Smackin' hard and true, and right into her. Though, thankfully, not into her head as he'd first intended.

And it had all started here.

Right here in this ballroom.

Cat could almost see it.

Or maybe, maybe she really did.

It was almost like that night simply sprang up around her. All those people dancing around her in their glittering jewels and fine, glistening silk, yet at the same time, they were like ghosts. Like if Cat reached out with her hand, glove and all, it'd go right through their misty, beautiful forms.

She, in fact, did just that.

Tugged off a glove and reached out with fingers a bit stained from the ash... and passed right on through.

Yes, it was a memory.

Either that, or they really were ghosts.

She'd believe both, in either case.

This time, though, she knew it weren't no ghosts she were seein' but memories. Knew it for a fact because when she looked down at her arm, she didn't see the sleeve of her heavy winter coat no more, but the fine tight-fitted silk of the dress she'd worn that night. And right there, touchin' her just so, gentle and warm and tingling all at the same time, was Blake's hand.

His touch, which had slipped right on through her and carried right down to her toes...

Just as it'd done that night... just as it was happening now.

Not ghosts at all, then.

Just her.

Blake was right there beside her in his own stunning radiance, his blond hair that about lit up the room, and the real gem among all the finery here, especially cause he went and had a conscience that matched it. Somehow even livin' in the kinda world he did.

Grace lightly touched Cat's shoulder.

The uninjured one.

"It's not easy to forget, is it?" she asked.

Cat would have lied. Could have done it.

But then, that simply wasn't who she was.

"I doubt I ever will," Cat answered. "Forget it, I mean."

Grace glanced down at Cat's arm, as if she could see Blake's hand on her. Probably could. She'd seen everything that night, make no mistake.

"No," Grace said, "I don't think you will. I have a feeling you don't forget much. Or forgive?"

Cat shook her head. "Not with myself, anyway."

"You should learn. It would be good for you."

Grace dropped her hand, which was now coated in a bit of dust from Cat's coat.

"Sorry about the mess," Cat said.

Cat slipped off her hat, lettin' her tangled hair fall loose around her shoulders, gettin' in the way as usual. Ash motes and dust motes and probably other bits carried in the air all thanks to those nearby smelters, drifted from her hair to the ground.

Laying there, just so, darkening the usually pristine, polished floors.

Except... not completely.

"At least... I think I'm sorry."

The floors here weren't as polished as they'd been that night, didn't gleam with her reflection as they should have. This, combined with the groaning doors that hadn't been tended to and probably needed constant tending, thanks to all the ash and smoke, and the lack of servants... maids... butler to open the door...

Cat turned to Grace, her eyebrows lifting in question. "Difficult times?"

A shadow of a smile crept onto Grace's face, before it was shooed away again.

"I have you to thank for that. Business has not been as... brisk as usual. My patrons are... unsure of me these days."

Which was a code for a hell of a big mess.

Grace, Cat knew, was an independent owner, but one who'd gone into a great deal of debt to the Nadeaus no less—which was why she'd even let them dictate their desires when they'd originally wanted Norma gone and out of the house for trying to blackmail one of their associates. See? Right mess. And Cat's finding herself a murderer here, and a close personal friend of Marcus Daly, one of the ruling Copper Kings... well, it sure made these things get tricky. And then there being a police raid on top of all that.

Cat winced.

She hadn't cared for Grace in the slightest, but then the woman had shown an inch of compassion and concern that night with Abigail and again now with Peter. So, just maybe her own feelings were starting to shift.

A little, anyway.

"Sorry about that," Cat said, more firmly this time.

"Don't be. It's a problem of my own making and my own poor decisions. You simply happened to speed it up a bit..." Grace tucked a strand of hair behind her ear. "You found the truth about Norma. I never did like that business with her and how it all ended."

It seemed as close as they were going to get with a handshake, so Cat let all her other feelings fall into the past where they belonged. She wasn't here for Norma, anyway. She was here for Evie and the promise Cat had made to her.

"Peter?" Cat called out.

He turned to her, blinking with those brown eyes of his, and it took a few moments before he actually seemed to *see* her and not the magnificence of a place like that.

"I don't... I don't understand," he said. "This place, you're saying it's a place where..."

But Grace saved Cat from answering.

"Where girls prostitutes themselves for money and trinkets and a better chance at life. You're here, Peter, cause she thinks you need to know the truth."

Grace tilted her head towards Cat.

"The beauty in my world," Grace went on, "and the darkness it hides. An honest-to-God darkness, and I'm telling you now, if I found out from anyone, from any other parlor house or brothel that you went and took one step inside after this, by Lord, you *will* hear it from me."

Grace drifted both hands to her hips and settled them there, all civilized-like despite the fire and no nonsense in her voice. The fabric of her dress didn't even stir at the movement thanks to the cinched-up corset she wore.

Death contraption, Cat called it.

"So, now that we've this matter out of the way..."

Grace waved away her little outburst and instead went and told him all about her girls, the kinds who worked for her and the kinds of men who visited. Grace was... kind in her words. Nothing vulgar or untoward, but at the same time neither her tone nor her words hid the truth from him, either. Peter, though, didn't seem to have a clue what to say next, if the shock on his face was any indication.

But then, Grace seemed to be on a roll cause apparently she wasn't about to let him off so easily.

"Let's continue, shall we? You promised to show him everything, Cat, so I think the next order of business is the place where all women—where they *all* eventually go—certainly if they don't pull themselves out of this business."

Peter came to Cat's side, his hand just brushing against hers, as if he were thinkin' of holding on.

For a moment, anyway.

Then it passed.

"What's she talkin' about?" he asked.

It was Grace who answered before Cat could:

"Why, the darkness, Peter. The darkness."

CHAPTER FORTY-FOUR

How dare you bring this darkness amongst us!"

The Reverend Jacobs stood there on Evie's small, creaking porch. The wood which was already splintering and pulling away from the few nails that managed to hold it together. Ones she'd nailed in herself after gettin' tired of asking Lou to take care of it. She'd been concerned the children would trip during one of their many mad dashes out the front to play with friends, going off to places Peter thought secret from her but were, in fact, not secrets at all.

Couldn't be, because as a child herself, she'd played in places just like them. Sometimes, even, the exact same one.

Yet with Jacobs standing there before her—towering, really—with his head a good two feet over hers, she felt so removed from that childhood, so far from the joy and the play she'd grown up with. Somehow they'd always had joy even when her family had so very little everywhere else. Food. Money. Clothing that wasn't falling off them in just about every spot. Still, there was joy. And now here was Jacobs, right determined to steal that joy from her children and their future.

Evie was under no illusion, absolutely none, that this wasn't his purpose here.

Including all those other people who'd gathered to watch, to witness. Those who she'd once called friends and neighbors, who even now flipped back their curtains to peer out at Evie and the confrontation on her front porch. Then there were those who simply came outside to watch. Plenty of men, least those not at work or sleepin' after working the evening shift. Most of... most of Lou's former crew, the ones he'd worked the Spectacular with, she was thankful to see, were absent. At work, most likely, though there were wives and mothers and relatives aplenty to make up for it. Everyone and anyone, really, opening up their doors and stepping outside. It hurt so much, seein' all those folk. Especially Marybell. Marybell, who Evie had once considered a friend, who Evie never spoke with about the thinning faces and stomachs of her children, the dulling light in their eyes, yet Marybell had gone and stood there on her own porch, holding onto that door like Evie herself was the one on trial right now and she was watching, witnessing, with her two young ones holding onto her skirts like they were about to get swept up and away from her at any moment.

It hurt, though, hurt something fierce... even more so when Marybell's boy, Buster, came out. Or Bugsy, as Peter likened to call him... and Peter's closest friend.

They'd not gone out to school yet, all these kids, all these who'd been Peter's friends. It must have been early, then, earlier than she'd first thought when she'd heard Dusty pounding on her door.

It felt like their old life, the whole of their old life, had come out to see her humiliation.

Oh, the shame was feeling so great now.

Tears swelled in Evie's eyes when that hard, angry gaze of the boy landed right on her, as if he were blaming her for everything that had happened—maybe even something more—for the loss of his friend, for the safe haven her home had been for more, for all those unspeakable somethings he lived with, carried close to his heart.

But in this moment, he had someone to blame:

Evie.

Everyone was watching now. From Marybell and Bugsy, to Flossie with her aging face and those even harder eyes. But there was a bit of triumph there, too, as if Flossie been purposefully waiting for this moment. Perhaps she had. They'd never been good friends, though Evie had always thought it was simply them being different, or maybe... maybe just too similar to each other. Evie didn't know a whole lot about Flossie's husband, Joe, except that Lou never had a kind word to say about the man.

It was all part of that mining world and fellowship, and she just didn't know a whole lot about it because Lou had purposefully kept her from it. She didn't even know exactly what jobs he'd gone and done—at least, when he had been working. And back then? Back when Lou and Joe and Harold, Marybell's husband, had all worked together at the Spectacular, working the same shift, working the same crew, that was all she knew. The men didn't talk about it and none of the ladies, least around Evie, had ever asked.

All Evie knew was that Lou had blamed Joe for him getting fired at the Spectacular. Never said how nor why, just that it was Joe who'd gone and cost him his job. And yet... curiously enough... it was Harold who Lou hated.

He'd never given Evie an honest answer why, just said that Harold had backed Joe up and never once had Lou gone and changed his story about it, either. Even when he was drinking. Well, during those times he usually did a whole lot more swearing and fuming, but the story—and just those few bits he bothered to share—didn't change. Lou blamed Flossie's husband, Joe, but Lou *hated* Harold.

And maybe that was part of the reason why Marybell had pulled away from Evie, why she stopped inviting them over. Or perhaps... perhaps Evie was wrong about that, too.

Why not?

She'd been wrong about so much already.

Still, it was strange seeing all her neighbors gathering around her small home. Falling apart in too many places and run down in all those others. Yet there they were. There to pass judgment and hatred all because it was happening to her and not to them.

Evie's grip tightened on the door knob, holding it half open behind her. Wanting to close it, to keep Rose safe, but not wanting to stand there with her back against the wall to this... this crowd. Everyone here who was gathering to hear this sermon that Reverend Jacobs would now make, listing out in perfect detail and clarity of the sins and downfall of Evie Blonberg...

And with her little Rose huddling inside.

None of them cared, either. Evie felt it, make no mistake. There, too, was this look in Jacobs's eye, one that told her straight he didn't care one bit about her children, as if he knew for a fact that Rose *was* there and didn't care one bit.

But... what was worse... Evie had this feeling, right there in her gut, that told her he was in fact *hoping* Rose was there. Hoping to hurt her, too. Her and Peter.

Evie closed the front door with hard, definitive slam.

Whatever Jacobs was wanting to say, he wouldn't be saying it to her innocent daughter. Except then her fingers gripped her shawl, and it was like that silly thing was all the reminder she needed of how just how badly she'd failed.

In her roll as wife.

As a mother.

The very shawl her nana had made for her wedding day, ill-fated that it'd apparently been, except Evie was suddenly feeling unsure of herself... hesitant... weak. She tried to find the steel she'd had moments before, but it was like suddenly she was reaching and all she touched was flowing water, droplets that fell away and were simply gone.

Maybe she really was the woman Lou believed her to be. All those unkind, unfaithful words.

She didn't have the strength.

Not for this.

Not for the condemnation by her entire neighborhood. Not with Rose in the bedroom hiding with Dusty. Not with Peter out there somewhere with a woman... a former prostitute and God knows what else and...

Evie shivered. Tried her very best to force her whole body to not tremble, as it so wanted to do, and yet her will was also like that water and she could do nothing to stop it.

Certainly with Jacobs standing before her, giant in both his height and more importantly, his presence. Jacobs wore his usual black. Black shirt and pants, only slightly stained about the knees and the cuffs of his pants. Even though he had no wife of his own, the community always seemed to provide with more than enough. Enough to pay the Chinese for their laundry services and for necessary mending. Always clean. Always presentable. Always a figure who drew the eye and held it.

As he did so right then.

Even with his cheeks flaming red, there was simply no denying the man.

Nor the look he gave her.

Punishment and joy, all seemingly mixed together towards some cruel delight of his own. It was a kind of look she'd never seen on Jacobs before, not once during his sermons or when he touched Evie's hands in thanks as they left the church to have their Sunday meal at home, askin' as he always did how Lou was doin' and passing on his complete belief that Lou really would change his ways if she were only patient enough...

A memory tickled the back of her mind.

That she was wrong...

That just maybe... she *had* seen that look on him before.

But it was hard to think, to focus—certainly when she stood there, right there on display for everyone and the sight she appeared, as well. Her dress from the night before, wrinkles from top to bottom. The soot and ash stains as well, not to mention the absolute mess her hair was now in. And no one, certainly not one person here, missed any of those details, their outright shock at her current state and dress...

Just like she didn't miss the whispers that followed.

Though such sounds could only be called 'whispers' if one were feeling generous, which she was surely not.

Despite all that, Evie's mind kept tugging on her, kept trying to tell her something.

It was still there, too, that gleam in Jacob's eyes. That familiar pull of his lips in a cruel, unforgiving smile.

She *had* seen it before. But where? When?

Still her mind, her memories, they kept on persisting—even as those whispers got louder, even as Jacobs stomped his feet and puffed up his chest like some great bull ready to charge... Bit by bit, she remembered. Remembered back to that night... and yes, yes it'd been night. She remembered because she hadn't been feeling so well. Food poisoning, she'd thought, though you'd never get her to admit such a thing, that her own cooking had caused her own upset. Regardless of the reason, she had been in bed, unable to sleep, unable to find some measure of comfort, when there'd been some knocking on the front door.

A knocking that continued, except this time, for once, Evie hadn't answered it...

Instead, Lou had.

And it'd been Reverend Jacobs who'd done the knocking.

"Thank you, my child," Jacobs said now, pulling her back to the present. "Thank you for doing the right thing. For opening the door and facing your judgment."

Except there was nothing thankful or kind in the way he looked at her, this fire in his eyes that burned hot and mean... and yes, there was no doubt about it. That was the very same looked he'd worn that night when Lou had opened the front door. And Evie, sick as she was, she'd forgotten Lou was even home. Even back then, back when he was still working at the Spectacular, she was getting used to him being gone all hours of the day, so before her mind even caught up with her, she was up and stumbling out of their bedroom, ready to answer that door. It wasn't until she was halfway out of the room before she registered that latch clicking open and then there, there was Jacobs. She couldn't see a whole lot, standing in the doorway as she'd been, or holding onto it more like. But it'd been enough for her to glimpse Lou and Jacobs in that flickering candlelight he held. And there was Jacobs... his face lookin' more like he was a livin' shadow than an actual man. Except for the fire lighting in his gaze... and a hard, cruel gleam that didn't once leave Lou's face.

Jacobs's presence, both then and now, was so strong Evie found herself backing up a step and then another.

She knew the look.

Knew it from living with Lou, especially when he got to drinkin'. A look that said she was nothing more than his by right. His property, ready to do with it as he willed. Not a human being with feelings and fears and joys all her own.

And yet, with Jacobs, it felt like there was something more.

"Evelyn?" Jacobs asked, using his forgiving, father like voice. "Is... is something wrong?"

A slight tick upwards of his lips. As if... as if he was aware of what she was thinking, feeling. As if... maybe... he'd even been aware of her that night.

Evie didn't dare let go of her shawl. Didn't dare even speak for surely her pounding heart wouldn't let a single breath out or word out.

"Something on your mind, Evelyn?"

Yes.

That night... that night Lou had changed. She thought back, hard as she could, trying to remember when... when it'd exactly happened. It'd been... been right after some accident at the Spectacular. No one talked much about it, just that there'd been some accident and no one had gotten hurt too badly. But then... then Lou had lost his job. He'd blamed Joe for it and hated Harold. After that the pattern it just continued. Lou'd get a job, then he'd lose it. Didn't matter if he ever went in with a smile on his face or even some semblance of joy, though both truthfully were rare occurrences, but always, always, he'd come home furious and railing how none of it was his fault.

Almost like that bad luck had kept on following after him.

And she sure felt that bad luck right then. Real strong, like it was wantin' only to suck her down with it and... and my lord, it'd be so easy to let it. To just accept her place in this world and just be that woman now.

Except then... as if from nowhere... came a comforting presence.

A reminder.

A better memory, in fact.

A pressure on her shoulders. Of arms holding her. Stroking her back as she'd wept. Cowboy Cat. She'd shown nothing but kindness and understanding to Evie as the other woman had held her on that couch while Evie went and did all that crying.

Strength.

That's what Cat had said.

Evie... Evie had *strength*.

Evie took in a deep breath. Felt her chin arch up ever so slightly. Thinking, thinking hard. Putting some of those small pieces together like. Lou and his drinking, the anger he'd always had, simmering right under the surface. How had she missed seeing it? Or, more truthfully, stopped believing in it?

Now... now there was Jacobs and all his cruelty, hiding right there in plain sight. How had they *all* missed seeing the signs, the truth of his character? How could she ever have thought of him as a holy man? How could she ever have trusted in his counsel and wise words?

And right behind those questions came another. One that nearly stole her breath.

Could... could Jacobs somehow be behind Lou losing his job? Or, or could he even have been the reason Lou had finally up and left her and their children behind?

Except she didn't know the answer to that. Didn't know if Jacobs had been to see Lou more recently. She was always so busy, picking up a job as a cook or a cleaner, when she wasn't busy mending clothes and caring for Rose and Peter. There could have been any number of times and places when Jacobs could have approached Lou without her ever being aware. Perhaps it'd happened many times and she'd gotten lucky enough to see... to see whatever it was she'd seen.

No.

Evie halted all those thoughts. Fast. She would not think on this, would not dwell on it.

The reason her family had ended up on this path simply didn't matter.

Rose and Peter, they were all that mattered to her. And besides, Lou had created his own mistakes and he would live with them and the consequences of them.

Maybe not today. Maybe not ever. But they were *his.*

"Evelyn?" Jacobs asked again, bring her fully and clearly back to the present.

No more thoughts. No more dwelling in a past that couldn't be changed.

"Have you nothing to say to me, to all of us?" He spread his hands out wide to include everyone who'd gathered. "Some apology or promise? Some willingness to atone for your sins?"

He lowered his hands, slow like, like he was some great magician in the center of a stage. That smile of his stayed right there on his lips. Cruel and very, very aware.

The truth was, Evie had been deceived by Jacobs just as she'd been by Lou, and what was worse, no one else saw any of this. Couldn't, really, not with Jacobs facing her and he having his back to them.

As if it would matter.

As if the equally cruel glares from her fellow neighbors and former friends would even see anything more than her receiving what she'd rightly deserved.

The thought, and her strength, fluttered away from her as Jacobs stepped closer to her.

The stomp of his foot so hard and loud... she watched as the wood there bent. The nails there pulling in place. Bending. Ready to snap. To break. As if he wanted to do the same to her. Shove her inside where no one else could see. Say what he wanted. Do whatever it was he wanted.

A shudder ripped through her. With that look in his eyes, that hard, hard gleam, she'd put nothing past him.

"We are waiting," he said, quietly. Only for her ears. "But we won't be waiting long. I'd advise... against that."

Fear took over. How could it not? How, when she'd been trained so well by Lou, had practiced the art of hiding and ignoring and cowering?

Evie backed up a step.

Then another.

Couldn't help herself. Couldn't help that desperate need in her chest to survive, to bow down, even, to allow him to give his sermon and judgment while all the rest would learn from her suffering, even if he demanded other favors, other—

She stopped those thoughts. Didn't dare to look at them closely— and couldn't dare *not* to.

Evie could almost feel Rose nearby. As if... maybe she had an eye peeking out from that door crack. Watching her mother. Learning. And what would she learn? What would *Rose* take away from what happened here?

Her hands tightened hard on her shawl.

And she felt Cat's presence again.

Cat... as she'd reached across that table at Mrs. Allen's. Touching her hand so gently the same moment as Evie felt her whole self crumbling into a thousand different pieces and shards.

"You do," Cat had said. *"You do have strength."*

Evie breathed in, lifted her chin, and then took another step forward and reclaimed her spot on the porch. She would not allow him to push her inside where others wouldn't see what happened here. Because in this moment she knew, without a doubt, this was the one power she had:

To be seen.

For this moment and perhaps only for this moment, she *would* be seen. And she would be strong.

"Is there something I can do for you, Reverend Jacobs? Or are you intent on waking entire households with your yelling?"

CHAPTER FORTY-FIVE

Jacobs took a step back, then another, at Evie's words. At her very clear daring.

His eyes widened, too. Not a whole lot, mind you, but there nonetheless.

Pure and simple shock.

Evie's attention shot to all those out on the street who were watching this exchange between her and Jacobs, and saw a similar reaction. That somehow, even with all that smoke and ash, they seemed to see just fine, right then. But what mattered was they weren't ignoring her anymore. They weren't acting as if she didn't exist as they'd done yesterday. As they would do tomorrow and the day after until they'd finally succeeded in driving her out of this little cozy neighborhood—which they surely would given enough time— forcing her from a place she'd once thought of as home...

Which was the exact point of why Reverend Jacobs had come here.

Hadn't Dusty said it himself? Who else would dare come pounding on the door of a known fallen woman? Who else would dare take up the mantle and toss out the unwelcome and fallen now living among them?

Well, there she had it.

Standing right in front of her, tall and imposing, acting as he if were, indeed, the word of God. And also, the one person who'd want to make an example of her and keep the rest of them in line.

Jacobs recovered easy enough, clearly having had practice deceiving others even while he stood before them.

"I come to you because the community demands it," he said. "Can't you see for yourself?"

He lifted his arms, indicating all those around them, all the others out there, seeing exactly what Evie herself was seeing. The whole neighborhood had indeed shown up to stand against her. Standing in collective union and agreement that she did not belong. That she was not welcome here and she must go... and go *now*.

It was like Evie could see Jacobs eyeing the odds, adding up the individuals and the precise level of power he held so very, very high above her and there wasn't a thing she could do to stop it. There was a slight tick upwards of his lips.

A grin.

"Can't you see?" he asked again. "I can. God can."

He was pleased with the turnout and now, now as he turned back to her, that grin turned right cruel again, as if saying now, now was the time to begin his lesson and she, the object of that lesson.

Of course, no one else noticed this. No one else saw.

Not that they'd care anyway.

"I come here," Jacobs bellowed in that deep, sermon voice of his, "because our community demands justice and repentance. So I ask you again, Evelyn Blonberg: How dare you bring such darkness amongst us? Amongst these good families here. Good men. Good wives who know their place and follow in the manner God himself demanded of us. Good boys and girls. How *dare* you live amongst us and in doing so, try to subvert and taint such good and honest families with your dark one."

The way he spoke, it was like he was laying down all the sins of the world right at her feet. A blame placed on her and only her.

He smiled again at her, kindly like the man she'd known and believed in.

"Simply accept your fate," he said quietly. "It will... go easier on you. And your children."

He absolutely believed it. Believed that all this was her fault. Or enough of her fault to make this all convenient for him, that she rightly deserved to be blamed for everything he wished to name as hers. Probably even for the air being dark and smoky and stealing many lives who struggled in such conditions.

And yet... and yet, she also found herself straightening.

Because there was that smile. And there was him trying to manipulate her, and whatever his purpose or desire was, Evie did not know. Nor did she care, really. Her mind and heart were full to overflowing with fear and love for herself and her children; she simply had no space leftover for this. Perhaps she could tell Dusty her thoughts after this, maybe even Cat... if she survived this moment. If she was allowed to walk back into her home and quietly close the door.

Which she doubted.

Doubted very much.

All she could do now was focus on surviving. On helping her children survive what was coming next in their lives, and this *would* demand everything she and they could give.

What Evie did know, right at this moment, was that they had an audience.

Exactly as Jacobs had planned.

Exactly as he'd wanted.

Yes... yes that had been his intent. She felt it like a bell ringing clear off some narrowed, rocky walls of a mine. Perhaps this had always been his intent, that destroying her and her family, for whatever reason, had been the desired goal from the start. Maybe even some vendetta against Lou, some slight between men.

She didn't know, and as much as it burned in her blood, she didn't have the capacity in her to care.

Couldn't.

Because as it was, she was trapped.

Trapped in this cage shaped for a woman alone with her two dependent children. Evie knew, without a doubt, that nothing at all she said or did here would change her fate—but that didn't mean she couldn't face it. That she couldn't fight for herself, for her children.

And she knew, too, she wasn't alone... even as she stood here. Alone.

Strength.

Evie pulled her shoulders back. Lifted her head higher.

She was not simply going to stand there and cower as he ranted and raved at her. She wouldn't be that woman anymore, the one who'd have done just that in the past, back when Lou was gettin' into his cups and his anger was slippin' free of him, controlling whatever parts of him it would and damn the consequences.

To hell with fate.

She would take hers back, much as she could, anyway. And she *would* protect her children from the likes of men like this.

Evie took yet another step forward. Gripped her nana's shawl so hard her knuckles turned white. She tilted up her chin, staring up at that brute of a man above her, and glared right back at him.

"How dare *you* insinuate that I am the unfaithful one when you know, quite well, who was to blame."

For the second time, and for the briefest moment, Jacob's eyes widened. Then narrowed.

A warning.

"Your husband—"

"Was a drunk. He was a terror and an angry force to be reckoned with, one that you and everyone else here knew about and did nothing. Did nothing to speak with him. Did nothing to come to my aid when you all heard, right clearly, what was happening in my house. You knew he could *not* be controlled when he did drink. Which was often. Which the Spectacular Mine knew of. Which his whole crew knew of. And which, I say again—"

Evie flung her arms out wide, encompassing all those who were there. "Each and every one of you *knew* about. And did nothing."

She lowered her arms and looked right at Jacobs. "And so did the entire city of Butte. And yet, the city and each one of you, conveniently forgets his character for what he *dared* to write about me and my character. Lies, every single one, and you do not care."

"You are his wife. It falls to you to keep your husband from sin. All his misdeeds and mistakes."

Of course, it did.

Which had always been the heart of those little chats she and Reverend Jacobs had shared. He always encouraging her to show her husband the path to goodness, the path to God and forgiveness and all the rest of that bullshit. As if it were *her* job to care for a grown man.

No more.

Evie slapped her hands on her hips. Every inch of frustration she'd felt since Dusty had handed her that classified suddenly came out right then in one big, rushing wave. It would not be contained. She and *her* truth weren't to be contained.

Even if not a one of them believed her.

"Says the man with no wife to guide him," Evie said, "but claims to be doing just fine on his own. Or is that even true?"

To say there were few gasps from the growing crowd—and yes, it was growing—was a bit of an understatement.

But she *did* remember that night when Jacobs and Lou had stood arguing on her front porch. All of that cold and manipulation, it'd burned so damn bright in Jacobs's eyes Evie hadn't needed a candle to see. And for whatever reason or purpose that had, once again, brought him to her doorstep and stirring up trouble, shaming her, blaming her—

"Why?" Evie whispered.

For this one moment, this one breath, she forgot what truly mattered. Seeing to her children, protecting her family. Instead, right then, right with that one word, was this burning need for the truth.

Why *had* Jacobs set out to destroy her family?

Cat descended down into the darkness that was the underbelly of Grace's Gardens.

Every stomp of her boots on those sagging, creaking stairs taking her further from all that beauty and elegance of upstairs. Each step makin' her stomach twist.

Another step, then another.

The twisting growing worse. Unbearable, even.

Dust and dirt kicked up as that wood groaned and shifted underneath her weight. Each step taking her down, deeper and deeper, to the one place she'd hoped never to go again.

Her shoulder burned, too, though she couldn't quite tell if did so in sympathy or memory, and she didn't much care either way.

It was hurtin' like hell and that was all that mattered.

It took everything she had to not stop right there and touch that spot on her shoulder. She could almost feel that moment, that slow pause in time as Mr. Rippi had stepped out from behind the staircase and the shadows there, swinging that heavy butt of wood. The wood which had almost whistled in the muffled silence a half-breath before it connected with bone. Breaking, shattering, fracturing. And then there was Cat, flyin' across that ground, doin' everything possible to avoid the fatal blow he'd intended.

Peter paused on the steps behind her.

The steps shifted and groaned underneath them both, pullin' Cat back to the present, though that was mostly cause she wasn't sure if the wood was gonna split open right then and there, dumping their behinds smack down hard at the bottom of the underbelly.

The steps groaned for another second, then quieted.

"Cat?" Peter whispered.

It wasn't until that moment that Cat realized she *had*, in fact, stopped moving and that she was indeed touching her shoulder. She glanced over her shoulder but couldn't see much of Peter in that dim light. There weren't no lanterns or candles or light bulbs lightin' the way, though there was still enough light from the upstairs for her to catch an outline of him. The shape and form of his hair, which was juttin' out in every which way.

There was no Grace, of course.

Not that Cat had expected her to wait for them, and she certainly hadn't expected Grace to follow them down, either.

All Grace had done was show them to the stairs before bowing her head, all grace and regal like, and saying in that delicate little voice of hers: "If you will excuse me, I have some other important duties to attend. And well, Cat, you know your way around, of course."

Cat had nodded, understanding perfectly. Though Peter, of course, hadn't.

"But," he said, "I thought you said you'd show me—"

"I know what my cribs look like," Grace had said, cutting him off. "I have no need or desire to visit them. You may do so and take as long as you'd like, though why you'd need much time is beyond me. Still, a promise is a promise, and Cat is more than capable of seeing to the rest of your... education."

Grace waved her little gloved hand, dismissing Peter, before turning once more to Cat. "And then you *will* be going on about your business, yes?"

Cat ignored her.

Instead, she gently touched Peter's shoulder. "What Grace means is—she doesn't need the reminder."

"Reminder?" Peter asked.

"About the girls who live there. The conditions they live in. What you don't see, what you don't know, means you can't be held account- able for it. At least, that's been my experiences with madams, though there were more than a few who *did* enjoy seeing such misery."

Grace straightened, clearly taking offense.

Cat didn't give a shit.

"I run a business, Miss Cat."

"Yes. I'm quite aware, and after this, Peter will be, too."

Cat didn't fault Grace nor did she hold her accountable. Not really. It was a business, after all. The flesh trade. One involving people and deplorable conditions because there was simply a need that needed to be met, and the other half of that business were all those who'd simply looked the other way. Peter may not know it, but he and his family, certainly his mother, had been involved in this business long before Lou had written that classified and published it for all of Butte to see.

Cat, though, didn't to explain any of this to Grace. Nor did Grace defend herself.

One thing was for sure—she and Cat weren't about to be good friends any time soon. Certainly if she went by that look Grace was givin' her right then.

No matter.

Cat had slipped her hat back on just then, touched the brim, bidding Grace farewell.

She was just fine with them not being friends. Just fine.

But before Cat could go on about her business, heading down into that darkness that was the underbelly, the place that was already makin' her insides tingle and twist, Grace had touched Cat's coat.

"Come see me when you're finished," Grace had said. "There's another... matter I'd like to discuss with you. Business, if you will."

Cat said nothing and turned to go again, but Grace held onto her coat. And believe it or not, there was a bit of strength in her grip.

"You made a promise, remember," Grace had said.

"I remember."

She did.

Just didn't plan on fulfilling any more promises that day. Not when her whole body was stiff and sore from all the activities she'd gone and done the past two days, when she really should have been back at home and healing... just like the good doc kept on reminding her about. And just like he was most likely gonna remind her when he finally came round to the house again and if she were finally, actually, home.

Cat shrugged.

Or a little shrug, anyway, seeing as how her shoulder was startin' to throb and a new pain was blooming there, one she felt all the way to her teeth, no kidding. But it was apparently enough for Grace cause she finally went and let Cat go, and then she and Peter crept down into that darkness. The place where Cat now stood, totally stopped, because of all them memories of being here last time, of the pain that seemed to hum right underneath her skin until it felt like there was a fire dancing right across the top of her grave.

She shook her head.

She'd no time for this. Not now, anyway. There'd be time later to dwell on it, to... remember it all. But not now. Not when Peter was relying on her. Not when Evie was relying on her to bring her son home.

Cat dropped her arm and kept moving.

She'd made a promise... to Evie, to Peter, to Dusty... and she *would* deliver.

Despite, despite what it was gonna cost her.

Even now she was feeling the ghosts from her own past closing tight round her. Almost as if they sensed her growing weakness, her growing... vulnerability. She did her best to put them all out of her mind, to focus instead of the details of this place, but her mind just wasn't interested in workin' in the way it usually did.

Maybe this here was her answer.

Maybe she'd finally know beyond a shadow of a doubt—least when she went and finished this one last promise—that she wasn't cut out for this kinda life. That she didn't have what it took to seek out justice, helpin' out those who needed it, those who no one else cared about. That maybe she *should* just hang up her gun and go find some place quiet where she could have a horse or two and let the rest of the world blow on by her. Let all the darkness and injustice, let all those who no one else cared about, suffer in silence until they became the silence themselves.

Except... of course, there was that promise she'd just gone and given to Madam Grace.

Damn it.

"Cat?" Peter said again.

"Yeah?"

"Was... was everythin' Grace was sayin' up there, was it all true?"

"Yeah."

"She didn't lie?"

"She got no reason to."

"And... and my mom?" His voice cracked on that last bit.

"What about her?"

"If, if she can't go to a place like the Gardens, does that... does that mean this place, down here, is where she's gonna end up?"

Cat could have lied.

Could have said any number of things, any number of promises, but then lying wasn't something she did... even if it would have made this moment easier for them both. Even if it would have made gettin' him back to his mother that much easier. But it just wasn't about this one moment here. It was about preparing him for what all was to come and that meant lookin' close at some hard, dark truths. The only way Peter was gonna survive was goin' forward with both eyes wide, wide open.

So Cat didn't lie.

Instead, she told the truth.

Least as much as she could, anyway.

"I don't know, Peter. Don't know the future and don't rightly want to know, myself. Maybe the place we find for your mother, callin' in favors as Mrs. Allen and I are doing, will mean she'll have a pretty good place to start. Maybe she'll last some time there, too. Maybe she saves enough to move you all away from Butte where no one knows her name or her reputation. Or maybe she doesn't. Maybe she grows old and her madam doesn't like girls who are lookin' their age and forces her to move on. Find another place. One that's not so nice and doesn't pay as well."

Even to Cat, her words sounded harsh and unyielding, but then... she just kept on going, least as much as she dared go.

Peter was a smart kid, his imagination would fill in the holes she, herself, wasn't brave enough to say aloud.

She was grateful for the darkness right then. Grateful that she couldn't see Peter. Couldn't see that look in his eyes when she went and took his hopes and dreams, whichever ones he'd still managed to hold onto, and shattered them again and again. And she wished like hell, too, that Peter hadn't followed her down here. That he'd made another decision, that he didn't actually want to see what the hell was down there in the underbelly.

At least part of her, anyway.

It was that part of her that was twistin' up so good and tight. That just wished he'd just gone and shrugged it all off. That he'd told her he didn't actually need to see any of this. That he was just fine and trusted her and all that.

But... Peter didn't.

Instead, he'd followed along beside her as if he knew the fine line he was walkin'. This narrow, knife's edge, and that the only reason he was here, following her down here when no one in their sane mind would go, was cause he needed to know. Cause he loved his ma and his sister and he owed it to himself to see.

So he was here, right now, waiting for Cat to get her own nerves under control, her own shaking and shivering that was makin' a mess of whatever senses she'd had left. Somehow, despite the tingles and the warnings racing like crazy up and down her body, Cat got one foot to rise and then dropped down on the next step. Then followed it with another and then another until she was nearly down at the bottom and gettin' a glimpse of the faded light slippin' out from the hallway of the cribs.

Each step she took bringing her own ghosts closer to the surface, each one makin' the memories of last time so real she was havin' a hard time tellin' the difference between what had happened then and what was happening now.

But then she heard Peter behind her, his presence just the kinda reminder she needed—and her own will to keep going.

His soft steps, barely brushing against the top of the stairs, barely causin' that wood to creak or groan, as if maybe he was just to darn scared to make any noise.

Peter.

He was the reason she was here, despite her better judgment and the judgment of all her friends—including the good doc's who certainly was gonna have something to say when he got to examinin' her shoulder again—but Cat put all that out of her mind.

Had to.

Had to focus on why she was here, on the promise she'd made to Peter, to show him the truth of this life, all its glory and all its ugliness —and she would.

After all, it was the only thing she *could* do. It was the only move she had left to convince him to give his mother another chance, to believe in her again... to forgive her.

Peter's breath was comin' out in short, shallow gasps behind her, like maybe his own control wasn't much better than Cat's right then.

She didn't blame him. Not one bit.

She also didn't know if seeing this place would be enough. Or if *anything* would be enough. Especially with the future Evie was now facing. Especially because, out of all the scenarios Cat had given Peter just then while they stood both together and alone in that darkness of the stairway, out of all them scenarios, each of them felt possible...

Except for the one that got Peter his happy ending.

Or if she were being honest, Cat's own happy ending. But then, she'd given up on that a long, long time ago.

For Peter, for Evie, for their family... they still had hope.

It sure wasn't a whole bunch of hope, but it was something. And it was more than Cat had ever had.

CHAPTER FORTY-SEVEN

W hy," Evie asked Reverend Jacobs again, "did you come to my home that night and confront Lou? What did you say to him?"

Jacobs stood there on her front porch in front of the gathered crowd and all those neighbors who now wanted her gone. He eyed her carefully, coldly, and to such a degree she nearly took an involuntary step back on her creaking wood porch.

"So," he said, "you were there."

With his words and the way he was lookin' at her with such disdain, such calculation... her own memory of that night got a tad bit clearer. As if he, himself, were the trigger her poor memory, sickened as she'd been at the time, needed to fill in those gaps. How Lou had been railing against Jacobs, his face red and to near burning while Jacobs... Jacobs had simply stood there. Detached. Cold. Distant. He spoke only a few words and without the kind of fire she was used to hearing from him, but just like that, Lou had froze.

No more anger.

No more face bright red with his usual, drunken rage.

Just... went still. Quiet.

"Yes. You *were* there." Jacobs's eyes narrowed at Evie. "And you *do* remember. I'd be very careful, Evelyn Blonberg, if I were you and just what exactly you might have overheard."

The truth was she *hadn't* heard any actual words.

It'd all been feelings and, and impressions. She'd simply not been close enough or her head was too full of being sick. But it was quite clear, however, that Jacob's thought she knew more.

It was a warning. She felt it, right there true in her breast and heart. Her children. They were what mattered and yet... and yet...

"Whatever you have to say," he said, "means nothing. You're nothing more than a fallen woman now. A soiled dove. A harlot. A whore. Someone no one will ever take seriously, or care for, again."

Strength, she remembered.

And... and to be seen.

That was what she needed. That was *all* she needed.

Right here. Right now.

Evie lifted her head even higher, and Jacobs, his eyes got to narrowing all the more as if he could see her stepping into her own.

"You," he said, "are greatly close to stepping over a line that cannot be uncrossed—"

"I believe that line *has* been crossed. By my husband, no less. You remember? The very man who swore before God to protect me, in sickness and in health, and who then ran off for a better life. A man which everyone knew to have been unfaithful to our marriage bed, but let's not dwell too closely on that. He is a man, after all, and is *allowed* such indiscretions. But waving aside that particular promise to me, what about all those others? He burned them up when he said what he did and has pretty much left me and my children for dead."

Evie dug her fingers into her dress, making those wrinkles there deepen. No matter. It wasn't like she'd ever be as respectable again.

"You dare come here and accuse me of walking into a life that I didn't want, I had no part in making, and have no choice now but to accept? My husband crossed that line when he wrote what he did, but like hell will I play the part you're expecting me to play."

Never again.

It was like Lou had rung a bell inside her, and Cat had helped show it to her.

One that couldn't ever be unrung.

There was a lot of darkness flashin' in Jacobs' eyes right then, and right then it joined in with that chorus of bells ringing inside her. And despite what she'd thought earlier, of not remembering, of words... Jacobs was doing the favor of filling in those gaps in her memory. Still not clear, no, but more so than before. They *had* been talking about Lou's job, specifically about the Spectacular, and she heard one thing clearer than all the other words:

"Accident."

And then... and then... Lou saying...

"Not my fault."

And probably for the first time in her life, right deep to her core, Evie believed him.

Especially since Lou *did* get all cold and quiet by whatever Jacobs had said to him. How he hadn't thrown no plate or kicked at the door or some innocent chair. Instead he'd just, just stood there... fists clenching and bunching at his sides, the muscles in his neck bulging. Yet he didn't let that anger out, even as he and Jacobs continued to speak of the Spectacular...

Evie closed her eyes a moment, trying to remember.

But the rest, the rest was just like smoke.

Whatever was said between Jacobs and Lou would remain between them two.

But what she did *know*, what she was feeling right certain in her chest, was that Lou had been the pawn.

Just as she was now.

Well... to hell with them. To hell with all of them.

Jacobs crossed his arms and bowed his head, as if he... he were actually praying for her. She wanted to scream at that, to slap him so hard for continuing to lay this blame on her when she'd done nothing but what God and marriage had asked of her.

But the real truth, the one her nana had conveniently never spoken aloud of, were these ugly bits right here. The truth that, when you were the woman wronged and left behind and lied about, you simply didn't matter.

Jacobs made the sign of the cross. "Despite your words, Evelyn Blonberg, I pray for you. I especially pray for your children and the darkness you've brought to them."

That... *that* did it.

"Is that right?"

Evie stepped forward. Let her shawl fall to the ground because she simply did not care about propriety anymore. Did not care about her role and what was expected of her.

All she cared about was one thing...

Her children.

"You say this all falls at my feet? This darkness, that it's mine? Fine, then. I accept the blame. I accept the misdeeds of my husband and *his* faults—but only because I am strong enough, I am woman enough to do so. To do the very thing that you and Lou could never, ever do."

Evie jabbed her finger into Jacob's chest. Hard.

"And I will keep on living here." She jabbed again. "And I will keep on surviving and so help me God, I will *not* let my children down."

He slapped her hand away. "How dare you, woman, to touch me so!"

"If you don't like it, then get off my porch and leave me and mine alone, or I *will* call on the police."

He grinned at her. He actually grinned.

"I do hope you will," he said, "then we can settle this manner in a civilized... nonviolent demonstration."

The Evie of yesterday would have been shaking, cowering. But not the Evie of today.

It was her turn to smile.

She remembered yet another promise given to her while she sat at Mrs. Allen's table, when she thought she was now all alone in a world that wanted nothing to do with her, except for this woman named Cowboy Cat and the officer who, despite Cat's former profession, still somehow considered her... friend.

"I'm glad you see reason in this, as we do seem to be disturbing the peace of all my neighbors." Evie nodded towards them. "In fact, after hearing the news which my husband thought to kindly distribute across town, I went to the police to see what recourse I had for his actions. Of course, as I learned, I have none, being a woman and all. And yet... my circumstance was met with surprising sympathy."

"Yes. Yes, I'm sure it was. Especially for calling in a favor or two."

There was no denying exactly what Jacob's grin was implying, but Evie did not lose her resolve—or her control.

Instead, she turned and opened her door and waved Jacobs inside. "Would you like to come in, Reverend? Come in and wait while I send for this officer?"

Evie's sudden move, her taking control of that game board if you will, her open and honest, *smiling* invitation, surprised him Jacobs. No doubt about it.

He did not move. A wolf, so used to being a hunter, now smelling a trap.

Evie's grin widened and she easily slipped back into the role of dutiful wife, and yet still, Jacobs stayed right where he was.

"Why on earth would I dare go inside your home?" he asked. "So you can tempt me and trap me the same way you've done with many others?"

"You? A man of God? I think you believe very highly in my charms, certainly more than Lou ever did. But to answer your question, no, the offer is simply to sit and wait."

"And what officer would you be sending for?"

"Oh... I'm sure you've heard of him. He's been in the papers recently, like me. Maybe that will gain your respect?"

Jacobs's smile vanished, but that cruel look in his eyes stayed right there.

Right on her.

"Yes, I've a feeling you know him." She had no idea *why* she thought this. It was just a feeling, an intuition, if you will, but she trusted it. Trusted in herself. "His name is Blake. Officer Blake, and he was one of those recently investigating a murder. The one everyone's been talking about. The one that's tied all the way back to Marcus Daly and a close, personal friend of his."

Evie's whole world might have been collapsing yesterday and her mind might have been twisted up in all those fears, but she'd still been paying attention. And she'd been listening. She'd also seen how those other officers had treated Blake, even when the news of her predicament became known to the whole police force. They hadn't ridiculed him for his kindness nor had they looked at him with the knowing gaze Jacobs had sent her way earlier, this, this understanding than when dealing with a fallen woman there was an exchange of... services for help.

Instead, when those other officers had looked at Blake, it'd been the opposite.

Trustworthy. Respectful. A healthy dose of fear and distance as if worried about getting too close.

And now Evie saw the same in Jacobs.

"Whatever it is you think I've done or overheard," she said, "or whatever business you had with my mean drunk of a husband—I do not care. All I care about is my children and keeping them safe, clothed, and fed. And seein' as how you're not interested in letting us be and settling into these decisions, ones that were done and made by someone other than myself, stealing my free will, stealing what few choices I've got left, and seeing as how you're *not* interested in acting in good faith and as a good neighbor, and certainly not as a good man of God..."

Jacobs's eyes narrowed at this but he stayed rooted to her front porch, with those nails ready to pop on loose, watching her wary like, like he wasn't sure what she was gonna do next.

Good.

"How about we go inside, Reverend?" Evie asked. "Let us speak about this justice? Yes? The one you're so keen on giving me but aren't willing to accept the weight of which is yours."

There was just that flicker right there of emotions, sparking in his eyes, and she knew, *knew*, that she had him.

Dead to rights.

CHAPTER FORTY-EIGHT

With Peter right at her heels and Grace as far from this place as she could possibly go, Cat dropped down from that last step of the stairway, completely leaving the Gardens behind and stepping into a whole other world.

Dust and dirt kicked up from where she landed, and just their presence alone, the way it billowed out about her like a suffocating cloud, caused the memory from last time to claw at her, tug on her, begging her almost to just let go and simply *remember*.

She shifted her feet, trying to breathe, trying to see through that stinging dust. The floorboards were so brittle and dry that they groaned with such a force she wasn't entirely sure they weren't just gonna snap right then and there.

Snap.

That sound, it went ringing through her whole body, her whole being. An echo that wasn't about to quiet any time soon. The very possibility of it again, it just went and vibrated right through her and carried straight to her soul and didn't let go.

Her breath caught in her throat.

Every inch of her goin' tense. Every inch of her aware and

checking to see if it was just the aging, uncared for wood or if there was actually someone else... someone laying in wait right there in the shadows of the stairs...

No one was there.

Just the wood and the stairs, both desperately in need of replacing and neither of which would happen would any time soon.

She was totally alone except for Peter and the girls she knew lived here.

And yet despite knowing this, having the truth and confirmation right there for her eyes, indisputable proof that there was no Mr. Rippi hiding there in those shadows—her heart had no intention of settling its pounding rhythm any time soon.

Nor did she expect it to.

Not after what had happened last time.

Cat forced herself to breathe. First one, then another. In and out. She recalled her pa's training, his soft words when he'd taken her out all those times to the woods, a rifle steady and nestled there in the crook of her arm. Lettin' the world still around her. Seein' with more than just the eyes. Seein' the details. Makin' sense of them. Putting them together, one after another.

Cat let out a breath.

"Breathe," he'd whispered to her. "*But only when you're wantin' to.*"

She did so again and miraculously, her own heart started to slow. The raging pulse in her neck quieted down.

A little, anyway.

For now, anyway.

At least it gave her enough room to separate herself out from the memory, to focus instead on the here and now and do what she'd come here to do.

And just like he'd taught her, she began seein' all those details of this place—and how almost nothing had changed.

The cribs still lined each side of the narrow, dark hallway. Those tiny little dark rooms, each sportin' a smudged and dirty window and a door that had no lock. Those windows, which looked so similar to the ones upstairs, allowing gentleman callers the chance to see the merchandise beforehand, selecting which girl was to their liking and taste, and which ones would simply "just not do." Yet even though the windows and their purpose were almost exactly the same as the upstairs, there *were* no gentleman down here.

And there was nothing gentle about their nature, either.

Cat didn't even have to look hard to see the mark those men and all their types had left on this place. A door jamb there, a knob there: shattered. Wood splintered in every which way and direction, clearly never bothered to be replaced or repaired, not even to hide such obvious violence. A living memory, if you will, of what had happened here.

After all, what was the point? It was all just gonna happen again. And again.

It was that feeling there, which literally hung in the air. A heaviness and a solemn weight that simply *lived* in the fabric of this world. In the ground. In the rafters above them. It was everywhere you looked and it was in every breath you took. There was no escaping it. Just like there was no escaping this life and the downward spiral it all meant. Each of those rooms costin' the girl living in 'em a near fortune to rent. More than likely their entire week's pay. Each of them rooms barely big enough to move around in. Each one of 'em barely big enough for the necessary bed which business was conducted in.

Peter came up beside Cat, steppin' lightly off those stairs and peering into the dim lighting all around them—

And he stopped short.

Just... just stopped.

His shoulders jerkin' back so suddenly it was as if someone had a noose tied round his neck and pulled that rope hard and fast. Even the bulging eyes looked too similar for Cat's liking. Especially for her stomach. Especially for the coffee she'd drank what felt like lifetimes ago, burning and churning in just that way.

"What is this place?" he whispered.

His whisper felt like a shout in this place. One that seemed to go on echoing off those walls and ceiling with all them dusty, dirty rafters. How could it not feel like a shout when only the nearly-dead and ghosts lived here? Those beings who actually called this place home?

"It's the underbelly of the Gardens," Cat said. "The cribs."

"But... it looks nothing like upstairs."

"No. No it doesn't." Which was the exactly point. "This place caters to another... kind of client. And this place," she nodded down the hallway to the cribs, "is what those kinda clients can afford and only that. Nothing more."

And all of it looked almost exactly the same.

Which in itself was almost impossible for her to believe. Everything that had happened here, how quickly this place had changed her, those... those events... and yet it was like she'd left no mark on it, or at least very little. No change. No difference.

None at all.

Yet for Cat, her entire world and who she believed herself to be, had changed. Perhaps might not ever be the same again. In that moment, she felt more kinship with these girls than she'd ever had before. Sure, she'd done this job, worked this profession, but it'd been in a whole other place entirely. Back in Miles City and she'd been one of the lucky ones, workin' for a good house, and her manner and look and attitude, dressin' more the part of a cowboy than a lady, had earned her a reputation and a respect few ever saw. Cat had never walked *this* life before, like these girls who'd no choice but to live here until they either expired or moved on. That despite all their suffering and pain and the never-ending torment they lived in, they left no mark. No mark at all that they'd even existed.

Except, of course, to add to the darkness, to the heaviness.

The memory of Cat's own time being here and what had happened, it was pullin' so strong she was having a hard time telling the difference from what was takin' place now and what had taken place then.

Cat dug deeper into herself, calling up her pa's teaching even more, hoping it'd give her the strength to see beyond all these feelings, holding tight as they were, round and round her heart and mind. Eventually, she did start seeing with her usual clarity.

Along with that little tingle of awareness, the realization that this place *hadn't* changed, and yet the upstairs, with all its glitter and elegance, had.

Why?

Because she'd been right earlier, and Grace had even told her about the fallout from the police raid, from Mr. Rippi and MacDonald who'd attempted to kidnap Abigail. Why had that place been affected but not here?

The lighting, which was now dimmer and that slow, growing accumulation of dirt on previously gleaming floors. The door hinges that creaked and groaned. The silence. No music and no delicate voices slowly waking up from feather-soft beds. It was as if the whole upstairs breathed in this difference, in that subtle shift as Grace's reputation took the hit because of what Cat had done. Yet down here in this darkness, in this musty, freezin' cold world, there was no change.

None at all.

Cat's instincts tingled. The hairs on the back of her neck rose.

Felt she was close to something, to seein' something that was just right there—

And she couldn't quite grasp.

The dirt still hanging so heavy and thick you felt it with every breath as those bits and particles scratched lungs. The naked light bulbs above, least those that were actually workin', barely pushed back those shadows. Each of them bulbs swayed, too. Just this slight back-and-forth motion—even though there weren't no stirring of breeze or no whisper of wind. Yet they each kept on moving nonetheless.

Everything seemed untouched and unchanged.

Mostly, anyway.

Cat moved forward, slowly. Felt herself pulled into this world and into that memory. Didn't want to go there but knew, too, such a wish was probably impossible.

Because this place *had* changed her.

Cat moved farther down the hallway, looking into those rooms, searching for some understanding, some knowledge that she wasn't alone in this. She found none... except for her memory inching ever closer to the surface, demanding to be acknowledged.

To be felt.

This time there were no girls tapping on that glass. No girls trying to get the attention of the wealthy man amongst them who'd dragged poor Abigail down here, burying his fingers and nails into the delicate skin of her arm.

Cat's hand inched towards her shoulder. The pain that was slowly growing there.

She tried remembering her pa and his teachings, tried to keep on breathing and focusing, but even his voice was startin' to slip away from her. Just like Peter, who was still silent, still following behind her, but it was like he was fading from her. Almost like he was turnin' into some ghost or ghost-to-be.

The floorboards groaned and protested with each step and quite loudly, too, but no girl seemed to notice. No girl stirred from where she huddled on her bed, just a dark form and threadbare blankets and sheets coverin' every inch of them... if they were lucky enough to have even that.

And those who didn't?

Cat swallowed.

They wouldn't be here long. The truth, every ugly inch of it, was right there in those small details. And what really made her stomach sick, made it twist so gosh darn hard that she just might lose her coffee right then and there, was those girls would be leavin' the *luxury* of this place. They'd be finding themselves workin' an even rougher corner of life. A street walker, perhaps. Or maybe even... the cribs in the underground.

Cat wanted to look away.

Wanted to just turn and walk out Grace's elegant doors upstairs and never look back. To pretend, as Grace did, that such places and conditions simply didn't exist—so long as you didn't look too closely at it.

But Cat didn't walk away, and she couldn't look away, either.

Nor did she deny herself those tears slippin' from the corners of her eyes and didn't bother hiding them from Peter, either.

He saw her tears right then, just like he saw those cribs.

And it seemed like he couldn't move no more, either. Like his whole body was simply frozen. Rooted right there to those creaking, aching floorboards, breathing in all that darkness and despair and trying his best to keep from losin' his breakfast.

Cat turned back to the girls and their unmoving shapes.

Part of her hoped that a few of them had found some release during the night. That their souls weren't no longer bound to this world, the one that didn't love them or want them no more. That maybe they'd finally left behind all this pain and darkness and loneliness, the kind of which they faced each and every day, without one kind word or smile ever being shared with them.

And she remembered Norma... Norma who'd been cast out of that glittering world from above and who'd done everything possible to get back to it, including ransoming her own life. And Evie... Evie and her family and her two kids were walkin' into this world and there weren't no promises that Cat could make—*none*—that would ensure them their happy ending.

This time, with that simple thought, Cat's ghosts and memories and all that regret, mountains of it, came roarin' right back. It was like they were good and tired of being denied. They were gonna come and say their peace and they were gonna force her to see only what they wanted her to see.

Alice.

Cat's own mother.

And her shoulder?

My God, it was just on fire right then. Burnin' so hot and bright she was nearly doubled over and barely breathing.

She half turned, walkin' past Peter and not really seein' him, not seein' anything at all, really, just those stairs that she was headed right for—

Then wished to God she'd stayed exactly where she'd been. Because right there, right in front of her, was that shattered doorframe.

The very one Cat had flown straight through. Her head and shoulders and body smashin' into that wood. Splintering it. Breaking it. She'd done her best to dodge that vicious swing from Mr. Rippi, but she hadn't been fast enough.

Cat gripped her shoulder, burying her fingers into that tender skin and healing bones, hopin' that pain from the here and now would be enough to wrench her free of the memory.

She wasn't some wilting flower.

But my God, it sure as hell felt real, like it was happening all over again.

Cat's whole body shook. Small shivers that she couldn't seem to control, couldn't seem to do nothing about. They were just... there. Her fingers itched, too, desperate like, to reach for her gun. To feel the warm of the butt in her grip. Reassurance. That she wasn't down here alone this time. Wasn't down here defenseless.

Even though... it sure as hell felt like she was.

Peter touched her shoulder then.

She hadn't heard him come up. Hadn't heard his quiet voice and whatever words he was whispering to her, but they sounded kind.

Gentle, too, like his touch.

She was surprised he'd even noticed her distress at all, seein' as how he was starin' into his own version of hell, staring right down into its hungry maw and realizin', too, that there just weren't no escape.

"This where it happened?" he asked. "Where you got hurt?"

His voice was quieter this time, as if recognizing that this place here was one where the living didn't dare go.

"Yeah," she said. "Last place I want to be, speakin' frankly."

Mostly, anyway.

Excepting any place near Blake, of course.

"But you came back," he said. "For me."

"For you. For your mother. For the promise I made you both. I hope in the end, you tell me it was all worth it."

He swallowed and his lips trembled a bit and she saw then that he was starting to understand. Starting to... except he couldn't because all he could see ahead was darkness.

Darkness and fear.

Lots and lots of fear.

"I can't tell you that," he said, "not yet."

But he surprised her when he offered his hand. Offered her this small comfort when he himself was drowning in all that fear.

By God... Dusty was right about this kid, about his strength.

Cat accepted his hand and straightened, though she did so slowly as if her shoulder didn't seem to care one bit that this was a phantom pain she was relieving.

It still hurt like hell.

Peter let go of her hand and turned to face the cribs, the underbelly of the Gardens, and asked: "Why, why is this place even here?"

"I thought that was obvious. Cause... it needs to be."

CHAPTER FORTY-NINE

Peter didn't understand.

To him none of this was obvious. None of it.

But... it was starting to. Slowly. Bit by bit.

The longer he stood there, his feet on that creaking wood of the hallway, the cribs or underbelly or whatever it was Cat had called this place, every inch of him wanted to turn and run. Run so hard and so fast he could escape what he was seein' from those flickering lights overhead, escape what he was smellin'—such a foul mix that made him damn glad they were down here today, on a winter's day, and *not* in the boiling heat of summer.

All the while there was those, those darkened cribs.

They just went on down that hallway, one after another and not a shape moving inside that he could see—

And it was in that moment that it was all startin' to make sense.

Peter didn't know what he was more afraid of. That it *was* makin' sense or the feeling of rage clawing its way back to the surface. Those angry fire ants movin' under his skin, just so. They were gettin' a bit faster, too, poking their heads out and takin' a long, long look around... and not liking one bit what they were seeing.

And the implications of why they were here.

That this place, this place here, was his family's future.

Peter tightened his hands into fists and stepped away from Cat. He knew what it had cost her to come here. Well, he didn't *know* know, but it was pretty clear watchin' her struggle as she was, memory so close to the surface, it was like he could see it all happening, see how she got hurt. Seein' that spot over there, the broken doorway nearest the stairs, and he knew without her sayin' a word.

And what did that mean for his mother?

Peter swallowed. He didn't think he knew a woman strong as Cat. Sure, he hadn't known her long, but he could *see* it. Could feel it, too, whenever she looked at him and told him truth.

Yet, he was seein' her suffer and suffer pretty darn deep, and she'd come to this place with him anyway.

And for whatever reason... Peter didn't want her to see this rage buildin' up in him. Didn't want her to see how his pa's legacy was already back inside him, desperate for a way out. Any excuse, really, to let it all go. He just... just didn't want to add to her problems and didn't want to let her down, either.

Or his mother.

Was that... was that truth? Was that what he wanted? To not add to his mother's problems? But if that was the case, then why didn't he just go on home?

He could.

It was a simple answer, the simplest one, really. Except Peter just couldn't get his feet to move and head up those stairs.

So then... where did that leave him? Where *did* he go from here? Cause this place, this place here, *was* a possibility for his mother and if that happened... what then? What would happen to Rose? There was no way, no possible conceivable way that she'd be here when their mother was—

Peter cut off the thought.

Had to.

The heat from all those fire ants were blazin' now. Angry and biting. Just the thought of Rose...

Peter shook his head. Hard.

He felt Cat's gaze on him again, watching everything, probably even seein' him fight against that rage—

He couldn't let her see. Had to get himself back under control. It was the only way he could... could help his family.

But... was that *really* what he even wanted?

The fire ants took another chomping bite. A hard one, right there above where his heart would be. He went and clenched his fists so tight he could feel the nails pushing through those thin gloves he wore. The fire ants, his anger, none of them were givin' him a chance to figure out what he really wanted.

And how could he expect them to? Especially now, when he was staring straight into his mother's future.

And possibly Rose's as well.

No.

He couldn't let that happen. Wouldn't let it happen.

"It's not obvious to me," Peter said, doing his darn best to keep himself sounding calm. "About why this place is here. Why? Why would Grace need it? All that—"

He couldn't even think of a word to fully describe the luxury and beauty he'd seen upstairs—

"Doesn't Grace have enough?" he said instead. "Isn't all that enough?"

"No."

Cat's voice was simple. Direct. It was like she was back to her old self and not the woman he'd seen struggling with the ghosts and demons of this place.

He turned, expecting to see that woman who'd walked out of the smoke and shadows at the side hill to find him, completely at ease, completely fearless, but that wasn't the woman here with him now. From what he could tell, Cat *was* more herself, but those ghosts were still there and they still had a pretty good hold on her. He could see it in her eyes staring right back at him, and knew without a doubt his eyes probably looked the same.

Haunted. Scared.

The realization alone made his throat tighten and he suddenly found it hard to swallow—

And find the words for what he needed to say next.

For a woman like Cat.... someone that others called Miss Justice, who went out of her way and made a promise to him, to his mother, people she didn't know from Jack and didn't seem to care, either... for her to feel this way, how on earth could his mother survive? How could *he*?

Peter wasn't strong enough.

His father had seen to that. Hell, his father had proved it to him, time and time again.

The image of his pa exploded in his mind, so damn clear, too, it was like he was there. Peter could *see* him... stumbling down that hallway, heavy body tilted this way then that. Face bright red from all that drinkin' and the fire literally burnin' in his eyes. How he reached up, with that half-empty whiskey bottle of his, and shattered it right there on the doorframe nearest him...

That time... that had been at home, in the room he and Rose shared. Except... except Peter could see it happening right here, right in this hallway.

"Peter? You all right now?"

"Yeah." *No.* "I'm fine."

"Doesn't look like it."

Peter shuddered. He closed his eyes, needing to get that image, get the ghost of his pa far away from him as he could—but it didn't do a damn thing.

His father was still there.

Still standing there, right in this hallway, glaring at Peter for all he was worth.

"Does it matter?" Peter asked.

He meant it. All of it.

Cat sighed. "Wish I could say it did, but then, then I'd be lying, myself."

And that, he realized, was the reason he was still there. Still standing there in this place of darkness and misery, that held not one ounce of hope for the future, and the fire in him was demanding him to see just that, to take it and act on it and screw all them consequences—cause they didn't really seem to matter no more.

His pa... *he* had taught Peter that.

Peter let out a breath and managed not to choke when he got a sudden stink of a kind he only smelled on those summer days when the wind shifted and all of Butte was at the mercy of the dump. Cat seemed to know, too, that he was fightin' his own demons cause she went and gave him space... didn't touch his arm or comfort him like his mother and all them other mothers would have done.

But then, she did one thing more: she told him the truth. Told him about these cribs and why they even existed.

"Madam Grace," Cat said, "is just that, a madam. She's a business woman first and foremost. Sure, she came up through the ranks of working girls, earned enough money and bought this place off Mrs. Allen. But then she did what she had to do to keep the money coming in. That there is the tricky part. You make some hard choices. Real tough ones. Of the kind that's gonna go and stay with you the rest of your life. This isn't a business for the faint of heart and I may not like the woman—I certainly ain't her friend—but I understand it. I understand her."

Cat nodded towards the nearest crib.

This one had no light that seemed to reach it because the bulb overhead was out. It was just hanging there, swaying a bit back and forth with the glass burnt on one side. How long had it been like that? How long had that woman, whoever who lived in that darkness, lived like that...?

"The cribs," Cat went on, "exist for the same reason as Grace's fancy parlor house upstairs does. To earn a profit. To fulfill a demand. I wish I could say it was enough. Wish I could say this whole... *profes-*

sion was enough and that the rich folk could support the whole damn thing and spare the rest of us this misery."

"But it can't."

"No. Cause there's still other fellows who've got their needs to be met and then there's women like me, women like... well, like your mother, who are needing to make a living. And we can't all go and be one of Grace's flowers."

Peter moved closer to the glass, the dark one, and he thought just maybe he could catch a glimpse of the shape inside.

Wasn't sure why he wanted to even see. Maybe... maybe to prove to himself that the woman in there was nothing like his mother and never would be. Or maybe... maybe it was just that fire in him that *wanted* to keep seeing. Wanted more fuel. More and brighter and hotter.

Either way, he got so close his breath went and fogged up the glass.

Couldn't see much of anything. Maybe a form there on the bed with a quilt that looked barely big enough to cover the woman's body, let alone the bed.

Dark. Despairing. Unmoving.

But the fire... it wanted more. Needed more. Just like he needed to know if he saw the ghost of his pa right there behind him. Whiskey sloshing down his face, stainin' his clothes, makin' that smell that burned Peter's nostrils wide open.

"And down here?" he asked. "What do they demand down here?"

"The gentleman who go upstairs?" Cat asked. "Nothing. Nothing at all. See, Peter, those kinda men who use these tunnels, they don't want to be seen. They want to remain invisible, which fits well cause all this..." She gestured to the cribs, to the hall... "All this is invisible to them. They don't actually *see* any of this. And those women they pass by in the underground? They certainly don't see them."

Peter glanced at Cat. "The underground? You mentioned that a few times. You mean there's some place else? Some place worse than this?"

"There is, and it is."

Cat pointed to a trapdoor down at the end of the hallway. He couldn't see much from here, not with this lighting, but it looked like a thin sheet of wood slapped down over the floorboards.

How... how was any of this possible? How could there actually be a place, a place worse than this?

"If there's one thing your mother would have kept from you," Cat said, "it was the underground. In fact, I imagine it's the last place any mother would want their adventurous sons exploring."

"They've only mentioned the red light before."

"There's a reason for that, Peter."

"But your friend, Dusty? He knows about it, about the underground."

"Knows it better than me, in fact. He needs to. It's his world, remember."

"The one you're trying to keep me from?"

"No." Cat shook her head. "Not keepin' you from. All I'm tryin' to do is you show the truth. What you do with it... well, that's still your choice."

"So you'll take me there?"

Cat didn't even pause. Didn't even look away from him.

"I will," she said. "I promised to show you—everything. I meant it."

But it was more than just the promise. It was the way she spoke about the underground, and he knew, without a doubt, that it *was* worse than here. Much worse. He saw it in Cat's eyes. Saw her pain and hurting, and had a feeling, too, that this this time it wasn't her own... he just, just got that sense from her, was all, like she was feeling pain for all those women who *did* live down there.

Like... like his mother?

Peter shuddered... and then that shuddering turned into some more. A rage shivering that wasn't to be denied or ignored.

Not this time.

"There are two types of men who come here," Cat said, standing along beside him and staring into the darkness of that window, though still keeping her distance. Not comforting him or reassuring him. "The gentleman who walk this hallway to get upstairs to the Gardens. They don't see any of this. Not the cribs. Not the girls. It just, just doesn't exist."

"And the second type?"

He couldn't keep the anger from his voice.

Not this time. Not when he really *could* see his pa right there, as he stumbled into one of them doorways, pushing that thin piece of warped wood open. That whiskey bottle, how it'd slosh out the top and splatter onto who knows what. Didn't matter cause his pa didn't care. Could even see his hand, jerkin' at the belt of his pants—

Peter closed his eyes, so good and tight, but damn it all, he could *still* see him.

The rage was building in him now. Sure and fast and so angry. So bright and burning.

Cat kept her voice low and almost... gentle like. A complete contrast to what Peter was seein'.

"The men who *do* see these girls, they are the only ones who can afford a place like this and nothing better. Miners. Blacksmiths. Anyone really."

"You mean," he said, "men like my pa."

There was a pause.

A silence that hung in the air right with the dust and dirt he felt scratching up his lungs, going down then coming right back out again.

"Yeah," Cat said. "Like him"

The fire was burnin' so bright now it was all Peter could see, even when he opened his eyes... all he saw were flames. And his pa standing right in the middle of it all, grinning widely, knowing that his son was some weak thing that couldn't, and wouldn't, do a damn thing about any of this.

"Though," Cat said, "I doubt he'd have visited here, least in recent months."

Cat's words slowly pulled back the flames, enough that he could almost see her in them. Her outline, really.

"What do you mean?" he asked.

She shrugged. Least, that's what he thought she did. "Probably couldn't have afforded it. Not after he lost his job. Not after your mother was havin' a hard time finding work."

So... then, that means his pa would have gone to those other places, worse places... like, like the underground. But for the first time, despite those flames and that anger lickin' at his elbows, he was finally seein' some clarity. Some... understanding.

Much as he didn't want to understand. Much as he'd rather go back to being that kid who played with Bugsy and their gang out at the side hill.

Truth was, he wasn't that kid anymore. Never would be again, neither.

Thanks to his pa.

Peter somehow managed to swallow. "Would... would any of the girls here know? I mean... know about him... about my..."

He couldn't say it. Couldn't speak it.

"I doubt it," Cat said. "It's... part of how you learn to survive down here. You just do what needs doing. But seeing? Remembering?" She shook her head, her loose hair slippin' over her shoulder. "And it would be kinder to not ask, either. Both for you and those girls."

Cat's answer again was... painful. It was hard to hear, but still... truthful. Again. She'd been nothing but honest with him, which was more than his mother had done, certainly more than his pa ever had. Just like he *knew* that his pa had been unfaithful—and maybe had always been. Hell, Peter wasn't no kid. He knew most of the fathers living in his neighborhood did the same, went to these kinds of place, but you just couldn't... just couldn't go and talk about none of that.

But this time, in this way, with his pa... it just felt different.

Probably cause he was forcing his mother into this life by doin' what he did, writin' up about that classified and lyin' like he had, and for what reason? What reason could possibly be worth it to hurt his mother that way? To hurt him and, and *Rose*?

He didn't understand.

And that was the problem.

Peter stood there, right in front of the glass of that darkened crib. His breath, still fogging up the glass that was so smudged it didn't seem to make no difference about being able to see inside or not. He pressed his palms against it. Felt that cool glass bite right into him even though it didn't do a damn thing to douse the flames roarin' in him.

He wanted to scream. To shout. To rail—cause all he wanted was to understand why. *Why* his father had done this to them... why he'd hurt them so bad.

This time Cat did touch Peter. Right there on his shoulder. It was a gentle touch but firm, as if knowing how close he was to losin' it, of turning into his pa.

"Peter. This ain't the place for that."

He shrugged her off him. Stepped back. Angry. Feeling that fire and all those biting ants inside him, desperate to come out.

"Why not?" he demanded. "Why not in a place like *this?*"

"Cause these girls don't deserve your anger. They've got a hard enough life. Least we can do is give them a peaceful rest... while they have it, anyway."

"A hard life. You mean like my mother. Like my sister, too, right? You telling me *this* is where my mother's gonna go? Down, down here? Cause, hell, you and Madam Grace made it clear she *ain't* welcome upstairs. So that means, that means—"

He cut himself off.

Tears swelling in his eyes and falling down, down...

Peter looked back at the window and jerked back when a face stood there, right at the glass, lookin' at him. He hadn't heard the woman approach. Hadn't heard anything, really. Yet there she was. And... he found he just couldn't look away.

Couldn't.

A face so lined and wrinkled. A face with stringy dark hair framing it. A face so pale it looked like she'd never once, in all her life, seen the sun. Never once had some glimmer of hope, of dreams, or just the promise of a good hot meal.

This... this couldn't be his mother.

Couldn't *ever* be his mother.

Cat, he noticed, jerked back, too, when the woman appeared, almost as if she knew the girl. As if she weren't prepared for what she was seein' and seein' nonetheless.

Whatever the reason, Peter just didn't care.

Couldn't.

Because all he saw staring back at him from those hollow, deep-set, smudged eyes—was his mother.

"I won't stand for it." His teeth ground together. Hard. So hard it felt like he could break each one of 'em. "I won't—won't let him do this to us. To her."

Cat reached up, as if thinkin' of putting her hand back on his shoulder, when she let it drop. There was nothing but sorrow and sadness in her eyes, and that just made the flames in Peter grow brighter. Hotter.

"It's already been done, Peter," she said. "Can't go and unring that bell now. Law can't do it. Your mother can't do it. Hell, *I* can't do it much as I want to."

"It's... it's his fault."

A sob broke out. From him.

Then another followed, and another.

"It's his fault," he said. "He, *he* did this to her."

"He did and I'm terribly sorry to say, there ain't nothing any of us can do about it. It's just... just the way the world works here. It ain't fair, but then those boys controlling the laws, the courts, they don't care what's fair—so long as it doesn't affect them."

Which it didn't.

Peter knew Cat was telling him the truth. And sure... this was what she'd been saying all along... and yet... yet it just wasn't good enough. It just wasn't. All he cared about was his mother and what his pa had gone and done to her, to them... and there just had to be something, anything at all, he could do.

Anything to change this, this life his mother didn't deserve.

And maybe Cat was right. Maybe... maybe he never could change it. But what he couldn't do was stand there and cry like Susan Hoy woulda done. Cat, she'd been right this whole time. That he'd needed to see, needed to see it all, the grand parlor house with all the crystals and glittering lights and then, then down here... down here where there weren't nothing at all like hope, certainly not sunlight.

But Cat had been wrong about one thing:

It wasn't enough.

Not for him.

Peter *needed* answers. He needed to understand, and maybe, maybe then, he could move on. Could just let go and just accept the crumbs fate had decided to throw his way.

But not before and not without understanding the full truth.

And as far as Peter figured, there was only one place, one person, who knew, who might feel guilty enough to talk with him despite his sudden... change in circumstance.

He looked at that sad woman behind that glass. Thin face and eyes that looked as black as some mine shaft, and swore this wouldn't be his mother.

Not her.

There was no way he was gonna let his pa win. Not like this.

Not ever again.

CHAPTER FIFTY

Cat knew darn well that Peter was angry. It wasn't hard to miss, either. Fists clenching. Shoulders hunching but more like a tight coil than sorrow. She kept her distance and knew beyond a doubt that's what the kid needed.

But she'd needed it, too.

Needed it cause there, right in that window, was a face she hadn't ever expected to see again—and a face that brought her own memory of last time crashing right to the surface, so strong and unyielding, and not wanting to let go of her.

Not one inch.

Which was why she hadn't been prepared, hadn't been ready for when Peter—instead of railing and banging his fists against whatever surface was nearby and handy, yelling 'bout the injustice of it all— instead of all that, he turned and fled down the hallway.

Not fled... *no.*

Purposeful. Determined.

He ran right down that hallway as if there were no thought involved. Steps determined. Hands movin' quick as he yanked open that thin trap door and flung it open as hard and wide as he could.

Which went and thudded so hard against the ground those rafters above her shook and bits of dust and whatnot tumbled down and coated her hat, jacket, hair. But loud as it was, loud enough to shake the glass in front of her, Peter didn't seem to hear none of it.

He didn't pause, not one bit.

Just... just disappeared down into that darkness and all them shadows below, like he wasn't bothered by it at all. A determined rage she saw in him, felt in him, even as he went and disappeared, so strong that it wasn't gonna let up, wasn't gonna let go until it burnt itself out—

Or consumed him alive.

There was a slight rub at the glass. Fingers trailing down that smudged, dirty surface. Fingers that went and touched that same spot where Peter's had been mere moments before as if feeling that heat and anger through the glass.

The thin shade of the woman. The same one who'd saved Cat's life.

Cat could remember it all, so clear it was like it was happening right there, right again in front of her, not being able to move, not able to do nothin' at all to stop it.

This was the woman who'd huddled there in the farthest corner of that broken doorframe. Cat sprawled out onto that dirty, dusty ground, shoulder on fire, head spinnin' in just about every which way. This girl, she'd been so scared as she hid in those shadows, hid from the terrible anger that was livin' inside Mr. Rippi. Cat's derringer, the small gun she'd had strapped to her leg had flown right out'a her hands when Rippi had swung that wood into her, crushing her shoulder there, those muscles, and doin' a good number on her bones, too.

But it'd been this girl, this one right here, who'd found the courage to pick up Cat's gun. To stand up when Cat had asked the other girls there for their support and strength. And this girl here, a woman whose name Cat still didn't know, which shamed her more than anything else she'd done so far, more than any of the numerous mistakes and blunders she'd made since... well, since walking into this life, of living in the shadow world and now trying to do this calling of justice, and hell, she didn't even know the name of the woman who'd saved her. Hadn't the courage enough to come back herself in the whole week she'd been recovering to simply say, "thank you," as the woman surely, completely deserved...

And all that, right there, was reason why Cat hadn't been prepared.

Why she hadn't sensed the fire building in Peter. Reaching to dangerous levels. Takin' hold of him and promising to never let go. She'd been so damn lost in her own hurts and memories, of being human, that she'd missed seein' him slid off that narrow edge—

And she still was.

Still missing the point.

Cause, she was still standing there.

"Well?" The girl—*no*—the woman asked from behind the glass. "You gonna go after him?"

Except Cat couldn't seem to get her body to move, to answer that powerful need to run after him.

Or maybe that's 'cause she already knew the truth.

That she'd good and lost him. That despite doin' her utmost best, it hadn't mattered. Hadn't been enough. Cause he'd still gone and fallen off that edge—hell, she'd watched him—and there wasn't a damn thing now that she could do about it.

She'd let Evie down. Let Dusty down.

Hell, she'd let herself down.

"Well, Miss Justice?" the woman asked again. "You gonna get him or just stand there feelin' all sorry-like for yourself?"

"Good question."

Cat adjusted her hat, unable to take her eyes off that trap door and at the same time, unable to turn away from this woman. Or the truth. The truth that was staring at her right in the face.

"I think... maybe this time, I'm not gonna give chase."

"Cause of what happened to you last time?"

"Cause I'm thinkin'... this time, it ain't gonna matter."

Though there certainly was some truth to what the woman had said, a deeper hurt that Cat might not ever heal from, but she still had this sense... this knowing that right now, Peter needed to be on his own. Hunt for his own answers. Survive and learn to control his own rage.

"So that's it, then?" The woman asked. "You just givin' up on him? I thought justice, thought the woman who lived by justice, never gave up."

"I'm not giving up."

The woman's eyebrows rose, practically disappearing into that thin hair framing her face. "Certainly looks the way from where I'm standing. From where we all standing."

And... to Cat's surprise, there, right there, was a spark in the other woman's eyes. One that was small—tiny, really—but there. Burning so bright even in that darkness, even with all that clearly haunted this woman, all the loneliness swirling right there.

Cat remembered it. Remembered that look. The sudden growth, that little flame sproutin' out of about nowhere.

Hell, how could she not remember it?

Cat had stood there, almost in the exact same place in that hallway, facing her own death at the hands of Rippi and MacDonald, with poor Abigail there caught in the middle, and Cat... Cat being alone. Completely alone.

Except she hadn't been.

And the eyes of this woman, the eyes that had previously been scared and soulless without a bare spark of life in them... had changed. Cat had watched them change. She'd changed them. Cat. Cat and her words, sparkin' new in the other woman's life, and something, too, that looked an awful bit like hope.

... a hope that was, somehow, still there even though it was darn clear this woman's life here and her circumstances hadn't changed one bit.

"Why?" Cat asked. "Why do you care? About me? About helpin' this kid out?"

A small smile curled up about the other woman's lips. A little thing, really, for thin, narrow lips, but still, it *was* a smile.

"Cause," she said, "I gotta chance to see what hope looks like. Feels like. It's... it's nice to know, too, that we ain't alone down here no more."

Cat's throat caught. Disbelief and a whole lot more suddenly slamming into her. Hard.

She shook her head. "I ain't that person no more."

"You sure 'bout that? Otherwise, what the hell you doin' down here, huh? Though, got to say, it's nice seein' a friendly face."

A friendly face.

Again, another disbelief. After all, Cat had been the one hopin' to never come back down here, that if she'd had her way, she never would have again. Hell, *she* been the one who wanted to walk away from this life, hang up her hat and gun—part of her still did, in fact— but it'd been Dusty and Mrs. Allen who'd pushed her not to. Dusty alone who'd pushed Cat to be in this place, to be in a position for crossing paths with Peter and his family...

So many mistakes. So very many, many regrets...

But maybe there was at least one she could... well, maybe not rectify, but at least make right.

Even if it were small.

"If you don't mind," Cat said, "I'd like to know your name. The name of the woman who saved me and all."

"All I did was pull a trigger. It was your gun and it was your words that put it there, in my hands. You be the one who saved me. Saved all of us here."

Cat didn't believe it... sure as hell didn't feel it, either. "Either way, I'd like your name, if you be willing."

"Sadie."

Cat... she had a feeling right there, a right powerful one in her gut, that it was the woman's real name. Not her stage name, not the one she went by to hide the truth from family and relatives and friends. Maybe it's cause that wasn't a worry for her no more. Or maybe it's just cause she really did believe all those things she'd told Cat, and this was her way of saying thanks.

And a name, a real name, was a pretty darn powerful way of showing it.

"Thank you," Cat said, and meant it.

Meant it with her whole heart and more, if she were honest with herself.

Sadie nodded towards the other windows, and Cat turned and saw that she was, indeed, not alone no more. Each of them windows were filled now with women lookin' not much different than Sadie herself now did. Dark, smudged eyes, some bright red and gleaming, others lookin' like they were shades that were simply holding on for God knows why...

Except when Cat went and looked closer, really looked at all them details she was so fond of noticing... saw that Sadie *was* tellin' the truth.

Many of the girls were standin' up a bit straighter. Shoulders back and almost... proud. Not a lot, but in their own way. A small way. A small shift here and there, enough to show that there was a strength in them, a strength in the way they done looked at her—and Cat was finding it mighty difficult to keep breathing nice and even like, and the tears from fillin' up in her own eyes...

Just like she was having a real hard time right then, denying what they were tellin' her.

That this, all this, was cause of her.

Her and her justice.

Cat's shoulder burned bright and hot right then and she grabbed at it, guilt, her own set of failures and ghosts that dodged at her heels, never lettin' up, never lettin' go. Alice. Her mother. All of them. So many names, too, of women she hadn't known for her time of walking the line and hadn't done a damn thing to help them when she could have... could have and yet chose otherwise.

She dug her fingers into her coat but it didn't do a damn thing to relieve the pain.

Sadie, of course, noticed.

"You still hurtin'?"

Cat nodded. "I will be. For awhile."

"But... it's not gonna keep you from us. Will it?"

Again, Cat felt that breath gettin' knocked out of her. Knocked good and tight, as if Rippi had gone and taken a swing right at her chest this time. Maybe even her heart.

"I don't know yet," Cat said. "I reckon... I reckon I'm startin' to figure it out though."

Sadie's eyes narrowed. "Don't take too long now. You're needed."

Needed.

It wasn't the kinda mantle Cat was sure she could carry right now —or ever again. Or even... even if she should, if she even had the right.

But Sadie, by damn, seemed to know her trade well, cause she saw right through Cat's own bravado and told her right out: "Now. What you gonna do about that kid? Just gonna let him run off into those tunnels or what?"

And this time, Cat knew her answer. It was the same as before, but with a certainty she'd not felt since... well, since comin' to Butte, since Rippi had gone and done a number on her body as well as her mind.

"Yeah." Cat dropped her hand. "Yeah, I'm gonna let him run. This time... this time I'm thinkin' he needs to. I've showed him all I can. He'll need to see the rest for himself, come to terms with it as best he can."

"And if he can't find his way out?"

Out of the tunnels, out of the underground, and to the sunshine... my God, Evie wouldn't forgive Cat. Hell, Cat wouldn't forgive herself if he got himself lost down there. But that wasn't *really* what Sadie was askin'. She was askin' if Peter would go and end up like Dusty, end up seein' what the life was like in so many ways, how much more control and freedom you had when you embraced that shadow world whole. Sure it was a dark place, a kinda place most wanted out of, yet there *was* a certain freedom in all that.

But really, it came down to what Cat *could* do it. And there wasn't much, truthfully. She'd done her part and now, now it was about lettin' go and keeping her promise to Peter.

Lettin' him make up his own choice.

But there was something more, too. Cat *had* glimpsed something in him, and it really was just a glimpse, but it'd been there. It'd been there, smoldering in its own quiet way underneath all that fire and rage that was the legacy from Peter's father. And she knew it, knew it deep in her gut, what that little spark was.

Justice.

"I'm gonna trust him to find his way out," Cat said, "and then, well, then I'm gonna trust him to find his way back to me."

And maybe even back to his mother.

"You think that's wise?" Sadie asked.

"Feels like."

Sadie gave Cat a long, long look. Those dark eyes of hers seein' what felt like every inch of Cat. After a moment, she nodded.

"I'll send word if we hear of them. All of us will."

"I'd appreciate that," Cat said.

Then she turned and saw all those faces staring at her, all that fire sparkin' in those eyes now cause of what she'd done here, cause she'd gone and cared about them and about Abigail, and she remembered what Doc Griffin had said to her earlier... my God, was that only yesterday?

These girls, these women, they needed her. Needed someone, anyone, really, to care what happened to them.

Justice.

Cat touched the brim of her hat to Sadie.

How the hell had she ended up standing here, standing in all this responsibility? Shouldering it? Holding it? She could almost feel Alice and her own ma nearby. Their shades so close she could almost feel their chill touch, one that went right through and carried to her soul. Neither of them letting go. Neither of them wanting to, either.

And how could lettin' Peter go off on his own fulfill all those promises he'd gone and made?

Trust.

That was how and that was way forward. Had to be.

Cat was gonna trust Peter to make his decisions, hopin' like hell they'd be the right ones for him, for his whole family... just like Cat was now gonna do the same. And... well, she was gonna make good on the rest of those promises she'd gone and made. Because she was far from being done with them, either... the promises she'd made to Dusty, Mrs. Allen—even, hell to Blake. And the doc, too.

Cat had made quite a few promises and hadn't really kept 'em.

And despite what she'd promised Evie, there *was* still the matter and questions about Lou and this whole mess, and Cat had a good feeling that Peter wasn't gonna rest, wasn't gonna let go until he found them out. And Cat had that feeling, too, that tingling right in her gut, that was exactly where he was gonna go next. Which meant that she was gonna need to find something out if that was the only way to get Peter back home, to keep him from really and truly falling off that knife's edge.

But for now, she'd another promise to keep.

A few of 'em, actually.

"Where you headin', Miss Justice?" Sadie asked. "Out a town? Back out to the range where the sun always shinin' and not one inch of smoke clouds the sky?"

"Home," Cat said. "I'm heading home."

CHAPTER FIFTY-ONE

Small footsteps creaked on the floorboards behind Evie from where she stood—alone—on her front porch. Jacobs and all his fellows, his followers and believers, gone.

For now, at least.

Disappeared into that black smoke and ash with neither outline or shadow remaining. No more Marybell with her sad eyes, ones that carried such deep hurt in them as she'd looked at Evie and with such... such betrayal. As if it really had been Evie's fault.

Which just wasn't fair.

Marybell had known the truth about Evie and the kinda man Lou had been, and she'd still looked at Evie in such a way.

It hurt, too. Hurt something fierce. Especially... especially since Evie had this feeling that it was all somehow tied back to their husbands, back to the worked they'd done together at the Spectacular, except none of that mattered no more. Lou was gone and Evie, Evie—

She wiped at her eyes, causing the ash and dust on her to smudge even more.

She didn't care.

At least everyone had finally gone. At least Evie didn't have to see that mixed look of contempt and joy from Flossie, who'd held her nose so high like all this had been done per her will and hers alone.

Everyone had finally gone.

Which meant, too, that no one could see her.

No one could see how badly her knees and legs were shaking, both somehow still holding her upright. Her dress still wrinkled, and her hair still in complete disarray. Still completely and totally unacceptable in her appearance and attire, but nothing at compared to her actions and words here today.

Neither of which she could take back—and neither of which she wanted to.

The small steps came closer and she felt Rose's hand intertwining with hers. Bare fingers to bare fingers and then holding on, squeezing Evie's hand hard in both reassurance and love. Neither seemed to shiver from the cold and even though Evie's shawl was within reach, bundled up on the uneven floor where she'd dropped it, Evie didn't reach for it.

Instead, she and Rose were shivering for entirely different reasons than the cold.

Strength.

Jacobs hadn't been happy when he'd finally left.

Far, far from it.

The look he'd sent her way when he'd finally gone and turned his back on her, and those parting words, both filled her with dread. A promise that this wasn't over. The threat of Officer Blake had been enough this time, but it wouldn't hold. It wouldn't keep her and her dear children safe. Jacobs would come back spouting lies all his own or perhaps lies from other families and other men.

He would see her gone.

She knew, without a doubt, he'd not stop until he succeeded.

And she, with no recourse at all. Even if she had proof or truth on her side of Lou's infidelity and lies, it simply wouldn't matter.

Evie's legs shook all the more and Rose tightened her grip.

Strength.

How much of it did she have? How much did Cat think she had?

Just the thought of the other woman somewhere out there with Peter, doing her best to bring her boy home—Evie's hands, her whole body, really, got to shaking like a leaf. A trembling that started in her fingers and swept through her so hard and fierce her teeth started chattering. And her body, too, it seemed to lose whatever strength it'd found because she was slipping down to the porch, her legs simply not having the strength to hold her up any longer.

And Rose was there, helping her sit down. Her hands gentle and loving, and when Evie turned and looked in her daughter's big eyes, she found something she hadn't expected.

Strength.

And Rose wasn't there alone with her, either. Dusty... Dusty was still there. Dusty, the boy who'd came knocking on her door and handed her the paper that changed her life, he was still there. He didn't need to be, specially with his own past being what it was, but he *was* there and helping her settle in comfortable as she could on a porch that was about ready to snap and a cold that bit right through her, promising it was gonna be a long, cold, and right miserable day.

"You kept your promise," Evie said to Dusty.

Dusty just nodded. "I try. From time to time."

She believed he was, in fact, quite wrong. She had a feeling that when he gave his word, he meant it these days because... because your word, and your honor, it was about the only thing a person had left to them when they started walking down this other side of life.

The fear she'd felt earlier back when Jacobs had been pounding on her door certainly was still there, but not as strong as earlier.. Yet somehow, somehow Evie had done the impossible and showed her daughter strength. Strength when it was the last thing it'd felt like she had.

Evie reached across and pulled Rose into her lap, and Rose came to her.

They sat there together, with Dusty standing above them. Just the three of them on that porch, lookin' quite the sight if someone bothered to sneak another peak at mad Evie sittin' out there. Peter should have been there with them, standing right there in that spot that Dusty now was.

Peter...

Evie sighed.

She didn't even know what Dusty was still doin' here, other than his promise. because there just wasn't much more he could do. Her path was pretty much set—despite what she'd said, standing up to Jacobs and her neighbors. She doubted very much that she'd a choice at all except to find a new place to live. One that wouldn't mind having a fallen lady living in their neighborhood, and hopefully... hopefully a place that'd be safe and welcoming enough for her children.

If she got them both back.

Evie's arms tightened around Rose and she pulled her daughter closer. Breathing into her tangled hair, then out again.

Rose hugged her. Hugged Evie so tight then and she found that her face was wet.

Her tears, she realized.

Not Rose's, but... but hers. Grieving for the home and the life they'd had, and one they couldn't ever get back.

"What happens now?" Rose asked.

Evie wiped her face. "I don't know, dear-heart. I don't know."

Sure, she'd found strength, the same one Cat had said she'd had in her, but Evie wasn't a fool. She knew it wouldn't be enough. She couldn't go on fighting her neighbors while doing... while doing the only work that'd have her. There was no way she'd have strength enough for that, for both.

Rose settled her head against Evie's chest. Strands of her hair tickled Evie's nose and she simply breathed in. Breathed in the scent and feel of her little girl even as she held her closer.

Tighter.

"What did papa do?" Rose asked.

"I don't know. I don't know."

Dusty was watching her too, those green eyes of his seein' if she were telling the truth, most likely.

She shook her head.

But Dusty's eyes narrowed as if he was seein' or hearin' that little piece there, that little lilt of her voice that remembered what few words Lou and Jacobs had spoken that night when she'd been greener than a dog.

"I don't like the bad man," Rose said.

"Me, neither," Evie said.

Certainly not now that she knew the truth about Jacobs, or at least his character. He'd come here that night she'd been sick to intimidate Lou, to manipulate him—

But again, she just couldn't find the energy to care. She'd no room in her life for curiosity.

"Will you find out?" Rose asked. "Find out what Papa did?"

"Not me," Evie said. "I, I need to find a job, little one. So I can keep doing my best taking care of you and Peter."

She felt Dusty still watching her.

This time she didn't dare look up.

"But what about that lady? The cowboy lady? She can help. She wants to help."

Evie's throat tightened. Her daughter... too thoughtful, her mind too keen. She wished, at least in this moment, it wasn't so. Wished it all just go away as Lou had.

"I told her not to," Evie said, "... about this. I told her to bring Peter home."

That was all that could matter now. Lou was gone. He'd done what he'd done and all Evie could do now was look to the future... and whatever kinda one she could even make.

"She could help," Rose said. "The cowboy lady should help."

"I just want her to bring Peter home. That's all I want."

Dusty shuffled his feet on those half-broken floorboards. "You know how that's gonna happen? The truth."

"Truly, I don't know."

Again, all Dusty had to do was look at her and Evie got to squirming... not so much for his gaze but cause she knew in her heart he was right. At least... least in this matter...

"There's something else, isn't there?" he asked.

Evie nodded. "A little thing, that's all."

"Might make all the difference in the world, you know. To Peter."

"I don't see how it can. It can't..." Her voice broke. "Nothing can change my path."

"I'm not asking for you," Dusty said. "I'm asking for Peter."

Evie met his eyes, and this time she didn't look away. Didn't even a blink.

"You're askin' your son to come home," Dusty said. "A kid like that is hurting. Hurting real bad. If you want him home, than he'll need answers. If he finds out you had any of them, small as they are, you'll never see him again."

Evie closed her eyes a moment. She breathed in the scent of Rose, holding her little girl close.

She opened her eyes and Dusty was still there, still waiting.

"Kids like us," Dusty said, "we don't come back twice. Most of us... most don't even come back once. Don't let him down, Ms. Evie, not after all Cat's doin' bringing him home to you."

Dusty was right. He was asking her to trust in Peter and so... so...

So, Evie told him.

Again, it wasn't a whole lot, just snippets and all, but Dusty kept that green gaze on her, and when she was finished, he tipped the brim of his cap, then he was gone.

And she wasn't, wasn't sure either if she'd ever see him again. And somehow, somehow that set all right with her. She hoped he didn't. Hoped he didn't have a need unless, unless it was simply something he wanted to do.

Like finding her. Like helping her as he had. Like caring about her when no one else did.

"Thank you," she whispered.

Yet even as she watched him disappear, knowing he was right in this matter, it still didn't change the fact that whatever Lou had been involved in—hell, if anything at all—it was simply done. Done and gone, just like Lou.

He wasn't ever gonna come back, either. Evie knew that; knew that right to her soul. And regardless of whatever *did* happen to Lou and that accident and the Spectacular, what happened afterwards with Lou losing his job, Evie knew without a doubt, that was on him.

That it was no one else's fault but his own.

Evie took a deep breath. She wiped away strands of hair from her face even as the chill of the day finally worked its way through her, settling deep in her bones, in her heart.

A* chill she knew wasn't gonna leave any time soon.

"Peter gonna come home?"

Rose looked up at Evie and with such seriousness, too. Such worry. The kinda worry that should never have been on a girl so young.

Evie wanted to lie, to smile and pretend that all was right in the world, that everything *would* turn out all right. But... but Cat had encouraged her to speak the truth, even to her little girl.

"I hope so, Rose. I hope—"

Evie's voice broke. She swallowed and tried again. "I hope he does. I hope he comes back to us. That's all I want. You and him, safe and happy."

Hope.

That was all she could do at this point. Hope it'd all turn out all right and plan... plan for the worst. Which... which she could do. She had the strength for that and more... more than she'd ever believed possible. She'd do what she could for her part, and despite the sickening swirl and that twisting feeling in her stomach, she wasn't as afraid as yesterday.

That... was something. A big something.

In the meantime, she'd trust in her new fellows and wait...

Wait for Peter to come home.

CHAPTER FIFTY-TWO

Cat wasn't the least bit surprised that Grace had gone and rang
ahead for a hack. Sure, Grace had said she'd wanted to talk
with Cat after her visit down to the cribs, but she'd taken one look at
Cat and said, matter-of-factly: "My business will keep. Head on
home, Cat, and get some rest. You look like hell."

To which Cat silently agreed.

Cause that was exactly the way she was feeling.

Like hell, that was. Specially the way her insides were twistin',
how her mind and body just felt so unsteady after everything that
had happened. Those girls lookin' at her and in the way that they had,
like she really was this hope for them, this, this justice—even as
broken as she was.

Hard to imagine. Even harder to believe.

Then, too, there was the memory of Rippi and the beatin' she'd
taken down there. And Peter... Peter running off into those tunnels
and that weighty feeling she had, right on her chest, that what
happened next... if anything *did* happen to him, well, it was on her.

She felt every inch of that weight pressing in on her, just like her
ghosts did.

So when that hack finally pulled up in front of the parlor house, it was a right wonder that Cat had managed just to get one foot in front of another. She needed rest and quiet. A chance to settle herself back into her own thoughts and her own body, 'specially with the way Alice and her ma were so darn close right then Cat was having a hard time tellin' if they were really there or if it was her mind—or her guilt—playin' tricks on her again.

Especially her ma.

Especially the way her mother's ghost went and looked at Cat, as if everything that'd happened was Cat's fault. Hers alone.

Her ma, she was just so clear to Cat right then. Her thick blond hair tied back as it always was in that heavy braid. Always perfect, too, without one strand outta place. Her hair, it'd gone white long before Cat had even started walkin' and the look sure fit her ghost just fine. So did the look she was givin' Cat, too. Disapproval. Complete and utter disappointment. That usual frown darkening her face in that same way it always had whenever Cat had come home. Face smudged in dirt and mud. Stockings ripped right through the seams, specially right there at the knees.

Every darn time, her ma would have that look on her face.

It never failed. Not once.

Didn't matter neither that Alice had been the older of the two, that it'd always been Cat who'd done the lookin' out for them both. Least until their parents were gone...

The wheels of the hack pulled up hard in front of her, pulling her either away from the ghosts or away from the memory, she certainly couldn't tell the difference between the two right then. Crushed gravel and rocks flew this way and that, pinged off the boardwalk she was standin' on and even a few off her heavy coat.

Her relief at having a quick, quiet ride home was short lived. Jack nodded down at her, tipping his tall black hat in greeting.

The drive would be quick, no doubt about it, but it sure as hell wouldn't be quiet. Considering the way her day was going just then, she wasn't the least bit surprised to see him.

Or that gleaming look in his eyes.

Yeah, she knew the look. That sparkle there that told her rightly he had some burning news to share. It was that look, this particular one on that thin, skeleton-like face of his, that he only got when he got to talking about her...

And Cat just didn't want to hear it right then.

Couldn't.

She was hungry, sore, and livin' all kinds of hurts right then. The physical kind and the not-so-physical, and just plain wasn't in the mood, not one bit, for this particular topic.

And she doubted, rightly so, that her heart or soul could handle it 'bout now, either. Not after... not after the cribs. Not after seeing Sadie and reliving all those moments. Cat's successes. Her failures... especially not knowing if she was adding Peter to that score, either.

All she wanted—no, *needed*—was to go home and rest.

Cat raised her hand, cutting Jack off before he got going with whatever it was he was burnin' to say. "Jack. I ain't interested right now. I'm hurtin', I'm hungry, and all I'm wanting is to get home."

His bushy eyebrows 'bout rose all the way to that black top hat of his. "Even if I've got some news for you?"

"Especially then."

Except he didn't really have nothing important to say, though, otherwise there'd have been no way, neither heaven or hell, that would've kept him from telling her so.

Cat knew it. He knew it.

So he said nothing, just went and frowned, pretty mighty and deep, as she climbed up onto his hack, the whole thing creaking and groaning as she settled herself in before slamming the door behind her. Which hurt. Hell. It hurt like *hell.*

Jack said nothing to this.

Oh he was pretty darn sullen, but he said nothing and she knew she was right on the money considering his so-called news.

"You missin' something?" Jack asked, nodding at the empty seat behind her. "Or someone?"

"No."

Jack knocked back the brim of his hat with a knuckle. "Did you lose him?"

"No." Least, not yet, anyway. "Just get me home, Jack."

"Well, alrighty then, Miss Justice," he said. "Have it your way. I'll get you home. Though I'm thinkin' you might come to regret not hearing what I've got to say."

"I'm thinkin' I'll live."

Cat pulled her hat down low over her eyes, as if that could block out some of that ash and smoke—it didn't.

"How 'bout you send word later on?" she asked. "Or find Dusty. He always knows where to find me."

If Dusty didn't already know for himself—which, he probably did. Either way, she'd find out in good order, but for now all she wanted was to close her eyes and rest a bit.

Just a bit, she promised herself, and then she'd be back to her usual self. Her usual sharp mind and figure out just how the heck she could help out Evie and Peter—if there was anything else she could *do* to help, which wasn't seeming likely at this point. But Cat didn't get a chance to think long on this before her mind just sorta hazed out.

And then, before she knew it, her rest was over.

Jack was just pullin' up in front of Mrs. Allen's house, which had a few more lights on than when she'd left earlier. Lights that gleamed out of the smoke like shining little beacons of hope. Cat slowly sat upright, pushing back her hat and getting a good, clear look at the house. Or thought she was, cause her mind was still dull and tired. Except for that word.

Hope.

She felt it. Felt that word there echo inside her even as she tried to make sense of it. Tried to understand how those girls down there, living in all that darkness, still saw her in such a way. Specially when she, herself, felt so far from it and instead felt quite the opposite inside.

A new light turned on, this time in the sitting room.

The very room where Cat had spent so much of this past week staring out that window, trying to figure if it was all worth it, if everything she'd done had been worth it. She still didn't quite know the answer to that, but those girls... no, those women, they sure seemed to believe so. Even though it felt to Cat like she'd done nothing at all to help them, nothing at all to change their lives.

It'd all sure looked like the dark seemed a mess to her.

Cat studied Mrs. Allen's house, her mind taking in those details, where those lights were and what they could mean, but it did so in a distracted way. Not really focused, not really seeing. Maybe more lights than when she'd left. Perhaps Mrs. Allen had returned from her errands. Maybe was sitting down to a nice meal with Chin or some neighbor. A neighbor who had managed to accept Mrs. Allen and her glorious past, least enough to enjoy a meal. Something that Cat couldn't ever seen happening to Evie and her family, least not out on that street they lived on. But hopefully, if God were willing, Mrs. Allen had managed to secure a better place for Evie. A home, maybe. And if not that then at least a decent place of employment. One more suitable than the likes of Grace's underbelly.

And regardless of what she'd told Peter, she sure as hell hoped Evie never found herself in a place like that.

One could hope, right?

Another light switched on.

Again in the sitting room, or maybe just the fire gettin' lit as this particular glow seemed more of the orange variety—though it *was* hard to tell through all that smoke. Maybe Mrs. Allen had picked up another boarder and was making the place all nice and cozy and welcoming, which was the exact opposite of all those feelings swirling inside Cat as she dragged herself off the hard seat of Jack's hack. Hard to tell the time of day, too, except for her stomach reminding her just how hungry it was.

Which it did, and quite loudly, in fact.

Reminding her, quite clear, that she hadn't actually had much to eat... or... at all, really, unless one went and counted coffee. Which she knew for a fact Mrs. Allen would *not*.

Promises to keep, a whole lot of them.

Jack got off the hack and swung the door open for her. He tipped his hat and damn it to hell, that gleaming look was back in his eyes as if askin': You sure about this?

Cat nodded. "Thanks, Jack. I'll see you round."

"I've no doubt, Ms. Justice. No doubt at all. Take care of yerself now, and get some rest."

Then he winked at her.

If Cat was feeling more like her usual self, she'd have done something real ladylike, like spit at him. As it was, she was just too damn tired and sore to do much else than shake her head and get her body movin' again. She stomped her boots on up those stairs, shakin' off as much of the mud and muck as she could—she really wasn't interested in all those things Chin said to her that she couldn't quite understand —and slammed that front door as she did so. The whole house shook, including those windows, and she sure as heck hoped it'd been a cue for Chin to grab her some bread or something of substance. Or hide the good china.

Her arms were feelin' a bit weak and tingling, and her stomach really was growling something fierce. And hurting? My God, she was hurting.

She didn't hear no one movin' in the house, which was a bit odd seein' as how many lights were on. Instead just the shifting of some floorboards, but really, she was just too damn tired to care much.

She stood there in the entryway pulling off one glove then the other before gettin' stuck on working those buttons of her coat loose. It sure wasn't goin' so well, not with how every time she moved a whole lot'a pain went shooting out from her shoulder.

Also, her fingers being half frozen from the cold weren't helping none, neither.

Someone moved about the house, but she was just too busy shovin' her hair out'a the way to give it much thought. Instead, wishin' she'd been well enough to work the whole knotted mess into a braid or been brave enough to just lop the whole thing off, at least until her shoulder healed.

Which wasn't likely to happen any time soon considerin' the pace she'd been going these past few days.

She kept on struggling with her coat when her thoughts drifted to Jack and that look he'd given her. The kinda look she'd only seen when he'd had something to say—usually about Blake.

Cat focused on one button, the dull brass refusing to go through that too-small loop.

She was just being silly, was all. Fanciful, even.

Blake had made his feelings about her quite clear. Quite clear. Just like he'd been clear there wasn't a damn thing he could do for Evie... even if he'd made his own promise, in his own way. Even if he'd later gone to the Spectacular Mine like Jack had said and asked about Lou...

Cat shoved aside more hair, this time being a bit too harsh as the movement pulled hard on her healing shoulder.

"Damn it."

God she was just a mess. And her thoughts? Dull and sluggish and silly. As if she should have expected anything different after what'd happened that morning, that... afternoon? God, she couldn't even remember what time of day it was. Afternoon? Evening? It all kinda went and blended together, certainly with the dark they was always livin' in. Then were there all those memories, too, each of them hurting, each of them clamoring about the surface and a heaviness that wasn't lettin' go any time soon...

All the while those damn buttons just wouldn't cooperate.

She grabbed her hat and slammed it there on that stand next to another hat. Another coat too, she noticed, but wasn't caring a whole lot seeing as how her eyes were waterin' right then. A tear or two slippin' out, the traitorous things they were.

It just weren't safe yet to really let go, to let all these feelings out, to really let herself *feel*. Certainly not safe enough to think about her ma, her ghost that was standing so close to Cat, whose shame and disappointment just went and speared right through Cat. She'd never been good enough, hadn't ever been the kind of daughter her ma had ever wanted. Too much like her pa. Too much spirit and independence...

Too much of Cat being Cat. Of simply being herself.

She hurt. Everywhere. Her heart. Her shoulder. All of it hurting. And she couldn't let go, couldn't think—

Especially when she looked up and saw Blake standing right there in the doorway.

Standing there watching her.

CHAPTER FIFTY-THREE

B lake."

His name slipped out like a whisper. Breathy and airy and nothing at all like her usual self.

A thought alone that did a whole bunch to her insides. Made them turn over and twist just so, like she was some young girl and this here was some gentleman caller... while at the same time it made her angry. Real angry. Because that wasn't the type of man he was and this wasn't the type of woman she was.

A lady.

It wasn't her and wasn't ever gonna be her. A fact which Blake had made clear, quite clear, certainly after this past week.

It wasn't helping, though, that her breath *was* catching there in her throat, making her feel a might bit dizzy and all. Which was perfectly reasonable considering she'd not eaten a damn thing all day, not to mention she was sore as all get-out... and feeling hurt and confused and uncertain on top of it all.

Cat glanced at the hat stand, and there, right beside hers, was his wide-brimmed black hat.

His.

It'd been right there and she'd missed it. And yep... there was his black coat too, just about as ash dusted as hers, as if he'd been out all hours of the morning and late into the day just like her. Yet, instead of going home... he'd come here.

Here.

To wait for her. To speak with her.

Cat closed her eyes a moment, feeling the mess she was on the inside, wishing like hell she'd had the calm and center to do this, confront whatever this was, right here and now.

She didn't, though, but then it didn't look like she had much a choice, either.

Blake clearly wasn't leaving.

Instead, he just kept on standin' there, right in that doorway, not saying a damn word. And there were a whole lot'a words he coulda said.

A whole lot that *needed* to be said.

But nope. He just watched her. Saying nothing. Hands resting at his side. Those blue eyes of his lookin' more like storm clouds right then than they'd ever had before. Well... almost. There'd been that one time, down there in the cribs, a time she doubted she'd ever forget —much as she wanted to. That smell of gun powder in the air, her ears ringing from the shot Sadie had fired, and then there was Blake bending over her, holding her. Hands both gentle and desperate. The way he'd gone and looked at her...

Almost like she'd mattered.

Mrs. Allen's house was silent. Not even the floorboards shifting from where they both stood, the sounds of a house slowly settling in as the temperatures outside dropped. No swish or movement of air. Just that shivering bit of cold that wasn't gonna leave, least until spring decided to rear its head and bringing the sun back with it.

Blake's large frame was a dark silhouette in the doorway thanks to a warm light flickering from the room behind him. There was a small pop, like from a fire. Maybe even a shower of sparks or two. Its light reflected off that stunning gold in his hair and she felt that twist in her again, right there near her in stomach, makin' her think back to that evening and the worry she'd seen shining right through his eyes—

Eyes that looked a heck of a lot like they did now.

Yet despite the way he was lookin' at her, didn't seem to mind one bit all these unsaid words between them. Least not enough to actually go and say them.

Cat, however, minded.

She was darn tired of tip-toeing around... around whatever this was. These words, these feelings or whatever the heck they were, hanging in that air between them. Heavy. Tense. Like they were living, breathing things all by themselves. Coming in and out of view like the ghosts who followed her—day and night, never letting go, barely lettin' her breathe.

And that heaviness?

It wasn't gonna go away.

She knew it. Knew it right there in her gut.

Couldn't because of the way he'd left their partnership. How after going and doing the impossible together, gone right into Grace's Gardens as they had, right into that den of rattlesnakes, trustin' in the other to keep 'em safe... something Cat hadn't ever felt before, hadn't ever trusted like before. How after all that, Blake had just, just left. Left without saying a damn word.

Cat breathed in, then let it out. She tried like hell to use all her daddy's teachings, but this time they didn't help one bit.

The hell with it.

She was who she was and Blake, for better or worse, knew it.

"I didn't fancy seein' you here." Cat crossed her arms. "Not any time soon."

"No? Thought Jack would have told you."

"He tried. I wasn't interesting in listening."

"Why not?"

"Usually when I'm too tired to listen, I don't. But no, that wasn't what I was talking about."

She looked at him. Really looked right at him, right in those blue eyes of his, which were swirling something fierce and growing darker by the second, as if warning her to back away, to not get too close. To not talk about what she was plannin' on talking about.

Except she wasn't gonna back down.

Not this time. Not ever again.

"Are we gonna talk about this, Blake?"

"Is there something to talk about?"

He was darn lucky she *wasn't* of the usual female variety, especially after everything he'd gone and put her through. All those questions, all that uncertainty. He was lucky he didn't have a fainting flower on his hands. Or the kinda woman who angered easily and acted on that anger.

Especially considering she carried a gun and all.

"Yeah, yeah, I think there is," she said. "I think there's a whole lot you and I need to get straight."

"We don't have to do this."

"Yeah, yeah, we do. You owe it to me. Owe me a straight answer. Cause I'd thought we were onto somethin', thought our partnership meant something, but then you went and stayed away and proved to me, pretty darn clear, that who I was and the work I did before still matters."

And... that it was always gonna matter.

Part of her wanted to back away, to let the whole matter drop and sweep it up under some rug or something. Except she owed it to herself to get an answer. To get the truth.

The truth... the same thing she'd gone and done for Norma.

"This whole week," Cat said, "and you never once came by. Never checked on how I was doing."

"I asked," he said. "Asked Mrs. Allen and Dusty, too. Told them I was busy with Norma's investigation—"

"Askin' after me and actually showing up are two different things and you know it. And if you were so busy, you wouldn't be runnin' around town helpin' a woman who the law can't *legally* do nothing for." Which she knew from both Fat Jack and that healthy dusting of ash on Blake's coat. "And you know I applaud, doin' what you can't, but that doesn't change the fact that you're here. You're here now."

Blake's eyebrows lifted. "I thought you hadn't talked to Jack."

"Not today, no. But that's not the point and you know damn well know it."

She knew he was trying to dodge, trying to shift her thinking, getting her to focus on Evie and her family instead of this lingering thing between them. She knew cause that was the exact kinda thing she'd have done in his shoes when she was huntin' for information or if she were trying to misdirect... especially when trying to keep her boots clear of a right big mess.

Blake ran a hand through his hair. "I'm sorry I hurt you, Cat. It wasn't my intent."

Hiding... denying... *that* had been his intent, and they both knew it. But she wasn't gonna hide, though, not anymore.

"Why are you doing this, Blake? Why are you here? You know who I am. You *know* the kinda work I did and you despise me for it. 'Cept now here you are helping Evie out and knowing the exact the kinda life she's walking into."

Why was Evie different from Cat? Why could Evie be forgiven, be accepted, but not her?

That part, though, she wasn't strong enough to say.

And yet there they were, these unsaid words, and it was like they *were* real, like they were still holding close in that small distance separating them. Like a deep ravine that no one, certainly not her, was ever gonna cross. And jumping over? Forget it.

And it hurt, knowing that.

Really, really hurt.

For the first time since she'd seen Blake standing there in that doorway, he was the one to look away first. "My feelings aren't... aren't so clear anymore. About this life. Yours. Evie's. Even Dusty's. And sure, I'd learned plenty from my aunt. How could I not when I was living under her house all those years? Seeing all those letters coming in, addressed to all those ladies. She was out of the business, but it was still part of her, like you. But mostly what I'm learning now, what I'm seeing, it's coming from you. It's because of you."

"That's not an answer."

Again, her voice, that breathy, airy whisper. This time, though, she didn't care.

"Why are you here?" she asked again.

"Because much as I resent all this..."

Blake nodded to Mrs. Allen's home and Cat knew he was referring to more than the house itself. The life Mrs. Allen managed because of her colorful past, the opportunities it brought her, the money she'd made.

"I'm a part of this life," he said, "much as I hate to admit it. Whether or not I want it, doesn't change the fact that I am. And Evie and her family? They're important, and I'll do what I can to help."

"Right. They matter. They're important."

Evie. Her family.

But not Cat.

She tried to feel like those words didn't tear into her the way they did... or if she were being honest, smashed into her as Rippi had done to her shoulder. That feeling as he'd shattered body and muscle. But this, though, this was worse.

Much worse.

Because try as she might, there was simply no denying it. No denying how what Blake was saying, and not saying, was hittin' too close to home, to some thoughts and feelings that had hidden in the back of her mind. Ones she'd known intellectually had never been meant for her, but apparently her heart, in some secret, hidden place, had hoped for otherwise.

Dreamed otherwise.

Foolish. Silly.

Blake still hadn't been fully honest with her, fully upfront in why Evie had mattered and Cat still got to hold onto this mantle of shame for the choices she'd made, choices where, like Evie, hadn't been much of a choice at all. But then maybe that was the best he could do cause at the end of the day, Cat had been a whore.

Even if now she was aiming to do something different, something grander.

Didn't matter. Not one bit.

"Fine," Cat said. "If that's how you want it. Evie will be glad for the help. Next time I see her, I'll tell her."

She concentrated on her buttons again. Hands shaking, though she wasn't sure this time if it were from all that pain lancing out from her shoulder whenever she so much as moved (something that she'd been better able to manage when she'd put the darn thing on earlier), or if it were from anger or from somethin' else she wasn't interested in —and certainly not interested in lookin' closely at.

Not ever.

Blake came closer then, his feet creaking on those floorboards. His steps determined and precise, just as they'd always been and somehow that they were now, just added to all the frustrations she was feeling. The very last thing she'd felt, ever since that night at the Gardens, was determined. Surety. Precision.

Ever since then, she simply hadn't been herself.

It felt, too, like that had been another thing Rippi had taken from her and she wasn't ever gonna get back, despite how much she tried. Cause... cause it hadn't been Rippi who'd taken it away, had it?

No.

In this, she'd only herself to blame.

Her.

Blake stopped in front of her, his boots so close they were nearly on top of hers.

Still, Cat didn't look up. Cause there wasn't no need. He'd made his stance, his opinions, perfectly clear, or as clear as he could. And she understood them. Understood that she was just a different breed of woman than Evie and there wasn't no shame in that—

Except then his hands went and touched hers.

Her fingers, fumbling with those stubborn brass buttons,

instantly and completely stilled.

"What I'm trying to say," he said, "is that this isn't clear to me right now. Hasn't been probably since I met you. And that night? That night in the Gardens?"

He waited, as if wanting her to look up and meet his gaze.

Finally she did.

Blake's eyes were a swirl of black. Storm clouds. Thunder and lightning and all that. She could practically feel it, thundering there in her own chest. Maybe even shining out her own eyes.

"What about that night?" she asked.

"I don't know what it's been like for you, probably like hell, but for me it's been a nightmare. Over and over again. I keep hearing that gunshot and then I'm running down those stairs, already knowing it's too late. *I'm* too late. To do anything. To save you. You're all down there alone in that damn dress."

He stopped. Frowned. No... there wasn't one speck of blue, not even a glimmer, left in his eyes.

"It's a nightmare," he said, "and nothing I do—I can't pull myself out of it. I thought staying away from here, from you, would help."

"Has it?"

"... No. Certainly not the way I'd expected."

Blake moved her hands aside and gestured to her coat. "May I?"

He was askin' a question that he wouldn't have ever asked another lady because the action itself wasn't one he'd have ever offered to a lady.

But Cat wasn't a lady and never would be. A fact they'd both clearly established. But then, despite the flush deepening her cheeks and it being a bit harder to breathe, she wasn't about to get out of this coat anytime soon.

She nodded.

Blake pushed one button through, then another. His fingers moving so sure and confident, just like his steps, but neither was he rushing. Not hurrying to finish the task.

They were so close his fingers surely felt the rise and fall of her chest, just like he musta known how their breaths whispered out and intertwined in that slightly chill air between them.

"So," Cat said, "you stayed away, didn't want to check on how I was healing, except now you're saying it didn't help. You gonna tell me why or are we gonna talk about this?"

He chuckled. "And that there's part of the reason. You're not like any other woman I've met, Cat. Cowboy Cat. Miss Justice. Not a one."

"Cat'll do just fine. Like I always told you."

"I know. I know. And I'm sorry. Sorry I hurt you. Sorry I stayed away and didn't say anything."

Out of everything she'd expected, it hadn't been that.

An apology.

But it was also more than that. It was also a truthful acknowledgement of her own hurt, her own feelings...and that she mattered.

To him.

Which meant it was only right that she speak the truth, too.

"I needed you," she whispered. "You were there. You knew what happened."

All week she'd been waiting for him to come by, to check in on her, how she was holding up—or not, as the case was. All uncertainties, all her insecurities. Because he'd been there. He'd understood.

And he'd understood her.

Least she'd thought so.

He finished with her coat and gently, carefully, moved her tangled mess of hair behind her shoulder.

"I am sorry," he said.

"You said that."

"I let you down and I can see, I can see everything that happened is still eating at you."

She wanted nothing more than to cross that distance and just lean her head on his shoulder. To just stand there and feel comfort, the same as Cat had done for Evie just yesterday. Just lettin' someone else hold her a moment and take on some of that burden.

She didn't, though.

"See?" He touched her chin. Briefly. Gently. "Still hurting. So I'll keep saying I'm sorry because it's what you deserve. We were partners that day and I should have been down there with you. And... I'd like to think that we're still partners. Least, I'd like to be. If you'd let me."

Cat closed her eyes a moment, feeling the relief rushing through her and... and something more. Something a lot deeper. Something an awful lot like hope.

The urge to cross that distance, to seek and accept comfort and kindness was so strong, but even for her with this need to stay separate and independent, to protect herself from the exact kinda hurt she'd been feeling all along. Yet even with all that, even though she didn't lay her head on his shoulders like she may have secretly wanted, she still felt it.

Hope.

Who'd have known, even after all these years, even after everything she'd been through and the complete disappointment she was to her mother, her mother's ghost that was lingering so close Cat could nearly feel her cold fingers brushing against her arm, even with all that... Cat still felt this little thing called hope.

And not a little thing at all. Far, far from it.

"I think I'd like that," she said. "I'd like that very much."

Cat stepped away from him and Blake's hands fell to his sides. Much as she regretted it, there were those out there who needed her. After all, she'd made a promise to keep—a few of them, in fact—and she aimed to keep them.

"I think we both know the right place to start." Cat nodded towards the front door, closed as it was to the smoke and darkness. "There's a family out there relying on us to do right by them. I'd like to do what I can, but I'll be needing that information from you."

"Always, Cat." While Blake's eyes got a tinge more blue in them, they were still mostly black. "Always."

And this time... she believed him.

CHAPTER FIFTY-FOUR

Peter finally stopped running.

He bent forward, hands resting against his thighs. That cold wind doin' its damnedest to make him shiver, but right then was failing pretty mightily. His chest heaved up, then down again. A cough racked right on through him, and the more he breathed in that foul air, the more he kept on coughing.

'Cept his body couldn't help it.

He needed the air thanks to all that running he'd done in the underground, and this was the only air he got. Smoke and ash and a whole lot more thanks to those smelters that just kept on burning, that didn't mind one bit the arsenic and whatnot they were done breathing in, again and again.

And right then... he just didn't care. Couldn't. Not with all those numb feelings inside.

Peter hadn't stopped running. Not once in the underground tunnels.

Not once.

The moment his feet had touched onto those rotting stairs leading down, down into that darkness, into the tunnels, he'd kept running. The tunnels themselves were narrow and tight. Hard rock jutting out in every which way as if someone had taken a chisel and made the way by hand, inch by painstaking inch. He'd tripped a few times. Felt those sharper bits tear into his legs as he'd moved.

But still, Peter didn't stop.

Couldn't.

It was like his body had overwhelmed his mind and he just moved with a single determination.

To learn the truth.

And he did. Boy, did he ever.

Learned the exact kinda life that awaited the end of this road for his mother, maybe even his sister. Specially if they weren't careful—if he wasn't careful.

There'd been a scattering of lights strung up along the ceiling of the underground. Most were burnt out, which didn't surprise him one bit, and the ones that somehow stayed lit cast more shadows than actual light. But still, for Peter, it hadn't mattered.

He'd simply... *moved*.

Never stopped. Never paused at the forks and debated if he should go left or right. Never climbed up when he found the different varieties of rope and wooden stairs. He'd stayed and he moved, all because he needed to. And just like Cat had said, he'd needed to see.

So he did.

Saw everything. Saw those poor women, creatures looked more like, as if they came straight out of one of his pa's scary stories. Those few he'd tell when he was feeling generous and fatherly, though they'd always been stories about ghosts haunting the mines, specially in the Spectacular. All those miners who'd lost their lives in some fire or accident or tragic way—and especially those who done died 'cause someone else went and got careless, made a mistake, decided bringing down whiskey went well with their lunch buckets.

All those ghosts... still searching for their way home.

Those stories hadn't been hard to believe, not when Peter and every kid and family grew up knowing what those whistles meant. Knowing that they did—and would—keep on happening.

But as far as Peter was concerned, the real ghosts didn't come from his pa's stories.

They were those women. Those women living down there, if you'd call them living.

They were ghosts, no mistake, just not exactly dead yet.

He didn't exactly get close, running as he was, but close enough to see into their eyes. He'd thought that one woman up there in the cribs of the Gardens had been bad. Well, Cat had been right again. He'd hadn't a clue what real death looked like.

He did now.

And those women, those who lived and worked down in those tunnels, not a one of 'em had an inch of life shining out of their eyes. Their light had gone out, they were just, just still breathing.

Peter had run and saw everything, every little detail.

Taking it all in, remembering it, least until it got to the point where his mind simply couldn't take it no more... or maybe it was that place there in his chest. That place nearest his heart that hurt and twisted and ached whenever he thought of his mother, whenever he saw her as she'd been yesterday... standing in the school yard and all those others mothers turnin' up their noses at her, whispering about her... and, and Peter.

Peter, who'd gone and said such terrible, terrible things.

Hated himself for that.

But he wasn't running away anymore. Not this time.

Eventually his mind shut down, or more like fixated on what he needed to do next. But even then, he kept on moving. Simply couldn't stop until he saw every inch of that underground in as much as he could find, anyway. There'd been a couple turns there that were so darn small he'd barely squeezed through, and there were a few he'd passed by *because* he couldn't fit.

Slime and muck coated both walls, hanging low from that ceiling, too. Also covered those naked light bulbs until a bare glimmer managed to peak on through. It'd all gone and brushed off on him, on his coat and hands, staining them a black he looked like he belonged down here.

And maybe, maybe he did.

But he was back up top now. Back under that same darkness as below because there was still no sun and not a whole lot of feelings like hope... but that determination? It was still there. And... and he wasn't angry with his mother anymore.

He was angry at his pa.

He was angry at himself.

Peter's sides were hurtin' something fierce and his heart beat—well, pounded more like—harder than it'd ever had before. Though he also wasn't so sure if that pounding was cause of all that running—or if, if it were on account of where he was standing.

Waiting.

Grant School.

His school, least it had been until yesterday. Yesterday when everyone had read the newspaper and saw his pa's classified. When his teacher, Big Eyes Bertha, had gone and stopped him after class and made it pretty darn clear that kids like him—with mothers like his—weren't welcome here.

Peter pulled off his hat and wiped some of the sweat and grime off his face. Probably just smeared it around some rather than actually getting it off. Didn't know why he bothered, either. How he looked wasn't gonna change nothin'. Not anymore. Not with any of them.

Which was ridiculous seein' as how most of them weren't too better off than his family, maybe even a bit worse. Most of 'em poor, barely making ends meet. Probably a few mothers who'd no choice either but to go... go where they could, where would take 'em, and earn what extra coin they could.

Difference was the whole town didn't know 'bout it.

Peter grunted and squashed his hat back on his head. None of that mattered now. All that mattered was what he'd done come here to do. Which wasn't exactly gonna be easy, seeing as how he couldn't see a whole lot still thanks to all that smoke and ash. Both of which were so gosh-darn thick he'd had to get a lot closer than he was comfortable with.

But that, well, that'd be okay. It'd have to be.

He was a different man, now; he'd been changed.

'Cept that, though, was the frustrating part.

He'd changed... a lot.

But the outside, or the upside world as more felt like, with all that smoke? That ash stinging his eyes until part of him wished he was back down there in that darkness?

None of it had changed.

Not one bit.

Sure he'd been down in that underground for what felt like hours, 'cept up here it was exactly the same. Mind you, not that Peter could see a whole lot... as it was, he was barely able to make out the other side of the street where Grant School was resting, that giant brick building with all those lifeless windows lookin' more like black eyes than actual windows. He might have seen a flicker or light or two from within, but he sure doubted it. Only way to see through that glass was if you'd gone and punched right through it.

Least it was brick, though. Meant that most of the brick, while stained black like the rest of Butte, it was still there. Some of those other buildings that likened wood panels, well, those had a habit of going missing during the rough, cold times. Specially on the East Side. Specially during winter and those certain panels that weren't on so tight as the rest of them. Maybe he'd be doin' that, soon enough, if his mother didn't, if she couldn't—

Peter shoved aside the thought.

Grant School didn't have that particular problem. Instead, she had Big Eyes Bertha.

And no one, not even Bugsy, was gonna get into anything while Big Eyes was standing there right at the front door as all them kids streamed on out. Arms crossed over her thin chest, the usual frown scrunching up her face. She was doing as was customary, glaring down at each kid, scrutinizing them, straightening hats and collars, all the while that yardstick of hers tapping right there in her left hand.

Where it always was.

The kids were hustling outside and no one said a peep of complaint against Big Eyes. Least not until they were far from earshot or Big Eyes finally gave up her station and went back inside where she belonged.

Still, even standing there as he was, both shivering as the cold finally seeped back into him—or maybe it was helped along cause of all that sweatin' and pantin' he was doing—Peter was actually a bit proud. He'd timed it right, gotten here right as the other kids were gettin' out for the day. Didn't have to try again tomorrow. Didn't have to go into his neighborhood and risk, well, risk running into someone he wasn't ready to see just yet.

Sure, he'd been down in those tunnels awhile, yet even still he hadn't lost his sense of time.

That was something.

Some small victory, sure, but he'd take it. Especially considering what he was coming here to do.

As usual, big ol' clumps of kids moved together. They went by neighborhood mostly. And sure, kids on the East Side had a right mix of neighbors, specially compared to a lot of those other neighbors. Even still, there were groups. And you stayed in your groups. Kids from Meaderville and McQueen, the Polacks, Cornish, all of them, and there, too, somewhere, were the kids from Peter's neighborhood.

The whole reason he'd come here.

He watched as all them kids pulled their hats down as far as they'd go and tugged coats up high on their necks. Heads down. Holed shoes kicking up frozen clumps of mud and whatnot. Not a one of them noticed him, but then they weren't looking his way, either, hiding as he was in the shadows. Probably pretty hard to see, too, what with all that grime staining his face, hands, whole body practically.

And yet... Peter found himself slinking even further into those shadows.

His breathing was finally starting to even out and his coughing was calmin' down some. And yet, still, he hid. It might... maybe... have had something to do with recognizing a few of his school mates.

Like there, in her pigtails, with eyes and face red as if she'd been cryin' again—and probably had been—was Susan Hoy. Not far from her was giant-sized Gibsy who gave her a good shove as he ran on by and a wicked grin as was his usual when it came to Susan Hoy.

His chest tickled pretty bad, right then. A cough ready to explode on out.

Peter covered his mouth to muffle the sound much as he could, even as his eyes got to tearin' trying to hold it on it. Just... just couldn't give 'em chance to see him and run.

And yet... and yet...

He was still hiding. Hiding in those shadows like he weren't good enough no more. Like who he was didn't matter no more.

And that thought, well, strangely enough, it didn't make those fire ants in him angry as they should have. Instead, he felt his grip loosening, his hold on being here, doing this hard thing, slipping away just like Susan Hoy as she finally found her mother. Those pigtails of hers, flapping behind her, a right skip to her step as she slipped away from Gibsy and all those other mean kids.

A mother who embraced her wholeheartedly. A mother who didn't get no dirty looks as his own mother had yesterday. All cause... cause she was one of the good ones.

The good mothers. The still acceptable kind whose reputation hadn't been smeared all across the papers.

For some reason Peter thought back to Cat right then, as she'd been standing there down in the cribs. Those tears in her eyes as she watched those other women, tears she hadn't bothered to hide from him. Instead just let him see.

Not hiding.

Which was the opposite of what he was doing.

Peter felt shame. Felt it burn hard right there in his chest.

Silly. He was being silly and foolish, lettin' his worry about others control him. And besides, he weren't no kid no more, not after what he'd seen. The kind of things that you couldn't unsee, either.

And he didn't want to. Didn't want to go back to being like one of them.

Peter straightened.

Let 'em see. Let 'em know he was there. He'd no reason to be embarrassed. No reason to be ashamed of what his *pa* had gone and done.

But even as he took that first step out of those shadows, leaving behind his little safe haven between them two buildings, came another thought. Another truth—

No one would notice him.

Even if they turned in his direction, got a good long look at Peter, they wouldn't see him. Not as he was covered in grime and filth. That's what they'd all been taught, after all, that's what all them mothers had done, poor as these families were, comin' in from all across the world no less, making sure that kids lookin' like Peter simply faded from view.

And how, if not for Cat, if not for the circumstance he found himself in, he'd still be that kid. Still be like Susan Hoy who went and smiled like nothing in the world mattered, even as her gaze *did* pass over him, outside of the shadows like he was. There was no pause, no spark or recognition in her eyes about the one boy who'd taunted her like no other, made her cry and put pepper in her hair. There was nothing. Nothing at all. Like she couldn't see the dark living right there underneath her toes.

Hell, *he* still wouldn't have known a place like the underground existed, wouldn't have known about those, those women who lived down there...

Peter felt the rage push in again. Finally. And for a moment took comfort in that.

Better than the shame, better than the resentment he was feeling towards himself, his old life... even if that rage was still part of his pa's legacy...

Course, to be fair, that sudden rage might have had something to do with him seeing those other mothers... the ones who'd given his own mother such dark glances. Mrs. Flossie and Mrs. Marybell and all those others, women who were supposed to have been his mother's friends.

He clenched his fists. Squeezing hard. Not letting go...

Mostly cause he couldn't stop remembering. Couldn't stop seeing all those looks they'd given him. His own friends. His school mates. Those mothers there. But more than anything, he couldn't help seeing and remembering everything in the underground.

He hadn't been able to stop running. Hadn't been able to hide or to retreat to that surface, either.

Cause... cause Cat had been right.

He'd needed to see. Needed to understand, especially, especially if he was gonna do what needed doing.

And now, now it was Bugsy's turn to see him.

CHAPTER FIFTY-FIVE

While Blake may have agreed to tell Cat everything he knew, he'd made it pretty clear that he wasn't gonna say shit until she sat down and got some food down in her. And... much as she wanted to run back out that door and do what she could for Peter and Evie, Cat knew, too, that she was doggone tired and sitting down to eat... well, it was probably best for all parties concerned.

So she did.

Found herself in her usual spot in the sitting room, staring out that front window and into the never-ending smoke and darkness that was Butte, trying her best *not* to remember the last time she was here with Blake and how that flaming rock went right through the window and barely missed her head—thanks to Blake. Yeah... she was better off focusing her energy on the food in front of her and getting it into her belly, cause that roast and buttered mashed potatoes wasn't gonna get there of its own free will.

Blake watched her, though those blue eyes of his every once in awhile darted to that window, as if thinkin' the same thing she'd been thinking but saying nothing, as promised.

All he'd said when they'd sat down was that he'd eaten early and this all here was for her.

It was an order, and make no mistake.

And Blake certainly smiled a bit at that because the order didn't come from him, but by the good ol' doc.

Yep. Cat wasn't surprised in the least that Doc Griffin wasn't too happy with her. He'd informed Chin, who'd informed Blake, that the moment Cat set foot in this house she was to eat every single bite off that plate, and if she dare thought about going back out there again without getting herself properly checked over, well, she was sure gonna be in a heap of trouble.

Blake, though, hadn't sent for the doctor. Not yet, anyway.

Neither had Cat, for that matter.

As far as she figured, Doc Griffin was one of those who'd been pushing her to keep working this life, helping out those who'd needed it. Course, he'd been talking about how important it was givin' her body a chance to *heal* before she went and did all that, but well, it wasn't like those folks like Lou cared too much about Cat and her healing. And besides, she made darn sure she ate every bite off this plate, so at least she could point out she'd followed *some* of what was asked of her.

Plus, she was pretty darn hungry.

Still, as much as she had let Peter go run off into those tunnels on his own, he was still her responsibility, and she'd given quite a few promises when it came to keeping him safe. And right now she had this feeling, right there in her gut, that he was gonna be needing her and real soon, too. But first *she* needed food—and whatever Blake had learned from when he'd gone up yesterday to talk to the big bosses at the Spectacular.

Cat was missing some pretty big pieces of the story here, and while Evie only wanted Peter home, Cat knew better. She'd seen that determined look in his eyes to know what the kid had really needed. It was the kinda shining look, that slanted way of looking out at the world, the kind that went and only concentrated on the gray and the shadows—a look that had reminded her so much of Dusty. And in doing so told her rightly just what Peter needed to come home.

He needed to understand the whole of the story and not just what his mother wanted him to believe. Or at least as much of the story as they could learn with his father having gone and left town as he had.

Well, come what may, Cat *was* goin' back out there to look for Peter and this time, she'd not be alone. Blake was coming with her. A thought which, well, it put a smile right on her face. Sure it was a bit small, but it was there nonetheless. And when Cat finally got to scraping off the last of her plate and focusing more on that glorious hot coffee as she finished up gettin' the last of that roast juice onto those mashed potatoes and into her mouth, Blake seemed to think this was a sufficient time to tell her about his venture yesterday.

Which, as Cat soon found out, wasn't much at all. Certainly not as Fat Jack had led her to believe.

Cat slowly lowered her fork and even managed to swallow the food she was chewing before speaking. "They don't remember him? You mean, at all?"

Blake shook his head, a few strands of his golden blond hair trailing right across his forehead just so. "I spoke with the foreman of the Spectacular myself. He didn't remember Lou Blonberg or the accident."

"That's... odd."

"Not really, if you think about it. Accidents? They happen all the time. You haven't been around long enough. In fact, don't think we've had a single warning whistle since you got here, which is a bit surprising. And the miners? They've got hundreds or more working for them, sometimes just on one shift alone. And a mine like the Spectacular? With the depths they're working at? It's no surprise the man can't remember something that happened nigh on a year ago."

"That's... surprisingly unhelpful. Jack sure made it sound like you had some big news."

Blake snorted. "I imagine the point of Jack's news wasn't the one you were thinkin' of."

Meaning him... and her.

Yeah, yeah that sure sounded like Jack.

And yet... maybe that's what he'd meant, and maybe that's what he hadn't.

She shook her head. Her long hair, still unbraided and still gettin' in the way, made a run for falling right onto her scraped-clean plate. Shoved the whole irritating mass aside.

Blake just grinned. Or a smirk, if truth be told.

"This just isn't makin' sense," Cat said. "The moment Jack picked me up he went on about how I was steppin' into a right heap of trouble again."

"And with what I've found out, that's not seeming to be the case."

"Or maybe it is but it's just... simpler."

Simpler than Norma had been, at least with those men living up higher in the world and all. Mr. Rippi? That had been simple enough to understand. Maybe... maybe this was something similar.

"Or maybe, too," Blake said, "it's a right mess because you've got a father who went and left his kids behind and damned his wife in the process."

There was a darker tone in Blake's voice right then, one that had her flashin' back to the man she'd first met and who'd followed her around Butte. Cat couldn't help but remember that it'd been Blake and his mother who'd come to live here with Mrs. Allen... no father. If that was the case, well, it wasn't a new story.

It was Blake's, though, and his to share only if he wanted it, so Cat didn't ask.

Still... she was getting a right headache trying to put her finger on some small detail she was missing about Lou and his whole mess of a situation, and couldn't help but wonder if it was her own lack, again, that was getting in the way.

Cat rubbed at the bridge of her nose, trying to think, to focus. Trying to be that woman with all that clarity like when she'd first stepped off that train into Butte, before she'd gone and made all those mistakes that ended up with her gettin' injured and a whole lot'a girls being in danger.

"You okay?" Blake asked.

"I'm just... I'm not myself. Ever since that day..."

How long had she wanted to confide in Blake? Now here was her chance and there wasn't time at all. Peter and his family, they needed her. Whole and sound.

Finally, Cat shook her head. "I'm just not feeling like myself."

But Blake just watched her, like he knew the undersides of all those she weren't saying, all those ones that weighed on her so heavy, were pulling her down and wanted to keep her under if she let it.

"It happens," he said. Kind. Simple. "We all go through it."

"We?"

"Police officers. Investigators."

Now *that* word caused her breath to catch right there in her throat, and it took a few moments before she got her breathing up and around it again.

"I doubt it," Cat managed. "We're pretty different, you and I."

Blake's eyebrows lifted and for a moment, there was that look back in his eyes, the ones that didn't have a whole lot of blue doin' any swirling but a whole lot 'a black.

"We can argue that part later," she said, waving him off.

Maybe that person was still there in her and thinking about Blake wasn't gonna help matters right then. So instead, Cat focused on Evie and all her problems that went tied right back to Lou.

Lou Blonberg.

Cat pulled up every detail, every scrap and memory of what Evie had said about Lou. *Had* he been drinkin' on the job?

She asked Blake this, but the foreman, he said, didn't know. And accordingly to Blake, it seemed *this* would be one of those times when a miner would be remembered, especially how damn dangerous it was down there.

Maybe enough of a reason to pass on the word to other mines?

Could that be why Lou couldn't hold down a job ever since?

Blake didn't know.

There was no actual evidence except what had been seen and known of the man himself, from what Fat Jack witnessed of carting off Lou to the train and then to Lou Blonberg's own family. But... but nothing more.

The piece she was missin', that she wasn't understanding, was the mining life, and that was simply because it wasn't a world she was part of or privy to. From what she understood the fellowship down there was pretty important, pretty close and tight. Even with all them nationalities thrown together down there, it didn't matter cause it *was* about life and death.

Least, that's what she witnessed every time she saw those miners come walking by her window, all those days she was healing and whatnot. Seeing that look in their eyes, when the smoke was light enough to see that far, anyway. Still, even from this distance, she'd managed to see the fellowship.

Cat's insides got to tingling right then, and those hairs on the back of her neck were rising. Felt, too, like she hovering just above something... some thought... some connection...

And still it alluded her.

Instead of swearing as she really wanted to do, to just toss up her hands and give up, Cat did the opposite. Sure she was hurting and sore and tired as all hell, not to mention the exhaustion she was feeling just from finally dealing with this thing living right between her and Blake. Then there were her own ghosts hovering nearby, like her mother really only wanted to coax her upstairs, chill, ghostly touch and all, and off to bed. Or to give up, more like.

Cat focused on breathing, just as her pa had taught her.

Pulling it into her, then out again. Nice and slow and even. And bit by bit, she felt herself slowly settling, almost... almost pulling together. And then with this new clarity, or centering if you will, she asked Blake to go over every little detail, every little bit that the foreman had told him.

Blake nodded and glanced one last time out the window.

Cat did, too.

Just in case.

This was exactly how that last incident had started, with her asking him to go back over each detail while her mind did its thing, pulling all them pieces together, seeing the larger whole while time itself seemed to slow...

At least, that'd been her before her injury.

Now?

She wasn't so sure.

Maybe never would be again.

But Blake certainly seemed to think so because he went back into the tale again without hesitation, pulling up even more than he'd said the first time.

"Lou Blonberg certainly *did* work there," Blake said. "And for quite awhile, too. Six years, nearly. The foreman was good enough to go on and open Lou's file, for my badge and all, though I didn't have much legal ground to be asking and he did it, anyway. In all Lou's time there, though, there wasn't much written up about him. Just that he did his job and did it well enough. A regular miner who showed up, did what was asked of him, got paid for it." Blake rubbed at his chin for a moment, those blue eyes now goin' a bit distant. "There was note in there about him, though, that he wanted to keep moving up, keep advancing, training for something but the ink was to smudged for either me or the foreman to figure out..."

"Advancement? Is that normal?"

Blake shrugged. "Common enough, actually. Nobody *wants* to be a mucker forever just like no one wants those real dangerous jobs, if they can help it."

Which made perfect sense.

Still... Blake really hadn't been kidding. There hadn't been much there at all. Or maybe they just weren't looking at this in the right way. Or maybe *she* wasn't, with all her own misconceptions getting in the way, muddying the waters.

"Jack..."

A memory tugged at Cat of the ride Jack had offered her and Peter, my God, was that only yesterday? And Jack, being Jack, had gone and told her much as he knew about Lou, all the while thinkin' that Peter had been sleeping.

"Jack said something about hoist engineer."

Blake whistled. "That *would* be a lofty reach, no mistake."

Cat sipped her coffee. Thinking and thinking hard. "Is it? I've no idea."

"Those are the folks who lower the cages down to each of the levels. There's some complicated system of bells and pulleys, a whole way of communicating because it's just too damn loud in there for talking. Ain't no way a guy like Lou would ever become hoist engineer."

"But he'd have to start somewhere."

Even as Cat said this, her mind got to thinking... he'd start at the bottom, that's for sure, and surely there *were* more miners involved in that complicated system than just the engineer itself. So maybe he was eyeing a job somewhere else, like maybe a fellow on the receiving end of those signals, someone even answering those bells at each of the levels? But did it really matter?

Yes.

Every bit of this puzzle mattered right now. Not for helpin' out Evie and her situation, but in helping Peter understand... even if the answer they were looking for really was simple...

"His old crew," Cat whispered. "They would know."

If they were even still there. If they remembered him. But... but if there *had* been an accident and if there *had* been drinking involved, than surely someone there would have remembered.

Cat thought back to Peter and his neighborhood. Her mind running back over those little bits and pieces as she'd held Evie, right here in this room, and let the other woman cry. There, right there, was another piece.

She knew it. Felt it.

"You onto something?" Blake asked.

Cat held up a hand, closed her eyes a moment, and breathed.

One breath out.

Then another in.

Pulling in a memory. Feeling herself almost knitting back together the way her shoulder was now doing, now healing nice and slow. As she and Dusty had walked through the ash and smoke and darkness, following behind that group of mothers and young kids to the school...

Blake said nothing. Simply leaned back in his chair. Arms crossed against his massive chest. Just watching her, giving her the time and the quiet she needed.

She was only half aware of this, though. The rest of her, or most of her, was following her breath, following those tingles and where they were guiding her. All those puzzles and pieces slowly turning round and round, until she had them turn just that way, then another... and saw how they all started to fit together.

Cat remembered.

Remembered those two women most of all. Flossie. Marybell. Marybell's words about how her Harold had worked with Lou—

Another piece slowly falling into place.

"What about the accident?" Cat asked, holding onto the image of those women even as she opened her eyes. "Tell me about it."

"Nothing much. The foreman had to go and check again just to get me that answer. But like he'd first told me, it wasn't much, either. Just a timber gettin' caught in a chute, one it wasn't supposed to be in. Two guys up top trying to get it loose, another guy working at the lower end who nearly got himself crushed in the process. Probably not expecting it to come loose when it did or maybe just faster than he was expecting. He lived with only a few broken bones, which is a big relief in those situations."

"And Lou... Lou got fired. Even though there were two men involved."

"That's what I'm thinking, but the accident report doesn't list Lou directly. Or the other fellow."

Cat huffed, getting pretty darn frustrated with the Spectacular's lack of records on these matters. "Well, what *does* it list?"

"Date, time of his firing, man doing the firing."

Cat felt like she was onto something... an idea, right there...

But before she could catch the darn thing, that front door was shoved open, good and loud and *hard*.

Cat and Blake were out of their seats. Hands resting on their guns. Half turning and crouching low—

The memory of that rock crashing right through that window right at her came back hard and fast. How Blake had grabbed her, slammed her down.

Cat's shoulder flared. Pain, pain living just underneath her skin until it felt like she could barely move, barely breathe, and it all went to try and seize her up right then.

She fought it. Had to.

Couldn't let herself get hurt, get injured again...

Blake was there, too. She didn't know when he'd moved. Hadn't seen him. Hadn't heard him. But then, it was hard to see much of anything when black and red were alternating with her vision right then.

Blake was holding onto her. Holding her upright even as that stomping came closer and right into the sitting room—

And Dusty himself, complete with his usual black cap that went and rained down dust and ash on just about everything, entered.

Dusty.

Not an another attack.

Dusty's chest heaved up and down real fast-like, almost like he'd gone and run a mile in that smoke.

And that glare he sent Cat?

It never waivered. Not once.

"What the hell did you do?"

CHAPTER FIFTY-SIX

Peter saw Bugsy.

There was no mistaking it. No mistaking his once closest friend. Peter saw the minute Bugsy came out of Grant School with all them others, ducking out of that brick building as was his usual. Head bowed low, doing his best not to seen or noticed or heard.

Like... like Peter was now learning to do.

Bugsy wasn't tall like his pa and even Peter had a good foot or so on him, but he was thin. Real thin. The kinda thin that'd let a kid slip past a whole bunch of others, bunched together as they were, moving too without even stirring any of them oversized coats. And he did it right then, too. One minute he was right in the middle of the group and the next he was free and jumping down those brick steps and out to freedom, all to avoid gettin' his own fiddling from Big Eyes Bertha.

Bugsy's hat wasn't pulled low like the others, though, but instead kept on flopping with each step, like it was barely stayin' on, like it wasn't fitting so good no more.

Or maybe... maybe never had. And his face? His checks? Even from here, he looked thin. Real thin, just like the rest of him. Too thin.

How had Peter not noticed? Missed seein' that yesterday? Missed seeing it the day before that? Didn't get much of a chance to ponder on that too long, though, cause that's when Bugsy glanced right in Peter's direction.

Peter had a chance, right then. A chance to hide back in those shadows and no doubt, Bugsy would never have seen him.

But that woulda been the Peter of yesterday. The kid who'd felt alone and ashamed and hurt.

And now? Now...

Well, he still felt ashamed and he certainly felt hurt... but he wasn't alone no more. And... and he wasn't as afraid, either.

So Peter stood there, right tall and proud, and looked right at Bugsy.

And Bugsy, he looked right at Peter and stopped, stopped right there in his tracks like he'd gone and seen a ghost.

Peter stayed right where he was, lifting his head even a bit higher. Then he nodded.

It was a short kinda nod. Precise, determined. Cause that's what he was feeling right now. Feelin' more so than ever before.

He *was* gonna get answers and make no mistake.

And instead of doing what Peter had expected, turning away as Bugsy'd done yesterday, pretending like Peter didn't exist no more, Bugsy dropped his head. Dropped it real low to the point where Peter could see his shoulders, all hunched and narrow and pointed and—

Thin.

He didn't get no chance to think more on it cause Bugsy looked right at him and nodded.

The two had themselves a little moment. An understanding.

Bugsy's mouth twistin' hard into a pointed frown. He looked back at that grouping of mothers, probably looking for his own no doubt, hopin' that she'd not see him getting anywhere near a kid like Peter. But even still, Bugsy didn't run to her as he'd done yesterday, like... like maybe he couldn't. Peter didn't know what, but he saw *something* flash right quick in Bugsy's eyes...

A knowing.

And right then, Peter had this feeling of his own. It went and tugged at his insides, like his gut maybe... and maybe he was onto something. Maybe coming here and talking with Bugsy was the exact thing he'd needed to do.

Because clearly Bugsy knew something.

And that was exactly why Peter was there, why he was turning to Bugsy first. Hopin' that somewhere deep down Bugsy cared enough about their friendship to at least meet with Peter. And, well, it looked like Peter was right.

Because when their eyes met again and Bugsy went and nodded... right in the direction of the side hill.

So that's where Peter went to meet him.

His heart was poundin' hard and his feet poundin' even harder on that crushed gravel, feeling every stone like it bit through his thin shoes. Except he wasn't feeling it so much, cause there was that part of him that was just scared silly... scared that Bugsy was gonna show up and scared that he wasn't going to.

Yet still he hurried.

Not quite as fast as before. His body just weren't interested in doing something like that, running in all that ash and cold, certainly so soon after the last time. Bugsy, though, apparently didn't mind cause when Peter got to their spot out in the mine yard and that bridge they used as a fort so many times, Bugsy was already there. Bent over at the waist, hands resting on his knees, chest heaving, his coat seemingly so large the ends went and draped on the ground just then. Looked like he'd gone and ran harder than his body could handle.

And maybe that was true.

Cause when Bugsy looked up and saw Peter, Peter got hit with this feeling that Bugsy... Bugsy wasn't done running.

Not yet, anyway.

"What... what you doin' here... Peter?" Bugsy said in between all that panting. "What do you want? You know... know... I can't be seen with you no more."

Bugsy didn't say he was sorry or that he was real sore about losin' himself a friend. That, there, hurt more than the actual words and the truth of Peter's new life. That he weren't wanted, weren't welcome in those places he'd always been before. Hurt like hell to hear it spoken aloud so... and that his friend, supposed friend, wasn't sorry 'bout it none.

Course, it wasn't like Bugsy was wrong, and if Peter were being honest, he didn't exactly blame him, either.

It just was... what it was.

There'd be no changing things. No goin' back to the way things were. And if it'd been Bugsy standing there with his mother been written up in a classified, Peter'd be doin' the exact same thing as Bugsy now was.

But at least... at least Bugsy had showed up here at all. That was something. That was a big something.

"Look," Bugsy said, straightening some, breathing a little hard and panicked and desperate. "I got nothin' against your ma. She was good to me. Took care of me and I respect that; I respect her. But you all know that's over with now, right? You know? And we... we just can't be friends no more."

Again, not one word of being sorry or that... that he was gonna miss Peter.

Didn't make it sting no less or his words no less sharp or biting.

And Peter found himself gettin' a bit mad. Angry-like. The kinda anger that woulda been so easy to let it all control him. To let those fire ants do their thing just as they always done with his pa. Except Peter now knew he didn't have to be his pa and didn't have to live like him no more.

Or be afraid of him.

Peter thought back to Cat right then, thought on how she always seemed to breathe whenever something hard got thrown her way...

like down in those cribs and that woman there, staring back at them from the other side of the glass.

So Peter breathed, too.

"I know," Peter said. "I know we can't be friends no more, that's not why I wanted to talk with you."

"Yeah? Why then?"

"I'm needing your help."

Bugsy snorted. "You know I can't help with shit, Peter. Can't do anything to help, especially with what everyone's saying now about your ma. You weren't there, but just this morning Reverend Jacobs had a word with her. Right on her front porch. Right in front of everyone. And you *know* how important the reverend is. A damn, damn good thing my pa wasn't there when, when..."

Peter's breath suddenly got real, real cold. Like it went and froze right there in his lungs and breathing suddenly wasn't so easy no more.

His parents might'a made him go to church every Sunday, made him tuck in his shirt and whatnot—well, his mother more than his pa —but in this, when it came to the reverend and when it came to religion, Peter took a page out of his pa's book. And didn't mind it one bit.

Peter wasn't the God-fearing type. Or the praying type.

He didn't care too much about what the Good Lord had to say 'cause the Good Lord wasn't livin' down here in hell with the rest of them, in the muck and the filth and this smoke-black air of Butte. As far as Peter was concerned, the Good Lord had shown just how much he'd cared about his family as Peter's pa's drinking got worse, his anger burning hotter. Brighter. And then he'd gone and lost his job at the Spectacular and kept losing every one after. Well, it was sometime in there Peter had fully and completely lost his pa, too. Not that his pa had cared, of course.

And the Good Lord?

He didn't give a shit neither.

And Peter? Well, he was right done with praying and believing.

He'd learned a long, long time ago that God didn't exist. Or if he did, he didn't give a shit about them stuck down here in the hells of Butte.

And yet... yet that didn't fully explain what Peter was feeling right then. That cold, hard ball suddenly swirling in his gut. Thinking about Reverend Jacobs confronting his mother on their front porch, with Rose more than likely huddling inside somewhere. All those mothers and fathers standing there, too, judging her and not a one of them jumping to her side.

They've should have stood with her. Should've supported her.

Which was what Peter should've done.

If... if he'd been there.

And he hadn't because he chosen to yell at her, blame her, and, and run. And wasn't he still running? Running from what was happening right now, and instead all wrapped up in the past and what his pa might have or might not have done.

Peter... he *should* have been there.

That cold ball, it went and twisted itself even harder. Especially, especially with Jacobs there, towering over his mother like Peter could just now see, could picture so very clearly...

And... he knew why, too, why he was so upset and so, so scared.

All those times when Jacobs had smiled at Peter, big and toothy and welcoming, especially after church when he was seeing everyone off, giving them a personal word or two, and Peter had backed away. Each and every time, and him pulling Rose with him. Peter hadn't trusted him because he'd seen, he'd known, what none of those others adults could see.

That smile of his weren't real.

Oh, it looked real and probably was, but not in the way his mother had believed, and not in the way all those other families had believed, too. It was self-serving and self-fulfilling. The kinda smile that knew exactly what it was doing, and it was going and doing it all for himself.

"Didn't you hear me, Peter? The reverend—"

"I heard."

But Peter didn't say nothing against the reverend. There was no point. There wasn't much point arguing, least in this. Bugsy and his family had right different opinions about Reverend Jacobs. He was the one now gettin' invited over for supper or for noon meals, especially on Sundays. The very place that Peter and his family used to enjoy back when their pas had been friends and working together at the Big S. They'd been friends, good ones, too, before it all went to hell, anyway.

And one thing was for sure, Bugsy was right about his pa not being there this morning when Reverend Jacobs went pounding on their front door. Bugsy's pa *always* had a kind word to say about the reverend, always passing on his sermons and whatnot, especially when Bugsy and Peter had gotten in trouble, doing something they shouldn't have been—which was most of the time. Neither Peter nor Bugsy had ever been allowed to say anything unkind about that man Jacobs 'cause Bugsy's pa had no issue settin' you straight.

He didn't even need the excuse of drinking to do it, either.

"You hear me?" Bugsy asked, shaking Peter's arm and bringing Peter back to the present. "I said Jacobs had a word with her. Right in front of everyone, too."

But not Bugsy's pa.

"So what of it?" Peter asked, shrugging his shoulders, too, like he didn't care.

The exact opposite, though, was true. His heart got to pounding again. Harder, too, like he'd just come running straight up and out of that underground.

Again.

"If you ain't gonna care, that's on you." Bugsy shook his head. "I'm just tellin' you what I saw, what I heard, and it ain't good, Peter, ain't good at all. Jacobs pretty much told her straight that she needed to get gone. And he's not wrong, you know. Everyone else? They was all right there, nodding their heads, agreeing with him."

"It ain't right."

Ain't right that they'd all gone and ganged up on her like that, and with Rose...

God damn it, *she* must'a been nearby, too, and not a one of 'em would have cared or thought about her. But what really was right was that Peter... Peter wasn't there.

He should've been there. Should've been standing right beside his mother when they'd come.

Which was when Peter noticed a look in Bugsy, that same one he'd seen right outside the school. It was an... an uneasiness, almost. But it was clearer now, the way Bugsy was shifting from one foot to other, hands shoved down deep in his pockets, doing everything possible to *not* look right at Peter...

As if maybe he simply couldn't.

Now *that* got his heart pounding. Real good, too.

"What happened?" Peter asked.

Bugsy shook his head.

Peter came forward. Grabbed Bugsy by his coat's collar and shook him hard. "What happened to her? To my mother?"

"Nothin! All right? Nothin' happened. Let go of me."

Peter did.

"She stood up to them, that's all." Bugsy pushed down his too-big coat from where Peter had grabbed him. "Told Jacobs... told everyone, really, it was their fault, about your pa and all. How they'd all known and did nothin'."

"Which you know is true."

Again, Bugsy wouldn't look at Peter, as if not lookin' meant he didn't have to accept the truth.

To hell with that.

Peter stepped forward and shoved Bugsy back a step. Not too hard but enough to get his attention.

"What the hell?"

"You don't get to look away. Don't get to hide from the truth."

"Yeah, yeah, fine. I know it's true, all right? But it don't matter. Now that your ma is gonna be a—"

"Don't even say it."

"It's true and you can't change that. I heard my mother and father talkin' about it all last night, even Jacobs came over, too, to have a word with them, reassure them that she—that you—was all gonna leave. But she just stood there, didn't back down none, even told Jacobs she had an officer friend they could go on inside and wait for."

Peter found himself smiling, just a little bit. Proud of his mother.

"We can't just go having someone, someone like *her* living here with us—"

The smile vanished. Just like that. "I'm warning you, Bugsy. One more time. I know a hell lot more 'bout it than you. Than you or your ma or your pa."

This time, it was Peter's voice who broke—at the thought, the memory, of everything he'd seen and witnessed down there in those tunnels, in those tears Cat had shed when she'd looked at that one woman down in those cribs—but Peter didn't hide none of those feelings. And it was all that... all them feelings... all this hurt and shame and his own part in this, that pulled him back from his own anger. From his pa's legacy that was hopin' like hell he'd just let go and take it all out on Bugsy.

Peter yanked off his hat and shoved his fingers through his tangled brown hair. Somehow felt the grime of the underground there, even though he'd been wearing a hat.

Maybe that was just it. This life... there wasn't no running from it, no hiding, no pretending. The dirt and grime was there and it was gonna go where it wanted, and there wasn't a thing you could do about it.

Except... Peter could.

He could understand, at least.

"Look," Peter said. "I'm not here to argue. I'm just aimin' to understand. You hear me? I'm just lookin' for answers. Can you help me? Just help me with that and I'll never speak with you again."

Bugsy eyed Peter for a long, long moment.

What he was thinking, what he was seeing, Peter didn't know...

but he got this sense that Bugsy was seein' some of those changes in Peter. Not the kind you could see on the outside, but that you went and felt on the inside. And lookin' at Bugsy... Peter got the sense that Bugsy had changed, too, but awhile ago—and Peter had missed it. Had missed seeing those signs, and missed understanding what it all meant.

He had this hunch, though, that now, now it was important. Real important.

And everything he'd missed seeing earlier, it all started to fit together. His pa losing his job, Jacobs coming in and taking their spot amongst Bugsy and his family. And then Bugsy not looking as well fed as before, clothes not fittin' right. How his own mother had never said nothing, just served up what she could to Bugsy even though they always had so little. But Bugsy's family... they *should* have had more.

By all rights, his pa still had a job and it'd been a good one.

Still was, in fact.

Bugsy's pa was a shift boss, just like he'd been when Peter's own pa had worked under him.

Peter breathed in, then out again. Realization dawning.

"It's about you, isn't it?" Peter asked, if his voice a bare whisper. "All this, it's about your family."

CHAPTER FIFTY-SEVEN

Cat nearly sagged back to her chair in relief to see it was only Dusty come stomping in like this and not someone with a gun or swinging a big chunk of wood right into her. She didn't though, cause of that hard line and grim, furious look Dusty was sending her way.

Real anger.

Right on furious, too. If those green eyes of his could'a set her on fire she'd no doubt they would have just then, no doubt at all. And then there were his words, which went and hummed through her, again and again.

What the hell did you do?

Cat didn't relax, but she did let go of her gun.

Slowly.

Blake did, too. He also sent a glance her way, it was a look and a question all in one, and she knew exactly what he meant. Cat nodded, and Blake, after only a moment, as if unsure, released her. To her own great relief, she didn't fall over, either. A good thing considering her whole left side was shaking right then, though whether it was from her injury or that intense adrenaline lightin' up through her, she didn't know.

Cat stayed right where she was, though, keeping that table in Mrs. Allen's sitting room between her and Dusty, all them leftover bits of her meal, her coffee that was still there and a little steam still managing to come up and over the top. Cat waited for Dusty. Waited to see what this was all about here, near Blake and also with the safety of the table between them. Too many years of survival taught her this. Too many years of living right on that knife's edge—

Just like Dusty himself.

Dusty's chest kept on heaving. Up and then down. Ash and dust falling off him like it were black snow, going down and dusting that once polished floor to the point where she was glad Chin wasn't here, though that meant he'd probably just go and blame Cat anyway as he usually did.

Cat's insides were dancing like crazy. Her instinct, who she was, not yet having abandoned her. And even with that tense atmosphere just about bouncing around the room, up and off the walls, the ceiling, she found herself noticing in all those details... about Dusty. Those smudge marks on his chin. His cheeks. The grime that went and coated his elbows and, too, around his knees like he'd gotten down and crawled.

Cat swore softly.

She hadn't thought to send word to Dusty... about Peter, about him going down into the tunnels alone as he had. She should have thought of it. Should have sent word—even if she'd no idea where to send it. But of course Dusty would find out and of course he'd be mad.

Hoppin' mad, it looked like.

It wasn't like Cat had been trying to hide the truth from him. Far from it, she'd just been about to ready to fall. A feeling that was still with her and pretty strong right then, too, what with the way her shoulder was hurtin', waves of hurting going all the way down to her toes. Still... still it felt like she'd gone and made another one of her mistakes. Like maybe she'd let Dusty down in the same way she'd done with Alice, her sister.

The kinda hurt that maybe couldn't ever be healed.

Dusty, she knew for a fact, had been down there in the tunnels. Had probably run right to the nearest entrance as soon as he'd heard about Peter. And he would have. Dusty's network in that shadow world and above, passin' on what they knew for God knows why, but sure enough, Dusty *would* have heard. Heard how Peter had been running right through all them tunnels in the underground—and all alone, too.

That was why he was mad.

Cat hadn't been with Peter.

She knew, too, that it was more than just Dusty being furious with her. She saw it right there in his eyes, a look that he wasn't even trying to hide from her. Not this time, anyway. Those green eyes of his, almost glassy, were flashin' with a kinda hurt she knew all too well...

All she had to do was look at the ghost of her ma to feel it. To know it. The hurt, the shame, the being let down, again and again.

"You mean about Peter," Cat finally said. "What the hell did I do about Peter."

"What the hell else would I be talkin' about?"

She didn't answer that; there was no need. "You heard and went down into the tunnels looking for him."

"Which is what you should have damn well done," Dusty whispered, his voice low and thundering. "But you didn't. You left him there."

"He got out, didn't he?"

Cat actually didn't know this for a fact, but she'd had a feeling about him, had known he'd be all right, least for a little while. That he'd needed his space and thoughts to himself for a change. And... she knew, too, if Peter *had* still been down there, Dusty would have known about it.

Which meant Peter was out and safe and this really, really, was about that other thing.

Dusty's hurt. His disappointment and betrayal... all 'cause of Cat.

Blake blinked, turning his attention to her. "What about Peter? You lost him?"

Cat let out a breath. She hadn't a chance to tell Blake yet about Peter cause he'd insisted on her sitting down and getting her belly full of food. And... Cat hadn't been worried about him. She'd known, known in her gut it'd been the right choice...

But what if she'd been wrong again?

A chill kinda cold slipped underneath her skin. If she let it, it'd steal the last of her strength right then and there, and she knew, without a doubt, she'd never be the same person again.

It was hard, real, real hard, but she didn't let it. Because... because she *hadn't* been wrong and everything she saw in Dusty, every little detail he was sending her way, *told* her this.

Trust.

Trust in herself for a change.

"Yeah," Dusty bit out. "Yeah, she lost him good, down in the underground no less. I gave him to her keeping and she *lost* him. How could you do that? How could you let him go down *there?*"

"I made him a promise, Dusty—"

"Yeah, well, you made one to me, too."

"He *needed* to see. He needed to know."

"He had no business down there. You let him go. Don't you understand? Don't you even care? You *let* him go. Into the tunnels? And by himself?"

Dusty came forward. He slammed both his fists on that small table, causing the china to shake and clatter. Spoons and forks slipped from their places and made an awful sound, and she hoped nothing got broke or chipped. Her coffee, the bit she had left, spilled over the top and stained that white cloth.

Cat held out both hands, palms up. "Peace, Dusty."

She didn't need to feel her instincts warning her, didn't need them telling her that even though this here was a different boy, she was, in fact, back on that knife's edge. All she had to do was push wrong, say the wrong thing, and Dusty would be gone, make no mistake.

Gone from her life forever.

She just couldn't risk it.

Couldn't not risk it, either. Because... because she just couldn't lose him. He'd become one of those few shining lights in her life, the ones that weren't cold and angry like all the ghosts that followed her were, like the way she often felt standing here in this room that reminded her so much of her childhood, the good parts, anyway, even if all those parts carried nothing but disdain and disappointment from her own mother.

Truth was, Dusty was family now. Whether or not she wanted it. Whether or not she wanted to risk that kinda hurt again.

That thought, that realization, stopped her breath right there in her chest and it held there, too, for a good long while.

"Dusty," she finally breathed. "I told you I'd keep my promise."

Cat slowly edged her way out from behind the table.

Blake stayed where he was, watching them both. He, too, seemed to understand what was happening here and... she wondered, too, if he'd seen it before. Maybe with other kids, other families, during his own time growing up and living in his aunt's house. Blake who'd grown up side by side in the shadow world but not truly in it. Maybe he'd seen all this before... and maybe this here was just gonna be another part of Dusty's story, the one he'd never let finish because he'd run out on them and ducked into the shadow life.

She didn't want their story to end here, though.

Then she let all those thoughts go and shifted her full focus on Dusty. On all the hurting she was seeing. All those old wounds breaking open as if they'd been waiting for this moment.

Or maybe, maybe she was just seeing herself in him.

"I said I'd keep my word," she said.

"Sure don't look it. You left him down there."

"He needed to see—"

"*You* could have taken him."

"He didn't *want* me to, Dusty, didn't want me there anymore than you wanted to share your past." Cat's voice softened, quieted. "You keep on going back to the underground cause you need to, cause something keeps holding you down there. I ain't gonna ask; it's not my place. Not my business."

"He was your business."

"Yeah, yeah he was, which is why I let him go."

Cat let out a breath. It was a heavy one and one that she felt from her toes to her heart.

"You should know," she said, "better than anyone, that he needed to go. That this last part, he needed to see on his own. Without his mother. Without me."

Dusty closed his eyes a minute. His fists clenching and unclenching at his sides. His whole body seeming to shake for a moment, then another.

Finally, he looked right at her.

"But how did you know? How did you know that he wouldn't go around and turn into me? Become me?"

"I didn't. I, I just had hope."

Dusty shuddered and look away from her. "Except he's not done, you know. He hasn't come home."

"No," Cat agreed, "I don't imagine he has because he's not finished yet, and we both know what he needs next."

"Understanding. About his father."

Cat nodded. "He's not ever gonna get the whole story, but he needs something, something to get him through the dark days ahead without, without all that anger in him taking over."

Like it had with Lou.

Cat gestured to Blake. "Blake and I've been goin' over what we know. It's not much, but it's there and it's something. I—no, we—were gonna head back out soon. To find Peter."

Dusty pressed his lips together, couldn't see much of the pink for all that grime and ash coatin' him. "You weren't gonna leave him?"

"Never."

Just like she wasn't gonna leave Dusty, unless that's what he wanted.

There was another long moment, just the three of them standing in that sitting room together.

Finally Dusty nodded... though he wasn't looking at her, and Cat knew, right there in her gut, that the trust they'd once shared wasn't there anymore. Not right now. Maybe not ever again.

She didn't let herself think on that, not right now when she *did* have these promises to keep.

"Can you tell me what you know?" Cat asked Dusty. "You want to sit? Want us to get a plate?"

Dusty didn't budge. She didn't much blame him, either, specially when she could only guess how close all this was to hitting home for him. Could only guess at who he was seeing right then when he finally did go and look at her.

Cat was sure, though, that whoever he was seeing was another ghost.

A ghost like her ma. A ghost like Alice.

The kinda ghosts who were gonna haunt a person for all eternity.

But Dusty told them all he knew. He told them about Jacobs coming over to the house and confronting Evie. The words that were exchanged between them, the ones that the whole neighborhood could hear—and then the ones that only the two of them, and Dusty, had heard.

Cat's heart was racing as she listened to all this. Her senses just about coming alive, like every bit, every little end was tingling and alive.

She breathed in, then out again.

Felt the whole puzzle itself finally coming together and clicking into place, just like that. All she'd been missing was that one final detail and now, now she had it.

Lou Blonberg's shift boss. The one who'd fired him. The one who'd dashed his dreams and then took up with another fellow, a righteous one, and called him friend.

Cat stood. Her hair once again falling over her front, the tangling mess that it was, and shoved it aside again. She headed straight for her coat and hat while Blake and Dusty followed behind.

"Where are you going?" Dusty demanded.

Cat shoved her hat back on her head and shrugged into her coat, best as she could, anyway, especially the way tears pricked the corner of her eyes at the sudden pain it brought. She didn't bother with the buttons this time and Blake didn't ask. Just grabbed his own coat and hat and donned them on.

"Where are you going?" Dusty asked again.

"To bring Peter home."

Cat look right at him. Good and long and hard. "Are you coming?"

CHAPTER FIFTY-EIGHT

Bugsy didn't move from where he was standing near Peter. His back, goin' back straight at tall. Head going high. His mouth twistin' hard in a grimace even as he went and shivered, that cold, cold air that seemed deepening all around them like it wasn't dare gonna miss this, not for the world.

"I don't know what the hell you're talkin' bout," Bugsy spat. "This got nothin' to do with my family. *Your* pa's the one who got himself fired. He's the one who left town and wrote what he did about your ma!"

For the first time since this had all happened, Peter didn't feel anger. Didn't' feel even one poking head of those fire ants, of his pa's legacy. They weren't there at all.

Instead he felt sadness.

And a real, real heaviness, too, like it was holding him down, pulling him right into that ground if he'd let it.

Peter, though, he held strong. Had to... for his mother's sake.

"It is about your family," Peter said again. "About your pa. I've got to admit, it never made sense to me, why our pas stopped being

465

friends. Why mine got so mad at yours after losin' his job. He never said anything, of course, but I think... I think he didn't need to."

Peter glanced in the direction, to the north, still farther up past the side hill, right where he knew the Specular Mine to be. Couldn't see nothing, of course, not with all that damn smoke cloudin' everything, holding onto them good and tight like it had no business anywhere else but the place that birthed it. Even still, Peter could picture it all clear-like in his mind. The head frame of the Spectacular, that big and mighty gallows frame dropping men down into that shaft, into the darkness below to whatever of the mine they worked on.

And Bugsy's pa?

He'd been shift boss of the level they worked together on. The nine hundred level, was it. Nine hundred feet down into that hard rock, that earth right below of their feet, and Bugsy's pa was in charge of all that, makin' sure his own boss and his boss's boss were happy with him, were gettin' all the right stuff done in the matter they wanted it in. Bugsy's pa... a man who went and got paid well, who'd fired Peter's pa because, as everyone was saying, it had to do with his pa's drinking at the time.

But in this... Peter knew it wasn't true. And remembered then something his mother had said, or maybe it was his pa on one of those nights when he'd not been drinking so bad, and those few times when it seemed his fury was sleeping... but they'd mentioned something about an accident.

Peter let out a breath. "That accident, the one that your pa fired mine over, it wasn't his doing, was it?"

Bugsy's lips got real tight and white. "What does it matter? Nothing's gonna change. Not for *you*."

"Matters to me. Truth matters to me."

Even if... even if there was no changing the past. Even if there was no changing the future.

Peter saw that now, he really did.

He looked right at Bugsy and told him so.

"I just want the truth, Bugsy. I just want to know why... why this all happened to my family. Why your family, and with your pa having a good job and workin' hard as he does, suddenly doesn't have much at all. Not enough food. Not the right kinda fitting clothes, warm clothes, even. Why your pa's never around much except no one is saying much about it."

"Shut up. You don't know what you're talkin' 'bout." Bugsy turned away. "There ain't nothin' wrong—"

But then Bugsy cut himself off, and Peter'd a feeling it was cause he really wanted someone else to know, really wanted...

A friend.

Even if they never could be again, not after his pa's classified, but he could be so, right now.

For this moment more.

"I hear you, Bugsy," Peter said, "and I'm seeing you, finally. I'm right sorry it took, took so long. I was holding onto a lot of anger from my pa and it kept me from seeing straight, specially what was right in front of my nose."

"Don't know what you're talkin' 'bout."

"Yeah, yeah you do. And I know that we can't be friends no more, but I'm here now, and I'm still your friend. Right now. If you want me to be."

Bugsy didn't look at Peter for a long, long time. He held himself up nice and straight and seemed to glare in the direction of the Spectacular Mine, same as Peter had done what felt like a lifetime ago 'cept it was only yesterday, when he was standing there, cursing his mother for damning them all as she had.

Except it'd never been her fault.

Hadn't even been his pa's fault... at least, at least to start.

"My pa's got a problem," Bugsy finally said. "With gambling. We all know 'bout it but ain't allowed to say nothing. That's why we ain't got much money. That's why he's not around much. Or eating much.

Or sleeping much. That accident? I don't know all them details about it, but I was actually there outside the door when... when..."

"When your pa was talking to someone, right?" Peter offered. "To Jacobs?"

Bugsy shook his head. "Nah, Jacobs didn't come in till later. It was Joe he was talkin' to."

Peter remembered a bit about Joe, though it was more a name his pa would curse from time to time—always with explanation, of course—but yeah, Joe and Flossie and their whole gaggle of kids. Most of 'em young, the ones that weren't were all girls, so Peter didn't have much to do with them, especially since Rose didn't seem interested in making friends with them, either.

"What's Joe got to do with it?" Peter asked.

"Joe was your pa's partner. I ain't sure of the details, but it sounded like it was *Joe's* fault that it happened, that they got the timber stuck in there the way it had. I got the sense that it was Joe who'd been drinking a bit extra down there, not coffee, if you know what I'm saying."

Peter frowned. "Then why blame my pa?"

Bugsy crossed his arms and looked away. Actually went and looked in just about every direction from those frozen clumps of dirt and black sludge to that rotting bridge behind them.

"Bugsy?"

"'Cause Joe knew, you know? About my pa's gambling problem. *That's* when I found out about it. My mother didn't even know at the time, but Joe threatened he'd go and tell her if my pa didn't save his job, so he did. Your pa got blamed for their mistakes. This time, this time it weren't his fault, Peter. And I think, think I just really wanted you to know that. Before, before you know..."

Bugsy's voice trailed off.

He didn't need to complete the sentence, not really.

Before Peter and his family simply disappeared from the neighborhood, from news around town, maybe even disappeared altogether, just like those women living down there in those tunnels did.

But... but Peter knew, too, that wasn't gonna happen. He wasn't alone in this even though, even though he wasn't continuing on with the friends he'd had to start with, or even... or even the same family.

His pa was gone.

He weren't ever comin' back, and his mother's reputation was ruined.

But at least, if nothing else, Peter had answers.

That's all he'd needed, he realized. Just, just answers.

It was time to go home, time to go back to his mother and apologize pretty darn fierce for running out on her as he did. Promise, too, that he'd do just about anything possible to help out with her and Rose, so she'd know that she wasn't alone in this, either.

"Thanks, Bugsy." Peter held out a hand. "I appreciate it."

Bugsy eyed him. "I just ruined your life. My pa ended up ruining your family's life, and you wanna thank me for it?"

Yes.

No.

All of it and everything in between. Because even though Peter's pa was gone, taking all his problems and his anger and his drinking with him, Bugsy still had his pa—and from the looks of Bugsy, it sure looked like he was still a far ways away from hitting rock bottom, to the point where Peter felt sorry for him.

A little, anyway.

"If you're ever needin' some help," Peter said, "look me up. I'll help, if you need it."

Bugsy sniffed. "I ain't gonna need it. My family's just fine. My pa's just fine."

It was like despite everything Bugsy had just said everything he'd just admitted to Peter, Bugsy still well and truly believed all that. That it would be fine. That there was nothing really wrong. The lie Bugsy told himself so he could go out and face the world, but at least Peter had faced his truths, faced what his new world was gonna be like, and really saw that gift for what it was. The one that Cat had given him.

Truth, in this case, was a hell of a lot better than holding onto some thin shade of hope, a hope, too, that wasn't really even there. Peter didn't blame Bugsy or fault him. Hell, he was the same way, too, until it had all gotten pulled out from under his legs and he face-planted in the frozen mud and all that.

One newspaper that had done changed his life... and maybe even saved it, too.

"See you around," Peter said. He nodded and turned away from Bugsy, possibly for the last time ever, when he saw a figure walking out of the smoke.

Bugsy stiffened beside him. "Who's that?"

But Peter, well, he only smiled. Knew exactly who it was coming up and out of the smoke like that, just as she'd done the first time. Coming, more than likely, to keep her promises.

"I reckon that's Cowboy Cat," Peter said, "keeping her promises, just like she said. Look, Bugsy, I know it's all fine for you now, but if you're ever needing help, well, that there's the first person I'd go to, if I were you."

If Bugsy said anything to that, Peter didn't know. Didn't care much, either. He was already walking away, heading to his own future, dark as it might be, but a free one.

Bugsy would either find his own way or he wouldn't. His choice.

Just like Peter had done.

Just like he was still doing right now even as he went to meet with Cat. And sure enough, it was her, though a bit different than the first time he'd met her. Blue jeans covered in a fair amount of ash and dirt and grime. Cowboy hat, which was still lookin' so out of a place in a place like Butte. Revolver hanging off her hip. Her coat was open, as if she'd not bothered with the buttons, and judging by the slight pull around her mouth he'd a feeling it was her shoulder again, hurting bad enough. Her hair was still unbraided and goin' every which it seemed, and was shade darker, too. Again, the dirt and smoke of Butte at work. But as he came closer, he saw something else, too.

A lightness in her eyes.

As if maybe, like him, she'd found something that she'd been missing. And from what he'd seen of her, down there in those cribs, he sure hoped she'd found it. Cause there'd be a heck of a lot more women like that, mothers with kids like him and Rose, that'd be needing some help. Some guidance. Maybe even a little justice.

Kinda like him.

Even if his pa was gone, even if his mother was still going to do the work she needed to do, his family had a heck of a lot more than if they'd never met Cat and.... Peter knew, without a doubt, he'd not be coming home. Least, not like this.

Behind Cat, Peter saw a familiar hack and familiar driver who still looked more like some specter or skeleton, 'specially wearing that tall, narrow black hat Fat Jack likened to wear. That goatee and mustache of his, too, each curling into a grin when he saw Peter. There were two unfamiliar passengers as well, but that didn't worry Peter none. He'd a pretty good guess of who they were. He could tell the larger man, who 'bout looked like he was made of muscle and whole lot cleaner and trimmer than his pa ever dreamed of (even when his mother had got after him). The police officer, no doubt. The one his mother had gone to for help which she'd threatened talking to Jacobs with, least according to Bugsy. The other one, well, it was no guess who that was.

A kid near enough to Peter's age, but older. Or maybe not so much as older, but just the way he went and looked at the world, saw through it, even, including Peter. It was sure something he felt when those green eyes narrowed right at him.

He'd a feeling that kid there, Dusty, didn't miss a thing.

But really, even with this new curiosity, Peter found his eyes drawn to Cat.

Cause, wow, she really did look like hell. Sure her eyes were lighter, but Peter could clearly see how these past two days took a toll on her, just as they'd done with him. Not enough sleep or food. The way she winced as she kept heading towards him, like her shoulder really was hurtin' her like hell and she was both too proud and too stubborn to admit it. That hair of hers blowing this way and that in what little wind decided to come tugging their way, though not nearly enough to make the breathing part any easier.

And when Cat got close enough? When she went and saw him, all of him, of which he'd no doubt?

Well, there wasn't at all a look or worry in her eyes, which he'd have surely seen on another other woman, certainly on his mother. But... not Cat.

"You weren't worried?" he asked.

"A couple of others were and didn't have any nice things to say 'bout me letting you go off as I did. I imagine if your mother had known, she'd have gone right for twisting my ears or something worse."

"Probably. Knowing her. But you weren't worried."

"Me? No. Not yet, anyway." She tilted her head a bit, even tipped back the brim of her hat. "I could see it in you, down there in the cribs. I saw the change."

Peter breathed in that smoke and ash-thick air. Had never realized how good it felt until just this moment—to breathe.

"Thank you for that," he said. "For trusting in me."

She nodded.

"How did you know where to find me?" he asked.

"Simple enough once I worked out the rest of the puzzle. Blake and Dusty," she nodded towards the hack, "they helped with that. I knew you needed answers and I knew the one person you'd go to get them. And, well, the one place you'd both go."

"Like old times?"

"Or past times."

"Yeah, yeah, I suppose it is." Peter took a moment, looking around the side hill, remembering all those forts they'd built here with the scraps of metal and wood, all those battles they'd gone and had, warring with other neighborhood kids.

All that, well, he wouldn't be part of that no more and, and he was okay with it. He really was.

Cat must have seen it, or sensed it in him cause she went and smiled then.

"Ready to go home?" she asked.

"Yeah, Miss Justice. I think I am."

CHAPTER FIFTY-NINE

Cat always kept her promises.

Sure, at times it took awhile to see them through to the end, but ever since she'd left her sister, Alice, that thin, pale woman she'd become, a woman who even though, at the time, she'd still been breathing but hadn't a spark of life left in her, ever since then, Cat had kept every promise she'd made.

And as promised, she didn't leave Mrs. Allen's house alone. This time, she'd brought both Blake and Dusty with her. Dusty who surprised her, especially when he didn't go running off into the shadows when the hack had bumped and jostled to a halt at the entrance to the half-fallen down side hill.

She'd paused, looked right up at Dusty, and had asked, "I thought you didn't want Peter to see you?"

"That was before," Dusty said.

"Before?"

"Before I talked with his mother. Before... before you."

Even as Dusty said all that, though, he'd looked away from her, which told Cat right clear that things still weren't well between them. Least not yet, anyway.

"Besides," Dusty kept on going, "Peter'll be needing some help... figuring out where to earn some extra coin and all."

Something, she knew, Dusty was a master at... along with how to survive life down there. In the shadow world. The underground. Yeah, she was under no illusion that was where Peter would go. Would have to. Still, she was glad for Dusty for finally breaking his silence, of letting Peter see him, get to know him. She hoped, too, that Dusty had managed to heal some of his own ghosts.

Maybe not completely, she wasn't so sure that'd ever be possible, but enough. Enough to maybe move on.

Or in her case, stick around for a bit.

Which she wouldn't be doing if not for Dusty.

Cat reached out with her good arm and gripped his shoulder. Gave him a tight squeeze.

Her way of saying thanks.

And Dusty looked back at her and nodded.

There it was, that exchange between the two of them again. An understanding. Both simple and complex all at the same time. Where it was gonna go from here was anyone's guess, but it was there and that was all that mattered.

Blake had kept his silence, and so, too, had Jack. Well, Cat figured that's 'cause Jack was doing all he could to hear every little bit and not miss out on some piece of the story, some minor detail.

And then Cat left them to fetch Peter and bring him home. As she'd been expecting, he'd been waiting for her. Not surprised at all, either, like he knew she was gonna come.

He was here at the side hill, just where she expected him, and talking with the person she'd expected him talking with.

They spoke a short while and then Peter had followed after her. No promises were needed this time. No reminders that the choices were his and she weren't gonna take them away from him.

Nothing at all like that.

Peter climbed in after her, nodding at Blake first, then Dusty, who he settled in next to while Blake scooted over on that hard bench to make room for Cat. Though, sure didn't feel so much like room as they were shoulder to shoulder and there wasn't one inch of her left side that didn't seem to be touching him.

Yet neither seemed to mind, and Cat found herself breathing easy, despite all that damn smoke.

For the first time since Mr. Rippi had gone and swung that wood right at her head, connecting hard with her shoulder instead, a blow that had set both mind and body off balance and a torn asunder... she finally felt centered. Finally felt more like her old self...

Or maybe a new self with bits of the old holding it all together.

This puzzle, though, this story of the Blonbergs and the justice they were wanting, turned out to be simpler than Norma's had been. No grand ol' plot accidentally reaching up and out to the very top of the hill, right to a Copper King no less. No corrupted and dead police officers this time. No Cat gettin' injured either, unless she counted having saved Peter from a right hard knock to his head. Still, it was just a story of a family who'd fallen on hard times and a father who'd skipped out on them.

Simple, yet... not so simple at all.

Not in the end.

But then, when it came to family, there wasn't no such thing as simple, which she well knew. All she had to do was look around in this hack, at the new family she was already gathering round her, to know that.

Still, there a few pieces of this puzzle Cat was missing, but she'd known the answers to them would be found with Peter and with the one person he could trust to give them to him:

His friend.

Bugsy.

The very same friend whose own father had been Lou's boss. Cat had known Bugsy's family was having problems and wasn't been doing so well—she'd seen Marybell that first day, walking with Evie and all the rest of them mothers. She'd seen the signs, then, of a family not doing so well but holding airs that all was well. Peter, for his part, filled in the rest of the story on that bumpy—yet surprisingly slow—drive back to his mother's.

Or maybe not so surprising 'cause Fat Jack was listening with both ears, make no mistake.

Though to be fair, Cat's injured shoulder was pretty glad he was takin' the route slow.

For once.

Course, seeing as how her injured side was pressed up nice and close to Blake gettin' jostled would have been a pretty challenging feat right then.

Peter told them all he knew, everything that Bugsy had said.

How all of it tied back to Bugsy's pa, Harold, and with Lou stuck right there in the center. Maybe if he hadn't been such a drunk and a mean one at that, he'd have had his wits about him more, maybe even the insight to do what Flossie's husband, Joe, had done. Sweet talkin' his way into a better deal than the pink slip he deserved, the same one that was handed to Lou and all the rotten luck that'd followed him.

Though Cat doubted it was as much rotten luck as it was character disposition at that point.

To Cat, it felt there was this whole coming together-like, a settling in, a knowing, as she heard the rest of his family's story.

She breathed out, then in again, feeling the world slow a bit as if the horses merely... paused... while there hooves were up in the air, before slowly, so slowly, touching back down on the ground.

Yes, there it was. The clear picture she'd been waiting for.

Her promise to Peter, finished.

Perhaps.

Cat looked right at Peter, who'd kept on eyeing her then Blake all throughout that bumpy ride. She asked him, "You've got your answers, but is that all you're wanting?"

She remembered right clear the anger that'd been coursing through him like it was a living breathing thing. She didn't sense none of that in him no more, but still...

She had to be sure.

"I made a promise to you," Cat said. "This goes back to Bugsy's pa and I'll see it through, if that's what you're wanting."

She felt Blake turn towards her, his gaze both warm and focused.

She didn't look at him.

Peter thought a long moment, his gaze moving off to the distance, to where she didn't know 'cause Lord knows no one could see shit in this smoke and blackness.

Finally, though, he shook his head. "There's no need. Won't change anything, anyway."

"No," Cat agreed. "It won't."

They arrived at Evie's home slower than anyone in that hack could have ever expected. Jack himself helped Cat down this time, to which Blake let him. Jack kept clear of her injured shoulder, to which she just gave him a wry half-smile.

"I told you, you was heading into a mess." Jack held onto her a moment longer, making sure she was good and steady.

"I thought you were talkin' about some grand plot as last time."

He shook his head. "In my day, Miss Justice, of all these rides I've given, I can promise you the ones with the biggest messes always come from the smallest places. The kinda hurt no one else sees or notices, certainly don't care about."

He tipped his hat to her.

"Until now, that is."

Then Jack hopped back on his hack, pretty darn spry for a man gettin' up in his age, and took off. Didn't even ask if she'd wanted him to wait until she was done and finished here, but then, she supposed her work wasn't yet done. While it was close, it sure wasn't complete.

Not yet, anyway.

First, she'd a promise to keep, of bringing a boy back home to his mother.

CHAPTER SIXTY

E vie peered out her window, with that curtain so threadbare it barely did a thing to block out the light. Squinting as she could through all that smoke and growing darkness, trying to see those bits of light that managed to peer through all that ugliness outside.

For a long, long moment, she just stood there.

Staring.

Unable to move. Barely, barely able to breathe or hope...

But no, the image she saw didn't change, even though she simply couldn't believe her eyes.

She pulled that curtain all the way back, all the way open just to see, just to be absolutely, perfectly clear... and, and no. No, it wasn't a dream. It wasn't her eyes playing tricks on her or her mind makin' up some fanciful aberration. Because he was there.

Peter.

Tears filled her eyes. Filled her heart.

Evie let them all fall. All of them.

Didn't bother to hide them. Didn't bother to grab her shawl, yes, that very one her nana had made all those years ago, filled with all those hopes and dreams and wants of what a dutiful daughter should become, especially when she became a married woman and then become a mother. Evie left that damn shawl right where it was, draped on the back of that off-balanced chair, the very one that Lou had refused to fix just like that front porch with the nails popping out that he'd refused to fix as well.

Evie didn't care about none of that.

All her eyes, all her focus, was on her son.

Her son, coming home.

To her.

And he did.

The hack had barely stopped before Peter was jumping out. His hat flying off his head into some frozen mud pot or something or other. He didn't notice or care and Evie didn't, either. Instead, Peter ran right towards her, and she to him.

Evie heard small footsteps following behind her, but then even that little detail was gone, simply vanished like smoke out'a her mind because then she was holding out her arms—and there was Peter, in them.

In her arms. Holding her tight, just as she held him.

Neither letting go.

Not ever, ever again.

Then there was Rose, launching into them both and in turn, they grabbed and held her, pulling her even closer, even tighter into their embrace.

Just the three of them, a family, crying together outside their home. It was a home that wasn't to be theirs much longer, but for now, for this moment, it was. And that was all that mattered.

Her family, those that mattered, back home with her.

Safe.

Evie looked up through tears and more emotions than she'd ever thought a person could feel, least until she'd given birth to her first child, and knew for a fact that her life would never be the same again. That her life would never again be... just hers.

"Thank you," she mouthed to Cat.

And Cat simply nodded back as if she knew and understood just how much Evie was feeling right then. Gratitude and so much more.

So very much more.

Her family... *home.*

CHAPTER SIXTY-ONE

Cat, Blake, and Dusty stayed back, letting the family have their little reunion. Each of them, smiling, as they couldn't help themselves—and didn't want to.

Cat tipped her hat back a little and took a long, slow look around the neighborhood, least what houses she could see through all that smoke. Her tangled hair pulling this way and that, as that little breeze kicked up between them. Her gaze went back to Evie and her small family and her home just beyond them. Cat noticed how those wooden boards on that front porch were warping and bending, like the nails were ready to spring out and dump whoever was standing there right on their rump. The door, too, that hung ajar, yet even from here she could see it was just as warped as the porch.

Every sign telling her true that Lou might have just left yesterday, but in truth, he'd been gone a real long time before that.

Cat continued looking around, taking in all those houses round them, how most weren't in a whole lot better conditions than Evie's, or if they were it was like they was living right on that edge, that balance there between having just enough, and having not nearly enough.

There were plenty of faces, too, watching out their windows, watching the reunion right there on that street that was filled more with holes and dips and rivets than gravel and crushed stones. But in each of those faces? Nothing but judgment and shame, and not one ounce of pity.

Was she surprised?

No, not in the least.

Just like she wasn't surprised when, after not too long, a hack came racing down that street and stopped with one full-on wheel lifting off the ground. And Cat knew, just from the way Peter had described the horrid man, that this was none other than Reverend Jacobs, himself. And oh my was his face set in a hard, angry line. Fury about ran straight through him to the point where she wasn't sure Doc Griffin should be sent for or not.

But then, that particular worry was taken from her as Blake touched her arm and nodded in the reverend's direction.

"You'll be all right here?" he asked.

She nodded. "You gonna enjoy yourself?"

"I sure plan on it." Blake gave her a grin, and his blue eyes got to flashing again, this time some of that black coming back. His hand stayed on her arm a moment more, as if he was wanting to say something else.

Whether or not he was goin' to, Cat wasn't gonna learn today cause Reverend Jacobs was already jumping down from his hack like he was gonna go storm the castle all by his lonesome.

Blake gave Cat another nod, touched the brim of his hat, then went to head off Reverend Jacobs ruining such a happy moment.

And, Cat noticed, there was a great deal of satisfaction in Blake's stride. Oh, it was still just as determined and hard as it always was, but she could see that small change, that small almost like a bounce to his step.

Blake's hands might have been tied by the law earlier regarding with Evie and her situation, but this? Right now?

No doubt he was gonna enjoy it.

"Cat," Dusty said, and nodded in the direction of another nearby house.

Cat turned and saw a woman standing there on her own front porch. A shawl wrapped tight as could be around her shoulders. Her knuckles just about white from holding it. Her face, too, was scrunched together so fierce and with such a volley of emotions Cat couldn't pick out just one out. But still, Cat knew the woman. Remembered, quite clearly, from that day they'd all walked to the school house together.

Marybell.

Earlier, before they'd arrived to his home, Cat had asked Peter if they were done with this business, whether or not he'd wanted to see it through to the end—all the way to Harold and the ill he'd caused Peter and his family.

Peter had said no.

Cat respected that more than the kid even knew—or maybe, or maybe not. Maybe he understood quite well, which had been his whole point in lettin' the matter go.

But there was someone else, maybe, that Cat could help.

Maybe.

Cat left Dusty watching over Evie and Peter and Rose, still kneeling together and holding each other in front of their house. Cat headed towards Marybell, who after a good long while, like she herself was just as lost in the reunion, in the love and the near loss of Evie's family, that she didn't notice Cat until she was nearly on top of that porch. Cat stopped and waited for Marybell to finally feel someone else's gaze on her, and when she did, flicking her attention to Cat, as if annoyed at the sudden interruption, Marybell stepped back.

Good and fast, and clearly surprised.

Marybell's dress, Cat noticed, was a bit frayed long the edges. The hem dragging a little lower than it should have, even a stray stand of thread there floating in that little bit of breeze, the same breeze that was tugging and playing with Cat's tangled hair, getting it right into her eyes, just in the way she truly hated.

Marybell twisted her mouth, pressing it into such a thin line her lips nearly gone and disappeared. Clearly, she was affronted by Cat's presence, by everything Cat represented and simply was, as evidenced by her nature of dress—or not dress, in her case. Yet, at the same there was a very clear wariness in Marybell's cool gaze... something that felt an awful lot like fear.

Least from what Cat could see.

She'd a feeling, too, that Marybell understood damn well the reason why Cat was standing there, why she'd even come up to her in the first place.

Cat saw it all, clear as day, clear as she would have steppin' off that train and into Butte, before her injury, before she'd gone and felt so unsure of herself, of what she was even doing there, if she should even continue on with what she was doing...

All that, feeling like it'd happened to her a lifetime ago.

Marybell tugged good and hard on the knotted ends of her shawl. "Is there something I can help you with?"

They both knew it wasn't what she'd *wanted* to say. Probably something real unkind, if that tightening around her eyes was any indication. But the fact that Marybell *hadn't* said it gave Cat some hope. And, too, that she wasn't wrong in coming over.

"Nothing, ma'am," Cat tipped her hat to Marybell. "Just saw you standing there alone. Thought I'd introduce myself. My name is Cat, Cowboy Cat, as some like to call me."

"You've no business here." Marybell sniffed. Her chin going up a bit higher. "Besides, I'm not alone."

Cat knew what Marybell had meant, especially when Marybell literally went and jerked her chin towards the direction of Reverend Jacobs, but Jacobs, well, he was a bit busy with Blake and getting those Blonbergs out of his neighborhood that he wasn't paying one bit of attention to Marybell... or to Cat.

"I can see you're not alone." Cat nodded towards the house. "See all your kids there, staring out those windows. You've got quite a few of them, I see. Must be real hard, keeping up with all them mending, keeping up with them growing bodies."

Marybell sucked in a breath. Her gaze shot towards the house, then back to Cat and finally... finally towards Evie and her little family. The worry? Oh, it was back in Marybell's eyes, shining, too, like she was almost maybe thinking of crying.

Or maybe she'd known more about Evie's situation and what had happened with Lou than she'd let on with the rest of her family.

Marybell said nothing for a short while, all her attention on Evie.

Sure enough, Marybell reached up and brushed at her eyes.

Cat said nothing to this, just... just waited.

She didn't have to wait long.

"You were there, yesterday," Marybell said. "Outside the school. I saw you."

"Yeah. That was me."

"Why are you here?"

"Because... someone needed help and I offered what I could."

"I don't need help."

Cat gave her a small smile, a sad one, if she were honest. A real sad one. "In that case, it was a pleasure meeting you, Mrs. Marybell."

Cat turned, ready to head home and get some of her own, much needed rest, when Marybell called back out again.

"I've heard of you. In the papers. But that's not the name I heard."

Cat glanced over her shoulder. "Oh?"

"Justice. That's why they call you. Miss Justice."

Cat just nodded.

"Is it true?" There was a slight... hitch to Marybell's voice, and again, another swipe at her eyes.

"Sometimes," Cat said. "And sometimes, I'm just a woman trying to find my way in this world."

"Have you? Found it, that is?"

"Sometimes yes, sometimes no. The aim, though, is to keep on trying. Good day to you, Mrs. Marybell. I hope it all works out for you."

Cat tipped her hat again and left Marybell standing there on her front porch. A porch whose wooden boards were also gettin' warped and twisting, just like Evie's. Like those rusted nails there were of the same quality and kind, like they were gonna give way at any moment though they might go and last another week, another month, maybe even another year.

One day, though, they'd give.

One day.

But at least, for today, Cat had done what she'd set out to do. Kept some promises and reminded yet another soul, as she'd done with Peter, that there was also a choice... even if that choice weren't the one you'd grown up believing in.

Just like her and this life here she was making for herself.

Cat saw Blake still dealing Reverend Jacobs, both men looking so opposite of the other. Jacobs red in the face and Blake completely calm and cool, assessing everything, missing nothing... like how she was looking his way, too. His gaze met hers and he gave her a grin.

It was a small kind of grin, the one they'd shared when they were heading off to the Gardens in all that finery and the dance they'd shared in the fancy ballroom. It was also the kind of grin that a person like Reverend Jacobs wouldn't ever understand—couldn't—because he'd never lived on that edge, on that shadow side of life.

Cat grinned back.

Yes, yes she'd stay awhile at Mrs. Allen's, see exactly where this life here was gonna take her. Finish helping Evie get on her feet with this new life and those kids, too, settling in. Then there was Doc Griffin who really *was* gonna have her head for doin' the exact opposite of what he'd recommended.

But yeah... she'd enough to keep her busy for awhile. Besides, Cat still had some promises to keep and just maybe, a dance or two waiting for her.

Maybe.

AUTHOR NEWSLETTER

To keep up with Chrissy Wissler's new releases as well as information about her other works, please go to ChrissyWissler.com and sign up for her newsletter.

SNEAK PEAK: WOMEN'S JUSTICE

A COWBOY CAT MYSTERY

A take-no-prisoners historical mystery about strong women, justice, and redemption.

Women's Justice: A Cowboy Cat Mystery, on sale now from your favorite retailer. Turn the page for a sample chapter from that book.

When Cat, a former prostitute, steps off the train in Butte, Montana, she walks right into hell. The dark smoke-filled air reeks of menace. And the stares—scorning her blue jeans, cowboy hat, and empty holster—don't help put her at ease.

Still reeling from her sister's death, Cat aims to find a purpose and help those who need it find even some small measure of justice. When she reads about the mysterious death of a local prostitute, she resolves to find the truth.

But the closer Cat gets to that truth, the more she realizes Butte, Montana, harbors some very dark secrets, indeed.

A take-no-prisoners historical mystery about strong women, justice, and redemption.

"Wonderful book, chockfull of unexpected surprises. If you like sports novels, you'll like this—even if you don't like romance. If you like romance, you'll like this—even if you don't like sports novels."

—Kristine Kathryn Rusch, *USA Today* Bestselling Author, on *Home Run.*

"Wonderful, wonderful book. Held me me from word one all the way to the end." —Dean Wesley Smith, *USA Today* Bestselling Author, on *Women's Justice*

PROLOGUE

Every sound imaginable filled the air: discordant keys striking hard on a piano, the shrill shriek of a violin. Yells and cheers as money was lost and won from one gambling house or dance hall or saloon; it truly didn't matter. They were all one and the same and they lit the chill, wintery night as Norma stumbled about in their shadows.

At least they would have lit the night, if not for the blackness. The smoke hanging so tight and close she could barely see one foot in front of her.

The noise throbbed against her head until it became nothing more than a dull ache no amount of alcohol could take away. Which was well enough. The noise, if not her eyes, at least told her this was the way home.

Norma accepted this small bit of comfort, for that's all it was.

That's all she had left.

That, and that light stirring bit of wind. Not enough to help her breathe or see. To push away that heavy, thick smoke hanging over Butte like a black halo, from all those smelters pourin' out their blackness, not caring a whit about the folks who lived there.

Day and night, they went on and on. Day and night, they kept on with their burning of the ore. Great heaps of it.

And the smoke, it stayed right where it was cause the wind, the little tickling thing that it was, wasn't strong enough to do much else than make her shiver. Make her wish for the coat that she'd... lost somewhere.

Which, for the moment, was no matter because the sharp sting of cold helped. It cleared her mind, just enough, anyway. The kinda cold that went straight through you. Right into your bones without so much as a by-your-leave. And it stayed there, too. Stayed in you as yet even more of it came rolling down off those far-off, snow-peaked mountains. Ones she'd never been to but had always dreamed of. She'd had many dreams as she'd gazed out the rickety door of her little one-room crib, gazing off into that distance, so close and yet so far.

A dream she'd almost had, too.

But almost didn't get you nothin' in this place, just kept on pushing you down into the muck and mud until that's all that you had left. Until it was just you stumblin' about in the blackness, stomach ready to revolt right up your throat, hopin' like hell you could actually make it home before that happened.

Not that wind cared 'bout her dreams. Or whether or not she made it home.

It didn't. It rolled straight on down the hill, laughing all the way. Taunting her with it presence.

Or perhaps the laughter was all in her head.

Laughing or not, the wind at least brought another small comfort. A small one, yes, but a comfort nonetheless: It stole away the bits of sweat lining her forehead.

Though why the sweat was there, she didn't know. And couldn't much think straight, either.

Had it been from the heat of the Lucky Horseshoe, all those hours she'd spent there, earning her coin just like the rest of them? Bodies stacked up against each other from one wall to the next, so tight, desperate, almost as if there weren't another four dozen just like it?

Her head spun. Black dots dancin' right about in that darkness.

Norma pressed one hand against a building's brick wall, which turned her fingers blacker than even this black, hell-bit of a night. Not that she could see much, eyes stinging red, burning from that sulfur-laden air. Smoke that was both bane and blessing. They and their mines, giving miners their steady stream of money, a steady need to laugh and relax, to seek comfort from any willing-enough woman they could find after trudging hours beyond imaging in that dark underground of Butte's great and rich Hill.

Norma welcomed them, as did many others.

And this time, she'd managed to claim some of that coin for herself. A decent bit, for once.

Maybe even enough to get home.

Home.

That very word... it sent a longing straight through her, seared through her. So powerful, so strong, she felt it right to her soul. The only way to keep it from burning her whole was to keep walking.

But... the word just wouldn't go away... wouldn't leave her with this small peace that she had, this little amount of coin and the chillness of the night, whether or not she could see. *Home.* As if such a place were still open to someone like her, her and her brother, but well, a woman could dream. Could... long for.

So, she did.

She longed, and she walked. It was the only way to survive in this town. The only way to keep head above water was to keeping pushin' forward, never pausing long enough cause if you did you'd sink right on down to that bottom and never get it. She was so close to that, too. So close to just laying down and giving in.

Because she'd been a fool.

She'd wanted it all, and what she'd really wanted, that whole time, was home.

Something she could never have again.

Norma followed along that brick building, feet thudding on the rotting, shifting, plank way. Her stomach, its ends, turning and twisting something so fierce she actually lost her grip along that brick wall a few times and nearly crashed right down.

Something... wrong. Not... not right at all.

Horses and carriages she couldn't see from beyond the blackness creaked by in the street. Except for the noise from the carriages, from the saloon whose steady beat she could nearly feel right through that blackened brick, it felt like she was completely alone.

Walking alone in that blackness.

Her other hand clung tight to her shawl, now dipping so low it'd give any passerby, if they was close enough to see in the smoky-dark, a glance at her bare shoulder. At some point while she worked the saloon, offering drinks to customers and offering a bit more to anyone with a hint of willingness, before the owner had declared her too drunk for good business and thrown her out, some-time then... her dress had caught on some piece of nail, or ripped, or...

She could no longer remember.

Something had happened.

Her mind got even more tangled. Sluggish. But she focused on that rip in her dress like it were the lifeline she needed to see her home.

It wouldn't be an easy easy thing to mend, let alone replace. And her missing coat, too.

Except... she couldn't quite understand why such worries mattered much.

Only that it hurt, this truth. As if her body alone were all the proof and reprimand she needed, that she'd never go home.

That she didn't deserve it, neither.

Once creamy smooth, her shoulder, where the fingers of the most wealthy had once caressed her, held her, devoted themselves to her, it was a changed thing, now. Smudged as it was with dirt and grease and black powder. She could even see the imprints of her last customer, the swirls of his fingertips as they'd ground down hard into her.

At least... if she could see straight, anyway.

Which she couldn't.

Norma moaned. Her stomach twistin' like it was about to knot itself good and tight and never untangle. Her head pounding, it was getting hard to think let alone breathe. She pressed a soot-smudged hand to her forehead and it felt like a fiery, hot poker was being stabbed into her, again and again. So hard and fast the rest of her was starting to go numb.

Fingers shaking.

Legs weak.

Could she have drunk more than she'd thought?

Not the opium. She knew the feeling well enough, and she hadn't had enough money to push herself into a more lengthy state of pure bliss and calm.

This, though, this was different.

Her stomach churned and burned, and she sagged against the wall. Felt like it was the only thing on this hill keeping her upright.

Something slipped into her own drink?

Possible.

She... she hadn't been in her right mind tonight. Not with the pain still so fresh, and then, her final... rejection. Too good to be true. She'd taken a risk, such a foolish one thinking it'd bring her happiness, and it'd failed her. And tonight, it had felt like every man in the place knew it, too, and wanted to enjoy their good fortune while she wallowed in her own misfortune.

It hadn't taken her long to lose her last shred of decency, the desire to be the lady she'd once been known for, certainly in the face of alcohol and its promises of dulling this too-painful world. She'd easily lost count of how much she drank, of how much and what exactly, as the others, no longer her gentleman callers for sure but men all the same, men willing and men spending, as they poured whatever they had right into her cup.

And she hadn't cared.

A swirling image of another man slipped through the pain tearing into her skull. A man who'd both fit and didn't. His clothing, looking like all the others, but treating her with kindness and caring like she was still one of Grace's ladies. And oh, he'd been her heaven in that moment, that little joy, the reminder of the woman she'd been before. And then he'd given her this brilliant, promising smile, and she'd soared. The sting from earlier, gone. Rejection after rejection, and knowing too the wrath that was about to fall down on her.

But for that moment, it had been enough.

He'd been her last customer for the night and he had paid her a hefty price. He'd caressed her forearm like she was indeed the treasure and not the coins he was parting with.

It was a touch she still felt, still caused a shiver of pride. Felt even through her splitting head. Even her breasts, too, as they pushed out her too-tight, breath-stealing corset.

She stumbled at that moment, her worn shoe catching some uneven plank on the walkway. It caused the ribbing of her corset to gouge into her soft skin.

She gasped.

Got only a mouthful of smoke that burned.

Her pride burning, too. Silly, foolish woman she was, she'd believed him, believed this man when he said she'd been worth every coin and more.

Once, she'd been that girl.

A girl with a smile, who lived with joy and enjoyed sharing it with others. No longer.

Red—a sudden pain seared through her head. So fast, so complete, her vision turned to blackness. It came so suddenly. Violently. Nothing like before. Nothing that she could see through, see around. It was her everything. Shrinking her whole world down to that one sight, that one feeling.

She cried out. Doubled over.

From somewhere far off—or close, she couldn't tell, not around the pain, not around the red—she thought she heard the clomping of horses. Hooves smackin' into the beat-hard dirt. They came nearer. Towards her?

Impossible.

She was no one. A nothing.

Now, anyway. She'd long ago lost the glittering jewels and silk and dresses fashioned straight from Paris, which she'd worn like the dazzling primrose she'd been while at Gardens. A world so far gone it felt like decades rather than months.

Her own fault. Her own weakness.

The pain came again. This time it felt like it split her in two. Right from her head all the way to her groin.

She crouched on the ground. Panting, moaning, crying.

Was... was she crying? Did she truly have any tears left?

Surely not.

There was a shout. Feet rushed towards her. Then... hands pressed against her head as if that would make it all go away. Soft and gentle hands, of the kind she hadn't felt in many long months. Caring hands, and they were cool, too, not like the wind cold, but cool. Comforting. Though they did nothing against the fire that was on her skin.

Those hands felt her head, lifted open her eyelids. She thought maybe something cool pressed against her chest, listening to her poor, straining chest. Her lungs that desperately fought for a clean breath of air, or any breath really, through her corset, through that smoke-thick air, and each time failing a bit more than the last.

"Norma? My dear girl, how could this possibly be you? What happened?"

What happened was she'd been a fool, thinking she was in love, and turned out she was wrong.

Yet again.

Somehow, she opened her eyes, and at first, saw nothing but the pain and fire and darkness.

"I, I can't see."

But that wasn't fully true.

The image of the man slowly came together. Blurry and full of shadows, but enough to make out his wrinkled, bone-white skin. The long, back cloak that looked close enough to the darkness she found herself in. A man she recognized.

A tear slipped past.

The man, this doctor who'd reluctantly tended to her before she'd given up her life of glitter in hopes of a better one, a decent one with the promise of a full life that, even now, burned like a secret flower in her chest.

"You're burning up," he said. "We need to get you to a hospital. Immediately. Driver!"

Who he called to, she couldn't see. Could, in fact, barely see him and his so sad face. Even now her vision was darkening as if it was reaching right up from her soul to finally take the rest of her.

The doctor had always looked at her, at all the girls really, with such overwhelming sadness.

His hands though, they'd always been kind.

"Who did this to you?" he asked.

Her hand, black from all the soot, black as her soul, lifted. Touched his cheek.

"Doctor. Thank you."

It was all she managed.

That, and one last smile. She had no idea she still had one in her, but it was there.

And for a moment, she felt that joy again. Just like she felt his kindness, one last time.

The pain became too great then. Too great, even, for the great and kind Doctor to heal.

She would die and no one, beyond the doctor, would care. Not for her, not for any of the fallen sisters like her.

No one.

CHAPTER ONE

Cat stepped off the Butte train and walked right into hell.

A heavy, black smoke hung about the hill. So thick, so dark, forget seeing any of those narrow, wooden frames she knew were out in the distance. Gallows, really, marking the entrances to hundreds of the copper mines the city was so famous for (and damned rich, too, if the stories held true).

And the railroad station? Those folks in charge were smart to string up lanterns all about the place, otherwise their paying customers would be lost right quick.

Hell, it looked like it were about midnight and she knew darn well it was just past noon.

Ashes drifted down, so fine and thin that at first she thought she'd imagined it. Then she saw those ladies disembarking from the train, all lace and yards of fabric bustled about their persons, wrapped up tight in their fancy coats and furs even though it weren't that cold, certainly for the mountains. They pressed their dainty, flimsy, pure-white handkerchiefs to their delicate little lips to keep themselves from breathing in the noxious, disgusting air.

As if that would do a damn thing.

Certainly not when those pearly-white handkerchiefs were already takin' on the ashy, gray color themselves.

The burning sulfur and what-not already stung Cat's eyes. Probably lookin' red-rimmed and bloodshot like she'd downed herself in the bottle the whole jostling ride over from Miles City.

There was a bit of wind, the late winter kind, so chill it reminded your bones that snow still lay hidden in those mountain peaks and had no intention of giving way to spring, just yet anyway. Or anytime soon. But as pleasing as that bit of wind was, it wasn't nearly enough to cleanse this poor air of the smoke that fouled it.

Butte looked like hell, no doubt about it, and she, the whole of the city herself, didn't seem to mind one wit about showing her true colors to the world. There was certainly some grace in that.

Honesty, too.

Just as Cat had been promised.

She tucked her scarf into the protective covering of her overcoat. The faint, flowery pink somehow still holding onto those dyed threads even after all these years. The rest of her could handle the ash and soot just fine. Her blouse, the best one she had even with all them stains and wrinkles, not to mention her blue jeans, getting a bit worn round the bottom, but still hugging her hips in all the right places.

Fact was, she drew about as many glances from the newcomers to Butte as well as the ones who lived there.

The men trudged around in tough-looking boots meant to carry a man miles underground, protecting his toes from heavy rocks and slabs ready to crush him silly. Nothing like the kind of boots that slapped-on spurs and carried about a pound of muck soon as you slipped 'em on. Then there were those smart, slim-cut jackets and more manner of shined shoes than she'd seen in a whole year workin' in Miles City.

Not to mention those squashed caps the newsboys wore, just as soot-stained as the rest of 'em. One in particular studied about everything and everyone shuffling off that train, those sharp eyes of his missing nothing, including Cat. All them newsboys cried out their headlines to the overflowing passengers, waving their ink-stained fingers like the whole stack was about to blow away if one didn't hurry on over and get the latest.

And not a cowboy in sight.

Butte was a city all right, but not like the usual ones out here in Montana.

All that put together, plus Cat herself not looking like the respectable part of a lady (or of any kind, for that matter), well, it made perfect sense why her fellow passengers tried to bustle past her. Those fancy, lacy skirts and dresses, and not an inch of fabric ever touching Cat's person.

Which, considering the flood of bodies flowing off the train then stopping right in their tracks as Cat had done, was fairly impressive.

Course, there were also those in their matchin' suits and vests best known as the upper gentry. They at least gave her the most curious of glances. More than a few were filled with revulsion, which was all right, but none of them could deny it:

They all looked.

They didn't dare come near, though. At least, not now, anyway.

Certainly not with the empty holster for her revolver hanging loose at her hip. The gun was stored away in her bag, as most cities likened these days, but the holster was reminder enough for most folks. They gave Cat her space, and she watched as they fled to the hordes of waiting hacks, drivers and horses seeming to appear and disappear right before her eyes, materializing in this unnatural light.

Or un-light, as the case were.

Through this all, this constant movement, the ringing of bells and whistles and clomping hooves, for the first time in years, Cat felt a weight slide off her shoulders.

Not a whole lot, cause it weren't ever gonna go away, couldn't, but now she felt lighter.

Comfortable. Content.

Part of her hoping, praying even, that her dear sister had found some measure of this same peace during her final days, all the while

Cat knew that she hadn't. Couldn't. That just weren't the way of the world, when ill luck fell hard on a woman, even a righteous and good one. *Especially* a righteous and good one. Especially, too, when they stuck to that path even knowing the end result, something neither God, nor man—certainly no woman—could change.

Alice had agreed to her fate, accepted it even, hardness and all.

Cat hadn't.

Or she had, but just in a different way. A path she wouldn't be on now if not for her sister. Of the last memory she had of Alice—her eyes, saddened, alive still but lifeless, and how she'd told Cat to leave and never come back. Standing there in that thin dress, the fabric barely hanging off her bones, and her straight, pale hair. It hadn't mattered that she was finally free of her wretched, hateful husband, who'd been inches away from finally stealing her dear Alice's life— and it hadn't mattered.

Not to Alice, the good and righteous woman that she was.

The memory would never, ever let Cat go. It would haunt her to the end of her days, but maybe, just maybe, Butte could help lessen that burden. Because perhaps, right here, there was a place for someone like her. Someone who'd do what she could for those the world didn't care none about. It might only be a small act, but it'd be something.

It'd be justice.

Cat had no doubt, none at all, that this was the place she was meant to be.

Needed to be.

CHAPTER TWO

T ruth was, there was only one place to find the happenings in any town, big or small, likened enough to hell or not.

In this, Butte was like any other.

The newsboys stood where train station met street, their squashed hats and ink-stained fingers waving about their papers and yelling about somebody who died out in the wilds of Chicago or New York. They didn't stop, not a once, even with the constant roll and crunch of hooves and wheels as hack drivers loaded everybody they could into their carriages. The whistling of those trains and whatnot. Even further off whistling in that blackness, which Cat only assumed came from the mines.

Dear lord, she'd never been to a place that made such a noise.

And those newsboys, why they were made of stern stuff because they kept on going without even a pause or need for breath, it seemed.

Except for the boy with sharp eyes.

He'd been studying Cat the moment her boots had smacked onto the hard platform, and unlike his fellows, he hadn't gone back to selling his papers. Instead, he kept on watching her. Waiting. Green-gray eyes of his, as if there was more than a mix of curiosity there, almost like a daring.

Now, however, his eyes narrowed, focused, right on her.

Somehow even in this blasted black smoke that green of his eyes cut through like a sharp knife. They never once left Cat's face.

She recognized him for what he was.

A shadow soul.

Someone living on the edge, on the fringes of society. Someone who hadn't yet failed, or if he had, he'd gotten back up before life trampled him under the muck and ash. Someone who made his livin' at surviving and didn't bother hiding it none.

A shiver slipped through her.

Carried right down passed her overcoat as if that chilly, still winter air was its own doing and not the actual truth.

Instinct.

Cat knew this truth, through and through. It tingled all up and down her body, and she'd learned long ago to trust in her feelings. Let them guide her.

Cat slapped her wide-brimmed cowboy hat on her head. Thing was, she couldn't stop herself even she wanted to, the urge was just that powerful. And never say curiosity itself wasn't powerful in its own right.

Cause it was.

So, Cat let it be what it was, and headed right towards him.

She kept the boy in sight as she moved around the passengers, trying not to trample on the enormously long and ridiculously impractical dresses some ladies thought travel necessitated. Not that the boy was trying to disappear or nothing, but she had this itch between her shoulders.

Instinct, again.

It dangled in her gut like a fish teasing her, ready to slip on free of its hook before heading back towards the murky-dark waters of home.

Something important, she simply knew, and she couldn't let it get away.

Maybe it was the way he looked at her, with that daring of his, or maybe it was leftover from her own resolution to come to Butte.

Whatever the reason, it was there, and this feeling, well, it stirred within her, pushing her forward and she followed. Besides, if there was anyone who knew about the inner workings of Butte, both above ground and what took place below, it'd be a kid like this.

Her boots clomped on the wooden platform and her bag slung across her shoulder, heavy and feeling just the way it needed to. Behind her, the train whistled something fierce, starting up a whole litany from others she couldn't see through the thick, heavy smoke.

"Offer you a paper, Miss?" the boy asked when she got close enough.

Not Mizz or ma'am.

She noticed, too, that he had a few different stacks with a few different names leaking across the fading pulp. *The Miner, Anaconda Standard, Butte Bystander*. All being sold by one boy? She hadn't a clue what was the norm in a city like Butte, but compared to the boys nearest him, they each had their one stack and that was all. Even the nearest kid, of the tall, beefy variety with narrowed, squinty eyes that about lost themselves in his freckled face. He looked the kind that wouldn't stand for some green-eyed, skinny kid outselling him.

Yet, there beefy stood and Green Eyes here, well, here *he* stood. Right on that corner, in the coveted spot and not a one of the others challenging him or his three papers.

Definitely a shadow soul, no doubt about it.

And exactly the person she needed to talk to.

"I'm looking for some news," Cat said. "Of the local sort."

Cat tossed him a coin. It twisted once and then twice in the air, just a glimmer of its copper-gold gleaming in the poor lantern light. The boy snatched it right quick from the air before it got even a second turn in. And whether he stashed it in his coat pocket or some hidden fold in his sleeve, Cat didn't know. His movement had been so fast and fluid.

Shadow soul, indeed.

Green Eyes tipped his cap up with an ink-smudged finger. "Local news, eh?"

"That's right."

"I'd recommend *The Bystander*, then. Some interesting bits in there."

She noticed he didn't bother to recite the headlines like the others, just told her, straight-a-way, which newspaper suited her needs.

"Course," he said, "depends on just how local a story you're lookin' for."

Cat felt the tingling again, crawling all up and around her spine. Testing her, perhaps?

"The kind not a whole lot of folk care about," she said.

He glanced at her hip, specifically her empty holster. "You plan on staying long, Miss Justice?"

There it was. The tingling.

She didn't fight it. Instead, she embraced it.

"Depends," she said, "on how the wind blows and what turns up."

"It's quite foul, I'll warn you right. When the wind turns wrong, you'll have never experienced anything of the like before, I promise you. You'll know it when you smell it. At least, that's when the wind blows wrong. When it blows right?"

This time, it was his turn to shrug.

"Well, fresh mountain air, for one. A thing of beauty, really, even here in this eyesore of a city. For the rest, though? I guess it'll just depend."

"Depend on what?"

"You, I suppose."

And there it was.

That look again. That kind that cut right on through her, taking her so far back like this kid could see back to the days of her being at home, when ma and pa were alive, when it was just her and Alice and when it felt like they had the whole world to themselves.

So naive and foolish they'd been. Little bitty dreamers that they were.

Dear God, did she miss those days... did she miss Alice.

Green Eyes slapped out the paper to her without a wasted movement or word. "Still interested in local?"

"I am."

She took it from him. Felt the weight on her shoulders shift yet again, settling almost. And... there was a feather-cold touch along her fingers, too, as if her sister were right beside her, reaching out for that paper and accepting more than they both realized.

Alice, of course, wasn't there, but this kid was, and Cat got a dusting of ash and ink on her hand.

She nodded to him. "I'd appreciate a recommendation of where to start. Rather big town you've got here."

"Page four, then. 'Bout midway down. Might just find a good place to rest your feet for a spell."

"Thanks."

Cat opened the paper, which crinkled in her hand. It rustled, too, as that chill winter wind suddenly swept up and between them, like it was planning on snatching the paper good and quick before she could stop it.

It didn't, though.

Cat held on, and for a moment felt like it was her breath that had been stolen. At least, what the smoke hadn't already burned right out and through her lungs. Especially as the words themselves, in that tiny, blocked print, like it was the most insignificant piece of news in the world, jumped out of the page and landed squarely against her chest.

The place where her heart still ached and beat because Alice was finally gone and Cat had failed her, time and time again. That same place that had driven her to Butte, and now to this boy.

But the words themselves were somehow clear, even in this shifting lantern light:
Woman Found Dead on Galena Street

To read more, visit your favorite bookseller for your copy of *Women's Justice.*

ABOUT THE AUTHOR

Chrissy Wissler's writing has garnered praise both from readers and professional writers. Readers love her characters and the emotional grip she engenders.

About her novel *Home Run, New York Times* bestselling author Kristine Kathryn Rusch said: "Wonderful book, chockfull of unexpected surprises. If you like sports novels, you'll like this—even if you don't like romance. If you like romance, you'll like this—even if you don't like sports novels."

Chrissy's short fiction has appeared in the anthologies: *Fiction River: Risk-Takers, Fiction River Presents: Legacies, Fiction River Presents: Readers' Choice, Deep Magic,* and *When Dreams Come True.* She writes fantasy and science fiction, as well as romance, young adult, and historical mystery.

Before turning to fiction, Chrissy also wrote nonfiction for publications such as *Montana Outdoors, Women in the Outdoors,* and *Jakes Magazine.* In 2009, *Inside Kung Fu* magazine awarded her with their 'Writer of the Year' award.

For more information please go to ChrissyWissler.com and sign up for her newsletter.

For more information:
www.chrissywissler.com

facebook.com/chrissywissler@chrissywisslerwriter

ALSO BY CHRISSY WISSLER

Cowboy Cat Mystery Series

Women's Justice

Mother's Justice

For more information about Chrissy Wissler's other works, go to
ChrissyWissler.com